S0-AFK-509

"Come to me before I die of wanting you."

A thrill of excitement coursed through Arianna's veins, but she needed to hear more. "You speak of want, but what about love?"

"The devil take it!"

Arianna swallowed hard. Why was Rob making this so hard for her, when all she wanted was to be in his arms forever? Knowing his pride would keep him from saying any more, Arianna realized that if they were ever to be together again, she would have to give in.

Solemnly, she pulled off first one boot and then the other, glancing up to see how he would react.

His expression never changed.

She rolled down her trunk hose and hose, taking a long time to pull them off, aware that he was watching her every move.

At least she had his attention.

Moving up close to him, she started unbuttoning the velvet doublet, taking an inordinately long time to do so, her eyes never leaving his face.

A bead of sweat ran down Rob's cheek, though the air was damp and cool.

When she was done unbuttoning her doublet, she slowly worked it off her shoulders, letting it slide to the floor. Arianna stood before him completely naked now, a wicked gleam in her eye. "You were saying?"

SANDRA DAVIDSON

THORN OF THE ROSE

ZEBRA BOOKS
KENSINGTON PUBLISHING CORP.

ZEBRA BOOKS are published by

Kensington Publishing Corp.
475 Park Avenue South
New York, NY 10016

Zebra and the Z logo Reg. U.S. Pat. & TM Off. Heartfire
Romance and the Heartfire Romance logo are trademarks
of Kensington Publishing Corp.

First Printing: May, 1994

Printed in the United States of America

Prologue

Fotheringhay, February 7, 1587

To my most precious son, James.

By now you must know that Elizabeth has decreed my blood to be spilled. Defying all reason, she has signed the warrant ordering my death. And so, having but a few short hours left in this world before I go to the next, I write these final words to you. You will note my hand is steady, for my heart is joyful to at last be rid of the troublesome burden of my painful existence.

Dearest James, I have lived long enough to regret many things, but none so great as losing you when you were but a babe. Though our separation was caused first by the Scottish lords and then by the English queen, I cannot help but take some responsibility, for I have not always acted with the greatest of wisdom. Because I let my heart rule my head, I have paid dearly, but never so dearly as to be denied the God-given right of every mother to raise the child of her womb.

How grand it would have been to see you once more

before I died, so that I could tell you how very much I love you, but since that cannot be, let this letter be my voice, and hear me speak of my undying love for you. Undying, for my son, though I be dead, yet will my love linger on.

Believe this truly, and in times of despair let that love surround you, protect you, and guide you toward the healing light of hope. And remember always that when you are in need of me, I will be there. Feel, then, the brush of my lips upon your cheek as truly as if I were standing beside you.

And now, as the candle of my life grows dim, let me brighten your life's flame with the greatest gift I can bestow. The gift of knowing you have a sister who shares your blood and mine. I know how incredible this revelation must seem, but I swear to you on God's holy blood that she doth truly exist.

Her identity must, sadly, remain a secret so that she will be protected from Elizabeth's revenge. The English queen hath sought her since her birth. And why, my son? Because, in truth, your sister was fathered by none other than Elizabeth's lover, Robert Dudley, Earl of Leicester, the man she loves most in this world.

The day will come, I'm certain, when your sister will make herself known to you. Mayhap, when Elizabeth is dead she will reveal herself, or sooner if she is certain that you will receive her warmly. And I implore you to do just that, for she is a loving lass who will make your life all the happier for having known her.

You will know it is truly she when you meet her, for the unusual ivory ring she wears. There is none like it in all of England or in our own fair Scotland. The ivory is carved in the likeness of a rose, and on one perfect little petal is embedded a ruby sliver, symbolizing the blood we three share.

And now, my beloved son, I must bid you adieu, praying that someday you will be united with your sister. Until that glorious day, I wish you great happiness and tranquility, and I hope that when you think of your mother, you will remember she died happy, a martyr to her beloved Catholic faith.

Your loving mother, in life and in death,
Mary, Queen of Scotland and the Isles

Chapter One

England, April 30, 1588

Sanctimonious nudged her velvet nose into Arianna's hand, sniffing the offered sugar cake fastidiously before deigning to take it into her mouth. Arianna rolled her eyes in exasperation, letting Rob know this prissy animal was not to her liking. She missed Pasha, her beloved stallion, and had accepted the white mare in his stead only to humor her husband.

Sighing resignedly, her gaze wandered back to the landscape as she listened halfheartedly to Lord Trumbull's voice droning on as he pointed out the boundaries of the lands that went with Brambly Castle.

This was their first visit to the castle Queen Elizabeth had given them a little more than a year ago, and Arianna's feelings about being here were divided. Only her thirst for revenge, along with the proximity of this land to London and Windsor, and therefore to the English queen, kept her from refusing the gift.

Her heart quickened in response to the thought of revenge for her mother. Revenge for the horrible way she had died at the hands of Elizabeth. Revenge for the nineteen long years her mother had spent locked away. Somehow, she would find a way to bring Elizabeth to her knees, and coming to Brambly was the first step toward that holy end.

"I'd give a gold sovereign to know what you're thinking right now, Rose Petal," Rob whispered into her ear, breaking through her bitter reverie.

Arianna paled and lowered her head.

It didn't take a soothsayer to tell where her thoughts lay, Rob thought, shaking his head in dismay. Damn. Double damn Elizabeth for giving them Brambly Castle on the occasion of their son Robin's first birthday. They dared not refuse the gift and, having accepted it, were obligated to make use of the castle so the queen would not be insulted.

If only Elizabeth weren't so confoundedly fond of Arianna, it would make his life considerably easier. But the whole of England knew of Elizabeth's affection for the Countess of Everly—Arianna Warwick—his beautiful, headstrong wife, and they whispered about it behind the queen's back, knowing how out of character it was for Elizabeth to warm so to another female.

How ironic. Because of that affection, Arianna was treated with great respect everywhere she went, making it all the easier to hide the fact that she was the Scottish queen's illegitimate daughter. How many sleepless nights had he worried over her safety, afraid that Elizabeth would discover her true identity and take her from him? Imprison her as she had Mary. And all because the Earl of Leicester had betrayed

Elizabeth by bedding the Scottish queen and fathering the child of that union.

But why dwell on that? The danger was past. Arianna was safe. Elizabeth would never know the young woman she was so fond of was Mary's daughter. No, if Arianna was at risk now, it was through her own folly. No matter how she might deny it, he knew the fire of revenge still burned bright in her heart. He would have to watch her like a hawk every waking moment and would not breathe easy again until they returned to Everly.

"Feel free to call upon me if you have any questions about Brambly. I am just a stone's throw away in Wimbledon," Lord Trumbull said, concluding his repertoire on Brambly's long history.

"What's that? Oh, yes. Right neighborly of you, Trumbull. Did you hear that, Arianna?" Rob dug Arianna in the ribs with his elbow.

"Yes, my lord. You've been most helpful." Arianna responded to Rob's nudge, knowing she was expected to act the gracious hostess. "Will you join us back at the castle for an afternoon cordial, or would you prefer a tankard of ale?"

"Another day, my lady, if you please. I am expected at Windsor Castle after I have concluded my business here. The queen is having a May Day celebration on the morrow, and I have been assisting her."

Arianna was amused to note how the ancient lord's chest rose appreciably at those words.

"I have been asked to personally invite the two of you to join her. She would have sent a formal invitation had she known you would be coming to Brambly

Castle at this time, and she begged me to tell you that she looks forward to seeing you once again."

It was Rob's turn to roll his eyes. He knew it was only a matter of time before Elizabeth and Arianna got together again, but he had hoped it wouldn't be this soon.

Arianna smiled, saying, "We will be very happy to accept, Lord Trumbull. Very happy."

Rob heard the underlying excitement in his wife's voice and cursed the day Elizabeth had been born, adding every one of her ancestors to the list, too, for all the aggravation he would soon be facing.

"But tell me, how does one dress for the occasion? I'm afraid I've not had much experience with that sort of thing, raised as I was in a convent."

Trumbull looked at Arianna with renewed interest. "Yes, yes. I understand, my dear. Quite. Quite." He stroked his graying beard as if the act enhanced his memory. "Why, as I recall, the ladies dress in their newest, gayest frocks. That's right. And wear ribbons and garlands in their hair. Smacks of pagan days, it does, but I don't object. Not a bit of it. Good to see ladies carrying on joyfully, instead of looking as if they've been stung by a wasp. Yes, yes. Enjoyable day. Enjoyable day. You shan't have a bit of problem fitting in."

Arianna absorbed Lord Trumbull's words, her mind quickly moving ahead to other matters. May Day. Spring. The time of new beginnings. But not for her martyred mother. And if she had anything to say about it, not for the queen of England. The time was drawing near when Elizabeth would pay.

"My lord Trumbull, you have no idea how you've

eased my mind. Thank you. And now, kind sir, if you'll help me seat my horse . . ."

Trumbull's chest puffed up further at Countess Arianna's request, surprised that she had turned to him for help instead of to her handsome young husband. Here was a girl who knew how to please a man. The stiffness he had been experiencing in his legs was forgotten as he bent over to cup his hands to receive the small booted foot placed there. Using all his strength, he boosted her onto her horse.

Rob watched with raised eyebrow. If he had any doubt before that she was up to something, it was dispelled now. He knew his wife well. Her coquettish way with the ancient Lord Trumbull was a sure sign she was experiencing a surplus of restless energy and was in need of an outlet. His throbbing manhood anticipated the outlet he had in mind. Since his marriage to his volatile bride, he had used long sessions of lovemaking to take her mind off her quest for revenge. Consequently, they spent a lot of time in bed. Time very well spent, indeed.

He watched as she clicked her tongue at Sanctimonious and started across the wide field, head held high, spurring the mare into a graceful gallop. Damned, but she was a magnificent sight to behold. It would be hard waiting until bedtime.

Arianna's nervous energy carried over to the evening hours as she set about preparing her garb for the queen's party. Clothing went flying as she sorted through the three large trunks that had accompanied her from Everly, settling, at last, on a gown of the finest French silk in an unusual hue of moss-green.

While feeding little Robin his supper, she pondered

the matter of what to wear on her head. She would have been happy enough to weave a garland of flowers, but wanting to impress the queen, Arianna knew she would have to come up with something bolder, more imaginative. But what? How could she hope to compete with the grand ladies of Elizabeth's court? They had been at this much longer than she. That was it! Why try to compete? She would do something totally different. Instead of wearing colorful flowers and bright ribbons, she would fashion a wreath of earthy things. Velvety moss over new shoots of grapevines to form the base, acorns and tiny pinecones for decoration, and for color, whatever berries could be found this time of year.

By the time she had Robin bathed and ready for bed, her ladies in waiting had scoured the grounds and forest nearby and had gathered enough materials to make several handsome wreaths.

Arianna worked late into the night finishing her garland by the light of the cozy fire in her bedchamber, whilst Rob, eager to bed his wife, pretended to be interested in the book on his lap.

Satisfied with her creation, she placed it on her head and studied her reflection in the looking glass. Rob moved up behind her, circling her waist with his impatient hands, his moist lips nibbling at her ear.

"Mmmm, my mouth doth water looking at you." His searching hands slid up her rib cage. "I've been eating you with my eyes all day, now let my mouth have its turn."

"My lord, you are incorrigible. How can you think of that at a time like this? Can't you see the state I'm in?"

" 'Tis far better than the uncomfortable state I'm in." His hands covered her breasts, greedily digging into her soft flesh with fingers that demanded surrender. "But . . . luckily, I have a remedy that will cure us both. Trust me, by the time I'm through with you, you'll sleep like a babe."

Arianna moved away from his grasping hands, removing the wreath before Rob's ardor caused it serious harm. "Forsooth, Robert, I am too distracted to—"

Far from discouraged, Robert began to undress, slowly, deliberately, his gaze never leaving her face.

Looking deep into the warm brown depths of his eyes, Arianna saw the fire burning there, and her pulse quickened as it always did. Her gaze shifted to his bare chest and then further down as he slipped out of the rest of his clothing and stood before her naked and ready.

Arianna felt a deep throbbing inside her at the sight of him, so masculine, so strong, so ready to pleasure her. "If you think the sight of your lively manpart is going to entice me to give in, you're mightily mistaken. I . . ."

Rob took her hand and pressed it to his manhood. Involuntarily, she wrapped her fingers around the hardened shaft, and the throbbing grew stronger.

"You were saying . . ." His voice was like velvet heat, the part of him she touched the same.

"I . . ." Arianna felt the movement beneath her fingers as Rob began to slide back and forth inside her grasp. "I . . . I . . . oooh . . ."

Before she knew it, she was naked, rubbing her body against the hardness in her hand, her eyes half closed, her lips half parted. The only thing that mattered was this moment, this desirable man.

It had ever been so.

She felt herself being lifted into strong arms, and Arianna surrendered to the pleasure as she always had. She had never been able to deny him the pleasure of her body. She would not deny him now.

His lips came down on hers hot, hard, enticingly, and she clung to him as he lowered her to the bed. Reluctant to release him, her hand moved to his manhood once more, in need of touching what was hers. He had started it, and now she would make sure he finished it.

In great haste, she guided him inside, eager to be joined to him, eager to feel the velvet heat of him inside. Ahhh . . . Yes! Her eyes closed dreamily as he thrust into her, filling every inch of her with his pole of pleasure, his magic wand that never ceased to turn her into a wanton slave to his vigorous passion.

Almost three years of marriage had lessened neither her desire for him nor the intensity of their lovemaking. Indeed, it seemed to grow by leaps and bounds every sensuous day.

Tightening her body around him, Arianna drew him in even more, thrilling to the sensation. "Ohhhhh . . . Rob . . ." He thrust again, plunging to the very depths of her being. And again. "Yes." Again. And again. "Yes! Yes!"

Rob heard her cries and knew well how she wanted it. He obliged by thrusting all the harder, freeing himself to give her all he had. They came together, straining at each other, intent on the need, the desire, the fulfillment, the passion building ever faster, ever more urgent, until he thought he'd die if he didn't send his seed bursting inside her.

And then he did and she took it . . . took all he had and gave herself up to the rapturous release that followed, her voice singing out her ecstasy, escalating until the very walls echoed from the primal female cry.

Later, whilst he slept, Arianna, still caught tight in his arms, tried to rekindle the rage for Elizabeth she needed in order to carry out her revenge, but the pressure of Rob's body on hers, the lingering afterglow from the rapture of his touch, were all she could feel, and content, she joined her husband in sleep.

Morning came, and with it the hustle and bustle of a household in near panic to ready the Countess of Everly for her day with the queen. When at last Arianna was satisfied with the way she looked and had decided Robert, too, was more than presentable, dressed in a velvet doublet the color of rich cream and trunk hose of gold and white stripes, she swept toward the door, her servants trailing behind in case there were last minute instructions from their mistress. Kissing her son goodbye, she was lifted onto the mare and the journey to Windsor began.

They could have gone by barge; the Thames was right outside their door. That would have been the civilized, practical way to travel, but Arianna knew well the value of a grand entrance. She and Rob would certainly have that, what with the horses decked out elegantly in bright trappings and garlands of flowers, as well as the unicorn horn she had fashioned attached to Sanctimonious's pretty forehead.

The mare looked the perfect unicorn and, seeming to know how truly spectacular she was, pranced regally down the road. Begrudgingly, Arianna felt a modicum of pride for the beautiful animal. Sanctimonious was not Pasha, could never take his place, but she was an elegant creature. Elizabeth should be quite impressed, and that was the point of it all, after all.

She must keep Elizabeth off guard at all costs. The best way to do that was to keep the queen entertained. That had never been a problem in the past. Contrary to what most people thought, she had not been raised in a convent, but rather in a peasant cottage by her beloved foster parents. Because of that upbringing, her demeanor was quite unlike the noblewomen the queen was used to.

Elizabeth always seemed to enjoy Arianna's simple ways, calling them fresh and unspoiled. Well, she would continue to act that way for the queen's benefit, though she was far from being that sweet, innocent girl anymore. It was her greatest weapon, and in this war she would use whatever means she could to win.

The first sight of Windsor Castle took Arianna's breath away. Long before she saw it in its entirety, the castle's towers, both square and round, had guided the way, but they hadn't prepared her for the magnificence of the structure. It was truly fit to be the royal residence of kings and queens. To think, if her mother had lived she might one day have resided in Windsor Castle. It had been said that Mary, Queen of Scots, had more rights to the English throne than Elizabeth, for Elizabeth's mother, Anne Boleyn, was not legally married to Henry at the time of her birth.

Another reason to hate Elizabeth. If not for her, she would be visiting her mother now, instead of the woman responsible for her death.

"What do you think of it, Rose Petal?"

Hiding her anger for Elizabeth, Arianna forced a light and airy voice. " 'Tis the largest castle I've ever seen. It must have taken years and years to build."

Rob laughed heartily. "Try centuries and centuries. It was first built by William the Conqueror, and expanded and renovated ever since."

"Then we should feel very honored to be here."

"Look, Elizabeth has sent an escort out to greet us."

Arianna watched as a party of horsemen dressed in the queen's livery of green and white rode toward them, trumpets blaring. In answer, a loud shout drifted down to them from the castle walls. Looking up, she saw a group of lords and ladies waving to them from the parapet. Smiling, she waved back.

As she watched, the group suddenly parted and a woman's head appeared framed in a glimmering halo of light as the afternoon sun glinted off her crown, sending rays of liquid gold into the air. Arianna felt her stomach lurch. Here was her bitter enemy. Here was the woman she would bring to her knees.

With a smile upon her face that belied the rage inside, she blew a kiss to the queen.

Chapter Two

In a few, too short moments Arianna was up on the north terrace, curtsying to Elizabeth, her nails digging into the palms of her hands to keep herself contained. Elizabeth smiled brightly and drew her into her arms, astonishing all that gazed on such an unusual occurrence. Elizabeth was not known for being overly friendly to beautiful young women.

"My dear, you astound me with your fantastical entrance to my celebration! On the back of a unicorn. It was just the right touch. I am so happy you are here at last. I was beginning to think you must be angry with me for some reason which I cannot fathom."

Arianna's heart quickened. Did Elizabeth suspect something? Was it possible she could no longer hide her hatred? But no, Elizabeth was just being Elizabeth, digging for yet another meaningless compliment. "Your Grace, how could you think such a thing! I could no sooner be angry at you than I could my sweet babe, Robin."

Elizabeth's smile deepened. "Robin, yes, how is the little one? I have not seen him since his first birthday."

"He's into everything, I fear. It takes three of us to keep him in check."

"And no wonder, considering his perilous birth on that wretched cliff. He is born to danger, I warrant. I shall look forward to watching him grow into a man." Then, pouting exaggeratedly, she added, "That is, if I am ever given that opportunity. You must promise to visit here more than just once a year."

"I shall try very hard, Your Grace."

A loud murmuring arose at Arianna's answer. Anyone else would have been sure to promise to visit more often, but it would be out of character for the Arianna that Elizabeth knew to answer in the expected way. Her unpredictability was what charmed Elizabeth the most, making her one of the queen's favored few.

"I am glad to see you haven't changed a bit." Laughing happily, Elizabeth took Arianna by the arm and led her over to a group of ladies. "Lady Trumbull, I call on you to make the Countess Arianna comfortable. I wish to steal her husband for a few moments."

As Lady Trumbull guided her from one elegantly dressed lord or lady to the next, Arianna had a hard time concentrating. But all seemed fine. Elizabeth was acting her usual coquettish self around handsome young men. And Rob was doing a commendable job of hiding his displeasure at being here. She had nothing to worry about. She would have relaxed and enjoyed herself but for the blasted new shoes she was wearing. They pinched her toes unbearably.

Scanning the faces of the stately lords, Arianna sought the beloved face of her father, Robert Dudley, Earl of Leicester. Ah, me, she thought, Robert was such a nice-sounding name. She was lucky to have two

Roberts in her life. No, not true, she was lucky to have three, for her son Robin was a Robert, too. It gave her a good feeling to know that the three males she loved most in the world shared the same wonderful masculine name.

It had been three long months since she had last seen her father. He visited whenever he could pry himself away from Elizabeth, but he had to be very careful. Elizabeth must never know her favorite man in all the world had fathered a daughter with her hated enemy Mary.

Her eyes suddenly lit up as they gazed, at last, on the Earl of Leicester walking toward her. The sight of him thrilled her, as always. Raised as she had been with no knowledge of her father until the day she married Rob, she never seemed to get enough of him now.

"Arianna, I'm delighted to see you here."

Silently, Arianna called out to him. *Father.* Then for the benefit of anyone who might be listening, she spoke aloud. "My lord, it is good to be here. I hope I find you in good health."

"As good as can be expected for a man of my advanced years."

Arianna laughed gaily. "Advanced years? Why, you are the perfect example of what a man in his prime should look like."

Leicester smiled, knowing Arianna was blinded by her love for him; he well knew how old he looked. His hair was now white with age, and though he was still quite slender, he had a portly pouch where once there had been a hard, lean stomach. And if that was not enough, he had been plagued of late with a weakness in his limbs, which grew worse with each passing day.

Pushing the dismal thoughts from his mind, Leicester turned his attention fully on the delightful company of his daughter. A sudden thought came to him, and he looked around to see if they were being observed. They were. Drat. There was something important he had to tell her and it couldn't wait.

Speaking in a low voice, he said, "Arianna, someone will be here any moment that you couldn't possibly be expecting to see. I want you to brace yourself."

Arianna paled. "Who . . ."

The blare of trumpets kept her from continuing, and through a hazy fog she heard the herald announce, "His Royal Majesty, James VI, of Scotland,"

Arianna felt her knees go weak, but Rob moved to her side, his arm going around her waist protectively, while Leicester gave her a reassuring look.

James Stuart! Her half brother. Mary's only son. She would be meeting her brother for the very first time. Her heart began to pound with a vengeance.

Rob squeezed her hand, whispering, "Easy there, girl. Keep your head. James has no idea you are his sister, and no one else does, either. You're going to be fine."

Unable to speak or even move, Arianna watched as James Stuart moved through the crowd of nobles, the object of everyone's attention. Without so much as a glance to the lords and ladies eager to catch his eye, he walked straight to the queen, his eyes locked onto hers.

Arianna gazed in awe at the tall, lean, man dressed in pale blue and gold. This kingly man shared her blood. Eating him up with her eyes, she tried to make out his features but was standing too far away. She could see, though, that his hair was a darker shade of blond than her own.

In a moment, the press of people around James obscured her view and she was able to catch her breath. Leicester whispered to her, "Sorry you had to find out so abruptly. Are you all right?"

"I . . . I'm fine . . . fine. Stars in heaven! I never thought I'd meet my brother. It's truly a miracle."

Rob shook his head. "Rose Petal, don't you go getting any ideas of letting James know who you are, because if—"

"Oh, Rob, stop being so protective. I'm not that foolish. But is it wrong of me to be happy to see my own flesh and blood?"

Rob's voice softened, "Of course not, darling."

Leicester put his hand on Rob's shoulder. "This is a shock to you, too, Robert. But don't be so concerned. By now, you should know our Arianna can take care of herself enormously well with kings as well as queens."

Arianna gave her father a grateful look, then catching the eye of Lord Trumbull, she moved away from her father and husband, wanting to share her excitement. "Isn't this marvelous, Lord Trumbull! I didn't know there would be visiting royalty today. You didn't mention that to me at Brambly."

"Didn't I? Just like me, it is. Ask Lady Trumbull. She swears I'll forget my name at the pearly gates. The king has been visiting England near a week now, but he'll be returning to Scotland very shortly."

Arianna tried to get a better look at her brother, but too many people blocked the way. If only she'd known. Why hadn't Father sent word to her? The answer to that was all too obvious. Despite his fine words to Rob, he didn't trust her to be around James for fear of giving away her identity. Well, he would soon learn he had nothing to fear. That is, if she ever got a chance to talk to James. She would just have to be patient.

Frustrated, she walked over to a table laden with food and leaned against it to take the weight off her feet. The new shoes were pinching unbearably now. She had a good mind to take them off. Why not? Under her voluminous skirts, who would know the difference?

Surreptitiously, she used the toe of one foot to push down on the back of the other shoe, then removed the first shoe the same way. Ah, that felt much better. The cool grass under her feet relieved the pain mightily. Looking around, she could see that no one had noticed a thing. She would stand at this spot for a few minutes and then put the blasted shoes back on again before dinner was served.

Her attention soon returned to James Stuart. She watched his progress around the terrace with eager eyes, until she was distracted by two young lords who insisted on conversing with her no matter how much she tried to discourage them. They finally left when the announcement came that the food was ready to be served.

Gazing casually up at the clouds overhead, so no one would realize what she was up to, Arianna searched for her shoes with her toes. Where were they? She hadn't gone anywhere. Maybe just a few steps hither and yon as she stood talking to those two young nuisances.

This was beginning to get embarrassing. Everyone was heading for the long trestle tables set up on the terrace, a few heads turning to look at her curiously as they passed by. Rob was nowhere to be seen. Again, she searched the grass for her shoes, her foot making larger and larger circles under her skirts.

"Is this what you're looking for, bonnie lassie?"

Arianna whirled around and stared into blue eyes exactly like her own. James! Holding her shoes.

She couldn't speak.

An amused look came over James's face. He was used to pretty little things too tongue-tied to talk in the presence of kings. "Allow me."

Arianna's eyes opened wide as the Scottish king knelt at her feet and began to lift her skirts. In response, she offered a stockinged foot, which was quickly covered with a shoe. Projecting her other foot forward, James took it in his hand, running a finger intimately across the bottom of it before covering it with the shoe. "Such pretty little feet, my lady. But not little enough, I fear, to fit these shoes properly."

James rose, and Arianna's face flamed bright red. "I fear you're right, Your Majesty. Thank you for coming to my rescue."

"Indeed, it was my very great pleasure. Shall we?"

Arianna was too flustered to realize what he meant, until he offered her his arm. Of course. He wanted to escort her to her seat. Her eyes searched for Rob, finding him escorting Elizabeth, and she realized she would be dining at the same table as Elizabeth and James. How thrilling. She would have a chance to talk with her brother. Turning back to James, she proclaimed softly, "It will be my very great pleasure."

James's eyes twinkled. This was a lady after his own heart.

In a moment, they were seated in the position of honor next to the queen and Rob. She was so happy to be with her brother that for the moment she could not find it in her heart to be angry at Elizabeth. In fact, the queen was being quite charming. Even Rob seemed to be enjoying her company.

Several times, whilst they dined on course after course of the sumptuous feast, Arianna caught James looking at her with a strange expression on his face, until he finally asked, "Have we met before?"

Arianna's heart constricted. "No, Your Majesty."

"I didna think so. I could never have forgotten you. But you seem so familiar, so . . . I canna put my finger on it, but I feel as if I know you."

Elizabeth heard and commented, "I know exactly what you mean, James. She has the same effect on me. But 'tis nothing more than her charming manner that makes you feel as if you know her."

Arianna smiled sweetly at the queen, but inside she was quaking. Her father had told her on more than one occasion that she greatly resembled her mother. Is that what James saw in her face?

The king of Scotland was surprised—and happily so—at how warm Elizabeth was to Arianna. Somehow, he knew he couldn't bear it if she came to any harm. What was it about this enchanting creature that made him feel this way?

Uncomfortable with this new turn of events, Rob claimed his wife as partner at the maypole, and as they weaved in and out of the ribbons held by the other revelers, he envisioned tying her up in them, hand and foot, to keep her out of trouble.

She had been a handful from the moment he first gazed at her, dressed as a boy and acting as her foster father's apprentice falconer. And she was more than a handful now, having gained considerable confidence as lady of his castle.

Rob gazed into her sparkling sapphire eyes as she ducked under his arm, laughing gaily, and he couldn't keep from laughing, too. Watching as she moved around the pole like a graceful nymph, his heart filled with pride knowing this beautiful woman was his wife. Yes, indeed, she was a handful, no doubt about that, but the great love he felt for her and the pleasure she brought to his life more than outweighed the problems she gave him. He felt a throbbing in his groin and decided they would leave the festivities early.

But Elizabeth had other plans. Knowing of Arianna's way with hawks, the queen asked her to look at a sick peregrine in the mews. Rob and James accompanied them there, watching as Arianna put her expertise to work. Her foster father had taught her well, and she soon found the problem and prescribed the proper medication for the bird.

"Elizabeth, I should like to steal your bonnie little falconer away to Scotland. But I fear I would spend all my time in the mews, instead of conducting my kingly business."

"My dear cousin, I do believe Robert Warwick would have something to say about that. He is quite devoted to his wife."

James could hear the slightest edge in Elizabeth's voice and knew he had overstepped his bounds with her. Amazing how protective she was of Arianna, when even the lady's own husband seemed to take no offense at his remarks. The young earl was very sure of himself where his wife was concerned.

"Well," Rob said, breaking the strained silence, "since Arianna has succored the bird and all is well, I will beg leave of you, Your Grace, so that I might take my wife back to Brambly to care for her poor neglected husband."

"I won't hear of it," Elizabeth answered curtly. "I require more than a day's visit from your wife. You may be excused if you wish, but I must insist that Arianna go hawking with me on the morrow. I'm sure James could benefit from her knowledge of the art. I warrant he's seen nothing like it in Scotland."

"Dear Elizabeth, if you are inferring that in my primitive country we know nothing of the finer graces, then I shall have to show you what prowess we Scots have."

Elizabeth laughed. "I was hoping you'd say that. What fun! Arianna and I accept your challenge."

Rob groaned inwardly. He knew it had been a mistake to come to Windsor. Now he would suffer the consequences.

Chapter Three

In the morning, Rob awoke sore and cranky from a night of restless churning, whilst Arianna awoke with roses in her cheeks and a cheery greeting for her husband. Rob answered with a curt good morning mumbled under his breath, then set about dressing in resentful silence.

Ignoring Rob's churlish mood, Arianna donned her hunting dress, sighing, "Isn't it a spectacular morning to go hawking? Spring is my favorite time of the year." The beautiful weather wasn't the only reason she was feeling so good. She thought she might be with child again, and oh, how very much she wanted it to be true. How wonderful it would be if all their intense lovemaking had finally conceived another child. She had begun to wonder if there was something wrong with her, but now she had reason to hope.

The news would make Rob very happy. He wanted to fill Everly Castle with his children. It had been very lonely for him growing up without sisters and brothers, and he vowed that Robin would not be raised the same. Then, besides his great love of children, there was another reason. To him children were a very visible sign of his masculinity. And oh, how he cherished his masculinity.

She wished she could give him the news this very day, but Arianna decided it was more prudent to wait until she knew for sure that it was true. It would be too great a disappointment for Rob if it turned out to be a false hope.

"I repeat, isn't it a spectacular morning to go hawking?"

Rob made his way to the chamber's privy closet in silence. The sound of his urine spraying against stone assaulted Arianna's ears, expressing Rob's feeling more succinctly than mere words ever could.

When he returned, she crossed her arms over her chest, declaring, "Is that how it's to be, then? You mean to punish me with silence because I obey my queen's wishes? A pox on you, then. I *will* hawk with my brother and the queen, so get used to the idea."

"Used to the idea? Ha! Woman, in the years I've known you, I have not gotten used to your willful ways. But have a care, I am about to change that. I'm going to tell the queen that something important has come up and we must, alas, leave for Everly right away."

"No, Rob," Arianna cried, her confident demeanor melting away as she realized she had pushed Rob too far. "You mustn't. You'll ruin everything. Don't you understand? I need to be with my brother. Have you no compassion in your bloody soul?"

"That's not what you're upset about, and you right well know it. James will be leaving on the morrow, so my actions will not interfere with you seeing him. No, it's your miserable desire for revenge on Elizabeth that you're thinking of now. Do you take me for a fool? I know you too well, my darling wife. If you knew me half as much, you'd not defy me now, else I'll—"

"I know. I know. Else you'll lock me in the tower room again. Damn you, Robert Warwick. Damn you to hell. If I didn't love you so, I'd already have had my revenge on Elizabeth. But, since I am condemned to love you, I am condemned to yield."

Rob felt a hollow victory at Arianna's concession. Arianna had no choice but to go along with him or risk endangering her family. But her desire for revenge was as strong as ever, and it was only a matter of time before she sought a way to carry it out.

A soft rapping sounded on the door and Rob moved quickly to answer it, eager for the distraction.

A tiny birdlike woman stood there. In a shy voice, she said, "Forgive me, my lord, but my queen bids me to direct the countess Arianna to the stables at once. The queen is eager to begin hawking."

Rob turned to look solemn-faced at Arianna. "Do you hear? The queen requests your presence. We shall continue this conversation when you return."

"Will you not accompany me?"

Without answering, Rob turned away from her and made his way over to the window, where he gazed out in sullen silence.

Arianna glanced at the stiff back of her husband, then spoke quietly to the maid. "Will you escort me to the queen? I fear I shall get lost if I try to find the way alone. I have never been in such a huge castle as this before."

Relief spread through Arianna as she was led down

the magnificent gilded corridors. Relief and a twinge of guilt and yes, something else, too . . . the knowledge that she must find a way to get around her stubborn husband if she was to carry out her revenge. As long as Robert was by her side she would not have the chance, but . . . what if . . . What if he were sent out of the country for a short time? . . . Yes. That would work.

No, it wouldn't. Not unless it was a direct order from the queen. Then and only then would he venture away from her side. She suddenly felt much better. That could be arranged quite easily. Arianna had only to use her guile on the queen, a task she found easier and easier to accomplish.

A smile came to her lips at the thought that the queen herself would be the instrument whereby Arianna could have her revenge.

It was only fitting.

Rob immediately regretted not accompanying Arianna, but his pride wouldn't let him remedy that wrong now. Instead, he made his way down to the castle's elegant great hall and over to his father-in-law, who was sitting alone at a table. He cleared his throat, and the earl looked up at him.

"Rob. I'm surprised to find you here. I thought you'd be out hawking with your wife."

"I warrant I could say the same for you, sir."

"Ah . . . well, in my case, I was not invited."

"Not invited? That seems out of character for Elizabeth. I thought she insisted on your presence always."

"My dear man, nothing is out of character for Elizabeth. No, she had no need of me this morning, since she has the handsome king of Scotland to entertain her, and of course, she has Arianna. You know how she doth dote on her."

Rob sat down across the table from Leicester. "We can be thankful for that, at least, but I tell you, sir, I am mighty tired of worrying over her. I mean to find a way to live with my family in tranquility."

"I understand well what you mean. But have faith. I have a strong feeling an answer will be found. And if not . . . the queen grows older every day. Her memory weaker. Mayhap even now she has forgotten all about Mary's daughter."

Leicester stood, suddenly cheerful, and clasped Rob on the shoulder. "Meanwhile, since we have the morning free, I'd deem it quite enjoyable if you'd show me how to perfect my use of the crossbow. I have the damnedest time making the bolts fly true."

Rob rose from the wooden bench in a better mood. Handling a crossbow was a subject with which he felt comfortable. "Then shall we ride out to Great Park to practice? Who knows, we might even run into our ladies. Quite by accident, of course."

Walking out the door side by side, Leicester rested his arm on Rob's shoulder. He liked his son-in-law tremendously. Tall, lean, and hard-muscled, Rob reminded him of himself when he was the same tender age. Damned if the fleeting moments of one's life didn't speed on ever faster with each passing year!

* * *

"There! You see! My little Merlon has again snatched its prey from the very jaws of your gyr falcon, Your Majesty."

James laughed, enchanted with the beguiling Countess of Everly. "I see all too well the Scots must keep ever vigilant of the English."

Elizabeth watched James and Arianna in amusement. The girl's earthy innocence captivated all who knew her and knew no bounds. Never had she seen her so happy. She couldn't help but be curious as to the cause of so much bliss. For a moment, Elizabeth felt a twinge of jealousy, but it soon disappeared. She would not allow anything to spoil her time with Arianna, for she was the one woman Elizabeth trusted, outside of her own loyal maids of honor, and the pleasure of her company far outweighed her petty jealousy.

As for James, this was the first time she had seen a side of him that perked her interest. And it had taken Arianna to bring it out in him. Too bad his visit was, of necessity, so short. He had been here only one week, and that for reasons of state only. Next time, she would make sure he stayed much longer.

Remembering there was yet a full day's work ahead of her, conferring with her cabinet about the infernal war with the Spanish, Elizabeth called out, "James, Arianna! 'Tis been delightful, but duty calls, I fear."

"As you wish, cousin. It has been a most enchanting morning. Thank you for suggesting this outing. I am most pleased."

Elizabeth smiled widely. Yes, it had been a good idea. "I'm glad you enjoyed it, James. You see now why I enjoy being with Arianna. There are times when

I feel the need to order her to attend me at court, but her husband would never forgive me. And in truth, I would hate to see her fresh innocence destroyed having close contact with the most jaded members of my realm. No, it is best that she take life at court in small, harmless doses. Though, I must confess, this is one of those times I wish her to stay here with me."

Arianna saw her chance and took it. "You make me blush, Your Grace, with your kind words. In truth, it is always a joy to be with you. So much so that I regret my husband is in such a hurry to return to Everly. I would dearly have loved to stay a few days longer." Forcing a laugh, she added, "I fear, he needs a mission some time soon to occupy him for a bit. So that I will be free to visit you."

A light came to Elizabeth's eyes. "That idea has much merit. I shall think on it. Now, shall we race back to the castle? I'm suddenly feeling very invigorated. The attendants can carry the falcons for us so that we may ride the wind." There was something about being with Arianna, Elizabeth thought, that always made her feel a rush of youthful vigor.

"Good idea," James replied. "There is nothing so pleasurable as riding fast and hard on one's mount."

Elizabeth smirked at the double meaning of his words. She was beginning to like him more all the time.

James pulled on his mount's reins, forcing his horse to ride in tight little circles, knowing well how masculine it made him look. "You see how well-mated I am to my mount? Do you recognize her, Elizabeth? The mare is from the exquisite stable of horses you sent me."

"I had no idea, James. It looks as if I chose the perfect animal for you, for without a doubt you are well-mated." Yes. She was beginning to like him more and more. She couldn't help wondering, though, if James favored his mother. For in all the years Mary had been prisoner in England, she had never met the woman.

In truth, she had never wanted to meet Mary. Only now, with the Scottish queen rotting in her tomb, could she even begin to understand the motive for that. It seemed so foolish now that she could have been afraid Mary was more beautiful than she. Hadn't she been reassured time and time again, by Leicester and everyone else she had asked, that she was the lovelier of the two blood-related queens?

If James's features were like his mother's, then she had had nothing to worry about. For though he was tall and slim, his chin was a mite too pointed. His large blue expressive eyes were the only thing that kept his face from being quite ordinary looking.

She laughed to herself thinking about James's attraction to the sweet and innocent Arianna, for she would not hesitate to wager Arianna was the one woman in England who would be unattainable by the king of Scotland.

The wind whipped Arianna's hair about as she galloped down the well-worn path through the thick stand of woods, making it fly around her face like a golden mist. It had been an exciting morning, one she would never forget, for she had spent it pleasurably with her brother. The only thing that could make it all the more perfect would be if James knew about their relationship. But she knew that could never be.

Suddenly, Sanctimonious stumbled, slowing to a lopsided canter. Arianna reined in, calling out to her riding partners that her horse was in trouble. Elizabeth and James and the entire entourage came to a halt, backtracking to Arianna as she dismounted and bent to examine Sanctimonious's right front hoof.

"Here, let me do that, Arianna. 'Tis no job for a lady," James said, making his way over to her before anyone else could reach her. Bending over, he lifted the mare's slender leg and looked at the underside of her iron shoe.

Restless to continue her ride, Elizabeth said, "Since you are in good hands, Arianna, I will keep on riding. Catch up as soon as you can." With that, she spurred her horse, setting off again at a fast gallop, her entourage following obediently behind.

James's heart quickened at the knowledge that he was alone with the beautiful Arianna, but he kept his eyes focused on the mare's foot for fear she would know what was in his heart. "Here's the problem. She's picked up a jagged rock in her shoe."

"Let me see," Arianna said, moving close to James. "Ohhhh, that must hurt." Involuntarily, her hand reached out to touch Sanctimonious's hoof, accidentally brushing against the king's fingers.

James felt a strange sensation when her hand touched his, and he wondered again what it was about this woman. "Hand me a stick of some sort. I think I can pry it out."

Happy to oblige her brother, Arianna ran to the edge of the path and reached up to snap a branch from a tree, then stopped in horror as she heard the low, feral grunt of a large animal.

James heard it, too, and dropping the mare's foot, he moved quickly to lift Arianna out of harm's way, setting her on his own mount. At the same time, out of the corner of his eye, he saw the wild boar careening around a tree, heading right for him. In sick fascination, he watched as the huge, deadly tusks of the animal moved closer and closer to him.

Commanding his body to move, he made ready to dodge out of the way, knowing in advance the impossibility of that act. Then, hearing the distinctive thrum of an arrow being released, he dared to hope.

The sickening thud of a bolt slamming into the boar's tough hide, lodging in its heart, was music to his ears. He watched, still frozen in his tracks, as the gigantic animal fell to the ground at his feet, its gaping mouth emitting an unholy shriek like a wraith from hell. The tremendous body shook violently for a few moments, and then death finally took it.

In a daze, James sought his rescuer, his eyes lighting on Arianna's husband and the Earl of Leicester standing on the path, crossbows in hand.

Arianna followed his gaze to her husband, taking in his enticing masculine image. Her heart thrilled at the sight of him looking every bit as heroic as the legendary Robin Hood himself. "Oh, Rob, thank heaven you were near. I don't know what would have happened if you were not."

Regaining his composure, James said, "I'll tell you what would have happened, Arianna. That overgrown swine would have had me for dinner. But now, I trow, we shall dine on him."

Striding over to Rob, he pumped his arm enthusiastically. "I canna thank you enough, Robert. I'm in your debt. If there's ever anything I can do to repay ye, ye have only to ask."

The looks Rob and Leicester exchanged left no doubt in James's mind that they had already thought of a way he could repay them. How curious. Leicester was the most powerful man in England; what could he possibly need or want?

The last night of James's visit was turned into a gala event. Elizabeth outdid herself with an extravagance she rarely expressed, turning the great hall into a magnificent spectacle of pageantry.

Word had quickly spread that Robert Warwick of Everly had saved the life of the Scottish king. The most prestigious lords and ladies of Elizabeth's court now awaited the arrival of that noble lord and his beautiful wife, curious at their prolonged absence.

In truth, Elizabeth had commanded them to be late. She knew well the value of a dramatic entrance and wanted to heighten the already-considerable excitement that prevailed in the venerable hall. It was a boon to her that an English earl had saved the Scottish king's life, and she would play it for all it was worth.

Suddenly, Arianna's words came back to her. A mission for Robert. She had the very one. She would send Robert to Scotland for a short time. Just long enough to gain more advantage from today's events. The Scottish people would receive him warmly, and they would no doubt be more amiable to a treaty she had in mind. And she would benefit most of all, with a nice long visit from Arianna.

In sooth, she sometimes wished Arianna had no

husband at all. But, if the dear child must be burdened with a man, at least he was an admirable one, like her own dear Robin.

A sudden hush drew Elizabeth's attention as she sat at the table of honor on the raised dais. Gazing down the length of the long hall, she saw that Robert and Arianna had finally made their entrance. She smiled craftily.

Arianna sucked in her breath at the magnificence of the hall. Never had she seen so grand a place. Her eyes swept to the right, taking in the row of beautiful arched windows that numbered over a dozen, their elegant lines a pleasure to her senses.

When she had her fill of that view she looked to the left, eyeing the exquisite paneled murals that lined the inner wall. Each one depicted a different scene, from stag hunt to victorious battle to satyrs frolicking in the woods with nubile nymphs. Her heart filled with pride at the thought that she was here, an invited guest. Nay, more than that, for because of Rob's brave act, Arianna and her husband were guests of honor.

Grasping tight to Rob's arm, she turned her attention to the queen of England sitting at the dais, her brother, king to another proud country, beside her, and drew herself up to her full height, slight though it might be. Tonight she felt like a princess royal and she would act the part.

Sensing their presence, James turned his attention to the entranceway, watching as Robert and Arianna began the long walk down the center of the aisle. The trestle tables on either side of the hall were filled to capacity, a tribute to Rob and his lady.

And oh, what a glorious lady she was. Dressed in a

green velvet gown so luxurious it befitted a queen, Arianna was a delectable vision. His heart leaped at the sight of her, but strangely, at the same time, he felt quite melancholy. What was it about her that caused such opposing feelings? He had never felt like this with any other woman.

Colorful pages escorted Arianna to his side, whilst Rob was directed to the seat beside Elizabeth. Composing himself, James remembered his manners and stood, clapping his hands together to honor the hero of the hour. A murmur came over the crowd and then as one, they stood and applauded, too, the hall reverberating with the great sound.

Robert was surprised and quite touched by the king's action. Gazing over at his wife, he saw the tears of pride gleaming in her eyes.

Turning to the king, amidst all the noise, Arianna raised herself up on her toes to whisper in his ear, "Thank you for that, Your Majesty. It was a lovely gesture."

Beaming, the king took her hand in his, raising it to his lips. The sight of the ivory ring on her finger brought a jolt to his heart and he froze, staring at the delicate carving of the rose that adorned the ring. He blinked and looked at it again. There was no doubt. This was the very ring his mother had described to him in her letter. And the wearer . . . Dear God, the wearer . . . Arianna . . . was his sister.

Bending his head very slowly as if he thought the ring might disappear, James kissed Arianna's fingers, his lips deliberately brushing the edge of the ivory rose in reverance. And then aware that everyone's eyes were on him, he lowered her hand, reluctantly breaking contact with his nearest living relative.

In a daze, he nodded to the applauding spectators, and the clamor ended as everyone again sat, unaware that the king of Scotland's life had changed forever.

The muted clang of tankards on wood made him aware that there was food to eat, wine to drink, and he raised his own silver goblet to his lips and drank deeply of its contents.

Fortified, James turned to gaze at the woman who shared his blood. Countess Arianna Warwick of Everly. Beautiful wife to the Earl of Everly.

His sister.

He understood now the strange feelings he had had before. It wasn't the ancient attraction of a man for a woman he had felt, but the ancient blood bond between a brother and sister. It was a kinsmanship, a fealty, a cherished reunion of like souls.

Arianna looked up just then and smiled sweetly, the expression on her face suddenly changing as she looked deeper into his eyes. How strangely he looked at her. Did he know? Did he see his mother in her eyes? No, that could not be. He had been but a babe when last he saw his mother. Then what? She stared back, enthralled. What did it matter? He was here with her now and that was truly a miracle.

Elizabeth's voice broke the magic spell between brother and sister with a whiny plea. "James, it pleases me that you find Countess Arianna so mesmerizing, but since we have such little time left to talk, I do hope you can spare me a few moments."

The urge to kill Elizabeth rose strong in Arianna at that moment. How was it the queen always found a way to come between her and those she loved? Arianna lowered her gaze to her trencher and took a large bite of venison, tearing into it with a vengeance.

"Cousin, I thought you happily occupied talking with Robert, and I wished not to interfere." James hid his disappointment, hoping he would have another chance to talk to Arianna. His ship would leave first thing in the morning; tonight would be his only chance. "But since that is not the case, I implore you to speak your mind."

Smiling coquettishly, the queen replied, "Word has come to me that a certain privateer in your hire was once a subject of mine."

"Whom do you speak of? I'm sure I have more than one stray Englishman in my service."

"None like this one, I trow. For he is the very one who helped Arianna give birth to her son as she lay on a wretched cliff in the middle of a horrific storm."

James stared at Elizabeth in disbelief. "You canna be serious? It seems too incredulous to believe a noble-woman would find herself in such a precarious situation."

Elizabeth laughed raucously, jubilant that she had so intrigued the king. "Not our Arianna. She indeed gave birth on the cliff after she had fallen whilst running away from a madman."

Astounded, James turned to look at Arianna.

Arianna blushed deeply.

"Then tell me, Elizabeth, the name of this noble knight. When I return to Scotland I will reward him most generously. For, to be sure, the world would be a poorer place without Arianna Warwick."

"Ha! No noble knight he, but a huntsman. Colin Colrain."

"Colin? Colin Colrain? Well, I'll be damned. But correct me if I'm wrong. I seem to remember he is a nobleman by birth, not a common huntsman. Although, now that I think of it, I remember hearing that you confiscated all his lands some years back."

Elizabeth pursed her lips. "No need to remind me. Arianna has already done that. In truth, I would have returned his property, but he vanished most mysteriously. It has only just come to my attention that he is now in your service."

Speaking softly to Arianna, James said, "You were in good hands then, Arianna, for Colin is an exceptional man."

Arianna's felt suddenly lonely thinking of the man who had been her companion for ten full months. In the year since she and Rob had been reunited, not one word had she heard about Colin Colrain. "How is he? Is he well? Is he happy?"

James heard the concern in her voice and knew there was more to this strange story than had been mentioned thus far. "He is fine. And couldna be happier since his marriage to Cassiopeia, a most beauteous lady pirate. How strange, I suddenly realize she greatly resembles you."

"Oh, my dear James," Elizabeth piped in, "to think you could compare Countess Arianna to a base female pirate. Really! If I were Robert, I believe I'd take offense."

Rob had been listening closely, unnerved to hear mentioned the one name he'd prefer never hearing again. "I take no offense, Your Grace. Not if this

Cassiopeia is as sweet and good as my wife. Colin's taste in women has always been superior." Rob stared at his wife and she quickly lowered her head.

James knew for certain now that something had transpired between Colin and Arianna. The queen would see it, too, if she weren't so preoccupied with entertaining him at Arianna's expense. A shudder coursed through his body, and he suddenly knew Arianna was in need of protection from this black-hearted queen. And by God, he would see to it himself. Elizabeth had murdered his mother; he wouldn't give her the chance to do the same to his sister.

"Robert, if you please, forgive me for changing the subject, but I have not yet had a chance to tell you how I wish to reward you for saving my life."

"Please, my lord, I have no need of a reward. In fact, I would be insulted if you offered me one. I doubt not that you would have done the same if the situation had been reversed."

James laughed. "Aye, I would have tried, but the outcome might not have been the same. My aim is not as true, nor my talent at the bow as great. But as for your being insulted, I'm afraid I must risk that for I intend to give you a castle in Scotland, whether you weel have it or not."

Arianna drew in her breath in disbelief. "A castle! Your Majesty, you can't mean it."

Rob caught Leicester's eye. This was exactly what they had hoped the king would do. It could be the answer to everything. Elizabeth could not harm Arianna or his son if they lived in Scotland under James's protection.

"Well, what do you say, Robert? Weel you accept

my gift? Take my word for it, I am not often so verra generous."

"Then I shall accept. Not for myself, but because my wife delights so in adding new castles to her holdings."

A happy Arianna heard little of the conversation after that. It wasn't until the king rose to leave that she came back to earth, knowing she must bid him farewell. How could she bear it?

Tears threatened her already-bright eyes as James took her hand in his, softly brushing his lips over it. Then, unexpectedly, he fervently kissed her ivory ring.

Her heart leapt. The ivory ring. Why did he kiss it? It had been given to her by his mother and hers, Mary, Queen of Scotland. She had worn it this night to honor her. Had worn the green velvet gown for the selfsame reason. It was the very gown that had been fashioned after one Mary had worn when Arianna visited her in prison.

The wearing of it made her feel closer to her mother. And on this night, this wonderful night when she was with her brother, with hopes of a new life growing in her belly, Arianna felt closer to her mother than she ever had before.

Standing straight once more, James gazed into Arianna's eyes one last time. "My lady, if you ever find yourself in need . . ." He nodded his head slightly, indicating the queen engaged in deep conversation with Rob. "Please send your friend Colin Colrain to me with a message, and I shall do all I can to help."

"I don't understand. Either you are very perceptive, or . . . Has the queen given you cause to think I may need your help?"

"Not at all. In fact, she seems to regard you very highly. But it is my experience that when it comes to monarchs, it is best not to be noticed at all."

"Then, surely, I am in danger with you, Sire, since you have singled me out."

James smiled sadly. "Sweet lassie, you are safer with me than you can ever imagine, but I'll say no more. I've said too much already. Just remember . . . if you need a friend, Colin will be at the King's Head Inn in London for another month or two. And if you need him after that, you have only to ask the innkeeper there where he is, for he is in Colin's employ."

Nodding his head in a wistful farewell salute, the king made his way to the queen to pay his respects, then quickly left the dais.

Arianna watched as the king of Scotland strode the length of the great hall, waving goodbyes as he moved, and already she felt his loss. Then, raising her chin high, she thought, He and I are of the same blood. Blood of the ivory rose. Blood of Mary, Queen of Scots. Fate will bring us together again.

Chapter Four

Brambly Castle, June 1588

Drenched to the skin, Arianna and Rob rode over the drawbridge and through the gatehouse, laughing merrily. They had been caught in the rain as they rode home from a picnic by their private waterfall, and instead of dampening their spirits, it had only heightened them more.

Arianna decided that just as soon as they donned dry clothing and curled up before a blazing fire in their own bedchamber, she would tell Rob the news about the child she carried. She was certain she was pregnant now, for her breasts were heavy and sore, and she had had no menses for yet another month.

An hour later, nuzzling his neck with her nose as they sat before the fire, watching their small son at play, she said, "Rob, I have something wonderful to tell you."

"Hmmm? And just what is that?"

A knocking sounded at the door, and Rob kissed her nose, saying, "Hold that thought, whilst I get rid of whoever is there." He opened the door, the scowl on his face turning to surprise when he saw the messenger standing beside two of his knights.

Thunder rolled over the castle, sending eerie waves of lightning dancing over the battlement like delicate golden banners as Rob unrolled the parchment with the queen's seal. What in God's name does she want now? It could not be good news, else the messenger would not have traveled after dark to get here.

Before reading the neatly scribed words, Rob had his knights escort the rain-soaked messenger to the kitchen for a hot meal.

"God's blood! I don't believe it. Elizabeth has ordered—do you hear—ordered me to sail for Scotland in two days time."

Arianna's voice quivered when she spoke. "Scotland? But why?"

"Why? That is the question, isn't it? She claims to need me to negotiate a treaty with James. Says that since I saved his life, he is indebted to me and that makes me very valuable as a negotiator. Have you ever heard such rubbish?"

Arianna hid her shaking hands behind her back. "It seems reasonable to me, Rob. And 'tis certainly a great honor. I shall miss you terribly, of course, but I cannot help being pleased that the queen finds you a great asset to England."

"Miss me? Why should you miss me? You will be at my side."

Arianna's heart sank. She had been certain the queen was using this as a ploy to get Rob out of the way for a while. Was she wrong? "Oh, Rob, I would love to go to Scotland with you, but do you think it's wise to leave Robin again so soon?"

"Why would you have to? He can come along."

Arianna was getting more flustered by the moment. "I . . . I . . . think that's a wonderful idea, Rob, truly I do."

Rob studied her face intently. Elizabeth's document clearly stated that she wanted him to go alone, but he couldn't help but wonder if this was a scheme of Arianna's to get him out of the way. He had hoped to trap her, but either she was too clever to fall for it, or she was truly innocent. Damn, he wished he knew which was true.

"Arianna?"

"Yes, Rob."

"What do you know of this matter?"

Arianna felt the color drain from her face.

"What do you know of this matter?"

"How could I know anything? Am I a reader of minds? I don't understand your question, and I don't like the way you asked me."

Rob took her face in his hands, his fingers digging into her skin, his dark eyes penetrating hers to their very depths. "If I find out you had anything to do with my sudden journey to Scotland, I'll . . . I'll beat you 'til you can't stand up. Do you ken?"

Arianna stared back without blinking. "I ken. Now you ken this. If you ever try to beat me, I shall have your strongest knight, Sir John Neal, lock you in the tower room until *you* are too weak to stand."

Little Robin's voice startled his mother and father. "Mama, lock Robin up, too?"

Two sets of eyes gazed down at the child they loved

more than life, two sets of arms reaching for him at the same time. "No, baby, Mama was only joking. She would never lock your father in the tower."

Lifting him up, Arianna snuggled her nose into his sweet-smelling neck. She gazed over at Rob with solemn eyes, and he pulled her and Robin into the protection of his arms.

"I'm sorry for accusing you, Rose Petal. It's just my great love for you that makes me act so. If anything ever happened to you or the babe, I don't know what I'd do."

"I know. I know. I feel the same way. Oh, Rob, I love you so. And suddenly, I can't bear the thought of you leaving. Mayhap, if you speak to the queen, she will release you from this obligation."

"You know her better than I. Do you really think she would do that?"

A strange feeling of dread suddenly washed over Arianna. Something was going to happen to Rob. She knew it. "No. It would be dangerous to even ask." Was that what made her suddenly afraid? Was it only that? Or was it something much deeper that made her suddenly shiver.

"I'm glad you realize that. For it gives me hope that you won't act rashly whilst I'm gone. I want you to promise me that you'll not spill a drop of Elizabeth's blood. Give me your sacred oath and I'll leave for Scotland with a much lighter heart."

Without a moment's hesitation, Arianna answered, "I promise."

"That was too easy, my darling. I need more assurance than that. I want you to repeat after me: "I, Arianna Warwick, Countess of Everly, wife of Robert and mother to Robin, swear on the life of my child that I shall not spill a single drop of Elizabeth's blood."

In a voice barely more than a whisper, Arianna said, "In the name of all that's holy, don't ever again say anything about Robin dying. You know how superstitious I am."

"Swear on his life."

"All right! I swear!"

"Say the words, Arianna. Say the words."

Closing her eyes tight, Arianna repeated the words that would keep her from killing her hated enemy. "I swear on the life of my child that I shall not spill a drop of Elizabeth's blood."

No. She wouldn't spill a drop of her blood, but that wouldn't keep her from obtaining her revenge in some other way. "There. Does that make you happy?"

Rob smiled, pulling her into his arms. "No, not until I have heard the wonderful news you were about to tell me."

Arianna paled. How could she tell Rob she was pregnant now? Either he would insist she come with him, or he would worry over her every moment he was away. She could not live with either choice. Better not to tell him until he returned.

" 'Twas just . . . just . . . Robin's training is complete. He no longer soils himself. Isn't that wonderful! Our babe is growing up."

Rob frowned. He doubted very much that that was what Arianna had planned on telling him, but he accepted the answer all the same. If he knew his wife, she would tell him in good time. It was impossible for Arianna to keep a secret very long.

Arianna immediately regretted the promise she made to Rob. She would have to work harder now to find a way to exact her revenge on the queen without actually killing her. But she would, of that one thing she was sure. Nothing could keep her from that. Not even her husband. When Arianna was done with Elizabeth, the queen would wish she was dead.

Getting ready for bed, Arianna was surprised to see how lighthearted Rob had become and she felt a twinge of guilt, knowing the oath she made to him had brought about the change. But her guilt soon faded away as she rationalized her actions. It wasn't her fault if he thought her promise meant she had given up any idea of revenge, and if it made him feel better to think that, then what was the harm? She went to sleep that night convinced she hadn't done anything wrong.

Next day, Rob and Arianna traveled the suddenly-too-short distance to London and St. James Palace, where the queen was now in residence. Whilst Rob was getting secret instructions from Elizabeth in her private chamber, Arianna was giving out secret instructions of her own to Rob's trusted knight, Sir John Neal, who would be accompanying her husband to Scotland.

Deferring supper in the great hall with the queen and her court, Arianna and Rob had a quiet supper in the chamber assigned to them. But not even the cheery fire crackling in the fireplace could brighten their somber mood. In bed, they slept locked in each other's arms and awoke the same way.

All too soon, it was time for him to leave. Arianna's heart beat heavily as she watched her husband gather his luggage, her guilt almost too much to bear.

"Time to go, Rose Petal. Will you come down to the dock with me? Say goodbye to me there?"

"Oh, Rob, don't ask it of me. I cannot bear to see you board the ship that will take you from me. Please. Let me say goodbye here."

Rob swallowed his disappointment. "If that's the way you want it. Come here, then. Kiss me goodbye."

Arianna ran into his arms, luxuriating in the wonderful feeling of protectiveness that always came over her at their touch. It felt so good. So very, very good. Lifting her face to his, she felt his lips on hers and kissed him back longingly.

Rob pulled from her embrace and, beckoning to the servants to take his luggage, walked swiftly out of the room.

A lump the size of a goose egg was lodged in his throat as he made his way down the stairs and emerged into the bright daylight. Hearing his name, he turned to see Leicester standing in the doorway behind him. "Rob, I wish you Godspeed."

"Leicester. I'm glad you're here. Will you watch out for Arianna while I'm gone? I'm truly afraid she's up to something. Keep her away from Elizabeth as much as you can, and try to get her to go back to Everly. Mayhap she will listen to you."

"I'll do what I can, son, but I'm afraid the bloody conflagration with the Spanish Armada is drawing near, and my time is not my own anymore. I spend more and more hours on the road, traveling from place to place, drumming up men and supplies to defend our coasts."

"I'm sorry, my lord, I've been so preoccupied with

Arianna I've not paid much attention to anything else."

"Better to occupy your thoughts with your beautiful wife than to wait as I do for the day when the Spanish sail down the channel and attack."

"Forgive me, my lord . . ."

"Nonsense. I quite understand your worry over my exasperating daughter, but I think you're wrong about her being up to something. The only thing she seems to have on her mind is you. She hates to see you go."

"So much so that she can't bear to go down to the dock with me."

Leicester heard a twinge of bitterness in Rob's voice. "Surely you know how much she loves you?"

"Aye. But her love for revenge is more powerful than her love for me."

Leicester slowly shook his head. "I wish I could tell you that wasn't true. But God help me, I really don't know."

Before boarding the ship that would take him away from Arianna, Rob turned his gaze for one final sweep of the wharf. He had hoped at the last minute she would decide to see him off. But that was not to be. Disappointed, he walked up the long wooden plank and stepped onto the ship, where Sir John showed him to his cabin, a twinkle in his eyes. Strange, John rarely showed feelings of any kind. Mayhap he was glad to be accompanying him to Scotland. Gazing down at the dock last time, Rob opened the door to his cabin and stepped in.

There, stretched out naked on the bed, was his wife.

Without blinking an eye, Rob reached behind him and fastened the lock on the door. His gaze never left his wife's luscious body as he worked at removing his clothing.

One boot and then the other thunked down on the wood-planked floor, followed by trunk hose, hose, and doublet, until he was completely and gloriously naked, his manpart stiffened to the hardness of a steel rod. He reached the bed in but two long strides.

"I thought you'd never get here," Arianna moaned just before he descended on her, cutting off her speech with his hungry mouth.

He kissed her until he could breathe no longer, then came up for air long enough to say, "I swear to you, when I die, it will be whilst making love to you."

Suddenly serious, Rob stared deep into her eyes, then lowered his head to kiss her forehead, then cheeks, then nose, then chin in solemn silence. He took her earlobe into his mouth and sucked on it, before finding the other one and repeating his performance. He kissed her neck and shoulders, and nuzzled his nose in her armpits, before moving to her breasts, taking one rosy nipple and then the other into his mouth. They hardened noticeably at his touch, and he bit them lightly, desiring to sink his teeth much harder into them. Instead, he tongued them lavishly, joyously, reveling in the feel and taste of the delectable, delicate little buds.

Arianna moaned softly at his touch, compelling him to cup her sweet, warm breasts in his urgent hands, his teeth grinding together in his need for penetration.

She concentrated hard on each fervent touch, to store away in her memory for the time when he was gone. A satisfied smile played across her face as he moved over her, playfully at first, then intensely as his desire became overpowering.

And then he was moving even farther down her body, bent on tasting the love nectar that belonged to him alone. Using his fingers, he slowly separated the delicate lips that guarded her entrance, enthralled at the sight of her, moist and ready for him. Stiffening his tongue, he used it like his shaft, moving in and out of her, until she cried out from the sheer pleasure of it.

And when her body began to shudder as ecstasy took her away, he withdrew and mounted her quickly, wanting to be a part of it. Pushing into her moist, hot cocoon, he felt it tighten around him, contracting in spasms that pulled him in deeper, sending his senses reeling. The luscious feel of her drove him wild, and he wanted it to go on forever.

Her body stiffened and her breathing stopped as she let the orgasm wash over her in wave after wave. And when it was done, it began again as she felt his penetration and the heat of him moving inside her. If there was a place called paradise, it was here, now, residing within every bliss-producing stroke of his, every treasured moment she was united with the man she desired most in the world.

Wanting to prolong the moment of his own release, he ground into her slowly, maneuvering inside her as he probed and explored her, enjoying the sensuousness of the moment, the velvet depths of her being. And when he had delayed it as long as he could, he gave in to the pleasure and let it carry him away, muffling his deep moan in her neck.

Arianna felt his body convulse and felt another

wave of ecstasy building. "Oh, Rob, Rob, Rob. I still need you. Don't stop. Don't stop."

Happy to oblige her, Rob moved his finger down to her little pleasure nub and stimulated it, rubbing it back and forth at the same time he moved inside her deliciously slippery body. It didn't take long before she was gasping her pleasure, her fingers digging into his buttocks.

They stared into each other's eyes, sated, blissful in the erotic bond they shared. Then slowly, oh, so slowly, through the love mist that surrounded her, she heard the muted voice of someone on deck cry, "All ashore who's going ashore."

"Oh, no! No one but John Neal knows I'm here," Arianna cried, rolling off the bed and pulling her gown over her head. "I've got to get out of here before I find myself in Scotland."

Rob laughed, too, as he laced up her gown. "Countess, I've a good mind to hide your clothes to ensure you do just that. Of course, by the time we got to Scotland, there'd not be enough left of me to carry ashore. But, oh, it would be well worth it."

Arianna suddenly felt the ship list and realized it was in motion. "Ohhhh, damn it all, the ship is moving. Where are my shoes? Where are my hose?"

Rob dangled her shoes from his fingers, then thrust them behind his back as she reached for them. "Uh, uh. Not until you give me a proper kiss goodbye."

"Robert. You idiot. Do you want me to swim back to shore?" Reaching behind him, she grabbed her shoes as he plunked a wet kiss on her lips. Then opening the door, she ran out to the deck. The ship was separated from the dock by several feet. "Damn.

Damn. Damn," she shouted as she gathered up her skirts and flew through the air, shoes in hand, hose trailing over her shoulder, landing with a hard thud on the dock. Immediately, a cheer went up as sailors and city folk alike watched the spectacular sight.

And . . . another pair of eyes watched, too. Deep brown eyes that lit up like amber fire at the sight of the delectable female hurdling through the air, half dressed. One bushy eyebrow raised as he watched, knowing all too well that she had come from bed just moments before. He wondered who the lucky fellow was.

Feeling deep regret that he had not the time to pursue the lusty beauty, Captain Elijah Longfellow, pirate lord of the seven seas, reluctantly turned his attention back to the business at hand.

Chapter Five

Making her way out to the sweeping expanse of the stone terrace built especially for Elizabeth, Arianna leaned wearily on the railing and gazed at the town below. It was tiring accompanying Elizabeth. So tiring she wished she were free to go back to Everly and be with her son whilst she waited for Rob's return. Ah, me, that was not to be. Elizabeth was enjoying her company too much. It would take a braver woman than she to ask to be excused now.

If she lived to be a hundred, she doubted she would ever get used to the queen's ways, to the constant infernal traveling from castle to castle that the queen was wont to do. At least, here in Windsor Castle she didn't feel as fettered as she had at St. James. Still, she had hoped to find solitude here, and was discovering how precious and rare a commodity that was.

Trying to ignore the high-pitched squeals of the ladies of the court clustered around the parapet, Arianna concentrated on her hatred of Elizabeth. Hatred that continued to grow as she learned more and more about the woman. For in the short time she had been accompanying the queen, a vivid picture had formed in her mind.

It was a picture of a very vain, very self-centered woman. A picture of a woman who would go to any lengths to protect the carefully cultivated image she had of herself as England's greatest beauty. A woman who had gone so far to guard that image that she had actually had a man beheaded for discovering her youth and beauty were a myth.

Incredible as that seemed, Arianna knew the queen was capable of just such an act. One of the queen's maids of honor, under the influence of cherry wine, had told her how it had happened. A young courtier, anxious to have an audience with the queen so he might impress her with his devotion, thereby furthering himself in his pursuit of a place in her inner circle of confidants, had made the terrible blunder of barging in to the queen's chamber as she was making ready for bed.

Unfortunately for him, the queen had just removed her wig, and he found her almost bald and looking years older by far. To the surprise of her attendants, Elizabeth had received the handsome young man as warmly as ever, which relieved him no end. He never suspected that it had all been an act. That, in truth, she was exceedingly upset. The next day he was arrested on some trumped-up charge and was eventually beheaded. All because he had dared to see Elizabeth as she truly was instead of as the fantasy she had created.

Hearing this, Arianna finally had the key to her revenge: the queen's great vanity. Somehow she would bring the queen to her knees . . . and in front of an audience of the most important people in the land. She would humiliate her beyond belief, and in so doing would avenge her mother. But how to do it without endangering herself or her family? How to do it and still keep her promise to Rob not to spill a drop of Elizabeth's blood? There had to be a way.

Excited feminine voices assaulted Arianna's ears. Looking up, she saw the queen and her entourage of ladies leaning over the parapet.

"Arianna, look. See how swift Sanctimonious is. She is outpacing Leicester's stallion."

Arianna couldn't believe her ears. Sanctimonious? Who dared ride her horse? Turning to the queen, she started to protest, then thought better of it. Only the queen herself would have been presumptuous enough to make use of another's property. Fuming, Arianna turned her gaze away lest the queen see how truly angry she was.

"Ah, look at her go. My dear, I'm truly jealous of your fine horseflesh. Methinks Sanctimonious is truly a horse fit for a queen."

Arianna was stunned. The queen was outrageously begging to be gifted with Sanctimonious. Well, she could wait till hell froze over before she would turn her sweet little mare over to that hateful woman.

Another boisterous shout shattered the air, and the queen turned her attention back to the two horses racing below. Arianna looked, too, and saw a third rider on the road. This one was obviously a messenger, and judging from the lathered look of the horse, he had been riding a long time.

"Oh, bother," Elizabeth muttered wearily, spying the messenger. " 'Tis bad news, I fear. Why is it good news is always a long time coming, whilst bad news travels on a swift horse? I wager, it will be about the Spanish Armada. Not a single day passes without a reminder of that infernal and endless threat of impending doom. Between the Lord Admiral and Drake, I am constantly besieged with correspondence of death and destruction."

The queen's words sent a shiver up Arianna's spine, and unbidden, an image of Rob flashed through her head. It suddenly occurred to her that she had sent him out to sea whilst the Spanish Armada prowled the very waters he traveled. Dear Jesus, she had been so blinded by her need for revenge that she hadn't even thought about the consequences. If anything happened to him, she would never forgive herself.

In a moment, the rider, sweaty and covered with dirt from the road, came bursting out onto the terrace. "Your Majesty, terrible news. My lord Warwick's ship has been captured by pirates."

Arianna heard the words but could not comprehend their meaning. Pirates? What would they have to do with her husband? It must be some terrible mistake. Dear God, please let it be a mistake. As the truth sank in, a low keening sound escaped her lips and she cried, "Tell me what has happened to my husband!"

The messenger wiped the sweat and grime from his eyes with his sleeve. "My lady, don't despair. The earl was taken alive."

"Alive? Of course he's alive. He has to be alive. But I don't understand any of this. Who took my husband and why? How do you come by this information?"

"My lady, forgive me. Let me start at the beginning. I was a steward aboard the earl's ship. Captain Longfellow, that bloody pirate, blew a hole in the hull,

crippling her. He boarded her along with a horde of
his men, outnumbering us ten to one. We had no
choice but to surrender. Next thing I know the earl
and his knight, John Neal, were trussed like fowl and
transferred to the pirate's ship."

Arianna grew pale as the seaman's words sank in.
"Longfellow? What would he want with my husband?"

"Enough," Elizabeth said, taking Arianna's hand.
"I'll speak to the man in your stead; you're too dis-
traught to comprehend what's going on. Just take
comfort in knowing he is still alive."

Comfort, Arianna thought. *Comfort. My God, I'm
responsible for sending Rob into danger. There's no
comfort in knowing that.* Faced with overwhelming
guilt, Arianna fled to her chamber.

Elizabeth shook her head sympathetically as she
watched Arianna leave, then turned to the messenger,
eyes narrowed to a slit. "Do you have anything else to
report?"

"Yes, Your Grace. This ransom note. Longfellow
himself gave it to me. Said I was to make sure the
Countess of Everly received it."

Elizabeth looked at the crumpled parchment in the
messenger's hand and in an imperial voice said, "I'll
take that."

"But, but . . . I was told to wait for an answer from
the countess."

"And you shall have it. I will write it with my own
hand. As for the rest of you, not a word to Arianna
about the ransom, I'll not have her upset any further."

Arianna sat at the window in her bedchamber, staring out at the grey sky, her eyes streaked with tears. A

loud rapping sounded on the door, intruding on the isolation she craved. "Go away!"

"Arianna, it's me. Please open the door."

Arianna heard her father's voice. Swiftly opening the door, she threw herself into his arms. "Oh, Father, it's all my fault. What am I to do?"

Leicester escorted her back into the bedchamber and closed the door. "Your fault? Child, I hardly think you commanded the pirates to attack Rob's ship."

"No. I did even worse. It was because of me Elizabeth sent Rob to Scotland. Because of me and my plans to revenge my mother. Rob always told me great harm would be done if I persisted in my hatred, but I didn't listen, and now it's too late."

"Too late? Do you give up so easily?"

Arianna gazed into her father's eyes, and a spark of hope ignited. "Oh, Father, you are the most powerful man in all of England. Is there something you can do?"

"Child, I will do everything I can. As soon as we receive a ransom note, I will make arrangements to pay it."

"Ransom? Is that why he was captured? For a ransom?"

"Aye, I doubt it not. So you see there is very little to worry about. They will return Rob as soon as the ransom is paid."

"And if they do not? Oh, Father, what if it isn't a ransom they're after?"

"We'll worry about that when the time comes. Meanwhile, I'll send my most trusted agents out to find out where he's being kept. They'll find him, I'm certain. Be patient, my dear."

* * *

But Arianna's patience wore thinner and thinner as each unfruitful day passed without a ransom note or word of her husband. It was as if the ocean had swallowed him up, and she could bear no more of it. She had to do something.

Frantic to find her husband, she sent a message back to Brambly Castle notifying her people to immediately go back to Everly with baby Robin. She wanted her son safe with Rob's mother Margaret in case something should happen. Having accomplished that, she promptly left Windsor, pretending she was just going for a short ride on Sanctimonious. She had no choice but to lie, for if she told her father or the queen her plans, they would never have let her go.

Away from prying eyes, she disguised herself as a boy, wearing the same clothes she had worn when she was forced to play the part of her foster father's apprentice falconer. Then she rode toward London and the only man who could help her—Colin Colrain. Thank the Lord, James had told her where to find him. She just prayed he would still be there, because if anyone could find Rob, it was Colin.

The King's Head was bustling with activity when Arianna arrived late that night. Gathering her courage, she started for the door, hoping her male garb would gain her entrance without attracting a lot of attention. She was grateful that her pregnancy would not show for another month or two.

Had it been just five short years ago when last she wore these clothes? She smiled, thinking of her first meeting with Rob. He had been attracted to her even then, having worried that his feelings were unnatural, for he thought he was in love with a boy. Ah, what a bittersweet time that had been.

Thinking back, she realized her whole life had been a lie—a masquerade of some sort. In her almost twenty-two years on God's earth, she had donned the disguises of a peasant girl, an apprentice falconer, a young noblewoman raised in a convent, and oh, yes, a wandering minstrel. She had disguised herself first to protect herself from Elizabeth, and then to win Rob's love, and now here she was again, playing the part of a boy once more.

So be it. If fate decreed that she spend her life in masquerade, it was a sacrifice she was willing to make as long as in doing so she protected the people she loved most in the world.

Arianna started to open the door, when it was flung open and a ruggedly handsome face appeared haloed by a pelt of curly red hair and beard. "Colin!"

Colin stared, in disbelief, into the familiar eyes of the woman he had loved and lost. He blinked, thinking the apparition had been caused by the blue haze of smoke that stung at his eyes or the tankards of ale he had so profusely drunk, but the image did not disappear. "God's blood, woman, what are you doing here?"

Grabbing her by the arm, he led her around to the side of the building, backing her up against the rough stone. "Where is that blundering husband of yours? I vow, he has the damndest time holding on to his wife."

Tears spilled down Arianna's face at the mention of Rob. Colin immediately regretted his outburst, but he felt compelled to continue. "And what in heaven's name are you doing dressed like that? I thought you were done with masquerading."

"I was. Oh, Colin, I was done with all the lies and deceit, truly I was, but Rob is in mortal danger, and I had to find you. You're the only one who can save him now."

"Hold on, there. Slow down. What is all this about Rob being in danger? What's happened to him?"

"That scurrilous pirate Longfellow captured Rob's ship and took him prisoner."

Colin blanched, knowing what Arianna did not . . . that Robert was in grave danger. For fate had delivered him to a man who bore a grudge against him.

He remembered the day Robert's father had died whilst riding a horse. Remembered Elijah Longfellow had been the stable boy then at Everly Castle. He had been negligent in cinching the straps on the old earl's saddle and it had come loose, twisting around the horse's belly. The old earl had fallen from his horse, striking his head against a large boulder, and had perished instantly.

Rob blamed Elijah and had him lashed severely, then banished him from Everly. Colin was sure Longfellow would never forget that. Truth to tell, he should be grateful to Robert for that banishment, because it was what compelled him to seek his fortune as a pirate. Because of his wicked heart he had made a damn good pirate, and Longfellow was now the self-imposed king of a wild little island called Devil's Harp.

But he could not tell Arianna any of that. For if she knew what danger Rob was in, she would want to storm the stronghold single-handedly. Trying to keep the mood light, he asked, "And just what was Rob doing out in the wild blue? Why wasn't he safe at home in Everly planting more babies in your belly?"

Arianna blinked at Colin's words. If he only knew. But no, she could not tell him of her pregnancy or he'd never allow her to go after Rob. "Because . . . because . . . oh, Colin, because I had Elizabeth send him on a mission to Scotland to get him out of the way while I plotted my revenge on her." Overcome with emotion, Arianna began to sob loudly.

Colin pulled her up against his chest and comforted her. "There, there, now. You know I could never stand to see you cry. Dry your eyes or you'll have me bawling like a baby, too."

Arianna smiled through her tears. Leaning into Colin's body, she nuzzled her head against his shoulder. "Oh, Colin, I'm so glad I found you."

Tipping her head up, Colin kissed her forehead. "And now that you have, tell me how this mischief began."

"Mischief is the right word, Colin. I, too, want to hear why this woman is all but fornicating with you."

Colin jumped away, and Arianna's eyes opened wide at the sight of the most exotic female creature she had ever seen.

Cassiopeia—for it could be only she—was dressed flamboyantly, brilliantly, unbelievably, in red velvet doublet and black silk pantaloons, a very pregnant belly straining from beneath the too-tight doublet. Her legs were encased in gold stockings and over them she wore knee-high leather boots. To complete the outfit she wore a lace ruffed shirt of finest white linen beneath the doublet, and perched cockily atop her head was a black hat adorned with a plume of pink feathers so large and full it dipped down to touch the ground behind her.

"Cass! Honey Toes!"

"Don't "honey toes" me, you . . . you . . . prodigious, philandering phallus. I've seen everything now. Dressing your lover like a boy in order to fool me. That is incredibly revolting."

Colin laughed heartily, and Arianna nervously joined in. It was a ridiculous notion. How could Cassiopeia be so jealous? Colin was one of the most decent, honorable men Arianna had ever known, and as trustworthy as her own Rob.

"Darling, your imagination is getting the better of you once again. This is the Countess of Everly. My old friend Arianna."

Cassiopeia's heart lurched at the mention of the name she dreaded above all. Rather than reassuring her, his words filled her with despair. Arianna. Here. In Colin's arms. Was she tired of her husband? Did she want Colin to warm her bed again?

Arianna saw the fear, pure and cold, in Cassiopeia's eyes. "Please. This is all a misunderstanding. I have no designs on your husband, Cassiopeia. I am here for one reason only: to implore Colin to help me rescue my husband from Captain Longfellow."

Relief flowed through Cassiopeia. "I believe you, and so . . . I shall keep from running you through with my saber."

"Good girl," Colin said jovially. "You're showing remarkable progress." Turning to Arianna, he said, "Last time, she pierced a serving wench's thigh before realizing the poor girl was only trying to wipe a wine stain from my trunk hose. Ever since she's become pregnant she's been jealous of every female I so much as cock my hat at."

"And with good reason. My growing belly has slowed me. Soon I'll be too big to take on the miserable wenches who flap their skirts at my husband in hopes of taking him from me."

Arianna couldn't believe her ears . . . or her eyes, either, for that matter. What kind of woman had Colin married?

"Cassiopeia, I wouldn't be here if I wasn't in desperate need."

Cassiopeia heard the fervent plea and her heart went out to the beautiful, fragile girl before her. She knew Arianna must be a woman of great worth, for Colin had once loved her deeply. For all her stupid jealousy, she knew Colin did not love lightly. "What is it you want of my husband?"

Sighing with relief, Arianna swept the boy's hat off her head and combed her long tresses with her fingers, happy her charade had ended. "I want him to take me to Longfellow's stronghold."

Cassiopeia laughed, "And just what do you hope to accomplish by that?"

"I shall plead with him, bargain with him in any way I can, to get my husband back, and if that doesn't work, I'll . . . I'll . . . take him by force, if necessary."

"By force? Ho, Colin, your little friend is very brave. Very foolish . . . but very brave."

"Arianna, you have no idea of what you speak. Longfellow is not one to listen to a plea, no matter the sweetness of the bearer, and he will not bargain. As for taking Rob by force, Longfellow's stronghold is just that. Strongly built. Strongly held. The whole of the queen's army would have a hard time prying him loose. No. What you ask is impossible."

Arianna started to answer, when the sudden glare of a lantern was thrust in her face. Startled, she shielded her eyes from the blinding light.

The tavern keeper shone his light on the three figures engaged in deep conversation. "Sorry for interrupting, me lord. Heard a ruckus and thought you might need my help."

"Thank you, Mel, but as you can see, nothing is amiss."

The man nodded his head, then disappeared around the corner, content that he had done his duty.

Cassiopeia stared at Arianna. The light from the lantern had haloed her face long enough to give her a good look at the noblewoman's features. Arianna looked familiar. Very . . . very . . . familiar. Dear God! Arianna was the very image of herself. Arianna and she shared the same blue eyes and oval face, the same slim, well-shaped nose, the same full lips. It was like gazing into a looking glass.

With a heavy heart, she spoke to her husband. "I always wondered what you saw in me, and now I know. Damn you. You wanted me only to reclaim the lost love of your life."

Colin was flabbergasted at his wife's accusation. Moving quickly, he folded her into his arms. "I swear to you until this very moment, seeing the two of you together, I had no idea how much you looked alike. Cass, I love you because you're you. You must know that by now. There's no one exactly like you on the face of this earth!"

Cass stiffened in his arms. "That is what I always

believed. What I've always been told. I've always prided myself on being one of a kind."

"And you are. That's why I fell in love with you and for no other reason. Accept that and let the rest go."

Cassiopeia hesitated for one short moment, then threw her arms around Colin's neck in relief. She had a reprieve. Colin still loved her. Despite everything, he still belonged to her.

Arianna watched Cassiopeia in awe. She couldn't help liking the woman, for she was real, honest, and certainly unafraid of showing her true feelings. Much like the image she had of herself. Arianna's face became suddenly animated. "I know how to get Rob back."

As one, the pair turned to look at Arianna as if she had gone mad.

"Don't you see? I do look like Cassiopeia. If I take her place, I can walk right into Longfellow's lair and no one will be the wiser."

Colin shook his head. "What is it about you that compels you to disguise yourself so often? Was your mother frightened by a reveler at a masque when she was pregnant with you?"

"She's right, Colin. She looks enough like me to get away with it. But there's no need. I'll go myself. I'll find your Rob."

"No," Colin shouted, "the risk is too great! I don't want you out to sea again until the babe is born. Have you forgotten that is the purpose of our visit to London? To find a proper home for you to await the birth of our child in?"

"I haven't forgotten."

Arianna's voice rose with excitement. "I know the

perfect place. She can stay in Everly Castle. It's safe, clean, and most of all, Rob's mother is there. She'd be of great help to Cassiopeia."

"It does sound like the answer to our prayer, Colin. Elizabeth is dragging her feet about giving you back your lands, even though she's promised you. We cannot wait any longer. In one month's time this child will be born, home or no home."

"I concede. It does seem like a good solution."

"Then it's settled. Cassiopeia will go to Everly and you will take me to Rob, and we'll all live happily ever after."

"Hold on there. I never agreed to take you. The Devil's Harp is a wild and lonely island. Unfit for a lady."

A shudder of fear and excitement made its way through Arianna's body at the mention of Devil's Harp, but she shrugged it off, intent on having her way. "Then I shall fit right in. Give in, Colin. With Cassiopeia on my side, you haven't a chance to win."

Chapter Six

Arianna was right.

Two days later, she and Colin sailed for Devil's Harp, the wild island a short distance off the western tip of England, aboard Colin's galleon *The Constellation*.

Although Cassiopeia and Arianna did indeed look alike, Colin soon discovered one very important difference between them. Arianna was a terrible sailor. Sick from the moment they left port, she spent most of her time with her head hanging over the ship's railing. '

"I can't stand much more of this, Colin," Arianna groaned, clutching at him for support when the ship listed violently.

"Nor I. 'Tis painful to see you so sick." Colin rubbed his hand down her spine to comfort her. "Praise heaven, we're almost there, else you'll have me in the same condition."

"Almost there? Ohhhh, thank goodness. I swear to you when this is over, I shall never set foot on a ship again."

"I'm sure Rob will be grateful for that. You should

be home watching over the affairs of your castle, not gallivanting around on the high seas. Leave that to the knaves of the world."

"You're a fine one to speak, with Cassiopeia as your wife. Why don't you practice what you preach and make her stay home like a dutiful wife?"

"Why? Because it is my very large misfortune to fall in love with opinionated, adventurous women who know well how to get their way." He stared at her pointedly. Arianna answered by making a face.

"I pray now that she is in the family way she'll not feel quite so adventurous, but believe me, I don't count on it."

"Colin, what ever possessed you to marry a lady pirate?"

Suddenly turning serious, Colin said fervently, "She saved my life."

"Truly?"

"Truly. Oh, not in the sense of clutching me from the jaws of death. It wasn't that easy. Are you sure you want to hear this, Arianna?"

Arianna blinked, realizing that what he was about to say involved her. "Yes," she said softly.

"After your mother's execution, when Rob found you with me and we all went back to Everly, I didn't know how I was going to stand losing you. I stayed long enough to know everything was going to be all right between you and Rob once more, and then left. . . ."

"Disappeared is more like it. And without so much as a fare-thee-well."

"It was the only way I could leave you. And it was, by far, the hardest thing I've ever done. But how could

I stay when my very presence was a constant reminder to Robert that you and I had lived as man and wife?"

"He would have gotten over it, Colin. He would have understood that you saved my life on that wretched cliff . . . saved his son's life, too. That I stayed with you because to save him from Elizabeth, I had to be dead to him."

"We lived together *as man and wife,* Arianna."

"Yes, but only because I thought my life with him was over."

"But it wasn't, and ultimately that is the real reason I disappeared. You belonged to Robert and he to you. Your love was a holy thing. I knew that then, I know that now."

"Oh, Colin, I knew that was the reason you left, and I truly understood, but I worried so about you. Where did you go?"

"I didn't know or care where I went. I only knew I had to get as far away from you as I could. I rode until I literally ran out of land to ride upon, ending up at a primitive place called Land's End. But even that wasn't far enough away. I drank myself into oblivion, hoping to escape you that way, and became a pitifully hopeless drunk."

"Oh, Colin, I'm so sorry." Arianna softly touched his cheek with her hand.

Colin reached up to take her hand, kissing it before releasing it. "Don't be. None of it was your fault. None of it was anyone's fault."

"Not true. It was all Elizabeth's fault. If she had not been a revengeful queen, if she had not pursued me from the day I was born, I would not have had to run away. I wouldn't have given birth to Robin on a godforsaken cliff. You wouldn't have had to rescue me."

"Ah, but then I would never have met you. No. I can never be sorry for that. Our ten months together were the most precious moments of my life."

"Oh, Colin, you are so very dear to me. I can't be sorry, either, but I can't bear the thought that you suffered so because of me."

"Shush. 'Tis over. I have Cassiopeia now and a child on the way. I have no regrets."

"If that be true, then mayhap it was all meant to be. I thought I could never have Rob again and gave myself to you willingly, for next to him, you are the most honorable man I know. Cassiopeia is very lucky to have you. Tell me how you happened to meet her. Was it at Land's End?"

"Aye, though I remember nothing of our first meeting. I was mindlessly drunk, laying in my own puke on the water's edge. She found me there. Took me to her ship. Nursed me back to sobriety. I'd probably be dead by now if not for her."

"Was . . . was she a pirate then?"

"No, by then she had become a privateer. The king of Scotland had commissioned her to his service after hearing the tales of her exploits. Like everyone else she met, he, too, was enthralled with her and bragged to everyone of having the most beautiful woman in all of Scotland in his service."

Taking her chin in his hand, he tilted her face up, his eyes scanning the details of her face. "I believe now that the king must have sensed something about Cassiopeia. She does look a great deal like you and therefore like his mother. Mayhap without knowing why, he felt a kinship with my wife."

"It is certainly possible. For when I looked into James's eyes, I saw my mother reflected there." Arianna smiled softly, thinking of her brother. Would she ever see him again?

"God's teeth! You've met your brother? That's astounding. Where? When?"

Arianna laughed. "How do you suppose I knew where to find you? 'Twas he that told me. I met him at Windsor Castle."

"And you told him you were his sister?"

"No. How could I? I have no way of knowing how he would react to that. I had to protect my family."

"You have nothing to fear from James, Arianna. He is a good man, though not as strong a leader as his mother. But he can't be blamed for that, can he? Since he was never raised by her."

"My brother and I have that in common, do we not? Neither of us were raised by Mary Stuart. Though she had the power of a queen, she had not the rights of every worthy mother. But, enough of that. Continue your story. What happened after Cassiopeia became a privateer?"

"She urged me to join her and I did." Colin laughed. "It has been a most entertaining life."

Arianna joined him in laughter, until another wave of nausea overcame her. "Ohhh, if I die before we reach Devil's Harp, tell Rob how much I love him."

"In a few moments you'll be able to tell him yourself. Look!"

Raising her head, Arianna looked out over the deep blue sea and saw the ragged cliffs of the island. Her heart thrilled, knowing Robert was there. As they drew closer and closer, the sun began to set, turning the sky a brilliant orange. It welcomed her, like the warm glow of a lantern, leading her to the man she loved. *Rob. I'm coming. Somehow, someway, I'll find a way to free you. And then . . . then, I vow to the God Almighty, I'll be the devoted wife you deserve to have.*

"And so the first act of our play begins. I pray you know what you're doing, Arianna."

"I know what I'm doing. Cassiopeia instructed me in how to act. It won't be hard convincing everyone that I am she. I just thank the heavens that she has never come in contact with Longfellow or his scurvy lot."

"Yes, at least we have that to our advantage. Cassiopeia never gets close to anyone but her own crew and the Terrible Four."

"The Terrible Four? You mean those fantastic men who pledged their allegiance to me when I came aboard?"

"Aye, the very ones. They're Cassiopeia's personal guards, devoted to their mistress and now to you. There's not a man among my crew who would ever betray my wife. They've protected her with their own lives time and time again. And now protect me as well. Whilst we're on this island, they'll be by our side every step of the way."

"Then we have nothing to fear, do we, Colin?" Her voice was soft and calm, but inside Arianna felt close to panicking. She needed to hear Colin's reassuring voice.

Grasping her small hand, Colin squeezed it reassuringly. He knew what she needed. "Aye, we've nothing to worry about." Now, if he could only believe that himself.

In a matter of moments the ship had dropped anchor, and Arianna was ushered into a small boat and rowed ashore. Her heart constricted thinking about what lay ahead. Listening to the rhythmic tapping of oars on wood and water lapping against the sides of the boat, she slowly gained control of her nerves, knowing that if she panicked now, she would never accomplish her goal.

By the time they reached shore the sun had set. The beach was dark and lonely, the only sign of life the torches that jutted from niches in the cliff that rose in front of them. The light emanating from the balls of fire dotted the steep pathway, showing the wooden steps built into a natural crevice that led to the top of the cliff and . . . to Rob.

To Rob and . . . to Captain Longfellow and God alone knew how many more cutthroats. Dear heaven, how could she, living her privileged life in Everly, ever convince these base villains that she was one of them?

Suddenly, an uneasy feeling crept over her. She could swear she heard something. But it was too faint to make out. There . . . there it was again . . . music. She could swear she heard music. The higher she climbed up the twisting stairs, the louder it became. A shiver of fear coursed through her as the eerie music continued. "Colin, do you hear that?"

Colin smiled. "Aye, the Devil's Harp. 'Tis a natural phenomenon, though some would tell you otherwise. When the wind blows from the north, it hits a certain rock formation and makes that sound. Like someone playing the harp."

Arianna hugged her hands to her chest. "The Devil's Harp. It's well named. I've never heard anything so spooky. And the torches . . . they're spooky, too. It looks as if they're expecting us."

"Indeed they are. No one can anchor ship off this island without being seen. Look out to the water."

Arianna gazed out at the dark sea and saw the faint flickering lights from *The Constellation*'s cabin. "Then they're waiting for us?"

"Aye. They're waiting, and if I know Elijah, he'll have his slaves set exactly enough trenchers at the table to accommodate us all."

Arianna paused to catch her breath. The steep steps had her gasping for air. "Did you say *slaves?*"

"Aye, and don't you be gawking at them. As Cassiopeia, you are well acquainted with the sight of people of other colors."

"Oh, Colin, what if I make a mistake? What if I? . . ."

"It's too late to think of that now. You wanted to come here. You wanted to rescue your husband. Well, woman, here's your chance. Make the most of it."

Hearing a gruff voice behind her, Arianna turned to look at the giant man who spoke. "You have nothing to fear, me lady. My brothers and me will take good care of you."

Arianna smiled gratefully and took the man's rough hand. "Thank you, sir. Thank all of you. You know nothing about me or my mission, and yet you brave your lives to help me. And I . . . I don't even know your names."

Displaying a friendly gap-toothed smile, the man declared, "I'm Terrence, and these be my brothers . . . Timothy, Thaddeus, and Thomas. We've guarded our lady nigh on five years now, kept her safe in situations that would raise the hair on your head. We'll keep you safe, too. You've given our lady safe haven whilst she awaits the birth of her babe. For that you have use of our strong arms as long as you be needing them."

A surge of energy coursed through Arianna at Terrence's words, and gathering her courage, she followed Colin and the wonderful Terrible Four up the rough-hewn stairs. With these five valiant men by her side, she could brave anything.

She would rescue her husband. She had to. Little Robin could not lose his mother. His father. No. She knew too well what it was like to lose a mother, and she would not let that happen to her son. Robin and her unborn child would have both their parents, and they would all live happily . . . happily . . . Yes! Happily ever after."

Filled with resolve, Arianna concentrated on her role as Cassiopeia, imbuing herself with courage. Taking a deep breath, she continued the climb. By the time she peeked her head over the top of the cliff and gazed at the primitive, rugged wooden fortress in front of her, she had once again become the fierce lady pirate.

Colin noticed the change in Arianna and smiled. He knew she could do it. She had spent her whole life in one disguise or another. Whether she would admit it or not, she thoroughly enjoyed playacting. It was a part of her very nature. "Are you ready, *wife?*"

Before Arianna could answer him, a loud clamor arose. Looking up, she saw a ragged group of men making their way toward her. "Act one begins," she said solemnly, then forced a smile on her face and raised her hand to wave vigorously at the advancing men. As if she were happy to see them. As if they were not the most frightening gathering of people she had ever seen. For they were. Their manner was rough, their clothing dirty and torn as if they had been fighting, and God help her, they probably had been.

Their voices were loud. Bold. Belligerent. But despite that, somehow nonthreatening. She watched as Colin was engulfed amongst them, his voice ringing with laughter. They knew Colin. But how? How could he know them and Cassiopeia didn't? It seemed incredible to her that he should know any of these people. He was so kind. So good. Could he truly be happy living this treacherous life?

In a moment the crowd parted and Colin appeared, along with the Terrible Four. "Cassiopeia. Come. Elijah awaits. He has heard of my marriage and is eager to meet my bride."

Arianna swaggered over to them, hands on hips. "It's about time you took notice of me. I was beginning to think your friends have something against *ladies.*"

The night air was suddenly assaulted with boisterous laughter and lusty remarks, and Arianna soon found herself surrounded by men. She preened like a peacock. "Hmmm, gentlemen, you have me at a disadvantage. If I'd known I was going to be in the midst of such handsome devils, I'd have worn my gown of pure white velvet."

Posing boldly, she seductively stroked the long pink plume that adorned her hat, knowing full well what the effect would be. And Arianna wasn't disappointed.

Admiration for the lovely lady pirate swept through the throng of men, and a path was cleared for her so she might pass through their midst. Each man dipped at the waist as she passed by, as if she were the queen of England and they her loyal knights.

Arianna smiled her brightest smile and strode by the men, playing her part to the hilt. It was easy dressed in Cassiopeia's bright and dramatic clothing. Pleasurable to be doted on so. Just as her mother had been. Just as Elizabeth was every day of her life. Yes. There was something to be said about being the center of attention.

Before she knew it, the heavy armored door to the fortress was opened and she strutted through, linking arms with Colin and one of Longfellow's pirates, who beamed at being so chosen. The pirate steered her toward the great hall, and in a moment they were walking through the door. Laughter bubbled from her lips, deliberate, enticing, showing all who watched that this was a woman unafraid. A woman who knew her worth and demanded respect.

Captain Elijah Longfellow heard the feminine laughter and raised his head from the dark breast he had been nuzzling. Pushing the naked black beauty aside, he rose from his seat at the table to get a better look at the dazzling female who had so boldly entered his domain. The hall became still as everyone followed his gaze, staring as he did at the wondrous lady pirate.

Elijah couldn't believe his eyes. He had known Colin ever since the days when they were both at Everly and had heard of his marriage to Cassiopeia, but he never expected her to be so magnificent a creature. Hmmmm, not only was she a beauty, but there was something else about her that struck him. He could swear he had met her somewhere before. But how could that be? He would never have forgotten meeting this one. Nay, for he would surely have stolen her for himself.

How had Colrain plucked so ripe a cherry for his own? And what was his reason for coming to Devil's Harp? Was it his friendship with the Earl of Everly that drew him here?"

If that was the case, then it was a useless journey, for though he had captured Robert's ship not knowing it carried the Earl of Everly, he felt fate had played a part in delivering his enemy into his hands.

Arianna smiled gaily, but inside she felt frozen and stiff. Blind with fear, she couldn't take in everything she saw. Nothing seemed to register on her brain. Nothing but the formidable man rising from a chair.

She knew instantly that this was Captain Elijah Longfellow. Tall, well-built, with long blond hair that reached his shoulders, he had a presence that would not be denied. Dressed in black trunk hose and black silk shirt opened down the front, a gold brocaded sash around his slim waist, he was without a doubt the most handsome man she had ever seen. Deliberately, she stared him down, then moved her gaze from his to let him know he was of no consequence to her.

That was a mistake, for her eyes took in the naked, ebony-skinned women surrounding the captain and another half-hidden man still seated at the table, obviously passed out. Never in her life had she seen such an incredible sight.

Elijah saw Cassiopeia's shocked expression and smiled to himself. So, the wench wasn't half as sophisticated as would appear. Addressing Colin, he said, "My friend, it is good to see you again, but I must confess, not half as good as seeing your new bride. I have been looking forward to meeting the beautiful wife of Colin Colrain."

Suddenly, a loud groan filled the air, and a muffled, drunken voice, shouted, "Colin? Here?"

Arianna recognized the voice of her husband and her heart began to beat erratically. Where was he? He couldn't be the drunken sot sitting with the naked women.

A scuffling sound was heard as a chair was scraped against the wooden floor and the naked females moved aside as Robert stood on shaky legs, his body swaying back and forth.

Arianna stared at him in shock. Dear God, it was him! Never in her life had she seen her husband as inebriated as he was now, and never in her worst nightmare had she ever expected to see him surrounded by naked women. Why, he didn't look like a prisoner at all, but a participating member of this . . . this bawdy band of buccaneers.

Laughing, Elijah said, "You see, Colin, I am not the only one interested in meeting your wife. My . . . ah . . . captive friend here would also like to meet her."

Robert's vision was blurred. He tried to focus in on Colin but saw two images. Two images of the man he never wanted to see again. Two images of the brightly dressed lady pirate beside him. A jolt of recognition coursed through him and his vision instantly cleared. Arianna!

Rage filled him as Longfellow's words penetrated his senses. He had called Arianna Colin's bride. Never. "You bastard. You miserable bastard. You'll not have her again. She belongs to me."

Arianna watched in horror as Robert staggered toward her. Dear God in heaven, what has happened to him? *What has happened to my beloved husband?* A wave of revulsion swept over her. Not for Rob, but for herself. It was her fault. All her fault. Turning her head away, she buried it in Colin's shoulder. How could she bear to face Rob, knowing the shame of what she had done to him?

Rob stopped, stunned, when he saw Arianna cling to Colin. Had he lost her to his rival? Mayhap she had never truly belonged to him. Mayhap it had all been a dream. But no, baby Robin was no dream, the passionate life they shared had been no dream. Something wasn't right. If only he could clear his head of rum, he might understand.

Elijah watched the spectacle with interest. He saw Cassiopeia bury her head in her husband's shoulder and wondered at the sudden timidity of this bold woman. Something more was happening than he was aware of, and by God, he'd find out what it was. This woman was intriguing. It would be quite entertaining to fathom the mystery that surrounded her.

"Miggs, Flynn, take our guest to the dungeon. Chain him to the wall before he murders the captain before our very eyes."

Hearing those ominous words, Arianna looked up in time to see two burly men grab Rob by the arms and drag him toward a narrow door to the right. She wanted to cry out to them to leave him alone but knew she couldn't. The only chance she had of saving Rob was to keep her true identity a secret. Longfellow must believe she was Cassiopeia.

Rob fought the men to no avail. His legs and arms

were numb, his senses dulled with drink. He had no choice but to let the men drag him across the floor. All he could do was shout his rage. "Hear me well, Colin. I'll kill you with my bare hands. I'll tear your heart from your chest and feed on it if you dare to touch her again. Do you hear me? *DO YOU HEAR ME?*"

Arianna felt her heart shatter into a million pieces. She would have slumped into Colin's arms, but for the words her friend whispered fervently into her ear.

"Stand fast. Remember, you're Cassiopeia. Queen of the high seas. Act like her or you'll doom us all."

Throwing herself back into her role, she assumed her arrogant manner again and addressed Captain Longfellow. "Do you throw all your guests in the dungeon? If that be the case, I'm thinking I'll not stay for supper."

"Guest? Robert Warwick is no guest. He's my hostage. A very confused hostage, it seems, for he seems to think you belong to him."

Arianna laughed. "I suppose I should be flattered to be desired by a nobleman."

Colin circled her waist with his arm and pulled her to his side. "But, my darling, what difference does that make? All men are the same. There's not a man alive who could resist your charms."

"I'm glad to hear it. I wouldn't want to end up like that poor fellow. Tell me, Longfellow, why do you hold the earl hostage?"

Longfellow looked at her with suspicion. "The answer would be obvious to most. Do you have any reason to think it is other than for ransom?"

Arianna suddenly realized she must be careful of what she said. She had almost given away the fact that she knew no ransom had been demanded of Rob. "Then, your prisoner must be worth a lot to you. I just wondered at your rough treatment of so valuable a prize. If anything happened to him . . ."

Longfellow laughed heartily, suddenly understanding. "Isn't that just like a woman. Pretending concern when all the while it is profit that softens your heart."

Striding over to her, he continued, "But don't concern yourself. It matters not what happens to the earl now. His value has been greatly diminished. His family has refused to ransom him. And that in itself is ironic justice, for because of his family, I suffered unjustly."

Arianna heard nothing but the news that Rob had been ransomed. Why was he lying? There had been no demand for ransom. "Surely you jest, Captain."

"I never jest when it comes to my purse."

"Mayhap his family never got the message."

"Oh, they did all right. A note was returned to me, informing me of their decision not to pay. It bore the seal of an authority no one in England would deny."

Arianna was stunned. What was he talking about? "It could have been a forgery."

Longfellow threw his head back and laughed so loud it reverberated throughout the hall. "No one forges the seal or signature of Elizabeth Tudor, Queen of England."

Blinking back her shock, Arianna felt a sliver of ice travel through her body. *Elizabeth! But why? Why would she send a message of lies? Why didn't she tell me there had been a ransom note?*

The answer came to her in another wave of self-revulsion. Once again the responsibility lay on her own shoulders. For thanks to her intrigue, she had given Elizabeth motivation for keeping Rob out of the way. But how could she have foreseen that the cold-hearted bitch would go so far? Dear God, how could she have known?

Not true. She should have known. All the facts were there. It was well known that Elizabeth hated for her favorites to be married. So well known that many of her people married in secrecy to keep the queen from finding out. Elizabeth was so selfish and so spoiled that she wanted them at her beck and call. With Rob permanently out of the way, she would be able to have access to Arianna whenever it suited her.

In a voice tinged with bitterness, Arianna proclaimed, "The queen is well known for her stinginess. The scrawny bitch would rather let loose of her famous virginity than to let loose of a single farthing."

Knowing well what had caused this outburst, Colin breathed a sigh of relief. He had feared she would give herself away in her rage. Why on God's earth had he agreed to this insanity? They'd be lucky to get off the island alive at this rate.

Longfellow heard the hatred in Cassiopeia's voice. The flaxen-haired beauty hated the queen with a passion. But why? What was it about this woman? And why did he have the feeling he had met her before? It would surely come to him sooner or later. And when it did, he was sure that the mystery would be solved. He would know everything he needed to know about the intriguing Captain Cassiopeia.

Chapter Seven

Slow fury inched its way up Rob's spine as he lay upon the dank, smelly straw that was his bed. Arianna. Here. Damn her to hell, she was truly here. He pulled on the chain around his wrist, knowing the futility of it. He had pulled on that miserable chain for hours, until his wrist was bloody from the effort, but it would not give.

God save me from this nightmare.

Since the first moment of his capture, when Longfellow had fastened the cold steel bands around his wrists the very first time, he thought he'd go mad if he couldn't free himself, but this . . . this was ten times worse. Knowing Arianna was here at the mercy of Elijah Longfellow was more than he could bear. Did she value her life so little that she would risk it to try and rescue him? Robin needed her. God in heaven, he needed her. If anything happened to her . . .

What had ever possessed Colin to bring her here? What had she promised him to make him act so rashly? He yanked furiously on the chain, a wild animal trying to free himself, driven by the thought of Arianna in Colin's arms once more.

He would never share her with another man again.

She had to know that.

As God was his witness, he would not forgive her this time.

Weary with fatigue and worry over Rob, Arianna was grateful when the dreadful evening ended. Elijah had tried to convince her and Colin to stay the night in his fortress, but Colin would have none of it. He insisted they return to *The Constellation* to sleep.

Arianna hated to leave, knowing Rob was there, but she knew Colin was right. They were safer on board ship. Not even the Terrible Four could stand up against Longfellow's entire crew and the other scurvy pirates that lived on the desolate island.

Tossing and turning in her narrow bunk, she thought of Robert and the shock of seeing him not only drunk but surrounded by naked female slaves. That was the last thing she had expected to see. Stars in heaven, the last thing she had wanted to see.

Stop it. How could she worry about Rob bedding other women when his very life was in danger? As usual, she thought only of her own wants, her own needs. Robert deserved a much better wife than she, and by God, she would give it to him. If he ever forgave her for this, she would never again jeopardize the love they shared.

The shrill trilling of a seabird woke her with a start. She had slept, though she had feared she would not. As the soft grey haze of early dawn hung heavy in the air, familiar sounds drifted to her ears. Rope rubbing tautly against wood. Water lapping against the sides of the ship. Mighty timbers squeaking tremulously overhead. In truth, she wished she could stay abed, escape into sleep once more, safe and snug in the cradle of the gently swaying ship. She dreaded the thought of facing the day, facing the pirate, and God help her, facing her husband and his wrath.

Rising with a groan, she dressed in Cassiopeia's pirate garb and was about to go out to the deck, when a pounding sounded on the door. Unfastening the lock, she opened the door to see a grim-faced Colin standing there, a bundle of clothing in his arms. "What is it, Colin?"

"Longfellow is boarding the ship."

"Longfellow here? But why?"

"God alone knows why. The important thing is, if he is to continue to think you're Cassiopeia . . . my wife . . . he's got to believe we share this cabin." Pushing her aside, Colin strode in. "Scatter my things around the cabin whilst I get a little more comfortable here."

Arianna watched in astonishment as Colin stripped off his shirt and removed his boots, throwing them on the floor. "I don't know what that black-hearted devil is up to, but obviously he must suspect something or he wouldn't be here."

Before Arianna had time to gather her thoughts, there was another pounding on the door, and a raspy voice announced, "Pardon, Captain, but we have visitors. Captain Longfellow and his *friend* the earl are here."

Arianna gasped. "Rob? Here? Oh, Colin, he can't see us together in here. You know what he'll think."

"Pull yourself together, *Cassiopeia.* Pull yourself together or I'll raise anchor and head back to the mainland, and you can forget about rescuing Robert. I'll not risk my crew's life or my own for a spineless jellyfish."

Eyes full of fire, Arianna answered, her voice lethal and low. "Damn you, Colin Colrain, you'll never get a chance to say that to me again. I'll show you. I'll show Longfellow and anyone else who stands in my way that no one—do you hear, no one—can get the best of *Cassiopeia.*"

Striding to the door with her newly gained determination, she flung it open and came face to face with Elijah Longfellow. "Well, Captain, to what do we owe this surprise visit? Were you lonely for our company already?"

Elijah smirked, his eyes grazing over her from top to bottom before looking over her shoulder at Colin standing by the bed, half-dressed. " 'Tis obvious you were not lonely. If I may step inside, I shall be happy to tell you why I'm here."

"Come in, Elijah," Colin said, "What game is afoot now?"

Laughing heartily, Elijah said, "You see, your husband knows me well. There is nothing I like more than playing games . . . of all sorts." His eyes fastened onto Cassiopeia's, before brushing past her. Entering the cabin, he closed the door behind him.

"The game involves my reluctant guest. I've brought him with me. You met him last night. The Earl of Everly."

"I remember. What about him?" Arianna had no idea what was going on, but she knew it could not be beneficial to Rob. Longfellow was like a cat with a mouse, playing with it before sinking his teeth into its vulnerable neck.

"You shall see in a moment when I bring him in here. Your part in the game is simple." Putting his finger over his mouth, he said, "Say nothing, else you'll spoil my fun."

Colin and Arianna exchanged worried glances as Longfellow opened the door and called out, "Warwick, dear fellow, come in."

Before Arianna had a chance to brace herself, Robert appeared in the doorway. The sight of her beloved took her breath away.

Robert's face showed no expression as he walked into the cabin, his gaze traveling from Elijah to Arianna, and then to the half-naked Colin. His jaw tightened, but he contained his emotions. It wouldn't do for Elijah to see how upset he was. Scanning the room, he took in the rumpled bed and Colin's clothing strewn about, and it was all he could do to keep from bashing in his face.

Trying to control himself, Rob turned his attention to Longfellow. The pirate was up to no good, of that he was certain, but he had no idea what form it would take. Whatever it was, Rob was determined not to give the blackguard the satisfaction of seeing him react. In the past few days, he'd learned that lesson well. Longfellow thrived on the raw emotion of others. Most likely, because he had no feelings of his own. Clenching his teeth together, he waited for the game to begin.

"Good news, Warwick. I didn't tell you last night

because you were too drunk to understand. The truth is . . . Colin and the beautiful Cassiopeia have brought the ransom money from your wife. You're free to go."

A stunned silence greeted Elijah's words. Arianna couldn't believe her ears. How could Elijah lie to Rob like that? It was cruel, inhuman. Fastening her gaze on her husband's face, she fought the urge to shout out that it was a cruel trick. But as much as she wanted to spare her husband, she knew it would be a mistake to speak. She had no choice but to play along.

Rob blinked, opened his mouth to speak, then closed it once more as he realized that Longfellow had called Arianna Cassiopeia. If she was still hiding her identity, then there must be a good reason for it. It was a trick. A miserable trick. And not a clever one at that, for Elijah had forgotten one little detail. He had brought along half his bloody crew to escort him to the ship. If he had intended to let him go, he wouldn't have needed them. No. They were along for one reason only. To keep him from escaping.

The one thing he didn't understand was why Arianna had never paid a ransom. Why had she felt compelled to come here, risking her very life? For the life of him, he couldn't fathom what was going on.

"Sorry to ruin your game, Elijah, but it was really not worth your effort. How pathetic to think I would fall for such a weak ploy. If you knew more about me, you'd know Colin Colrain is the last man on earth who'd deliver a ransom for my release. The last man who would take me back to my wife. And the truth is, I'd rather swim back to Everly than spend another moment on the same vessel with him and his slut."

It was Cassiopeia who flew at Robert, Cassiopeia

who raised her hand to strike his face, but it was Arianna who was jolted by the touch of skin on skin as Rob's strong hand grasped her own, deflecting the blow. Arianna who felt the love for this man course through her body, so strong she became instantly weak in the knees and could only stare into his eyes with fierce longing, knowing that he above all men was the man she wanted, needed, cherished.

Rob held tight to her, feeling her life's blood throbbing through her hand into his. It filled him with strength, power, the will to live. It fueled his heart with love and his loins with longing. Arianna. This was the woman he would always love. The woman he would always desire.

The air crackled between them. Though they touched for only seconds, the emotional vibrations were powerful enough to be felt by Colin and Elijah.

Elijah stared at the man and woman in fascination. It was obvious his captive earl and this luscious female were lovers, and . . . and. . . .

Yes! He knew now where he had seen this woman before. On the dock in London whilst he had looked through his glass at Robert's ship. 'Twas the same day he followed Warwick out to sea and took him captive. The day he watched a lusty female leap across the open span of water to the dock, after a romantic liaison with someone on the ship.

It was Robert she had bedded that day.

And Colin she bedded now.

No wonder the animosity between the two men. It seems he wasn't the only one who liked to play games. Well, well, well. A tingle of excitement shot through Elijah as he anticipated the pleasure he would have playing against this formidable and very exciting woman.

"My dear Cassiopeia, I must commend you. Your beauty drives even the most gentle of men wild. You had better watch her carefully, Colin. For so great a treasure, a man would do most anything."

Robert felt a chill run down his spine at Elijah's words. Staring into his wife's eyes, he sent her a message of warning, his rampant jealousy over Colin fading into the back of his mind as his concern for her safety overpowered all other emotions.

Arianna turned away from Rob's gaze, letting him know that it was too late now to heed his warning. She had to play it out till the end.

"And now, since Robert refuses to play my little game, I'll bid you adieu, hoping you will join me in my fortress later this day. *The Sea Vixen* dropped anchor this morning. And there will be a grand celebration this evening for her captain, Black Bess."

Elijah's eyes grazed over Arianna's shapely body. "I'm looking forward to the meeting between the sea's two most notorious women."

It was obvious Elijah was trying to frighten her. And he'd never know just how successful he was at that. Who was this Black Bess? The very mention of her ominous name sent chills up her spine. "And I look forward to meeting Black Bess. It will be good to talk to another female. The constant company of men can be very . . . tiring."

Elijah raised an eyebrow, knowing the little witch's words had a double meaning. Damn, but he was going to enjoy this game. "Good. Tonight, then . . . And Cassiopeia, wear your most extravagant feminine attire. If I know my Black Bess, she'll be decked out like a gilded peacock."

When the door closed behind Elijah and Rob, Arianna ran to the porthole to look out. She watched as the little boat carrying her beloved grew smaller and smaller, her heart aching at the scene that had just been played out. Squeezing her eyes shut to block out the painful image of her husband as he called her a slut, she thought, He'll never forgive me for this. *I'll never forgive myself.*

Chapter Eight

Arianna's hands shook as she made ready for the ordeal ahead. The thought of facing a female pirate frightened her more than the thought of facing a hundred lusty males. She would not have her femininity to fall back on with Black Bess, and that made her feel very vulnerable. And as for Elijah, he had seemed almost rapturous at the thought of her and Black Bess together. That worried her further. What kind of woman was this Bess? Would she feel animosity or rivalry toward her because she was another female pirate or, heaven forbid, just another female?

Damn Elijah Longfellow. It was no more than an amusing game to *him,* but it was a very dangerous game for *her.* A game she must win, because the stakes were high. Her husband's life depended on it.

But how? How could she keep Elijah off guard long enough to steal Rob away from under his nose? She would have to plan her moves with care. She remembered how carefully she had planned her entrance to Windsor Castle on the back of Sanctimonious decked out like a unicorn. The queen had been greatly entertained, making Arianna feel more secure. It always made her feel more secure when she was entertaining others or wearing a disguise of some sort, as if she could hide her real self from unfavorable scrutiny.

She remembered, too, the first time she had met Rob. That had been just as carefully thought out. She had worn a simple white velvet gown without the artifices of lace ruff or corsets or stays of any kind. It had been exactly the right thing to do, for Rob had been enthralled.

Was it possible to repeat that performance? She had brought that very gown along to wear on the journey back to Everly with her husband. She had hoped that wearing it would make him remember the beginning of their love for each other. Make him forget her deceit.

It was worth a try. She would wear the innocent but paradoxically very sensuous gown for Longfellow's benefit. The clinging fabric hugged her breasts and waist, following the curves of her hips before gracefully flaring out and sweeping to the ground. It looked for all the world like a gown Queen Guinevere might have worn for her husband King Arthur. She prayed it would have the same effect on Elijah as it had on her husband, and she couldn't help hoping that when Rob saw her in it he would remember and go easier on her.

Arianna smiled bitterly. 'Twas obvious she was still hiding her true self behind disguises. Why could she not face the world as herself? She was no better than Elijah, playing games to get her way. But she didn't care. She would do whatever she must to get her husband back.

Filled with resolve, she dressed quickly, then combed her hair until it shone. Ready, she smoothed

her dress with her hands, sliding them down the clinging fabric. When a man went into battle he wore heavy
metal armament. All Arianna had between herself and
her enemy was this thin, soft fabric.

Mayhap, it was all she needed.

Once again she and Colin rowed ashore accompanied by the Terrible Four. The rest of the crew followed in the other small boats, filling the air with the
rhythm of the oars as they made their way to the rocky
coast. It gave Arianna great comfort knowing she was
not alone. That Cassiopeia's men were there for her.
Her admiration grew for the real Cassiopeia, thinking
she must truly be an unusual woman to garner such
loyalty and respect from these hardened men. Colin
was a lucky man, indeed.

Securing their vessels, they made their way up the
narrow path to the top of the cliff and then to the gate
of the fortress. Arianna's throat was dry as she waited
for the gate to swing open. Pray God, everything
would go as planned. She felt a touch on her arm and
turned to gaze at Terrence standing beside her. She
watched as he spit on the hem of his shirt, then raised
it toward her face.

"Here, me lady, there's a spot of dirt on your face."
Without further ado, he reached up to wipe her face
with his shirt. "There you be. Good as new."

Arianna smiled fondly at the rough-hewn pirate.
"Thank you, Terrence. I wouldn't want to meet Black
Bess with a dirty face."

"Aye, I thought as much." Terrence was pleased
with himself. "Here, now, let's get a move on. And
have no fear. Me and me brothers will not stray far

from your side. You'll be as safe as if you was in your mother's arms."

Arianna blanched at Terrence's words. Safe in her mother's arms. *Her mother was dead.* She could be, too, if she didn't keep alert.

Terrence and his brothers led the way, and in a moment Arianna was walking through the door to the great hall, her eyes scanning the hall for Rob, widening in surprise when she spotted him.

He was deep in conversation with the most exquisite-looking brunette she had ever seen. Tall and stately, the woman had an aura about her that demanded homage. So this was the infamous Black Bess. But unlike Longfellow's prediction that she would be decked out in flamboyant garb, Bess was dressed like a man, in black velvet doublet and pantaloons, her face framed by a collar of exquisite Holland lace.

Arianna's heart tore in two upon seeing the way Rob smiled into Bess's face. It was obvious he was enjoying her company. Had she lost him already?

Still smiling from something Black Bess had said, Rob turned his head and saw Arianna standing in the doorway. The smile quickly left his face.

Black Bess and Elijah turned their gazes to see what had caught Rob's attention. Elijah's face took on a strange, elated look, and she knew he was impressed with her clinging gown of white velvet.

That knowledge gave her the fortitude to continue walking toward them. Ignoring the men, she held out her hand to Black Bess and said, "I'm Cassiopeia."

Black Bess lifted a dark, perfectly formed eyebrow and gazed down at her from a lofty height. "Cassiopeia? You're not what I expected. Elijah has been filling my head with talk of the brave and brazen Cassiopeia, and here I find a slip of a girl dressed like a virgin about to be sacrificed to a pagan god."

"From the way Elijah described *you,* indeed I thought you to be that pagan god and I the designated sacrifice."

Taken aback by Cassiopeia's unexpected honesty, Black Bess took her hand and shook it vigorously. "I think I'm going to like you."

Colin and Robert exchanged looks, the animosity between them forgotten for the moment as they breathed a sigh of relief. Arianna had proven once more she was capable of taking care of herself.

"Good," Arianna declared enthusiastically, relieved that Black Bess was a civilized woman instead of some mad heathen. "I'm happy we shan't be dueling on the parapet. My clothing is hardly suited for that."

Bess laughed. "Well, now that we're done with the amenities, shall we join the men in drink and merriment?"

Taking Arianna by the arm, Bess led her to a table. Every head turned to watch their progress, taking in the contrasting beauty of the women, one small and fair, dressed all in white, the other tall and dark, dressed in ebony to match her hair. These were women any man would be proud to call his own.

The two women sat at a table, engaging in animated conversation, obviously enjoying each other's company, and soon the hall grew noisy again as the pirates got down to the serious business of drinking. Longfellow and Robert joined the women at their table, and the Terrible Four did, too, taking up residency at either end, removing men from their seats so they could sit.

No one was brave enough to protest. The four were large and exceedingly mean-looking. Arianna smiled to herself. If they only knew what softhearted bears they truly were.

Feeling more at ease, Arianna looked across the table at her husband. "I see you are unshackled this evening. One would never know you were a prisoner. But then, things are seldom what they seem, are they?"

Rob looked into her eyes, saying, "Is that your observation?"

"Yes, life has taught me that. But, of course, that doesn't apply to my husband and me. My love for him is so great, he must surely know the way it is between us and never doubt when it seems otherwise."

Robert knew she was trying to tell him she had not slept with Colin, even though it looked as if she had. He wanted to believe her. Oh, God, how he wanted to believe her.

"How right you are," Longfellow chimed in. "Things are seldom what they seem. That's what makes life so damnably interesting. For instance, who would have believed that Bess would become the earl's angel of mercy and talk me into allowing him free rein of my fortress?"

"Mercy?" Black Bess laughed lustily. "It has nothing to do with mercy. I'll show him no mercy when I get him in my bed. I've never seen a man better suited to pleasure a woman."

Color flamed Arianna's cheeks. She had to bite her tongue to keep from saying what she longed to say. *Keep your bloody hands off my husband.* But she couldn't say it. She was Cassiopeia. She must act her part. Cassiopeia would boast about her own husband. "He is a fine specimen, to be sure, but my husband Colin pleasures me well enough."

Arianna dared not gaze in Rob's direction. She did not want to see the hatred shining in his eyes, but it didn't matter, for she still felt the heat of his gaze boring into her. *Oh, Rob, you must know I didn't mean it. You must know how truly much I love you. Give me some sign to let me know you understand.*

Speaking in a cynical tone, Rob answered, "Well enough, my lady? Is that the most you can say about your husband's prowess? I would be insulted if my wife spoke of me in such an indifferent fashion."

Arianna couldn't stay her tongue from speaking what her heart wanted to say. "You speak of a wife, my lord, and yet you gaze at Black Bess with such ardor."

"What should it matter to you, Cassiopeia? It is not your husband that strays," Rob said mockingly.

Black Bess handed Cassiopeia a tankard of ale, "Here, my friend, drink. Don't give these rutting males another thought. They're all alike. Ready to jump the first female they see when their own woman is out of sight." Black Bess gave Elijah a dirty look, then drained her own tankard.

Things were not going as Elijah had planned. He had thought to have Bess and Cassiopeia at each others throats, but instead they seemed to like each other. And Bess's sexual interest in Robert Warwick was totally unexpected. Longfellow had believed, until now, that he had been man enough to satisfy her needs. It was a blow to discover she still craved other men.

He had always been sure of his prowess in bed and his power over Bess, and he didn't like the idea of her sharing her abundant charms with Warwick. True, they had always agreed they could bed whomever they chose. But up until now it had always worked in his favor.

Bess rarely strayed beyond the confines of his bed-chamber. But this was different. Robert was a noble-man. He had wealth beyond anything Bess had ever seen before, and damn it all, there was no doubt of the earl's effect on women. He had only to look at Bess and Cassiopeia to see that.

"Bess, you wrong me. You know how devoted I am to you. Almost as devoted as the lovely Cassiopeia is to her husband."

"Devotion." Rob spat out the word as if it were venom from a poisonous snake. "Such an overrated word. I think there's not one woman in ten who knows its meaning."

Arianna's face flamed, but she held her tongue. What could she say?

"Such a cynic. I'd never have thought it of you, Robert. But then, on further thought, I suppose I can't blame you, since your own wife lacks sorely in that virtue, else she would have sent the ransom to free you. Which, alas, leaves me with the dilemma of trying to figure out what to do with you."

"I'm sure you'll think of something, Longfellow," Rob answered sarcastically.

"Give him to me," Bess murmured seductively, "I know exactly what to do with him."

"That's why I shan't give him to you. I'm entirely too selfish for that. How about you, Cassiopeia? Do you want our handsome young earl?"

Arianna's heart felt as if it would fly out of her chest. Did she want him . . . sitting there, so masculine and tall, handsomer than she had ever seen him before? Did she want him . . . staring at her with eyes that pierced her very soul? Dear God, she would die if she didn't have him! Shrivel down to dust and blow away if she never felt his arms around her again. But how could she trust Elijah? Was he playing another game, or would he truly give him to her if she said yes.

Feeling everyone's eyes on her, she answered, "Yes . . . I want him."

Arianna saw the look of triumph that flashed across Elijah's face and immediately continued before he could say anything. "I want him . . . to serve in the galley of *The Constellation*. It is so hard to keep good help nowadays."

Colin and Rob had been holding their breaths and now exhaled at the same moment. Good girl, Colin thought.

Rob's thoughts were more complicated. He was glad she hadn't fallen for Elijah's trick, but angry at the same time at the game she was playing. Damn it all, Arianna grew more and more like Elizabeth, the very woman she despised so much, thriving on intrigue and duplicity. Mayhap she would never again be the sweet, devoted wife he longed for.

Elijah's triumphant smile turned to a sheepish grin. "Ah, I should have known. I repeat, Colin, you are a lucky man to have so devoted a wife. Now I shall have to think of some other use for Robert. Meanwhile, it's back to the dungeon with you."

Robert gritted his teeth together as two strong-armed men grabbed him by the arms at Elijah's command. Someday, as God was his witness, it would be his turn and it would be the black-hearted pirate who would be tethered in a dank cell. "What's the matter, Longfellow? Have you no confidence in your own manhood?"

Elijah looked piqued. "What are you blabbering about, Warwick?"

" 'Tis obvious to me and everyone else here, you're afraid if I stay up here, mingling with the ladies, they will prefer my company over yours. Isn't that why you keep John Neal isolated in the dungeon day and night? Because Black Bess found his attentions more desirable than yours? By all means, then, hide me away if you feel so unsure of your manhood."

Elijah motioned to his men to let Robert go. "Robert . . . you wound me. You know damn well I do not allow your knight John Neal the privileges you have because he tried to escape. He is being punished for that and no other reason. But if you are so eager for a night away from the dungeon, then it is done. You see how amiable I am."

Rob had known Longfellow would react that way. He was beginning to understand all too well the way the man's mind worked. "Do you hear that, ladies? You shall not be deprived of my company this night."

"I didn't know you had any interest in the women of Devil's Harp, Robert, but I understand a man has needs. Which one do you want? Choose and she shall be yours for the night . . . if she's willing, of course. I will reprieve you from your nightly stay in my dungeon."

"Your hospitality knows no bounds." Rob said, happy his ploy had worked. Then, thinking of another way to get to Longfellow, he continued. "Or . . . mayhap it does. Did you say I can choose any female?"

"Any *willing* female, my lord."

Rob looked first at Arianna, fire showing in his eyes. "I choose Black Bess."

Silence crept through the great hall like a malignancy, starting with the people closest to Robert Warwick and fanning out farther and farther, until not a word was spoken or a chair moved. The very air itself seemed to linger over the five strong figures who were the center of attention. Black Bess, with a stunned expression on her face. Arianna, looking whiter than death. Colin Colrain, standing like a rock, and Robert and Elijah, facing each other in stony silence, like two stags, horns locked in battle.

Everyone waited expectantly, eager to hear what would happen next.

Black Bess broke the silence with her piercing laughter, and the hall came alive once more. "I most heartily accept." From the corner of her eye, Bess watched to see how Elijah would accept the news. She cursed to herself when she saw that he didn't so much as blink an eye, and she realized, without a doubt, just how unimportant she was to him. Swallowing her pride, she took Rob's arm and steered him toward the stairs leading up to the sleeping chambers.

Arianna stood frozen, staring after Rob in horror. No longer was she the brave and brazen Cassiopeia; no longer was she capable of hiding what she truly felt.

It was too much to ask of any woman. She opened her mouth to cry out to him, but Colin covered it with his hand. No one saw. All eyes were focused on Robert and Black Bess.

At the top of the stairs, Robert turned and looked down at his wife, a tiny, frail-looking figure in her soft white gown. It was the gown she had worn the first time he saw her in female clothing. He had always loved to see her dressed in it. Loved to take it off her and glory in the beautiful body beneath. What in hell was he doing with another woman when all he wanted was to have her in his arms again?

Black Bess opened the door to her chamber and, taking his hand, pulled him inside. The room was bright from the light of several candles standing in an exquisitely designed Spanish candelabra. Colorful trinkets and fabrics, plunder from her pirating, were displayed everywhere, and on the bed was a coverlet of cloth of gold.

He swallowed hard. How was he going to let this lusty woman know he didn't want to bed her? That all he wanted was to hurt Arianna enough to drive her away from this evil place? Every moment she stayed put her in greater peril.

And yes, he had another, more selfish motive as well: to put a dent in Longfellow's ego. Turning to Bess, he said softly, "I'm afraid I'm here on—"

"False pretenses?"

"How did you know?"

Black Bess smirked. "A woman knows when a man is interested in her. And . . . when he's interested in a certain pretty little golden-haired girl in a white dress."

Rob sat down on the gilded bed and held his head in his hands.

"As bad as all that, eh?"

"If you only knew."

"I think I do. That woman down there is no more Cassiopeia than you are. Her hands are too soft for a seasoned sailor. No calluses or rope burns, no grip of steel. And the way she walks, like a countess, not the distinctive gait of a sailor who's spent months at a time aboard ship. If Longfellow thought with his head instead of with his cock, he'd realize that himself. Who is she, really? Your wife?"

Knowing it was useless to deny it, he decided it might be more advantageous to take her into his confidence. In any case, he had nothing to lose that wasn't already lost to him. "Aye, and the mother of my son. A son who I intend to see does not become an orphan, so . . . if you have any intentions of telling Longfellow . . ."

"Hold on, Robert. You needn't worry about me. I have no desire to tell Elijah any of this. In fact, it would please me very much if you were to escape his greedy grasp."

Rob looked deep into Black Bess's eyes. "I believe you, but that doesn't mean I understand. Why do you want to hurt Longfellow?"

"Because he wants her. Wants her bad . . . so bad, he's willing to let me sleep with you so that he can have her."

"Don't tell me you love that bastard!"

"Is that any worse than you loving that little baggage downstairs?"

"I can't argue with you there."

"Then we're in agreement?"

Rob grinned and nodded his head. "And the first thing we must do is drive Arianna away. Until she's safely out of Longfellow's reach, I'll not leave this place."

"That shouldn't be too hard to accomplish after this night, I'm thinking. We'll just have to put on a good enough performance to convince Arianna and Elijah that we thoroughly enjoyed ourselves tonight. So, your lordship, make yourself comfortable while I fill your ears with some of the little personal things I do in bed. Elijah has benefited from them all. If he is aware that you know about my little tricks, he'll think I've been treating you real good."

"Hmmm, you have my full attention. Tell me your bedtime tales whilst I rest on your soft bed—if you don't mind, that is."

"I don't mind. From the looks of you, you can use a good night's sleep in a real bed." Black Bess smiled. "This will be an interesting night. I haven't shared my bed with a male for sleeping purposes since I was a girl and had to sleep with my brother. He wet the bed every night."

Kissing Bess on the forehead, Rob said, "Rest assured, I gave up wetting beds a long time ago."

In the hall below, Colin led a defeated and broken Arianna to a chair and sat her down. Taking a pewter tankard from the tray of a passing servant, he handed it to her. "Here. Drink this. And for God's sake, take that look off your face. Do you want Longfellow to figure out what's going on?"

"Colin, how can you be so cruel? Rob is upstairs with another woman. Why? Why is he doing this to me? No matter what I've done, I don't deserve this."

"My God, Arianna, don't you trust your husband?"

"How can you ask that when he flaunted Bess before my very eyes?"

"Because I know Robert Warwick. Because he is an honorable man. Because he loves his wife very much. I know that if he went upstairs with another woman, it was for a good reason. A damn good reason."

Arianna looked at Colin with tears in her eyes. "Oh, Colin, I want to believe you. I pray you're right."

"Did you see her?" Longfellow's voice boomed behind her. "She practically pranced up the damn steps, so eager was she to bed him. I swear to you, Colin, I do not understand the female mind. I've a cock on me of a size that women swoon over. What can he offer her next to that? What can—?"

Arianna started out of her chair, her voice escalating in anger. "Is that all it means to you, Elijah? Do you think that's all lovemaking is about? Well, let me tell you—"

Colin pulled her down on his lap. "Sweeting, this is none of our business."

"No. Let Cassiopeia speak. She knows how a woman thinks. She's right. There is more to the act of love from a woman's viewpoint. I should never have tested Bess like that. Didn't think she'd do it. No. I didn't think she'd do it. *I was so damned cocksure she wouldn't do it.*" Shaking his head in frustration, Elijah wandered off in search of spirits to dull his mind.

"Stars in heaven! He actually cares about Black Bess. 'Tis unfortunate he didn't realize that before he started all this. I'm frightened, Colin. What if he kills Rob in a jealous rage? What if he—?"

"That's not Elijah's way. He doesn't fly into rages. He doesn't do anything before thinking it out from every angle. No, if I know Elijah, he'll find some diabolically evil way to get even with Rob without drawing a drop of blood."

A shiver of ice crept up Arianna's spine.

"Come, let's go back to the ship. We can—"

"If you think I'm leaving here, you are truly insane. I'm staying. I want to be here when that door opens and Rob and Black Bess come down the stairs. I'll know when I see them if there was anything between them."

"My dear Cassiopeia, how curious that you should be so interested in the earl's sexual activity."

Arianna jumped. She hadn't known Elijah had returned.

Colin quickly covered for her. "My wife cannot abide men who cheat on their wives. That is her only interest in the earl."

"So you say, but I'm afraid the truth of it is, Colin, women find the earl a toothsome morsel. Your wife included. Why, they've shown so much interest in the man, I've a good mind to auction him off to the highest bidder." Slapping his knee, Elijah continued. "Upon my sword, that's just what I'll do with him. Since there is no ransom forthcoming, I shall add handsomely to my coffers from the wealth of the island's lusty ladies. They'll pay dearly, I'm thinking, for the privilege of being serviced by him."

Arianna couldn't believe what she heard. "You can't be serious. Why, no respectable woman would lower herself to pay for a man's attentions."

"Respectable woman? Do you jest? I warrant

there's not a respectable woman on this godforsaken island. Present company excepted, of course. But then, my dear Cassiopeia, I don't expect you to bid on him. You have a husband, after all, but I'm betting there are a few women on this island who have the wealth and the inclination to bid on the earl. I shall turn a handsome profit."

And at the same time get him out of Bess's bed, he added to himself. For Bess was known for her stinginess every bit as much as she was known for her dark beauty. Everyone knew she could not bear to part with a farthing. It was one of the reasons she had become a pirate in the first place. Instead of paying for what she wanted, she took great pleasure in stealing it from others.

Curling her fingers around a tankard of wine, Arianna drew it to her lips, not conscious of what she was doing. She downed it in one gulp, then filled her tankard again, drinking it just as quickly. *Robert. What have I done to us?*

Chapter Nine

Hours later, a very inebriated Arianna reached for yet another tankard of ale. Her vision was blurred, her senses almost numb, and she doubted she could even stand, but it didn't matter. She wanted to drown herself in wine until she could no longer remember that her husband had gone to the seductive Black Bess's bedchamber.

"Cassiopeia! No more!" Colin warned.

Defiantly, she lifted the full tankard to her lips, missing them altogether and spilling the dark amber liquid on her chin.

Colin made a slight motion with his head, and the Terrible Four stood and made their way to Arianna's side. Terrence gently uncurled her fingers from the tankard and took it from her, whilst Thomas lifted her in his arms.

Grinning sheepishly at him, she proceeded to lay her too-heavy head on his broad shoulder and promptly passed out.

"Our lady here is too ill to go back to *The Constella-*

tion. What room will you provide for her?" Thaddeus asked, his large frame hovering over Elijah.

Longfellow raised his head from his own drunken stupor and waved in the general direction of the stairs. "What matter. Take mine. I'll not be using it. 'Tis the one next to Black Bess's."

Thomas carried Arianna up the stairs whilst Timothy lit the way with a candle. One down, one more to go, Colin thought, relieved that Arianna had gotten through the night without giving herself away. Turning his attention back to the drunken pirate, Colin wondered how long it would be before he, too, passed out.

He had been watching Longfellow's slow deterioration all evening long, noting that the longer Bess and Rob were gone, the worse he had become. The pirate had long ago given up pacing the floor and had switched to drinking as much spirits as he could consume, finding a willing drinking partner in Arianna, who made a point of matching him drink for drink. It would have been funny watching the two of them together if it weren't so dangerous.

Every time Arianna spoke, Colin was afraid that in her drunkenness she would forget she was supposed to be Cassiopeia and would give herself away. Every time Longfellow spoke, he was afraid it would be to order his men to kill Rob. It had been a harrowing night, and Colin vowed that if he got out of this alive, he would give up the dangerous life of a privateer and live in Scotland under James's protection.

Longfellow focused on Colin, and in slurred speech said, "Colin, my friend, methinks you, too, have reason to want revenge on the Earl of Everly. Let's hope he's bought by a monstrously ugly woman with cold tits who drains him of his manhood and forces him into repulsive sexual acts."

Laughing at his own speech, he stood up, holding on to the table for support. "Yes, I would pay for the privilege of seeing that."

"And I would pay for a good night's sleep, but I fear I shan't get one. Unless I miss my guess, Cassiopeia will be sick all night after everything she drank."

"Women! Just can't hold their drink like we can," Elijah said, burping loudly.

Colin grinned. " 'Tis true. Shall we have another?" Colin hoped that if he couldn't get Elijah to bed, he would at least get him to pass out. From the looks of him, he didn't have far to go.

Elijah fell backward into his chair. "Don't mind if I do." Downing Colin's offered drink, Elijah's eyes suddenly glazed over and he went limp.

At last. Wiping his brow with his hand, Colin poured himself a stiff drink and downed it in one gulp.

Arianna awoke with a start and found herself in an unfamiliar bedchamber. A bedchamber that most definitely belonged to a man, she thought, panicking at the sight of the masculine clothing strewn about. How . . . how had she gotten here? Obviously, she hadn't made her way here by herself. The last she remembered she was . . . Oh dear, it all came back to her then. The tankards full of wine and ale, Longfellow urging her on. Rob and . . . and . . .

Rob!

Had he spent the entire night with Black Bess?

She started from the bed, then sank back, grasping her head in pain. "Ohhhh, it feels like I fell off the blasted cliff and landed on my head."

She tried to get up again, this time moving much slower. Climbing off the bed, Arianna padded across the wooden floor, groaning at every step. Hearing a noise on the other side of the wall, she stopped and listened. Someone was moving about over there.

Creeping as quietly as she could, she made her way over to the wall and put her ear against it, the pain in her head forgotten as she envisioned Rob and Bess together. She heard Rob's voice and then a female laugh, and her heart sank. It was true. Rob was still with Bess. How could he do that to her?

The muted voices grew louder, and hearing the creaking of their door as it opened, Arianna quickly made her way to her door and opened it a crack. She had to know the truth.

Rob's low voice drifted to her. A purring voice; a sensual voice that spoke of a satisfying night. She opened the door wider and peeked around the corner . . . and saw Rob and Black Bess framed in the doorway of the next room. Her heart stopped. The two of them were kissing, their bodies entwined intimately.

She watched in horror as Bess murmured something into Rob's ear as her hand caressed his chest, then moved down to take his manhood in her hand.

Rob heard a gasp and knew he had an audience. Good. If this doesn't drive Arianna away, nothing will. Whispering in Black Bess's ear, he said, "She's watching. Let's make this good."

Rob took Bess's hand off his privates and brought it to his lips, nuzzling his nose in her palm. "Your hands deserve my praise. They are so very talented. Who taught you how to use them so provocatively?"

Arianna couldn't bear to hear any more but her feet were frozen to the floor, her knees so rubbery she thought she was at sea once more. And oh, how she wished she were. How she wished she had never come here . . . that she had never sent Rob off to this terrible fate.

But it was too late for wishes, too late for her. For Rob must surely hate Arianna if he could humiliate her by spending the night with Black Bess. How could he do this to her? How could he do this to their son? Thinking of baby Robin gave her strength, and she stepped out of the door to confront her husband.

Pretending surprise at her appearance, Rob pulled himself out of Black Bess's arms. "Arianna, I didn't realize you were here."

Arianna stared at her husband without speaking, the pain in her heart a fierce thing. A stray lock of his hair covered one eye, giving him a roguish look that had always melted her heart. She thought he had never looked more handsome, though his shirt was untucked and disheveled, the lacing undone, revealing most of his naked chest. Her gaze traveled down to the part of him that Black Bess had been caressing and she flexed the fingers of her aching hand. A hand that wanted nothing more than to touch him as Black Bess had. A hand that wanted to claim him as her own.

Memories of their life together flooded her brain. Of the husband who had loved her more than life itself. That couldn't have changed so quickly. She would stake her life on it. A rush of hope swept through her body, and it suddenly dawned on her why he was acting this way. "I know why you're doing this, Rob, and it won't work. I won't leave here without you."

Rob's eyes flickered, caught off guard by her words. Dropping his act, he spoke softly, using the only other weapon he had that could work. "Would you deny our child his mother?"

"Would you deny Robin his father? I will not. Not as long as I can draw breath. Not as long as there is one chance in a hundred that I can find a way to free you."

Black Bess touched Arianna's shoulder. "You're a brave woman, Arianna, but a very foolish one. You have no idea what you're up against. A fine lady like you has no idea how contemptible the human race can be."

"After your performance just now, I think I'm beginning to get the idea."

Black Bess laughed. "Methinks you have a very jealous wife, Robert, but then I don't blame her. If you belonged to me, I'd guard you with my life. Go back home, little girl. And let a woman do what you are not equipped to do. I will help your husband escape. I would have done so already, but he insists that you be safe from Longfellow before he consents to leaving. So you see, you traveled here for naught."

"I don't believe you for a moment. Why would you risk your life for Rob, unless . . . unless . . . Dear God, you want him for your own, don't you?"

In a solemn voice, Black Bess said, "It isn't Rob I want, but another."

Arianna searched Bess's face and saw the truth. It was so obvious, she wondered that she hadn't seen it before. "You love Longfellow."

"Now that you know the truth and have nothing to fear from me, will you leave so I can free your husband and send him home where he belongs?"

"Black Bess, I'm . . . sorry I wronged you. I knew the moment I laid eyes on you, you were someone very special. If you can free my husband, I'll be eternally grateful. I just wish—"

"What do you wish, Arianna?"

Arianna turned to gaze into her husband's eyes. "I wish . . . I pray . . . that someday you can forgive me for causing this to happen."

"Well, Robert," a booming voice called from the stairway, preventing Rob from answering, "I'm surprised to see you up already. Was the beautiful Bess a disappointment in bed?"

"To the contrary, Longfellow. She tells me I should thank you for teaching her all the delightful little tricks she performed on me."

Elijah gripped the stair railing hard, his muscles tightened to a mass of knots. "Is that so? My memory escapes me. Just what little tricks are you talking about?"

"How could you forget that wonderful leather device that she wraps around—" Rob stopped, hearing Arianna's gasp of horror.

Making his way up to the earl, Longfellow said, "You can practice your new trick on the ladies who bid on you. That should raise your price considerably."

"What are you talking about, Elijah?" Bess asked warily.

"Why, didn't you know? I have decided to auction Robert off to the highest female bidder."

Arianna froze. She had thought before that he was just joking when he said he wanted to auction Rob off. It was a shock to realize he was serious.

But Bess knew all too well what Elijah planned to do. It was so like him. "You can't do that."

"Oh? And why not? Because you want him? Well then, my dear, loosen your purse strings and bid on him yourself. That's the only way you'll have him in your bed again."

Realizing, finally, what Elijah meant, Arianna's mind raced. This could work to her advantage. She wouldn't need Black Bess's help after all, and she was happy of that. She would hate to be indebted to another woman for her husband's life. Much better to borrow gold from Colin and make the highest bid.

"Am I to understand, Longfellow, that any woman can bid on the earl? Any woman at all?"

"Aye. Do you have any one in particular in mind?" A sudden thought came to Longfellow and he cocked his eyebrow, looking at Arianna with suspicion. "Surely not you? And just how would you explain that to your husband?"

"Explain? Cassiopeia explains to no man. If I want, I take. It's as simple as that. Besides, my plans for the earl are strictly business. But I will say no more. I don't want you changing your mind about selling him. That would be too disappointing."

"You intrigue me, Cassiopeia. Nay, *intrigue* is too weak a word. You fascinate me. I have never met a woman like you. I'd like to delve into your mischievous brain and find out everything there is to know about you."

"Don't even try, Longfellow, for you'd get lost in all the mazes."

"Hmmm, I think you may be right. I guess I'll have to console myself with your fifty pieces of gold."

"What do you mean?"

"As an added incentive to bid high on Warwick, I am rewarding one hour with him in the privacy of his dungeon cell to any female who pays fifty gold pieces. Surely you won't want to miss out on that. The thought of Warwick chained to a dungeon wall whilst one woman after another has her way with him is very appealing, don't you think so . . . Bess?"

Bess's eyes sparked fire. "You've done some really despicable things since I have known you, but none so despicable as this."

"I doubt Madge Miggs or Big Alice will think it despicable. Methinks they will enjoy spending the night with a handsome nobleman. They've already paid their pieces of gold."

"If that's the way you want to play it, Elijah, watch out, because I mean to bid the highest."

Elijah hid his disappointment. "As you wish, but last night's passion will count as your time with the earl. Tonight will be Big Alice's turn, and then Madge Miggs, and if any other females pay the price, they shall have their turn on adjacent nights. If you wish to bid, you have until noon to give me your gold."

Elijah started for the stairs, then turned back, "Meanwhile, I want him shackled at his wrists and ankles so he cannot wander far. He's too valuable a prize to lose now."

Arianna listened to Bess and Elijah talk about Rob as if he were a farm animal to be bought and sold instead of the dearest man she had ever known. *If only this were all a bad dream. A nightmare I'll soon wake up from and find myself cuddled up against my husband in the safety of Everly Castle. But it wasn't a dream. It was all too real. It was all well and good to bid on Rob with borrowed gold, but to stand by whilst other females took their turn with him . . . How can I bear it? What can I do to stop it?*

Chapter Ten

In a daze, Arianna walked out to the courtyard, her mind awhirl with pictures of her husband locked in the embrace of one lusty lady pirate after another. She must find Colin right away. Find him and tell him to take the stronghold by force. Tell him to kill Elijah Longfellow, if he must, and rescue Rob before anything happened. But where was he? Why wasn't he there when she needed him? He was the only one who could help her now.

Spotting one of the Terrible Four—Arianna didn't know which one, because she still couldn't keep their names straight—she cried, "Where's Colin? I have to find him right away."

Thomas heard the urgency in her voice. "What is it, me lady? Can I be of service?"

"No. Please. I need Colin."

"Then you'll find him up in the guard tower. He climbed up there looking for a quiet place to slee—."

Before Thomas could finish speaking, Arianna was running to the rugged wooden ladder that led up to the crudely built open-sided guard tower. Gathering the

skirts of her gown between her legs to keep from tripping over them, she made her way up the ladder. When
she reached the top, she peered over the edge and saw
Colin curled up on the floor asleep. "Colin. Colin.
Wake up."

In an instant Colin was awake and on his feet, helping Arianna through the small embrasure. "What is it?
Has Elijah done anything to hurt you?"

Throwing herself into Colin's arms, she cried, "No.
It's not me, it's Rob. Longfellow is going to auction
him off to the highest female bidder. And that's not the
worst. He's . . . oh, dear God, he's going to let any
woman who pays fifty gold pieces spend an hour in the
dungeon with Rob."

Colin laughed uproariously. He couldn't help it. It
seemed like such a ludicrous idea. Pulling her out of
his arms, he held her at arm's length. "And just who
would pay fifty gold pieces for that? Don't take it so
seriously, Arianna. I'm betting there'll be no takers."

"Then you'd lose. Already two women have paid
the price. And . . . and . . . I won't have it. I just won't
have it! I want you to get all your men and . . . and
. . . take this place. It's what we should have done in
the first place, instead of—"

"Calm yourself, princess. You're asking the impossible and you right well know it. We don't have
enough men to take this place by force. You say Longfellow is going to auction Rob off? Well, there's the
chance we've been waiting for. I've enough gold in my
treasure chest to assure that we can bid the highest.
We'll buy him back and no one's blood will be spilt."

"No. I can't wait that long. Half the women on this

island could have slept with him by then. Oh, Colin, don't you understand?"

"I understand all right, but for once in your life, Arianna, you're going to have to suffer the consequences of your actions. It's a hard lesson to learn, I'll grant you that. But it is a smaller price to pay than the shedding of my men's blood. So grit your teeth and take it, then forget it ever happened and go on with your life. If you don't, you'll destroy whatever you have left of a life with Robert."

Arianna hadn't expected so little sympathy from Colin. She blinked back the tears that stung her eyes, her lower lip jutting out in a puffy pout.

Colin's heart melted at the sight. Cradling her gently in his arms, he pressed his lips to her forehead.

Inside the great hall, a very angry Rob spoke to Bess. "We've got to talk."

With a stern look, Bess cautioned him against saying anything more, nodding her head toward the courtyard. "It will be safer there."

Rob followed Bess outdoors, blinking at the bright sunlight. "Longfellow isn't making this easy. Arianna won't leave now because she's sure she can bid the highest."

"In sooth, she may be right."

"Well, I don't trust Elijah. Not for one moment. And even if he does free me, there's still the problem of getting my knight John Neal out of here. I'll not leave him behind."

"I didn't expect that you would. But that's the least of our problems. You see, there's one little thing I haven't mentioned before. 'Tis my men who guard the dungeon cells."

Rob's face lit up. "Your men? No wonder you were so confident you could free me." Rob laughed happily, tilting his head back to enjoy the warm rays of the sun, as he all but tasted his impending freedom.

A glint of golden hair in the crude wooden tower that stood in the center of the courtyard caught his attention and he narrowed his eyes, focusing on Arianna in Colin's arms. His face turned to stone.

Bess followed his gaze. "What is it between those two, Robert? It seems odd that a countess would have a privateer for a close friend."

Rob's gaze never left the figures in the tower as he spoke to Bess. "He wasn't always a privateer. He was a nobleman, until Elizabeth stripped him of everything he owned, and then . . . then he became a huntsman for me."   .

"Is that where Arianna met him? At your castle in Everly?"

"It wasn't as simple as that. No, she met him on a lonely cliff as she was giving birth to my son. He rescued her, brought her back to his cottage, and nursed her back to life. She and Robin owe their lives to that man."

"If that's how it is, I don't understand your hatred of the man."

"Would you understand if I told you that Arianna lived with him for ten long months as a man lives with a wife. That she willingly chose to stay with him, thinking she was protecting me from the queen's wrath by doing so. *That she wanted me to think she was dead.*"

Seeing the astonishment on Bess's face, he laughed bitterly. "Oh, yes, 'tis true. For ten months I grieved for my dead wife, dying myself a little more each day, never knowing she still lived and that the child she had been carrying lived, too."

"My God, Robert. Why did she let you suffer so?"

"Because she thought she had no choice. It is a long story. One I care not to conjure up now." No, he couldn't share the long and twisted story of the Scottish queen's birth to Arianna. Her secret identity must never be told.

"But you found her again. How? Tell me that at least."

Rob smiled bitterly. "I found her all right. At the beheading of Mary, Queen of Scots. Arianna was there dressed as a boy. She fainted at the sight of Mary's blood and was carried out. That's when I saw her. I thought I was truly going mad. That I was hallucinating. But it was her. I followed her back to the inn where she was staying with Colin and claimed her as my wife once more."

"You are a forgiving man, Robert Warwick. Not many men would do as you did."

"Not many men have a wife like Arianna. But, in truth, we've led an idyllic life since her return. At least we did until she had the queen send me off to Scotland and Elijah Longfellow captured my ship."

"I wonder that you still love her. It seems to me you'd be happier loving some—"

"Some boring little obedient lady who always says and does the right thing? No. God help me, I love every gut-wrenching moment of my life with her. You see, the hard part isn't loving her; that's easy. The hard part is to try and stop loving her. I've never been able to do that. In truth, the only regret I have is that she ever met Colin Colrain. Damn her, she still cares for him. Still turns to him when she needs help."

"Would you have it any other way? Would you have her so callous she could live with a man for ten months, then forget about him in an instant? Arianna is a decent woman. Of course she still cares about him, but you're the lucky man she loves. I'd settle for that in a heart's beat."

Rob knew Bess was thinking about Longfellow. "He does care about you, you know."

"I know. But not enough. Not as much as I need. I want what Arianna has. A home, a family, a man who loves her dearly. If I can't find it here, then I'll try somewhere else. The king of Scotland has promised safe refuge for the privateers who work for him. I can go there. Give up this bloody business and live a respectable life."

"Or you could come to Everly with Arianna and me. You'll never want for anything there. It's the least I can do for you."

Patting Robert's hand fondly, Bess said, "Thank you. Who knows, someday I may take you up on that. But as for—"

"Here now, Black Bess, you've had him long enough. Let me and Miggs, here, have a go at him."

Rob rolled his eyes at Bess in consternation, then turned to face the two women who stood ogling him as if he were a bit of sweetmeat.

"Yeah, 'tis our turn to check the merchandise, so to speak. We wants to see if he's worth bidding on," Madge Miggs said, squeezing Robert's arm. "He's on the thin side, but I guess I can fatten him up. I likes a man I can hang on to, if you knows what I mean."

A look of panic came into Rob's eyes as it suddenly occurred to him that he would be having nocturnal visits in his cell from these two women, and God alone knew how many more. *Starting this very night.*

When the women had pinched him and poked at him to their content, trying twice to fondle his private parts, they finally left and Rob drew in a deep breath. "What in Hades am I going to do about them?"

Bess laughed, enjoying Rob's discomfort. "You've got to learn to be more devious, Robert. You'd be amazed at what you can accomplish that way."

"I've spent my life believing that being honest was its own reward; I'm afraid I can't change now. But . . . if you have a solution to my problem, I'm willing to give it a try, devious or not."

"Good. It's very simple. Listen closely." Bess whispered into Rob's ear, outlining her ingenious plan, and a wide grin broke out across his face.

By nightfall, the great hall was crowded with pirates and village people alike, all eager to witness the strange goings-on. They knew that whenever Longfellow came up with a new game, they were sure to enjoy it. He had a great knack for finding new ways to while away the lonely hours of island living.

Dressed in Cassiopeia's flamboyant pirate outfit of red doublet and pink plumed hat, Arianna entered the hall, her gaze intent on searching the throng for Rob. She hadn't seen him all day and feared he was deliberately avoiding her.

It wasn't hard to find him, for he stood in the center of the hall, the object of everyone's attention. Arianna was sure every available female from here to the Tartugas was swarming around him. She felt the heat rise in her face. What was wrong with these women? Didn't they have a man of their own?

Suddenly, the air was filled with the erotic throbbing of some exotic drum. The beat was unlike anything she had ever heard before and the air was heavy with sexuality as Longfellow's naked female slaves danced into the room. They moved suggestively, their hips and breasts, arms and legs keeping time with the beat of the drum. Never had Arianna seen anything like it.

The oil-slicked ebony-skinned women made their way over to Rob and undulated their bodies against him in a blatantly erotic way, until Arianna wanted to take them by their hair and throw them across the room.

But Rob, oh yes, Rob looked as if he was enjoying their attentions, and Arianna wondered again if she had lost him forever. She had never seen him like this before. She had always been the only woman he ever looked at, and it came as a shock to her to know that he might find other women attractive.

But then, he was a man, above all else, wasn't he? And as a man, how could he fail to be attracted by these naked females who displayed their bodies so openly?

Arianna watched in fascinated horror as the women danced around her husband and, unconscious of the fact, absorbed into her brain every enticing movement they made. She couldn't help herself. She wished it were she dancing for Rob. She alone, in the bedchamber of Everly Castle.

A hard lump came to her throat. *Oh, Rob, I want you so.*

Bess could see that Arianna was close to losing her composure and she made her way over to Rob, intent on drawing him away from the seductive females. Playfully, so as not to make her true intentions known, she led Robert over to the table where Colin and the Terrible Four sat.

Arianna joined them, sitting across from Rob, her eyes sparking fire. "I'm surprised you could tear yourself away from those beautiful naked women. Unless, of course, Black Bess appeals to you even more than they. Which is it, Robert?"

Rob hid his smile. "Would you have me to yourself, Rose Petal? There is a way. Leave with Colin. Go to his ship. Sail for home, and I promise you I will escape and join you."

"And what if Bess cannot free you? What then? Am I to be deprived of my husband when I could have so easily bought you back? No, I won't take the chance."

"You're a fool, then, if you think you can trust Longfellow."

"He'll keep his part of the agreement. Just because he's a pirate doesn't mean he isn't an honorable man."

"Then let this be on your head. When I lie with these women, I hope you'll remember it didn't have to be that way. It will be on your conscience, not mine."

Arianna didn't have an answer for that. All she could do was plead, "Rob . . ."

"Listen to him, Arianna," Colin said, hoping she would come to her senses. "There is just so much a marriage can survive. We can leave now. Go back to the ship. Bess will free Rob and he can join us soon."

Watching as Big Alice swaggered over to Rob, Arianna wanted to do just that. It was obvious how Alice had got her name, for she had the largest breasts Arianna had ever seen. They bounced up and down with every step she took, as if they had a life of their own.

The thought of Rob's hands on that enormous bosom was more than she could bear. If she didn't do as Rob asked and leave right away, Alice would be exposing those obscene mountains to Rob . . . and more, much, much more.

Alice sidled up to Rob and slipped her arms around his neck, nuzzling his nose with her own. "I'm ready for a good hard ride, your earlship. No need to wait any longer, I says. Shall we get started now?"

Rob stared into Arianna's eyes. If she didn't give in now, if she didn't leave the island after Alice flaunted herself in his face, she never would. Holding his breath, he taunted her with, "What say you, Cassiopeia? Shall I get started now? Shall I invite the voluptuous Alice to join me in the darkness of my dungeon cell?"

Chapter Eleven

Big Alice didn't like the intimate way Robert was speaking to Cassiopeia. "Here now, what are you asking 'er for? You don't belong to 'er, but to Captain Longfellow."

Rob's lips curled into a sad smile. "Do you have anything to say to Alice, Cassiopeia?"

Struggling for a way out of the desperate situation, Arianna answered, "Yes, I do. Uh . . . Alice, I was wondering if you would trade nights with me."

"Trade nights? What? Give up me time with the earl tonight?"

"It's only for one night. You can have him tomorrow."

"And just why would I be doing that?"

Arianna's brows drew together in a deep frown. "Why, just because it would be a friendly thing to do."

Alice looked at Cassiopeia as if she'd turned mad. "Friendly? Next thing you know she'll be wanting me in 'er bed because it's the friendly thing to do. Sorry, me lady, but I don't do it with girlies."

Before anyone could stop her, Arianna balled her hand into a fist and struck Alice in the eye.

Alice staggered back, her face caught in an idiotic expression as she tried to recover from the blow. Shaking her head to clear it, her hand reached for a dagger in a sheath at her waist.

In an instant, the Terrible Four surrounded Arianna, their swords drawn and ready.

It all happened so fast that Arianna hadn't had time to do more than blink in surprise.

The hall became deathly still as everyone waited to see what would happen next.

Alice sheathed her dagger. "I see now why you're always surrounded by guards. If they weren't here, I'd be gutting you down the middle." Bowing grandly, she declared, "I yield to the might of the Terrible Four." But her voice turned lethal as she hissed, "Heed my warning, woman. Stay out of my way, else I change my mind."

Rob was stunned at Arianna's violent outburst. She was clearly on the edge of breaking down. The only way he could protect her now was to keep Alice away from her. "Ladies, ladies, ladies, please . . . There's no need to fight over me. I've energy enough to make you all very happy. But, as I understand it, Alice has been selected as my first liaison of the night. Be patient, Cassiopeia. Your turn will come."

Arianna had no doubt he meant those words as a threat. She started to answer him, when she heard Elijah's voice behind her.

"My, my, my, the earl is certainly in demand. I'll be most eager to hear if he was worth all the fuss. Report to me in the morning, Alice. I want to make sure you get your money's worth."

Arianna's heart sank. Elijah was going to make sure Rob went through with it.

"Meanwhile, Robert, I'll escort you back to your cell and make sure you're secured for the night. I don't want Alice or Miggs absconding with you in the heat of the moment."

Bess cursed to herself. Elijah was going to spoil her plan if he personally conducted Rob to his cell. Did he suspect something?

Thinking fast, Bess slipped her arm around Longfellow's waist and kneaded her fingers into his skin. "Must you be the one to go with him? All this activity has given me an itch that must be scratched. And the sooner the better. But if you're not available, I suppose I will have to—"

Elijah pulled her into his arms. "I knew you couldn't stay away from me for very long."

"You did, did you? Then what are we waiting for? Bart can secure the earl just as he does every night, and you and I can get started all the sooner."

In the blink of an eye, Longfellow scooped Bess into his arms and started for the stairs. "Bart, see to the earl. I have more important matters to attend to."

Black Bess laughed naughtily, winking at Rob over Longfellow's shoulder.

"Not to worry, Captain," Bart answered, smiling wickedly at Alice. "I'll chain him to the wall. If I know Alice here, that won't slow her down a bit."

Arianna watched as Rob was taken away. Each step he took was a piercing pain through her heart. Colin's words came back to haunt her then: "There's just so much a marriage can survive."

Dear Lord, how could it survive this? How could *she* survive the night? Hearing the taunts and lusty encouragements of the spectators, Arianna turned her attention to Alice. The miserable woman seemed to enjoy being the center of attention. Finally, after several suggestive comments to the spectators, Alice wiggled her hips erotically, then strutted out the door that led to the dungeon.

Arianna hated her with a passion.

Arianna hated every last person there.

But she hated herself even more. If not for her desire for revenge, she and Rob would be safe in Everly with Robin, a happy, loving family.

Tears streaked her face as she looked around, helplessly seeking she knew not what.

Colin saw her anguish and placed a goblet of wine in her hand. "Here, drink this. 'Twill take some of the pain away."

In a mournful voice, she cried, "Nothing but death can take this pain away."

Suddenly scared, Colin said, "Don't be talking that way."

Arianna heard the fear in his voice and answered, "Oh, Colin, I didn't mean it that way. I'll be all right. After all, Alice will be with him for only one short hour. One hour out of a lifetime. I can live with that." If only she truly believed that. If only . . .

Gently, Colin forced the goblet to Arianna's lips and she drank, unaware she was doing so. Unaware of anything but the door that separated her from Rob, the door Alice had gone through to join him.

Each moment seemed an eternity to Arianna as she waited for Alice to return. An eternity of pain, an eternity of anguish.

Rob with that terrible woman.

Doing what?

Would he touch her the same way he touched Arianna?

Would he feel the same ecstatic sensations that she alone had given him? Rob had been a virgin when she married him. Rob had never held another woman in his arms. And she had always held him in the highest esteem because of that. Would her feelings toward him change now?

And what about his feelings toward her? After tasting the charms of other women, would he find her too tame? Arianna bit her lip until it drew blood.

Seeing how close Arianna was to breaking, Colin and the Terrible Four tried hard to distract her from her horrible watch. They plied her with drink and meaningless chatter, and she joined in, not wanting them to suffer for her.

She laughed at their jokes, but there was a tinge of hysteria to her voice that broke the hearts of her companions.

Colin couldn't help but wonder if Arianna wouldn't have been happier staying with him in the cottage in the woods. At least she had been protected there. And she would have had a modicum of happiness. Not the great happiness she had with Rob, but great though it might be, it was also fleeting. For their life together had been full of strife, full of fear, full of . . .

Hearing Alice's unmistakable laughter, Colin and

Arianna exchanged glances, then focused on the door as it opened and Alice stepped in.

Arianna watched in dread as the woman made her way into the hall. Her disheveled clothing and hair made it all too obvious that Rob had given her what she wanted. One swollen breast escaped the unlaced bodice, and Arianna's blood froze at the sight of a bite mark displayed like an oval banner just over the nipple. It was silent testament to her husband's betrayal.

No. It couldn't be. It couldn't.

Madge Miggs saw it, too. She gave out a long, low whistle. "I was goin' to ask if he was worth the price, but I think I have me answer."

Alice strutted over to Madge. "Never had better. Them earls is right rambunctious. Eager to please, too. And I'm betting he'll not let up on you. Right full of energy, he is. Done it to me twice."

Arianna couldn't believe what she heard. The woman must be lying. That was it. She was just bragging to make herself look more desirable. Oh, how she wished that it were so, but Alice had a well-satisfied look about her that she could only have gotten one way. Was this Rob's way of punishing her?

Grabbing a bottle of wine, Madge headed for the door, waving it over her head. "To build up his strength. Don't count on seeing me for the full time I've got coming. I mean to make the most of it."

One more hour, Arianna thought. I can last one more hour. But she didn't really believe it. Feeling her stomach heave, she made it outside to the courtyard just in time to throw up.

Chapter Twelve

Next morning, exhausted and sunken-eyed from lack of sleep, Arianna made her way out of the stronghold to the edge of the rugged cliff, in need of being alone. It was a gusty day, the wind from the north pushing at her, playing with her clothes, doing its best to blow away her somber mood, but to no avail. Arianna was too deep in troubled thought.

Tonight would be her turn to go to Rob, and she dreaded the thought of facing him. She had returned to the hall last night, waiting for Madge to reappear. Arianna had endured the woman's detailed description of Rob's prowess whilst Madge bragged about the intense pleasure she had experienced in the pitch blackness of the dungeon, the sound of Rob's chains chiming in tune to the rhythm of their lusty lovemaking. Arianna had listened to every word, her heart dying a little more each second.

How could she go to him after that? But if she didn't, someone else would go in her place. *Oh, Rob, I didn't think you could behave so callously toward me or betray our sacred vows so easily.*

Staring out at the graceful lines of *The Constellation,* so pristine and beautiful, sitting high on the water, Arianna wanted nothing more than to escape to the sanctuary it offered. Where the lines between right and wrong were clearly defined. She wanted to set sail for home and never see this hated island again.

Rob was right. She should have gone when he begged her to. Gone before it was too late. Before she lost her dignity and her self-respect. But it was too late now. She would have to play this game out to the end. She would go back to the stronghold and tell Rob what she had decided . . . that despite his betrayal, she would not be driven off. She could not, would not leave until she knew he was safe.

Arianna became gradually aware of the wind blowing around her as it grew suddenly stronger, causing the Devil's Harp to sound. She listened to the eerie music, drawn into its magic spell, and closed her eyes to let it wash over her. It was an entrancing sound, a magical sound that soothed her very soul.

After a while, the wind shifted just a little and the music changed, a different sensation washing over her. A sensation of deep erotic longing brought on by the strange siren's music that filled her ears and flooded her senses.

A picture swam in her head, of being locked with Rob in a passionate embrace. She could see his body undulate, melting into hers, as they moved to the sultry song of the Devil's Harp. It haunted her with memories of past lovemaking, reminding her what it had been like to lie with her husband.

Her longing grew, until slowly . . . very slowly

. . . a growing awareness came to her that she wasn't alone, that someone else shared this siren's song.

Still wrapped in the sensuous spell of the music, she turned, expectantly, mouth parted, eyes half closed, dreamy with desire, and found herself gazing into the fervent brown eyes of her husband.

Rob stared back, his gaze intense, looking for all the world like a sensuous Lancelot, his body adorned in white. And for one glorious moment, he was her lover again. He was her beloved husband again.

For that one hope-filled moment she believed that he hadn't been intimate with the other women and, relieved, Arianna took a step toward him.

The wind died then and the erotic music ended, breaking the magic spell that had bound them. In the blinking of an eye, Rob's face had turned to that of a hard-faced stranger. She had lost him once again.

A sudden anger took hold of her. Anger that he should give up so easily on the love they had shared, anger that he could humiliate her like that, and she lashed out at him, striking his face.

Rob stood his ground, never moving a muscle.

She slapped him again and still he took it, his face a mask she could not penetrate.

She raised her hand to hit him again, when she felt an enormous meaty hand grasp hers.

"Me lady, you don't want to be doing that now. The earl doesn't deserve that, believe me."

"Be quiet, Terrence," Rob warned, speaking in a low voice.

Arianna suddenly felt a spark of hope. Was it all an act to drive her away? No, Alice and Madge had not been acting.

But . . . but if he had made love to them, why was he trying to keep Terrence from speaking to her now? What was he trying to keep from her? "Rob, what is it? Tell me. Dear God, I've got the right to know if you made love to those women."

Rob's jaw tightened. Without answering, he turned and walked away, and she was suddenly too weak to stop him.

Why was he doing this to her? Why had he walked away without an answer? Her heart ached to learn the truth. Was it possible he still loved her? Dear God in heaven, she had to know.

Shouting over the wind, she said, "I'll know the answer tonight, when it's my turn to be with you. I'll know then, Robert. God help me, I'll know then."

Robert kept walking, his fists clenching the accursed chain that weighed heavily on his wrists and on his soul.

Back in the hall, he strode over to Colin and, through gritted teeth, warned, "Get out of here today, or so help me, when I get free I'll tear you limb from limb and feed your bloody body to the sharks."

Colin took the outburst in stride. It was no more than he expected. Rob had been a lot more patient than he would have been under the circumstances. "I'd be more than happy to oblige you, but you know as well as I how stubborn your wife can be."

"Then reason with her. Show her the danger she is in every moment she spends within Longfellow's grasp. If he ever finds out she is my wife, God only knows what he'll do to her to get back at me."

"There's no reasoning with her where you're concerned. You try if you don't believe me. You'll be alone with her tonight. Take advantage of that time and make her understand. *She's your wife, not mine.*"

"And you wish it were otherwise."

Rob's words washed over Colin like the low rumble of thunder. He shook his head in frustration. "You're just as stubborn as she is."

Looking over Rob's shoulder, Colin saw Longfellow approaching and warned the earl in a low whisper.

Rob's demeanor immediately changed, and in a placid voice, he said, "Seems I'm the envy of every man on the island. Longfellow has no idea what a favor he's done me."

Rob's words penetrated Elijah's skull, echoing through his head in mocking laughter. *Blast it all, Warwick leads a charmed life. No matter what I do to hurt him, it seems only to benefit him more.* "You won't think so once you're sold. You'll be singing a different tune then. Having to perform for your mistress whenever she's a mind. Whether you're *up* to it or not."

Hoping to antagonize Longfellow, Rob answered, "If Bess wins, I'll be *up* for it all right. I'll be *firmly* up for it. 'Twill be no chore to pleasure her every night."

Elijah came close to losing control just then. Blind with rage, he wanted nothing more than to strike out at Robert, but he wouldn't give him the satisfaction of knowing his words had been lethal weapons. Feigning boredom, he said, "I'm growing weary of this game. It ends tonight. Cassiopeia has paid her fifty gold pieces and shall have her turn with you, and on the morrow the bidding will begin."

Robert and Colin never changed their expressions. With a demonic grin, Elijah continued, "It's time to begin a new game. A game where *I* shall be the sole recipient of pleasure."

As luck would have it, Arianna appeared in the doorway just then, her golden hair fanning around her face as a sudden gust of wind swirled about her before abandoning her to the three mortals who gazed at her with admiration.

"Yes," Longfellow said, eating up the beautiful woman with his eyes. "It will pleasure me well."

Rob felt a chill go up his spine. Danger was closing in on Arianna, of that he had no doubt. "I'm tired of your petty little games, Longfellow. If you wish to destroy me, go ahead and try. Don't strike at me from behind women's skirts. Combat me with your fists, or your sword, or your axe."

"You'd like that, wouldn't you? A chance to show off for Black Bess and Cassiopeia. You'd like to have them both fawning over you as you play the part of the dashing knight, ready to do battle to defend their honor."

"Longfellow, don't you think—"

Colin never got a chance to finish as Elijah interrupted. "Stay out of this, Colin. It has nothing to do with you. And don't try to fool me with your devoted husband act. Cassiopeia has told me about the arrangement the two of you have."

Colin was taken aback by Elijah's words but kept his thoughts to himself. He knew what Arianna was up to and had to play along. "The same arrangement you have with Black Bess, I'll warrant."

Arianna could see the anger on the three men's faces and she put on her prettiest smile, hoping to defuse it as she joined them.

"Ah, the island's prettiest occupant. Is that not so, gentlemen?" Elijah hoped Cassiopeia's presence would cool the hotheaded nobleman. He had an aversion to fighting that went back to his early childhood. It had been a hard life for him then, the youngest of seven brothers, having to fight every day of his life to survive. Even for the stale bread and ale that his slovenly mother threw on the table at mealtimes.

No, he much preferred ambush, manipulation, and devious plots to get his way now. It was a much more civilized way of living. But it was also a lonely way to live. For he could trust in no one, and certainly no one trusted in him. If he had it to do over . . . But no use dwelling on that now. He would use whatever device he could to win Black Bess for his own, and he would revenge himself on Robert Warwick for daring to make love to her under his very roof. And . . . above all . . . he would bed the incredible Cassiopeia. She would be his greatest conquest.

Tension between the three men was strong, Arianna quickly noted. She had no idea what had transpired between them, but from the way they stared at her, she had a feeling she was the cause of it. The thought of that gave her a modicum of pleasure. Smiling prettily at Longfellow, she crooned, "Why, thank you for your kind words, Elijah. My life, of late, has been bereft of such sweetness."

Taking Arianna by the arm, Elijah answered, "Then Colin is a fool. If you belonged to me—"

"If you belonged to him, he'd treat you just as he does me," Black Bess said, walking up to Arianna. "If you would hear the intimate details, join me whilst I feed Troubadour."

Arianna's eyes lit up upon seeing the beautiful parrot on Bess's shoulder, and she was happy to walk away from the three brooding men. It was stupid of her to think she could gain anything by flirting with Elijah. That would only make matters worse.

Stroking the bird's feathers of bright blue and gold and red, Arianna exclaimed, "She's beautiful."

"He, not she. But unlike the human males hereabouts, he is loyal to his mistress."

"I understand what you mean all too well. May I hold him? I've never seen such an exquisitely colored bird. It fair takes my breath away."

Bess's voice softened at the words of praise. "Troubadour doesn't take to strangers, I'm afraid. He has a nasty bite."

"Go ahead and let her," Colin said, his voice filled with pride. "Ari . . . uh . . . Cassiopeia has a way with birds that is truly amazing."

"Is that so? I'd like to see that."

"I do have a way with hawks, it's true, but I've never handled a parrot before, let alone seen one."

Arianna gazed into the intelligent, mischievous-looking eyes of the bird and made noises with her tongue. The bird responded with interest, and encouraged, Arianna made a motion for it to perch on her arm.

The parrot obliged as if Arianna were an old friend. Happily, Arianna nuzzled the parrot's colorful feathers with her nose and the bird responded by giving her a friendly peck on the cheek.

"You see, not even the males of the bird species can resist Cassiopeia's charms," Longfellow said. "Watch

out, Bess, or she'll steal him away from you altogether."

Bess fumed inside but hid it from Elijah. Instead,
she took Arianna by the arm and steered her away.
"As I was saying, come join me whilst I feed Troubadour and we can have a nice long chat . . . female to
female. 'Tis not often I get the chance. Too few
females in our trade, as you well know."

Arianna nodded her head, handing Troubadour
back to Bess. "I'd like that."

Walking to a long trestle table laden with breads,
cheeses, and fruit, Bess and Arianna chatted whilst the
parrot fed on bits and pieces of the food.

Sated, the bird ruffled his feathers, then to Arianna's
astonishment cried, "Give me a kiss."

Arianna's mouth flew open. "He can talk!"

"Aye, he talks, too long and too loud. Sometimes I
wish I hadn't taught him. Especially when I've overin-
dulged in spirits and have a terrible headache."

"*You* taught him that?"

"I did. That and other useful things." Suddenly
laughing impishly, she said, "Shall I show you my
favorite trick?"

"Oh, yes. Do."

"Watch this." Bess said, then coughed loudly.
Arianna wondered if she had choked on a piece of fruit
and was about to voice her concern, when the parrot
suddenly took flight across the hall, diving at Elijah
and knocking his blue feathered hat from his head to
the enjoyment of everyone there.

Cursing at the parrot as he flew back to Bess's
shoulder, Elijah picked up his hat and dusted it off,
then glared at Black Bess suspiciously.

"Did you teach him to do that? But how? I didn't see you give him any commands. No hand movements, no whistles. How?"

" 'Twas my cough that commanded him to move."

"Your cough? But why? Why didn't you teach him a proper command?"

"To keep Elijah from knowing that I have trained the bird to attack him."

"He's never suspected?"

"Never, and it drives him mad. But he can't blame me, now, can he? He just thinks the bird has it in for him. But sooner or later he will begin to suspect, and I shall have to think of another trick."

"I'm intrigued by this, Bess. How did the bird know to go to Longfellow's hat, instead of Robert's or Colin's, since they were both standing there, too?"

"Because only Elijah wears a hat adorned with a blue feather."

"I see. How wonderful. You've trained Troubadour to attack a blue feather. Does the bird think the feather is another bird or a rival?"

"I have no idea, but it's great fun, isn't it?"

"Oh, yes." It was more than fun to Arianna. It was information to be stored in her brain for future use. She had trained many a hawk and falcon to her commands, but had never thought of other uses for her expertise with birds. Bess had opened her eyes.

Troubadour's antics soon had Arianna feeling better than she had since she came to the accursed island. She couldn't get over hearing the bird talk, and she laughed happily whenever she heard a new word or phrase emanating from the beautiful parrot.

Her crystal laughter drifted to Rob's ears and he

was without the will to stay away. But as soon as he approached Arianna, her face lost its beautiful smile and the laughter died. At a loss for what to do, he floundered a moment before turning his attention to Bess, pretending that it was she who had drawn him across the hall. "Bess, have I told you how lovely you look today?"

Bess's eyebrow arched as she gazed at Robert. Out of the corner of her eye, she saw Arianna's stricken look. "Why, thank you, Robert. A woman never hears that enough. But I wonder that you don't mention how beautiful your wife looks, too, since it is most obvious."

Rob gazed deeply into Arianna's eyes and forced himself to keep his voice from betraying his feelings. "She has always looked beautiful to me."

A hard, hurting lump came to Arianna's throat. "Really? Even now? After you've known other women?"

The muscle in Rob's cheek twitched. "Search your heart and you'll find the answer to that."

"My heart hurts too much to probe it."

"Here now," Bess said, knowing well how much this man and woman truly loved each other, "don't you think 'tis time to heal your wounds?"

Breaking her gaze from Rob's beloved face, she answered, a tinge of sadness in her voice, "Some wounds are too deep to heal."

Chapter Thirteen

Sitting at the small window in Bess's bedchamber, Arianna watched the tide coming in, contemplating what she should do. But it was no use, for she had changed her mind as many times as the waves she so fervently studied washed against the rocky shore. Should she go to Robert and make him love her again, or should she tell him she could not forgive him for being with other women? Or should she take the coward's way out and set sail for Everly, leaving Rob's rescue to Black Bess?

Hearing a light rapping on the door, she opened it to see Bess standing there, a bundle of clothing in her arms. "Oh, Bess, what am I to do? 'Tis almost time for me to go to Rob."

"That's why I'm here. May I come in for just a moment?"

Arianna nodded her head and held the door open wider. "Of course. 'Tis your bedchamber. Thank you for offering it to me. I didn't want to go back to Longfellow's chamber for fear he might take it to mean something else."

"Too true. Men think in such simple ways. So easy to understand them. So difficult for them to understand us. That's the way 'tis always been. The way 'twill always be."

"Oh, Bess, I never thought Robert was like other men. How could I have been so wrong? I cannot bear to even think about what happened between him and Madge and Alice."

"Then don't. Go to him. Show him how much you love him. Trust him, Arianna, for he deserves that much. Your husband is an extraordinary man, and you have no idea how lucky you are to have him."

"You can say that after last night?"

"After last night or any other. Don't let Longfellow win. And he will, you know, if you let his manipulations come between you and Rob."

"I know that's true and . . . and I will go to him, but I have no idea what I'll say or do when I see him."

"Just give the man a chance to explain; he deserves that much. And . . . to make your visit all the more exciting, I want you to wear this." Bess held up a white velvet doublet for Arianna to see and dangled a pair of white hose with specks of gold in front of her nose.

"I don't understand. You want me to wear a man's jacket and hose and nothing more?"

"You can wear my boots as well," Bess said, tossing a pair of white leather boots on the bed.

"No stays or trunk hose or shirt? 'Twould be indecent."

"Not quite. Your privates will be covered. The only thing that will show is a glimpse of bosom and your legs."

Arianna was hesitant, but she had to admit the

thought of wearing the revealing outfit for Rob was enticing. It suddenly occurred to her that Bess's clothing was identical to what Rob was wearing. "Bess, did you give Rob the garb he's wearing now?"

"Aye, and for a reason. You see, I had the doublets made up for Elijah and me. We were to be married in them. But I realize now that the fabric will rot away before Elijah is ready to marry, and so I give them to you and your husband so they'll not go to waste. Robert looks incredibly handsome dressed in white, don't you think?"

Arianna nodded, seeing him as he looked at the cliff, and a lump came to her throat. If she dressed in the same clothing, would it have the same effect on him? "Does he know how I'll be dressed?"

Smiling softly, Bess answered, "No. I thought it would be lovely to surprise him."

Squeezing Bess's hand, Arianna proclaimed, "You are truly a hopeless romantic, Bess. And I love you for it. I only wish that soon you'll forget all about Longfellow and find a romantic hero of your own."

"I'll hang on to that thought. Now, woman, get dressed. You've punished Robert long enough with your absence. He's in agony wondering if your visit will be one of pleasure or of pain."

"Then that makes two of us."

In a moment Arianna was dressed in the provocative white doublet and hose, feeling terribly exposed. She would have felt naked but for the white hose that covered her legs. To finish the ensemble, she pulled on the pair of soft white leather boots that Bess had provided, knowing without asking that she looked spectacular.

Bess confirmed that with a low whistle. "Poor Robert. One look at you and he'll be lost."

Bess spoke the truth.

Robert lost his composure completely, seeing his wife in that unbelievably sensual garment. So much so that it took a minute for him to realize she wore the same exact clothing that he did. But, damnation, it looked so different on her. The doublet fitted her body like a glove, outlining it and showing off her magnificent breasts, her tiny waist, and her legs. God's blood . . . her legs. He had forgotten how beautiful they were until this moment. A frown creased his face as he realized every man in the hall was seeing the same.

Arianna dared not look in Rob's direction. Instead, she made her way over to the Terrible Four, where she knew she would be welcome . . . and safe. Indeed, the hurrahs and cheers they shouted helped her to relax and their comforting presence finally gave her the courage to look at Rob. He was standing but a few feet away, drinking from a goblet, his eyes staring at her over the silver rim.

His gaze sent her heart careening out of control. She had his full attention and that made her feel like a queen. No, not just any queen, but Queen Guinevere herself, and he was her Sir Lancelot of the Lake, a knight so pure and good that it took her breath away.

Here was the only man she would ever love. The only man she would ever want. And she wanted him now, this very minute, even knowing that he had betrayed her.

Why did it have to happen? Why couldn't they have

spent the rest of their days together? It was so unfair. She had been denied his love once before. Why must she endure the same again? And both times because of Elizabeth. If it took her last breath to do so, she would revenge herself on the English queen.

Arianna waited to see what Robert would do, hoping beyond hope that he would come to her. Tell her he loved her still. Tell her it had all been a terrible mistake. That he had never bedded those women. But the only motion he made was to take another goblet from the table and bring it to his lips. Happy endings happened only in fairy tales, not in Everly, and certainly not on this remote, primitive island. She was a fool to think otherwise.

Pulling herself together, she joined in conversation with Terrence and Timothy, Thomas and Thaddeus, her wonderful Terrible Four. But as time passed, her eyes sought Robert's more and more often, unable to concentrate on anything but the moment when he would be sent to his dungeon cell and she would go to him.

Arianna was suddenly glad that she had given in to Bess and worn the provocative clothing, because she wanted him to desire her, ache for her. When he saw her dressed like this, she wanted him to know and remember exactly what he would be losing. It was a petty, mean, and spiteful thought, but at this moment, she didn't care. She wanted him to suffer the same way that she did every time she looked at him.

Time became Robert's worst enemy as he waited to be taken to his cell. Would she come to him? And if she did, what then? Would she come with love in her heart, or hate, because of everything she had observed last night? And if she did still want him, then what? There was still the bidding on the morrow.

Even if Arianna had the highest bid, Rob was far from sure Longfellow would keep his end of the bargain. He dared not even think of that. The man was a viper, his enemy twice over because of what had happened between them in Everly when his father was killed and now because of Bess. It had been a mistake to pretend to make love to her. For a jealous man was a dangerous man.

"Warwick."

Rob turned to face his enemy.

"You should be down on your knees thanking me for giving you the lovely Cassiopeia for an hour. An hour in paradise, wouldn't you say?"

"You've been thanked enough with all the gold you've made on me and will make on me tomorrow. It is you who should thank me for being so desirable to the opposite sex. For that is the reason you have become suddenly richer."

"You give yourself more credit than you deserve. It is not your desirability that entices these women, but the chance to sleep with a man of noble blood. Any nobleman would have done."

"Is that so? And having done so, why will they now bid a fortune on me? You wouldn't have thought of having females bid on me unless you thought I could bring you a profit."

"There is more than one way to profit, my dear boy. And gold is the most boring way."

Robert was taken aback by Longfellow's cryptic words. And once again he felt imminent danger for Arianna. "Hmmmm, I suppose that's true, but I like to feel the weight of gold in my hand. It lasts a lot longer than some petty little revenge."

"Revenge? Yes, that is one way to profit." A sneer crossed Longfellow's face as he spoke, shifting his gaze to somewhere beyond Rob's shoulder. "A very satisfying way to profit from one's enemies."

A shiver crept up Rob's spine. Slowly, he turned to see the object of Elijah's attention and his eyes lighted on Arianna. *Satan's blood! Does he know who she is? The bastard. I'll kill him with my bare hands if he dares lay a finger on her.*

Rob felt a hand on his shoulder, at the same time he heard Bess's voice. "Elijah, don't be so cruel. Send Robert to his cell so he can get this over with."

"My dear, you speak of Cassiopeia's visit as if it were an odious duty. On my honor, it will be a far cry from that. I daresay any man would give his sword arm for an hour alone with her."

"And does that include you, Elijah?"

Longfellow laughed. "Do I detect a tinge of jealousy? My, my, my, I think I shall hate it when Cassiopeia leaves; she keeps you on your toes."

Bess bristled at Elijah's blatant teasing. "Well, will you send Rob to his cell or not?"

"One would think you were the one going to him, as anxious as you are. I have to wonder why."

"Why? Because then this stupid game of yours will be ended."

Elijah understood that reason very well. It was what he had been feeling since it began. For the first time in his life, he was the victim of one of his own pranks. "If that's how you want it, that's how it shall be. Have Bart take him away."

Bess motioned for Bart, and in a moment the guard was escorting Robert out of the hall. Rob paused at the doorway and looked back in time to catch Arianna staring at him. His eyes swept over her, taking in her luscious beauty, drinking in her image as if it must last him a lifetime. Then feeling Bart tug on his sleeve, he walked out the door.

Arianna stood rooted to the spot. The gaze he sent her caused her belly to contract as if he were already making love to her. And he was, oh yes, he was. He had made love to other women, but he still wanted her. She didn't know whether to be flattered or angry. She only knew she would listen to what he had to say before deciding what to do about it.

But what could he say to make it right between them once more? That he was punishing her for being with Colin? She couldn't accept that answer. The more she thought of it, the more it seemed impossible that things could ever be right between them again.

In a few moments she would have his answer, and suddenly she was afraid to go.

Feeling a tap on her shoulder, Arianna looked up to see Bart. He was ready to take her to Rob. Smiling wanly, she took one last drink of wine to fortify her nerves, then followed him out of the hall, looking at no one but the man who would guide her to her husband.

The way down to the dungeon was narrow and dimly lit. The walls were cold and sticky to the touch. And the air, the terrible rancid air, reeked of mustiness, the odor growing stronger the farther down the winding stairs she went. When she stepped off the last stone step, Arianna sighed with relief and held on to the back of Bart's doublet, afraid of being separated from him in the dim light cast by the candle he carried.

Shuddering, she said, "It's so dark."

"Aye, dark as Hades, to be sure, but never fear, my mistress has ordered me to leave a lit candle for you to see by. You're luckier than the others, for they had to go about their . . . uh . . . visiting in the dark."

Arianna remembered Madge Miggs talking about making love in the pitch darkness. "The others? You mean Madge Miggs and Big Alice? They did come down here? They did go to the cell?"

"Why would you think otherwise?"

Yes. Why would she think otherwise? She had been grasping at straws.

Coming to a halt, Bart turned to face her. "Here we are. Take the candle whilst I unlock the cell."

Arianna took the candle in her nervous grasp, unable to keep her hand from shaking. The flickering light danced furiously, casting furtive shadows all around her in the narrow passageway.

She heard the iron door creak open, and her heart raced with anticipation and with dread. Raising the candle, she peered into the fathomless black.

Her eyes opened wide in astonishment. "John Neal!"

"My lady, you're a veritable sight for sore eyes."

"But . . . but I don't understand. Where is Rob?"

John rambled on, too excited at seeing her to stop. "You can't imagine how good it is to see your bright face and those beautiful blue eyes of yours. It makes my heart sing just to look at you."

"Dear John, I, too, am happy to see you and know you're alive. I do believe you look even better than last I saw you."

"Is that a fact?" He smiled broadly. "There's a reason for that, you can be sure."

"Aye," Bart said, "and a mighty good reason it is. I'd be feeling pretty good myself 'bout now if I had the pleasant companionship this here lucky knight has had."

Arianna's heart raced with happiness at those few simple words, for they cleared up everything immediately. "Oh, John, you're the one who's been entertaining Alice and Madge. It was you all along, and not Robert!"

John grinned sheepishly. "Aye, and a fine entertainment it's been. Bart's so used to bringing women here, he forgot and brought you to me, too. Rob is in the next cell over."

Bart looked puzzled for a minute, then remembered his mistress's instructions. "Oh, yeah, this is the one that goes to the other prisoner."

Arianna had to hang on to the door for support. She began to laugh, but it soon turned to sobs as tears welled from her eyes. The release of tension choked her with the emotions that rolled swiftly to the surface, and her sobbing escalated as she realized Rob had not betrayed their sacred oath after all. She should have known. She should have believed in their love no matter the evidence to the contrary.

Bart was taken aback by this strange pirate lady's emotional display. "Hey there, let's not have that. If you don't want to go into Warwick's cell, I'll not force you. I'll just—"

"Oh no, please. Take me to him now. I want to be with him. Truly I do."

Shaking his head, Bart said, "Well, then, follow me."

Arianna didn't have to be told twice. She wiped her eyes and, with a light step and a lighter heart, made her way down the dismal corridor to the next cell, rejoicing in the knowledge that her husband had not betrayed her.

She heard the grinding of metal on metal as the guard unlocked the door, then heard the heavy groan as the door swung open and she stepped in, eager to see her beloved husband, holding the candle above her head so she might see farther.

What she saw brought a gasp from her throat.

Rob was naked.

His arms were outstretched, his hands chained to the wall on either side of him, his body forming a living cross. Arianna stared at him in awe, too astonished at what she saw to speak. She had expected to see a captive dressed in white, but instead she found a naked man who, despite his chains, looked for all the world as if he were in charge of his destiny and master of her fate.

He stood boldly, legs spread apart, his manhood erect and ready, pointing directly at her.

She suddenly felt weak in the knees.

The door slammed shut behind her with an unearthly screech and she gasped again, her nerves jangled, her emotions stretched to the maximum.

Rob had stopped breathing as she stood before him, the very image of all that was female in her seductive clothing. He had hardened at the very sight of her and cursed the chains that kept him from taking her in his arms.

Taking one timid step toward him, Arianna hesitated to go any further. Why didn't he say something? That he wanted her was obvious by the condition of his manhood, but that only meant he desired her as any man might. It didn't mean that he still loved her or wanted her as his wife. But oh, she wanted to be his wife, wanted to be the one he loved most in the world.

If he could not come to her, she would go to him, even though she faced being rejected. She was about to move, when his voice caressed her ears with his fervent words. "Come to me, Arianna. Come to me before I die of wanting you."

A thrill of excitement coursed through Arianna's veins, but she needed to hear more. "You speak of want, but what about love?"

"The devil take it! If you can question my love, even now, then you are not worthy to receive it. Go back to Colin or Longfellow or your Terrible Four. I will not play word games with you and I will not ask you to come to me again."

Arianna swallowed hard. She hadn't expected that outburst from Rob. Why was he making this so hard for her, when all she wanted was to be in his arms forever! Realizing his pride would keep him from saying any more, she knew that if they were ever to be together again, she would have to give in.

Solemnly, she bent over, setting the candlestick on the earthen floor, and pulled off first one boot and then the other, glancing up to see how he would react.

His expression never changed.

She rolled down her trunk hose and hose, taking a long time to pull them off, aware that he was watching her every move.

At least she had his attention.

Moving up close to him, she started unbuttoning the velvet doublet, taking an inordinately long time to do so, her eyes never leaving his face.

A bead of sweat ran down Rob's cheek, though the air was damp and cool.

When she was done unbuttoning her doublet, she slowly worked it off her shoulders, letting it slide to the floor. Arianna stood before him completely naked now, a wicked gleam in her eye. "You were saying?"

Rob strained against the chains. "Damn you, woman. I'd rather have my fingernails pulled out than endure another moment of this torture. My need is great, but my love for you is even more powerful. Come to me now."

That was all she needed to hear. In an instant she was up against him, arms outstretched, her hands in his, mirroring his position. Together they formed a united cross, united in their desire and in their love for each other.

Rob felt every inch of her warm skin against his own cooler skin and a shiver went through him. The touch of her was an exquisite sensation that heightened his already-fierce desire.

"In the name of all that's holy, I love you." He lowered his head as she raised hers and they kissed, each drowning in the soft mouth of the other, rejoicing at their lover's touch so long denied.

They stayed that way a long time, content in the contact of their bodies and their mouths. Lovers, mates, friends; everything to each other that they would ever need or want. Each saying a prayer of thanks that the other still loved so passionately.

Then realizing their time together was so painfully short, Arianna took him in her hands, in need of completion, in need of feeling him inside her where he belonged.

Rob groaned at her touch, bending his knees so that her petite form could climb up his tall frame. She knew what he wanted and pulled herself up over him so that he could penetrate her. Eagerly, she guided him into the hot wetness that throbbed to have him inside. Her eyes were shiny with desire as she took the full length of him inch by delectable inch, savoring every moment of intense pleasure it gave her. A long, low moan escaped her lips as the wonder of him filled her with great need for more.

When he could penetrate no farther, she wrapped her legs around him and he stood his full height, imbued with great strength in his love for her. His arms strained to be free of the binding chains, needing to hold her, but even his superhuman strength was not enough to break through iron. To make up for his loss, he thrust mightily, plunging to the very depths of her. And it felt so good he thrust again, reveling in the exquisite sensation.

Arianna moaned with pleasure with each deep, rewarding thrust of his manhood, crying, "As God is my witness, I will love you through all eternity."

Rob laughed and thrust again, and Arianna closed her eyes and held tight to his neck, eager for the strenuous ride ahead.

Though he was chained, Rob was in full command, guiding them through the ancient dance of lovers, until he was too far gone to do anything but respond to his own need.

It was then they each became masters of the other's desires, giving, receiving, demanding, lost in a world where only they existed, the desire so strong between them that nothing short of death could stop their fiery mating.

Wave after wave of intense pleasure coursed through Arianna's body and she held on to Rob with all her strength, taking his powerful thrusts eagerly and giving back her own with the squeezing of her legs. "Oh, more, more, more," she cried, in such need she thought she'd die. Her frenzy brought Rob immediately to satisfaction and he could not contain his fierce pleasure, letting it out in a cry that sounded like the baying of a wolf.

Arianna felt his convulsions and she exploded in a sea of white-hot heat as his seed flooded her. Then, with the last of her strength, she slid down Rob's body, sobbing softly as her need for him was at last fulfilled. She gazed into his eyes, wanting to share the wonderful moment, and saw the love shining brightly there, the heat of his gaze warming the coldness of the cell with light as bright as any stars in the faraway galaxies.

Nothing had changed between them.

They were mated for life.

After a while, when Robert could finally think of something besides Arianna and his need for her, he spoke to her in a serious manner as she dressed once again, aware of the too-short time they had left.

"Promise me that no matter what the outcome of the bidding, you'll leave this place tomorrow."

"How can you ask that of me? You are my love, my life, the very air I breathe. I cannot leave you here."

"You can and will, for Robin's sake and for mine. Bess has the keys to my shackles and her men the keys to the cells. As soon as you are safely away, she'll free John and me."

"How can you trust her? She's a pirate after all."

"The same way you trust Colin. Is he not a pirate, too?"

Arianna could see this was getting her nowhere. "It's not the same, and you well know it. Colin is a trusted friend."

"To you, not me. He betrayed my friendship when he took my wife. How dare you mention his name to me?"

Arianna realized Rob's pain was still strong, still too close to the surface to be able to discuss Colin in a reasonable way. She had hoped he would have forgotten that terrible time by now. The fact that he hadn't proved just how much she had hurt him. "Enough. Please. I will try to do as you say. I'll leave on the morrow, if I can."

"That's not good enough, Arianna. You must leave tomorrow, do you understand? Elijah is up to something. Some horrible new game he wants to play, and this one involves you, of that much I'm sure. If you don't leave tomorrow, it may be too late."

"All right. I'll leave, if it comes down to that, but all this is really so unnecessary. Colin has brought enough gold along to assure that I will have the highest bid."

Arianna hated lying to Rob, but it was such a little sin compared to letting him worry needlessly over her. For she had no intentions of leaving this island without him. No matter what. She would do whatever it took to get him back, and not the devil himself would stand in her way.

Chapter Fourteen

Bess listened as the exotic slave drums spoke again, filling the air with their strange sound. They were telling the women from the small village on the lee side of the stronghold to come. Come to the auction. Come see the nobleman sold to a female. And they were indeed coming, bringing with them their female children. All eager to be spectators at this unusual sport.

Bess knew what they were thinking. She had lived with them on this small island for some time now. She knew they were thinking the auction of the nobleman would be a memorable event in their dull lives. One worth remembering and repeating to their grandchildren for years to come. She knew, as they did, that they could never hope to bid on Robert themselves. They had not the resources. But that didn't matter. It was enough to see any woman triumph over a man.

For, without a doubt, the lives of the village women were not what they had dreamed they would be. Talked into coming to this godforsaken place by their men, they lived a life of deprivation.

Not so the men. Their lives were much easier, oh,

yes, for it was truly a man's world. They sailed the wide blue ocean in search of treasure, discovering the pleasure of female flesh in every new exotic port they sailed to. The only treasure the women had grew inside their bellies: a new child each year. Another mouth to feed. Was it any wonder they eagerly awaited this spectacle?

Arianna watched too, as the women filed in, fearful at first as she tried to pick out the ones who might bid on Rob. But then the realization came to her that these pitiful women were here not to bid, but to watch. The only serious bidders were Bess, Big Alice, and Madge Miggs, and Bess was on her side. Or was she? It was possible she had intended to have Rob all along.

No. That wasn't true. Bess was a good woman deep in her heart, Arianna knew that. It was her own petty jealousy that made her think ill of Bess. There was a time when she would have been above that kind of behavior. What was happening to her? What was happening to her mind? She was afraid it was deteriorating more and more each day, and Arianna didn't know what she'd do if she couldn't free her husband.

But this was not the time to think of that. She had to keep up her strength a little while longer. That's all, just a little while longer, then it would all be over and Rob would be hers.

Garbed in the white doublet and hose once again, as a reminder to Rob of their wonderful lovemaking in his cell, she wondered now if it had been the right decision to dress so provocatively. She noticed that her outfit was attracting a lot of attention from the village women. Arianna saw them whispering about her behind their hands, looking her over with raised eyebrows and frowns upon their weathered faces.

Then Rob was brought in, dressed identically to Captain Cassiopeia, and a different attitude prevailed. The island women sensed a bond between the two, not only because of their like clothing, but also because of the possessive way the earl and the beautiful pirate looked at each other. Whispered words turned into exclamations of wonder as the knowledge swept over the hall that there was more to this strange auction than met the eye. Without a doubt, something exciting was about to happen.

Rob's eyes sought Arianna's, shining bright with love as he gazed at her beautiful form. This was his woman. This was his life. He would do everything in his power to keep her safe. Yanking hard on the chains at his wrists, he smiled wryly. Power? He had very little of that at this moment. His fate was in the hands of a godless pirate, a man who had good reason to hate him.

A twinge of jealousy marred Longfellow's otherwise perfect evening as he watched the glances exchanged between Cassiopeia and the earl. But, what matter? Soon he would have the perfect revenge, and that would set him on his stride once more. Ever since he had captured the bloody earl, nothing had gone as he wanted. But tonight it would. Of that he had no doubt. For he was the only one who knew what was about to happen.

Longfellow's gaze scanned the hall, taking in Bess dressed in a gown of pale pink. He had never seen her in clothes so subdued or feminine and was delighted. Was it an indication that her attitude was softening toward him? He watched as she approached Robert, smiling at him in a conspiratorial way, as if they shared some delectable secret, and his imagination went wild thinking of what that secret could be.

No. It was not for him that she changed her looks, but for the bloody nobleman. He cursed the gods of fate for having been born a lowly stable boy whilst the earl enjoyed so much. Clenching his jaw, he made his way over to Robert. "Warwick. Time to begin. If you'll take your place on the platform where the ladies can see what they are bidding on, I'll soon have you off my hands."

Longfellow indicated the raised platform that had been built especially for this occasion. It was time to finish what he had begun. Time to take that smug look off Warwick's face.

"Oh . . . and, Warwick, take off your doublet. Let the women get a good look at you."

Rob steeled himself, shedding his doublet before making the short journey up to the platform. He walked straight and alert, in need of showing Longfellow that he was not diminished in any way by this miserable situation. But inside he felt like a fool, an object of ridicule, and he hated the very idea of women bidding on him.

He had no idea how very appealing he looked, a virile, romantic figure dressed in his white trunk hose and silk shirt with long, full sleeves, the shirt opened down the front to reveal his masculine chest, the flowing sleeves moving around him invitingly. Immune to the sighs of longing emanating from the women he passed, he was intent on only one thought: to survive the ordeal.

Finding Arianna once again in the crowd, Rob saw Colin Colrain standing close beside her and he became all the more determined to survive. Without him in her life she would fall prey to Colrain, for it was of no reassurance at all to know the lusty privateer was now married. It was obvious to Rob—and to anyone else who had eyes—that Colin had married Cassiopeia because she looked so much like Arianna.

His jaw tightened as he saw Colin whisper into her ear, then nod his head slowly when Arianna answered him. Damn Colrain. That small intimate gesture and the protective way he was treating her left no doubt in Rob's mind that Colin still loved Arianna. He couldn't help wondering if Arianna knew that, too.

Then, unexpectedly, Colin left her side and made his way to the door that led to the dungeon. That was odd. Why wasn't he staying by her side? Arianna would need his support if this ungodly auction didn't go as she so foolishly hoped. Surely he knew that. It suddenly occurred to him that Bess had most likely enlisted Colin's help in her plans for freeing him and John Neal, and Rob groaned inwardly at that thought. As much as he wanted to be free, Colin Colrain was the last man in the world he wanted to be obligated to.

Arianna was unaware of the conflict inside her husband. She gazed up at him with pride shining bright in her eyes. He handled himself like a prince, unbowed and handsome beyond belief. But pride soon turned to sorrow as Longfellow shackled Rob to a board nailed to the platform for that very purpose. Why did he have to humiliate him like that? There was no need.

Longfellow began talking and the hall became hushed. "Ladies, it gives me great pleasure to be able to offer you such a fine specimen for auction. Robert Warwick, Earl of Everly. Turn around, my lord, so that the ladies may get a better look at you."

Robert answered with a dark glare aimed at Longfellow.

Elijah grinned, knowing full well how humiliating this must be. "And open your mouth. Let's see if you have all your teeth."

"We ain't interested in his teeth. Show us the size of his cock; that's what we want ta see." The woman who shouted turned to face the other women, laughing at her own joke.

"Ladies, please, let's try to keep this on a higher level. After all, the man is an earl. He deserves a little respect."

"And that's just what he's getting, a little respect." The woman laughed at her own joke again.

Arianna wanted to scratch her eyes out. How dare she talk about Rob that way. "Captain Longfellow, are we to be subjected to this meaningless drivel, or are we going to get down to some serious bidding?"

"Ah," Longfellow said, pointing at Cassiopeia. "A woman after my own heart. Yes, indeed, we'll start the auction now. Would you care to be the first to bid?"

Arianna wasn't prepared for that. She had no idea what she should bid. "I . . . uh . . . offer fifty gold pieces to add to the fifty I paid last night."

"Is that all he was worth as a lover? Do you hear that, Warwick? You ought to be ashamed of yourself. Didn't you give the lady a good time?"

The earl glowered at Longfellow but maintained his silence, finding it more and more difficult to contain himself.

"We have fifty gold pieces. Do I have another bid?"

"Let's stop fooling around here. I'll make it one hundred." Alice folded her hands over her ample chest, sure she had won herself an earl.

"One hundred and fifty, I says," Madge Miggs proclaimed proudly. "He did give me a good time."

"The hell you say," Alice countered. "I had a better time. He likes me the best. I'll bid another twenty-five."

"And I'll bid another fifty. So there."

"Ladies, please, a little decorum. We haven't heard from you, Bess. Will you part with your gold to win this man?"

Bess lifted a large leather sack high in the air. "What do you think?"

Elijah gritted his teeth. "Then make your bid."

"One thousand pieces of gold."

Madge began to cough, whilst Alice's eyes bugged out.

Without so much as batting an eyelash, Longfellow shouted out, "Do I hear two?"

Silence reigned.

Longfellow began to sweat. "How about fifteen hundred?"

Cassiopeia's lovely voice rang out. "Yes."

Relieved, Elijah shouted, "And now two thousand."

No one spoke a word.

"Now, really, ladies, surely someone will bid higher. This man is a valuable piece of property. Think how much he can do for you. Give me two, Alice."

Alice waved him away. "He ain't worth that much in bed. No man is worth that."

Madge slapped Alice on the back. "You tell him! That's my sentiments exactly."

"I'll ask one more time. Will someone bid higher?" When no one answered, Longfellow grinned and said, "Then he is yours Captain Cassiopeia . . . or should I say Countess Arianna Warwick of Everly?"

Arianna was too shocked to even gasp, but as one, the women of Devil's Harp gasped for her. Not one of them ever dreamed something as exciting as this could possibly happen. They waited eagerly for the response.

Arianna didn't know how he had found out who she was, but it didn't matter. The important thing was she had just won back her husband. There was no use in pretending to be Cassiopeia anymore. Gathering her courage, she curtsied prettily at Longfellow and blew him a kiss.

Elijah couldn't help but admire Arianna's bold response. She was truly a woman of substance. He almost regretted what he was about to do to her.

Opening his mouth to speak, he noted with pleasure that the hall immediately became silent. No one wanted to miss a single word he said. "Of course . . . there is one minor stipulation that I failed to mention."

Arianna's heart sank. She should have known it wouldn't be this easy.

"After all, fair is fair. You had your hour of pleasure with your husband last night. Now . . . in return . . . you must spend an hour with me before I will turn him over to your waiting arms."

Robert strained at his chains, hatred burning in his eyes. He had deliberately set up Arianna to be hurt.

"Do we have an agreement? Will you spend an hour with me in my bedchamber?"

Every set of eyes in the audience turned now to gaze at the beautiful woman in white.

Arianna could barely speak, so much in shock was she. "I . . . I don't . . . know. . . ."

"Think it over quickly, my dear. Wait too long and you forfeit your claim on the earl."

Arianna looked to Rob for help. "I . . . I . . ."

Rob could take no more. "No," he shouted. "Don't even consider it. Don't—"

"Please, Warwick, let the lady speak for herself."

"Go to hell, Longfellow. She's not going to dirty herself with slime like you. Go ahead and forfeit, Arianna. Show this greedy satyr you will not play his games."

"What is your answer, my dear? Quickly."

Arianna was numb with horror. She knew there was only one answer she could give. In a hurt little voice, she whispered, "Yes."

"What was that? I didn't hear you. Speak up."

"Yes! I said . . . yes."

A loud clamor went up as the women in the audience all spoke at once, excited over this turn of events. But their voices weren't loud enough to drown out the agonized shout of "Nooooo!" that Robert bellowed as he pulled furiously on his chains, trying to get to Longfellow.

Arianna heard Rob's yell and ached for him, ached for herself. But she couldn't give up now. Not when she was so close. She would endure an hour with the devil himself to free her husband. "Please understand, Robert, I beg of you."

Rob knew there was only one way he could save his wife now. In a low voice, he spoke to the pirate. "It's obvious you want to humiliate me, but must you do it at my wife's expense? She's done you no harm."

"True. But, alas, I cannot think of a way that would hurt you as much as that."

"I can."

Longfellow gave Rob a curious look, almost afraid of what he was going to say, almost regretting that he would say anything. "How?"

"By bending me over, here and now, in front of all these women, and sodomizing me."

Longfellow felt a stab of pain. Warwick had no way of knowing that as a child Elijah had been subjected to just such a humiliation at the hands of one of the old earl's knights.

For a moment, he forgot his need for revenge, remembering how it felt to be the one humiliated so. But Longfellow had gone too far. He couldn't turn back now. He would lose his hold on these people if he weakened now. In a compassionate voice, he answered, "Robert, you must love your wife a great deal to make such a sacrifice. I admire you for that. But . . . unfortunately, not enough to change my plans."

Robert curled his lips in hatred, his voice low and lethal. "I'll kill you if you go ahead with this insanity. I'll kill you if it's the last thing I do. But before I do, I'll hack off your cock and shove it down your throat."

Elijah laughed triumphantly. At last, he had the response he wanted, the high emotion that was proof of Warwick's anguish. "Go to my chamber, Arianna. I'll join you there in a moment."

Arianna couldn't move. How could she go through

with this, even for Rob? She didn't know how she could do it. But . . . if she didn't . . . if she didn't . . . she would lose her husband.

She could only pray that alone with Elijah she could talk to him, appeal to his humanity. Then everything would be all right. Yes, she would talk him out of it. Somewhere deep inside, Elijah had a heart. She had only to find a way to reach it before . . . Unable to finish that horrendous thought, she began the hardest journey she had ever made. Her body was stiff and wooden, her heart in a shambles, but somehow she made it through the wall of spectators to the stairs.

"Arianna! Nooooooo!"

Rob's voice carried to her as she started up the steps, hovering over her, surrounding her with its desperate plea. "If you love me, you will not do this. If you want our love to survive, don't go any further. It needn't be this way. Believe in me."

Arianna opened the door to Longfellow's chamber and walked in, closing it and Robert's voice behind her.

Below, Elijah gazed around him, eager to see the reaction on everyone's faces but realizing the one face he wanted to see the most was missing. Where was Black Bess? He wanted her to see Robert's humiliation. To see that he, Captain Elijah Longfellow, was the victor. It was important that she be witness to that.

But not quite as important as Robert Warwick's complete humiliation.

For that, Warwick would be witness to his wife's violation. But one step at a time. First he would have to send these stupid women home. Proclaiming the auction over, he had his slaves usher them out of the hall, over their loud protests.

When the hall was at last empty, except for Elijah's chosen few, he proclaimed, "Remove Warwick's chains. They make too much noise for what I have in mind now. Bind him with rope, gag him, and take him up to Bess's bedchamber . . . and be quiet about it. I don't want Arianna to get an inkling of what's going on."

Bart had a bad taste in his mouth about following Longfellow's orders, but Bess had directed him to obey Elijah to the letter. She had told him she had a plan of her own and had taken the keys to John Neal's cell from him, reassuring Bart that all would be well and that they would soon be going to sea again. He hoped it was true and that she had at last had enough of Longfellow's cruelty.

When Warwick was tied with rope and gagged with a clean rag, Bart sent for the Terrible Four, the largest men he knew, and had them carry Robert upstairs to Bess's chamber. They obeyed too easily, making Bart wonder if they, too, were a part of Bess's plan to free Robert and John Neal. It didn't matter to him one way or the other, for Robert Warwick was in Bess's hands, and he trusted her to have every option covered.

Longfellow watched as the four men carried Warwick upstairs, and with a wide grin, he gestured to the two shapeliest and attractive black slaves to accompany him up to his chamber.

His pleasure was about to begin.

Chapter Fifteen

When Longfellow didn't immediately follow her up-stairs, Arianna felt a spark of hope that someone had intervened on her behalf or that he had possibly changed his mind. But that hope was short-lived, for the door was suddenly thrown open and Elijah strode in.

And he wasn't alone.

Behind him, two naked slave women padded silently into the room, their eyes large with fright. She knew then there would be no reprieve for her. She would have to endure whatever he demanded, so that Robert could be freed. Trying to contain her own fright, she lashed out at him, saying, "Must you have witnesses to my degradation?"

Elijah was taken aback for a moment. How could she know her husband was on the other side of the door? Then, realizing she meant only the slaves, he smiled and answered, "Indeed, there is someone from whom I would derive great satisfaction from witnessing what shall take place here, but no one in this bedchamber. These women are not here to bear witness. They are here to participate. Does that make you feel any better?"

Arianna's mouth flew open in shock. "You can't be serious!"

"My dear, I've never been more serious. Since this is my time, bought and paid for by your husband's freedom, I shall conduct myself in any way I wish. But don't look so shocked. You may find it very enjoyable. In fact, I'm counting on it. For if I think you're not enjoying yourself, why then, I believe I would want to keep you here until I am sure that you do."

Arianna couldn't believe the man's arrogance. Not only must she submit to the bastard, but she was expected to enjoy it, too. "Captain Longfellow, you repulse me so much, I couldn't even pretend to enjoy your touch. I fear, instead, that I should faint from the horror."

"Ah, you'll faint all right, from ecstasy at the very sight of the instrument that will pleasure you. After me, no other man will ever satisfy you again, and that includes your husband."

Elijah's reference to his manhood was making Arianna very uneasy. Trying to take his mind off it, she asked him a question that had been bothering her since the bidding began. "How did you find out that Rob was my husband? No one from *The Constellation* would ever betray me."

"There was no need. Your husband himself gave it away."

"What do you mean?"

"After I brought Warwick here to Devil's Harp, he took to drinking to while away the empty hours of captivity. It amused me to see him deteriorating and so

I encouraged it, letting him leave his cell each day so that I might watch his descent to hell. One day, when he got exceedingly drunk, he started ranting and raving about his wife Arianna and the white velvet gown she had worn when he met her. Having no interest in women's garb, I paid no attention, but Big Alice hung on his every word."

Arianna blanched, knowing where he was leading.

"That's right. You wore that very gown the other day, and it nagged at Alice until she remembered Rob's vivid description. Naturally, when it came to her last night, she informed me. You can't imagine how happy that made me, hearing that. For I knew then I'd have my revenge."

"Revenge? What has Rob ever done to you that you should hate him so?"

Laughing, Elijah said, "Where shall I begin? How about his making love to my woman, right under my very roof? Is that enough for you, my lady?"

Arianna laughed, relieved that she might have her reprieve after all. "Even I knew that Rob and Bess only pretended to make love. It was to make you jealous and to drive me away. I saw through it right away, because I knew how much my husband loves me. And Bess loves you the same way. If you weren't such a fool, you'd have seen through their act as I did."

"You're the fool if you believe that. Didn't you hear him speak of the leather device that—"

"I heard, and I almost believed him then, until I realized that it was all a part of the act. That Bess had told him what to say so you would be convinced."

What Arianna said rang true. He should have been

relieved, but instead felt a bad taste in his mouth at being deceived. No one played him for a fool and got away with it.

"Too bad, then. Warwick will have to suffer the consequences without benefit of tasting the fruit."

"You can't mean that you're going to go ahead with this, even knowing the truth?"

Longfellow's voice became almost a whisper as he said, "The truth is, Arianna, I have wanted you since the moment I first saw you. You'd want me, too, if you gave yourself half a chance. Stay with me willingly and I'll send the women away. We can spend the night in sweet bliss."

"Captain Longfellow, you've been playing games so long, you can't tell fact from fantasy anymore. I despise you and will submit to you for one reason only: to free my husband."

Elijah's face hardened to stone, his voice to steel. "Very well, if that's the way you want it." Without further ado, he began to strip his clothes off, his eyes fastened on hers.

Arianna felt close to panic. Dear God, he was really going through with it. Forcing herself to stay calm, she stared back, her head held high to show that he could not daunt her. But, oh, it wasn't easy. She would much prefer calling him the monster that he was. How could so handsome a man have such an evil heart! She almost felt sorry for him, for it suddenly came to her that he had to be the most miserably unhappy man to act this way.

But her sympathy soon vanished as Longfellow lifted a chair, carrying it over in front of the door that led to Bess's room and sitting down, his legs spread wide apart so she could not help but see his manhood.

He motioned to the two slaves and they walked over to him, each straddling a leg with their naked bodies. Arianna had no idea what was going on, but she grew uneasier with each passing moment. He snapped his finger and immediately the women began to rub their naked bottoms across his leg, then back again, over and over again.

Arianna's face turned a brilliant red. How could he subject them to that? How could he subject her to this? Did he have no decency at all?

In a moment, the erotic rubbing caused Longfellow's manhood to move as if it had a life of its own. Arianna watched in horror at the tremendous size it attained. Oh . . . my . . . God! Was he going to put that inside her?

Longfellow grinned lustily. "You see now why I am named Longfellow. It was no coincidence. I earned my name."

The slave women stopped moving, and Longfellow snapped his fingers again. Immediately, they started rubbing his legs once more.

It was hard to keep looking at him. Arianna wanted nothing more than to close her eyes, but that would give him too much satisfaction. She would endure. But oh, it was a wicked thing to see. Him sitting there with legs so far apart it made his swollen member all the more obvious. The naked women rubbing their private parts back and forth over his legs. Dear God, what would he do next?

On the other side of the door, Rob could only guess what was happening. Although he was forced to stand there, listening to what went on in Longfellow's room, he could not tell from the conversation exactly what was happening. He knew, though, that Arianna was being subjected to humiliation of some sort and his rage grew stronger, knowing how helpless he was to help her. Bart and one of Longfellow's men held tight to his arms, making sure he didn't move. Longfellow wanted him to hear everything that went on.

Where was Bess? She had left to rescue John before the bidding ended, whilst everyone was preoccupied with the auction. Had something gone wrong? If she didn't get here very soon, it would be too late for Arianna.

Longfellow spoke again and Rob listened in dread, knowing in advance what would happen next.

"Take off your clothes."

Arianna's blood turned to ice upon hearing those words. Biting her lip to keep from crying, she started to undress. A sudden noise from Bess's room stilled her, and for a moment she dared to hope someone would come to save her. But the door remained closed and the room became silent as death. Had she just imagined it, wanting so desperately to be saved?

She continued to undress, her skin crawling as Longfellow watched, his eyes sliding over her body, lingering at her breasts, lusting to see more. And then she was naked. Exposed to his greedy gaze, cringing inside as his eyes devoured her.

The slave women began rubbing faster on Longfellow's legs, and by the glazed look in his eyes, she knew he was ready for her. Her stomach churned.

"Kneel down in front of me, Arianna."

Arianna did as she was told, fear and hatred fighting for prominence inside her.

"Is it not beautiful to behold?"

Arianna said nothing.

"Take it in your hands."

Arianna hesitated for only a moment, realizing that the faster she did it, the faster it would be over with. Reaching between his legs, she grasped the grotesquely huge rod. It jerked spasmodically at her touch, and she quickly let go.

"Take it."

Arianna grasped it again, curling her fingers around the stiff, hot thickness that was so different than her beloved's. She had always thought Rob's manhood a beautiful thing to behold, but not so Longfellow's. His seemed an obscene object and she hated the very touch of it.

In the other room, Rob's rage grew beyond control, knowing what Longfellow would be demanding next. But his arms were bound tight to his sides and he was unable to move. He wanted desperately to warn Arianna that he was there, because if she knew he was listening, she would not be able to go through with it. But how could he let her know when he was bound and gagged?

In desperation, he thrust his head forward, hoping to hit the door with it. But the men holding him anticipated his move and pushed him back far enough so he couldn't reach it.

He heard a sound behind him and twisted his head to look. Bess, gorgeous, beautiful, lifesaving Bess, was walking into the room. His heart beat harder, urging her onward with his eyes.

Bess walked over to him, followed by his knight, John Neal, and Rob knew his liberation was at hand.

But would he be in time to save Arianna? Bess and John had no knowledge of what was going on in the next room, and he had no way of telling them.

Bart pulled out a dagger and held it to the throat of the other man who had been guarding Rob, while Bess and John worked frantically at the knots for what seemed an inordinate amount of time. Rob used his eyes to try and tell them of Arianna's danger, but Bess put a finger to her lips and hushed him, afraid it would attract Longfellow's attention and thwart their escape plans.

In the name of everything holy, he prayed they would take the gag out of his mouth so he could talk. Every second that passed was a second lost in saving Arianna from Longfellow, and dear God, she didn't have many left.

Sweat beaded up on his furrowed brow as he counted the time with the beating of his heart.

Longfellow was primed and ready for the next step.

"And now, my dear, take my cock in your mouth."

Arianna looked up at his face, pure hatred emanating from her eyes.

"Now!"

Arianna closed her eyes so she would not have to look at the obscenity before her, but she saw it yet in her mind. She feared she would see it in her dreams from this day forward.

Willing her mind to escape if her body could not, she visualized a green pasture dotted with wildflowers of every hue and slowly opened her mouth. Gentle rain fell on the petals of the flowers.

Rob heard Longfellow's dirty command to his wife and, in a fury, broke through the rest of the ropes and threw open the door. Longfellow was sitting in a chair, his back to the door, a naked female on each knee.

At first Rob couldn't see his wife, but as he grasped the pirate in a neckhold, trying to choke the life out of him, he looked down and saw his naked, vulnerable wife, kneeling in front of Longfellow, her glistening mouth opened to a round, surprised "Oh."

"You bastard! I'll kill you for th—"

Rob felt the blinding blow to the back of his head, then knew no more.

Chapter Sixteen

Black turned to a dull grey fog as Rob started to come to his senses. For one contented moment he was a child again, safe in his mother's arms, rocked in a gentle sleep.

As awareness grew, he realized the rocking was the sway of a ship. He tried to remember why he was aboard, but his mind was full of mist, the throbbing in the back of his head growing stronger and stronger, blocking out rational thought. Rob groaned and opened his eyes.

A crack of thunder rent the air, and in an instant he remembered the blow to the back of his head. Expecting to see Longfellow grinning down at him malevolently, he turned his head to scan the room and found his good knight, John Neal, standing there instead.

John spoke, forcing a jovial cadence to his speech. "So, you're finally awake. I feared you'd sleep like a babe all the way back to Everly."

"John, what in God's name happened?" Rob tried to sit, but the pain drove his head back down. "Who cracked my skull open? It couldn't have been Longfellow, for his head was in my grip when it happened."

" 'Twas . . . 'twas I, my lord."

Rob sat up again, this time managing the painful move. "You, John? Have you lost your senses, man?"

John cringed as if expecting a blow. "I had no choice, my lord. You were about to bring the whole of Longfellow's men down on us with your noisy attack on him. It would have ruined our plans to escape."

"Would you have me stand by whilst that miserable pirate violated my wife? Dear God! Arianna! Where is she?" Rob jumped off the bed, almost fainting from the pain. John reached for the earl, supporting him until he could stand on his own.

"My lord, never fear. She is safe."

"Where?"

"She is aboard ship. Outside on the deck."

Rob heard the pounding rain upon the cabin's roof and looked at John as if he were crazy. The door flew open then, driving in the rain as Colin entered, drenched from head to foot.

"She won't come in."

"Damn your hide, Colrain, what's going on?

"Robert. Glad to see you're among the living. For a while there, I thought your knight had done too good a job in silencing you."

Rob glared at Colin. "We have a score to settle, Colrain. Don't think we haven't, but right now my only concern is Arianna. What in God's name is she doing out in that storm?"

"It would seem she is cleansing her soul."

"What?"

"Is it so hard to understand, Robert? She bared herself to Longfellow and came near to being defiled by him. He humiliated her, made her feel unclean, unworthy of your love. Is it any wonder she wants to wash away the scent of that man? Go to her. You're the only one who can bring her out of it."

The vision of Arianna kneeling in subjugation before Elijah Longfellow brought an ache to Rob's heart that competed with the pain in the back of his head. He quickly willed it away before it grew too strong to bear.

Setting his jaw, he opened the door and walked into the blowing rain.

Colin called after him, "The cabin is yours and Arianna's. We're going down below so you can have privacy."

Rob's jaw tightened all the more. Closing the door behind him, his eyes searched the deck, lighting on the small, delicate form of Arianna standing at the rail. Her clothes were plastered against her body, her hair against her head, but she seemed unaware. He felt the urge to protect her as he always had before but he fought it, knowing things were different now. Arianna stared out to sea, unaware of his presence until he spoke her name. "Arianna."

Her head jerked around, her eyes wide with surprise. "Rob! Oh, thank God, you're all right." Moving close to him, she touched his cheek with her icy hand. "I was so wor—"

Rob grasped her hand with a firmness that surprised even him and removed it from his face. "Come inside before you catch your death."

Arianna swallowed, a hard lump forming in her throat. She tilted her chin up in defiance. "Not until you say that you'll forgive me."

Rob stood wooden, his voice colder than the wind-blown rain that pelted her face unmercifully. "What shall I forgive you for, Arianna? Tell me. Which sin do you need my forgiveness for? The sin of lying to me? The sin of deceit when you connived to have me sent away? Or do you need forgiveness for the sin of disobeying your husband? That is one sin you are all too familiar with, is it not?"

"Oh, Rob, you don't have to tell me how wrong I've been."

Ignoring her confession, he continued, "Or is it the sin of adultery that eats at your soul?"

"I never lay with him."

"But you would have! You would have if I had not burst in on you."

"Rob, please, I beg of you—"

"How can I ever trust you again? How can I ever forget the sight of you ready to perform an abomination on that satyr. All the water in the ocean cannot wash away that sin."

"I did it to protect you. And I would do it again. I'd lie with the very devil himself to free you."

Rob raised his hand to strike her, then caught himself in time. He took her by the elbow and steered her toward the cabin, his anger so great he couldn't speak.

Arianna didn't protest. What was the use? She was beyond redemption now. Her only hope was that when his rage was gone, he would realize he still loved her.

When they entered the cabin, Rob was surprised to see the two slave girls who had been in Longfellow's chamber. They were dressed in garments belonging to Arianna. "Help my wife change into dry clothing and stay with her through the night. I'll be sleeping below with the other men."

Arianna looked stricken. "Rob, please, stay with me. Hold me in your arms. I need you."

"You don't need me. The only thing you seem to need is the revenge that consumes you. Very well, then. Sleep with that. Be comforted by that, for by God, you've driven everything else in your life away."

Rob left, slamming the door behind him, the lonely silence that followed too terrible to bear. Arianna turned to the young slave women, her arms outstretched in a helpless gesture, shaking her head in bewilderment. "What am I to do now?"

Exchanging sympathetic glances, the women comforted Arianna, smoothing back her sodden hair.

Defeated and shivering from the heavy wet clothing she wore, she let the women prepare her for bed. Arianna responded to their tender care, in need of sympathy after Rob's cold rejection and her callous treatment at the hands of Longfellow. Unsure if they understood her language, she pleaded, "I cannot pretend it didn't happen, but . . . I pray you will not speak of my ordeal to anyone. I would die of humiliation."

The younger of the two women looked into Arianna's eyes in a questioning way, then opened her mouth wide, pointing inside. The other woman did the same. Arianna thought that was a very strange thing to do, but curious, she drew closer, gasping in horror at what she saw. "Your tongues have been cut out."

That discovery was the last horror she could stand, triggering the hysteria that had been waiting to burst forth. She started sobbing loudly, unable to contain the emotions that swept through her. "My God, I've

. . . been worrying . . . about my reputation . . . when all along . . . you've suffered so very much. I'm . . . so . . . sorry, so . . . sorry."

Arianna's heartbreaking sobs soon had the two women in tears. No one had ever cared enough about them to cry for the mutilation they had suffered. Encircling Arianna in an embrace, they gave and received comfort as they let all their pent-up emotions carry them away.

Once started, it was impossible for them to stop, and their voices escalated until they carried through the wooden door to the ears of the men standing just outside. Fearing something terrible had happened to the women, Rob, Colin, and John burst into the small room, stopping dead at the strange but appealing sight that met their eyes. Three young women, one fair as the morning mist, the other two a rich, warm brown, their contrasting beauty enhancing each other most wonderfully, stood crying in each other's arms.

Rob knew not what had set them off. He only knew that the sight of Arianna crying so heartbreakingly set his heart to aching all the more. She was so young, so beautiful, so vibrant. How could he even envision a life without her?

Arianna raised her head and saw Rob, the man she loved more than life itself, and her sobs stopped, hiccups taking their place.

Rob almost smiled then. Arianna looked so adorable, her chest heaving with each powerful hiccup, sending the soft fabric of her shift moving around her. He felt compelled to pull her into his arms but fought the urge. He would have to guard his feelings. The last thing he wanted was for her to think he had forgiven her. For he hadn't.

He couldn't help it, though, if the mere glimpse of her sent up a crescendo of emotions too powerful to contain. "Since there doesn't seem to be cause for alarm, men, I think we should leave the women to their female tantrums."

A chorus of ayes echoed his sentiments and all three men left, closing the door very softly.

Arianna hugged herself with joy, twirling around and around in the small cabin. "Did you see the way he looked at me? He still loves me, I know he does. I'll win him back. Just you watch. I'll win him back."

Then turning suddenly solemn, she crossed her hands over her heart, palms flat against her chest, and in a fervent whisper vowed, "Let there be an end to my suffering. I've shed enough tears to last a lifetime, suffered enough for a score of lifetimes, but no more. No more. The blood of powerful kings and extraordinary queens flows through my veins, and I will not forget that again. Watch out, Robert Warwick. I've just begun to fight for you."

Chapter Seventeen

In complete awe of Arianna and her fervent speech, the dark-skinned women clapped their hands together with great enthusiasm, caught up in the moment. It was obvious their new mistress had reached an important turning point in her life and they wanted her to know their hearts were with her.

The applause brought a smile to Arianna's face and she brushed away the tears. These women had seen her at the lowest point in her life, had shared her humiliation and her sorrow at the hands of Elijah Longfellow, and it was obvious they fathomed everything she had said. Suddenly, it was very important that she understand them as well. "Can you read or write?" she asked hopefully.

The women shook their heads no.

"Then how can I talk with you?"

One of the women gestured with her hands.

It only took a moment for Arianna to understand what she meant. "You talk with your fingers? How ingenious! Then you shall teach me. That is, if you want to be my attendants and come to Everly with me."

Both women nodded yes, their faces beaming.

"Then that's settled. And since I don't know your names, I shall call you Ruth and Naomi. They are proud names of honorable women who also traveled far from their homes. You shall be Ruth," she said, pointing to the shorter girl, "and you, Naomi," to the taller one.

Having something to occupy her mind beside the hurt of Robert's rejection, Arianna immediately set about learning the strange finger-talking used by Ruth and Naomi. By the time she went to bed, she was able to communicate with them, albeit in a much slower, clumsier fashion.

That didn't matter. She was pleased at her accomplishment, even when she used the wrong motion of her fingers, because it delighted Ruth and Naomi so. It was good to hear their happy giggles, good to know that though their tongues were cut out, still their voices could be heard in laughter.

Sometime in the middle of the night, Arianna awoke feeling the warmth of a body against her back and for one happy moment thought Rob had returned. But then she remembered she shared her small bed with Ruth and Naomi, one curling up beside her, whilst the other slept at the foot.

Oh, Rob, it's so easy to be strong in the light of day, but in the dark of the night, my courage vanishes and all I can do is ache for you.

Unable to sleep, Arianna crawled out of bed without disturbing the other women, wrapped herself in a cloak, and walked out onto the deck. The rain had stopped long ago and the wind had gentled to a caressing breeze that sighed in her ear. She yawned and looked around for some place to sit, but there was nothing close by save a giant coil of rope with strands as thick as her wrist.

Rather than venturing too far from her cabin, she curled up on the coil, the pungent smell of hemp filling her nostrils. She felt much better out in the open and was grateful that her seasickness had abated considerably. She had another thing to be grateful for, too, a pregnancy free of the sickness that had been a part of the early months when she carried Robin.

Staring up at the melancholy moon, Arianna felt more relaxed than she had since they had left Devil's Harp, and in a few moments her eyelids began to droop. Out here, under the stars, everything seemed possible. Possible . . . hopeful . . . Sleep pulled at her one more time, and she gave in to it.

Lying on a pallet of straw, Rob tossed and turned, hating himself for walking away from Arianna when he wanted her so much, then in the next moment, grateful that he had had the strength. His inner struggle finally wore him out and he drifted into a dream-filled, troubled sleep.

A tap at his shoulder woke him with a start.

"Me lord, 'tis me, Terrence."

Rob groaned and rubbed his eyes. "What is it, Terrence? It better be important waking me in the middle of the night."

"She's at it again."

"What? Who? . . ."

"Your wife, me lord. She's up on the deck again."

Rob sank back on the pallet. "Well, leave her there. She'll get tired soon enough and go back to her cabin."

"Not likely, me lord."

"And why is that?"

"She's sleeping like a babe in a cradle of rope."

Rob groaned again and pulled himself up. "Very well. Go back to your post. I'll call you if I need you."

And he had a feeling he would have need of Terrence's help. Arianna seemed bound and determined to make life miserable for him. Emerging on the deck, he looked around. Where in blazes was she?

Spying the coil of rope and the small form curled up there, he made his way over to her, determined to be firm. Kneeling to tap her on the shoulder and wake her, he stayed his hand when he gazed down at her lovely face. She was fast asleep, her head resting on graceful hands, a faint smile upon her face. He could do nothing but drink in the beautiful sight, everything forgotten but the pleasure of the moment.

She looked almost like a child, innocent in her sleep, and he felt a pang of regret that she had borne him no daughter. But he quickly came to his senses, realizing how lucky he was. For if he had a daughter, she would most likely be just like her mother, headstrong, stubborn, strong-willed, and he would have twice the trouble he had now.

Still, he couldn't help regretting that she hadn't become pregnant again in the past year. It certainly wasn't from lack of trying, considering the intensity of their lovemaking. He had wanted to have more children, not only for the joy of hearing their laughter ring out through his castle, but also as a way of taming his wife.

But what use in thinking of what might have been? What use in thinking of what will be? It was too soon. His hurt was too great for him to think of his future, of the future of his family. Right now he had to deal with his sleeping wife.

"Arianna . . ."

Arianna opened her eyes and stared up at her husband framed in the light of the moon. "Rob? Is that you?"

"Aye."

Rubbing her eyes, Arianna stretched languidly. "What . . . what do you want?"

Rob's jaw tightened. "Terrence told me you were here. I came to take you back to the cabin."

"Will you stay with me there?"

Her voice blended with the breeze, caressing his body with desire. Damn her! "You know I cannot."

"But I can't sleep without you."

Or I without you, he thought. "You'll learn."

The hurt penetrated Arianna's heart and she struck back in pain. "If that's all you have to say, then go. Leave me."

"You know I won't go till you are safe in your cabin."

Jutting her chin out, Arianna remembered she was the daughter of a queen. "In that case, you'll have to carry me there. I suddenly find I'm too tired to walk."

"If that's the way you want it . . ." Without another word, Rob reached down and scooped her into his arms, regretting it as soon as he touched her. Her arms went around his neck, clinging tightly to him as he carried her across the deck. Oh, God, but she felt so good.

Her breast rubbed against his chest with each step he took, causing him to harden unbearably in jolt after jolt of desire. It was the longest walk of his life. He wondered if he would have the strength to tear her out of his arms as his mind dictated. Or would he do as his heart and body desired and take her?

Arianna laid her head on his shoulder, as if things had already been settled, and Rob's anger won out over desire. Did she think he would forgive her so easily? That all she had to do was lie in his arms and everything would be all right?

He flung open the cabin door and lowered Arianna to a standing position as she still clung to his neck, his manhood throbbing, in need of penetration. By all the saints in heaven, her body had been designed for his.

It didn't matter that she was a full foot shorter than he; that made him feel all the more powerful and protective of her. It didn't matter that he had to bend to kiss her. It only mattered that when he lifted her into his arms, she melted into him; when he took her in passion, she accommodated him so wondrously.

Making love was the one part of their life together that had always been perfect. *'Til now. 'Til Elijah Longfellow.* Turning on his heels, Rob left the cabin, locking the door behind him as if trying to lock her out of his heart.

"Terrence!"

Terrence was there in a moment. "Yes, me lord."

"I want you and your brothers to take turns guarding this cabin. Under no circumstances are you to let anyone in or out, and that includes myself. Do you understand?" The last was almost a plea.

"Yes, me lord. I quite understand. She's a handful, all right. And fearless. Why, on Devil's Harp . . ." Terrence's words faded away as he saw the icy expression on Lord Robert's face.

"We'll dock at Land's End in the morning and be on our way to Everly. I'd like you and your brothers to ride with us. Colin informed me Cassiopeia is in Everly with my mother and son. You can do double duty and escort her and Colin to wherever they want to go after she's had her child."

"Aye. We'd like that. And, me lord, rest assured, we'll be at your service until we leave. You never know when a strong arm might come in handy."

Inside the cabin, Arianna leaned against the door, reliving the touch of Rob's strong arms around her, still lost in a haze of desire. But instead of feeling miserable, she felt light at heart. He had rejected her, that was true. But only with his mind. His body had been all too willing to forgive her.

She had no doubt about that, for as she clung to his neck, she felt the unmistakable stab of his manhood against her belly. It pressed against her, ready to give her what she wanted, and only his anger had kept him from relenting.

If this was a war, then she had won the first battle.

By mid-afternoon the next day, the small party was well on its way to Everly, having stopped at Land's End only long enough to rent horses for everyone at an exorbitant price. Robert, however, was taken with a handsome stallion and bought him on the spot. The animal was a huge dappled grey, awesome to look at and sturdy of build, with a broad back that could easily accommodate three men. Never had Rob seen a horse as mighty as this one, and he envisioned himself riding his borders astride the back of this giant stallion. Immediately, the name Border Lord came to mind and he dubbed him that, right there and then.

They were a strange-looking group, to be sure, Arianna thought as they galloped down the rugged dirt road. Two black slaves, a quartet of privateers, two noblemen, a knight, and she, moving like the wind across the lonely landscape. Rob had sent one of Cassiopeia's men ahead to let Margaret know they were safe and on their way home, and Arianna wondered what her reception would be.

She glanced over at Ruth and Naomi and realized they, too, must be wondering the same. Both women had refused to ride their own horses and had to be cajoled into riding behind Colin and John. But once well on their way they had relaxed, enjoying the ride and finger-talking to each other when they became at ease enough to let go of their escorts' sturdy backs with one hand.

The castle was a welcome sight, and even more welcome the sight of the people standing on the drawbridge awaiting their return. As she drew near, she made out the tall, dignified figure of Rob's mother Margaret, and beside her the pregnant Cassiopeia holding Robin in her arms. Arianna burst ahead, eager to be reunited with her son.

She almost wept, but remembered her vow of no

more tears and blinked them back. What need of tears on this happy occasion?

Up above, lining the parapet, were town and castle folk alike, all cheering her on as she drew closer. Reining in, she waved to the people—her people—as Rob pulled up beside her.

Forgetting for a moment Rob's anger with her, Arianna sighed. " 'Tis good to be home." She smiled warmly at Rob, and he answered by scowling and spurring his horse forward, ignoring her completely.

With Naomi holding fast to his doublet, Colin rode past both Arianna and Rob and stopped in front of his wife. A knight helped Naomi down from the horse, freeing Colin to leap from his mount and take Cassiopeia in his arms, engulfing little Robin in his embrace as well.

Arianna swallowed hard, seeing the beautiful familial scene of husband, pregnant wife, and child, and longed for it to be that way with Rob and her.

Robert dismounted and walked over to Arianna's horse, lifting her off, his body stiffening at the soft touch of her against him. He forced his arms to hold her at a distance, as if she were a polite stranger, but his body knew different. It ached to pull her up against him, and his heart mourned the loss of his beautiful, sensuous wife.

Little Robin saw his mother then and cried out for her. At the sound of his voice, she ran over to take him from Cassiopeia's arms. Hugging her tight, Robin planted a wet kiss on her cheek.

Arianna kissed his sweet little face, noting how much he had changed while she was gone. Guilt overwhelmed her. "Mama missed you so much. Have you been a good boy for Grandmama and Cassiopeia?"

He nodded solemnly and she hugged him to her chest, content. She was home. That was all that mattered now.

Cassiopeia looked into Arianna's eyes and saw the sadness behind her happy facade. "I'm thinking you've paid a dear price for Robert's freedom."

Arianna smiled sadly. "A very dear price." Turning to gaze at Rob, she found him in his mother's embrace.

Margaret clung to her son for a long moment, then taking him by the hand, she led him over to Arianna and Robin. "The messenger told me how you braved the fortress on Devil's Harp to rescue Robert, my brave, wonderful girl. The whole of Everly knows it. Their cheers are for you, my dear."

Arianna smiled at her husband triumphantly. "Do you hear that, Rob?"

Rob's voice was as cold as stone. "Would they cheer, I wonder, if they knew you are also the one responsible for my having been captured in the first place?"

"Why don't you tell them, then? What are you waiting for? Here's your chance to diminish me in their eyes, because I'm thinking what bothers you most is your injured male pride."

Rob glared at her in silence.

"That's it, isn't it? You can't stand the thought that it was two women who rescued you."

With a voice edged with steel, he answered, "If that's what you think, then it's obvious you have no idea of how grievous your betrayal was."

"Enough!" Margaret said. "I don't know what transpired between you two, but you will keep it to yourselves. The people of Everly rejoice that their master and mistress are safely returned, and for their benefit you shall behave accordingly."

Kissing his mother's cheek, Rob said, "Forgive me, Mother. You're right. This is not the time for harsh words. I am glad to be home and happy to find you well."

Turning to Arianna holding tight to their son, he held out his arms. "Robin, come to your father. Give me a kiss, or have you grown too big for that whilst I was gone?"

Robin reached over to clasp Rob around the neck with one small arm, still holding tight to his mother with his other.

Forced into the close proximity of his wife, Rob kissed his son, his eyes locked onto Arianna's. He saw the sadness there and felt a pang of regret, but the memory of her naked in Longfellow's chamber soon dispelled that ache and a stone wall of anger hardened his heart, protecting him from further hurt.

Chapter Eighteen

Rob's coldness drained Arianna of the last of her strength. She had worked hard at staying strong throughout the ordeal, doing what she must, no matter how hard it was, to reach her goal. Now, having accomplished that, her body protested, begging for rest to nurture her unborn child. But she had to hold on just a little longer, just enough to make it through the gatehouse and the inner ward, and up the winding staircase to her bedchamber.

Robin laid his head on her shoulder, content to have his mother back, and the touch of his small arms around her neck revived her enough to go on. She tightened her grip on him, took a deep breath, and started through the gatehouse.

Margaret saw the state her fragile daughter-in-law was in and took her by the arm, leading her through the throng of people who lined the way. "My dear, I'm sending you straight to bed and I'm thinking you'll not object. I've never seen you look so exhausted."

Arianna squeezed Margaret's arm to her side with her elbow. "You're right. I shan't complain. I'll go right to bed if you'll see that my new attendants Ruth and Naomi are taken care of."

Margaret laughed delightedly. "You have a penchant for bringing home the most unlikely women to serve you. I hope they last longer than Buttercup did, running off with our master builder."

"They shall, I'm sure. But . . . there is one thing you need to know about them right away. Ruth and Naomi cannot speak. They have no tongues."

Margaret stopped dead in her tracks. "No tongues? But how? No, I take that back. Don't tell me. I have a feeling I'm better off not knowing." Shaking her head in wonder, she said, "Child, what would we do without you around to make our dull castle lives more interesting?"

Arianna sighed. "Too bad your son does not share your sentiments. Oh, Margaret, I'm afraid I've truly lost him this time."

"Fah! That's utter nonsense. He loves you dearly. What terrible thing could you possibly have done to change that?"

Arianna kept her silence. How could she tell this good woman about Longfellow? If she ever found out, it would only be because Rob told her. But that wasn't likely. Rob wasn't the kind of man to cry on his mother's shoulder. No, he would bear it all in silence.

When they reached the stairs, Arianna hugged Margaret and went up to her chamber, still carrying her son. She settled him beside her in bed and recited one of the familiar stories he loved so well. He drifted off to sleep so quickly she suspected he hadn't been sleeping well while she was gone.

Brushing a lock of his hair from his eyes, she whispered, "My sweet babe, Mama is going to be here from now on. You and your baby sister or brother will have the kind of mother you deserve to have. It may be too late to be a good wife, but it's not too late to be a good mother."

Arianna remembered nothing after that. The wings of sleep took her and the next thing she knew it was morning. She stretched, revived considerably since the night before, and turned to kiss her son good morn. The bed was empty.

A light rapping sounded on her door and it opened to reveal Fiona. "Good morn, my lady. I beg pardon, but I cannot find your . . . uh . . . your—"

"My what, Fiona?"

"Your new attendants, Ruth and Naomi. I thought they might be in here disturbing you and I was going to chase them out."

Arianna scowled at Fiona. "The only one disturbing me is you, Fiona."

Fiona started backing out of the room. "I'm truly sorry. I'll leave and—"

"Fiona! Can't you tell when I'm teasing you? You need to develop a sense of humor. It will keep you in good stead."

"Humph. Seems I need more than that, what with the castle being overrun with heathens."

"Heathens? Oh, Fiona, really. Just because they have a different color skin doesn't make them heathens. Why, for all we know, they could be more devout Christians than you or I."

"You mean you don't know if they're Christians, my lady? Why, we could get murdered in our sleep!

And I'd be the first since they share the same bedchamber as me!"

Arianna shook her head in frustration. "Really, Fiona, you get more crotchety every day. I'm thinking you need a man to share your bed. At least then you wouldn't be worried about being murdered in your sleep."

"A fat lot of good it's done you having a man. I don't see him sharing your bed." Fiona was sorry as soon as she said the words.

"At least I have a child to love from that union and another on the way. You'll die childless if you do not marry soon."

"My lady! You're with child again? How marvelous! My lord Warwick must be very happy. I know how much—"

"He doesn't know, and you are not to tell him. Do you hear? I only mentioned it to you because it would be hard to hide it from you much longer."

"But, my lady! If you told him, it might make things right between you again."

"No. I want my husband back because he loves me too much to stay away from my bed. I don't want him because he is obligated to take care of me. I'd rather leave here forever than to have that kind of marriage. I've learned a lot about myself on the journey to Devil's Harp and back, but most of all, I've learned that I can take care of myself. If Robert Warwick cannot handle that kind of woman, than he is less the man for it."

Overwhelmed by Arianna's outburst of independence, Fiona plunked herself down on her mistress's bed. "My lady, you astound me. You . . . you make me proud to be of the same sex. Don't worry about me. I'll keep your secret. I'll—"

"What secret is that?"

Fiona and Arianna jumped at the sound of Cassiopeia's voice. As one, they turned to see Cassiopeia standing there holding a tray brimming with food, and behind her Ruth and Naomi, one carrying little Robin, the other carrying another tray of food.

"Cassiopeia."

"Hope you don't mind. I stole Ruth and Naomi away early this morning. I wanted to prepare a meal worthy of your return. After all you've done for me, that's the least I could do."

"Mmmm, put that tray right down here. I'm famished. And please, join me for breakfast."

Robin and Cassiopeia joined Fiona on the bed, and Arianna gestured to Ruth and Naomi to join them as well. In a moment, all five were busily engaged in eating, giggling, and enjoying each other's company.

Rob heard the tittering from the hall as he passed by and, curious, pushed the slightly ajar door open far enough to peer in. He was prepared to be angry, but what he saw almost made him laugh out loud. Robin was bouncing on the bed, upsetting the bowls of porridge and sending the cheese flying through the air.

The women took it all with good humor, salvaging what they could and stuffing it down their mouths before Robin spread it all over the bed. A dollop of butter sailed through the air, landing on the tip of Arianna's nose, and the women all joined in laughter. Robin saved it from sliding off his mother's nose by licking it off with his little tongue.

Rob watched, his face lit up like a bonfire on a cold

winter night. Only Arianna could get into such mischief. Only his wife . . . his wife . . . Turning suddenly somber, Rob backed away from the door and continued down the hall, his mind awhirl with conflicting emotions.

Later that day, trying hard to take his mind off Arianna, Rob decided to go for a ride with his son on his new stallion, Border Lord. Robin always loved to sit in front of his father and pretend it was he who was taking his dad for a ride.

Taking the steps two at a time, Rob walked into the nursery, which was between the master bedchamber and the small one shared by the attendants, and found it empty. Making his way into the servants' room, he saw Fiona. "Where is my son? I thought I'd take him for a ride."

"Oh, you startled me, my lord. A ride, you say? I'm afraid you're too late. My lady has already gone out with him."

"Out? Where?"

"Why, they were quite sticky from the young master's breakfast and decided to ride out to the forest pool to bathe. I'm sure they'll be—"

Before Fiona could finish, Lord Warwick was gone. Fiona smiled craftily. Arianna had given her strict instructions not to let the earl know where she was, but . . . It could be the very thing that could bring them back together again. After all, Arianna was a beautiful young woman. If the earl should happen on her naked, well . . .

Robert strode to the stable and saddled Border

Lord, unsure of just what he intended to do. He had planned on going for a ride, hadn't he? So, he would do so. And . . . if he just happened to ride by the forest pool, well then, what was wrong with that? It was his property, after all, and . . .

As he made his way out of the castle and down the path leading to the water, Rob tried not to think about his real reason for riding to the pool. It was the same private spot where Arianna had swum before he married her, and he remembered the enchanting sight of her swimming on her back, her beautiful breasts bobbing in the water like exquisite water lilies.

He felt an ache in his heart and in his groin, and Rob rode all the faster. He just wanted to make sure Robin was all right, that's all. It could be dangerous for a small child there. He could drown, he could . . . Rob knew he was trying to fool himself, and it wasn't working. There was only one reason he was riding to the pool, and that was because the thought of Arianna naked drew him there like a bee to a nectar-filled flower.

Dismounting from his horse far enough away not to be heard, he tied Border Lord to a tree, then walked down the path. He hadn't gotten very far when he heard the sound of female laughter, and his heart beat harder. Stepping off the path, he crept into the woods, kneeling behind the thick ferns that grew at the edge of the opening.

All he could see of his wife was her head as she swam through the water, carrying Robin on her back. His son was laughing delightfully and kicking his legs. "Mama, me swim, too."

"Oh my, what a big boy you are. Before you know it, you'll be swimming better than your mother."

Robin's head suddenly dipped beneath the water, and he came up choking. Arianna immediately swam closer to shore and stood in the water, pulling Robin off her back. "Are you all right?"

Robin shook his head yes. "Me drank some water. Me was thirsty."

Rob heard Ruth and Naomi laugh, noticing them for the first time. They, too, were naked, entering the water to take Robin from Arianna. He saw Arianna gesture to them with her hands and realized it was some kind of communication. Leave it to her to find a way to talk with the tongueless women.

Naomi carried Robin to the edge of the limpid pool and sat with him there as he contentedly kicked his feet in the water. Arianna wrung her long hair out with her hands, then started out of the water. Rob held his breath as she waded toward shore, the sun catching the dewy crystals of water on her skin, light beams radiating from her body.

God, she was a beautiful sight. He watched as she strode up the bank and lay down on the mossy ground, stretching out languidly. The sun beat down on Arianna and warmed her, and she made little mewing sounds of contentment.

Her nipples, hard when she walked out, now softened before his eyes, and he saw the golden hair of her woman's mound glisten and move as it dried in the hot sun.

His manhood, hardened from the first glimpse of her naked body, now throbbed with desire as he watched her lying there as if it were the most natural thing in the world to do. She seemed completely comfortable in her naked state, like Eve in the garden of Eden, before the snake . . . before Longfellow. Damn her to hell, why did she have to be so beautiful? Why did she have such a hold on him? He was a prisoner to her love as much as he had been a prisoner in Longfellow's dungeon. He had escaped from there, but could he ever escape his captivity to Arianna?

Rob tore himself away, feeling out of place watching her when she was unaware, and rode back to the castle. Mayhap it was time to do some serious thinking about his wife. About his life. He couldn't go on forever in this hell. He must either forgive her and live out his life with her as he had once planned, or send her away from him so that he could live a life without heartbreak, without a woman he could no longer trust. Yes, it was time to think it out, painful though it might be.

That night Rob entered the great hall for the evening meal, in as much of a quandary as he had been that morning. It wasn't easy to come to a decision about Arianna. She was so deeply ingrained on his heart that he couldn't think clearly. He looked around the hall, seeking his wife's form, and could not find her. He swallowed his disappointment and made his way over to his mother. "Mother, will you tell my wife her presence is needed here? Would you remind her that as long as she is mistress to this castle, she has obligations she must—"

"Tell her yourself, son." Margaret nodded her head toward the entranceway and Rob turned to stare at the beautiful sight before him. Arianna was dressed in a gown of pale peach, almost the same hue as her creamy skin. It brought a lump to his throat just looking at her. And her hair, her golden hair, shimmered with light, brushed out to its full length behind the cream-colored lace ruff at her neck.

He blinked from staring too long, then stared again, unable to do anything but gaze at her wondrous beauty. It was the first time he had seen her in that gown, and if he was to survive, it had better be the last. There wasn't a man alive who could look at her now and not desire her.

At that moment, Sir John Neal made his way up to Arianna, bowing deep at the waist before offering her his arm. For the first time in his life, Robert resented his best friend in all the world. But it was so like John to be the gallant; he had always been so with Arianna, and until this moment, Rob had always been grateful for that, knowing John would always be there to protect his wife if he were absent.

Arianna smiled sweetly at John and took his arm, feeling her husband's eyes upon her. She knew how spectacular she looked and, armed with that knowledge, felt wonderfully confident in herself.

In a moment, she was surrounded by her people, each one trying to talk to her, and she turned her full attention to them.

Rob watched as Arianna conversed with everyone, and he wanted nothing more than to order them all away. Realizing he couldn't do that, though, he walked out of the room in frustration. Damn her, she seemed so sure of herself, so happy, so . . . so righteous, as if she had done no wrong. 'Twas obvious she was not repentant.

Striding down the path that led to the stable, he

decided to check on his stallion. Earlier in the day Border Lord had seemed out of sorts, and since he was so new to Everly, Rob had no idea if there was something wrong with him or if he just had a stormy personality.

He entered the stable and immediately heard a thumping on wood. Border Lord was trying to kick down the door to his stall. Damn. Had he been stuck with a crazy horse? He remembered Pasha then, Arianna's beautiful white stallion that he had had to destroy after it had killed Judith Deveraux, that poor demented woman. The last thing he wanted was to have to repeat that agonizing moment.

Soothing Border Lord with his voice, he opened the door and led the stallion out into the night air. Immediately, the animal calmed down. Mayhap it was just the strangeness of his new surroundings that had him spooked. He would settle down soon.

Laughter drifted over to Rob, and he turned to see Arianna outside in the courtyard talking to Colin and John. A frown came to his face and he forgot all about his stallion as he watched every movement his wife made.

The moon shone bright that night, caressing Arianna with its magic light. She looked even more heartbreakingly beautiful out here than she did in the glow of the torch-lit hall. A groom walked by, and Rob gestured for him to take the stallion. Without awareness of anything but his wife, he started toward her, pulled by the power of the shimmering moon . . . by the light of it enveloping Arianna in its glow . . . by the power of his endless love.

Arianna watched Rob approach, his long, lean

body seeming to eat up the distance between them. His movement was sensuous, lithe, every inch of him radiating masculinity so strong and vibrant that she wanted nothing more than to be touched by him, mastered by him, in any way that he desired. It was a need so great she felt as if she would die if she did not have him this very night.

Raising her head high, she sent him that message as he came closer and closer, holding her breath, so intense was her desire.

Rob felt his flesh tingle with excitement as he drew closer to his wife. There was a strangeness to the air, like the crackle of energy just before lightning struck close by. He felt it to the very marrow of his bones, and though he knew not what he'd say when he came to her, he could not stay away.

He stood before her, gazing into star-lit eyes. "Arianna . . ."

She stared back, expectantly, waiting to hear what he would say, hoping against hope that he had forgiven her.

He watched as she parted her lustrous lips, the tip of her tongue showing as she started to speak. Then the blare of a trumpet rent the air between them and the spell was broken.

"My lord, a messenger approaches the gate," the voice from the parapet cried.

"Do they carry a banner?"

"Aye, my lord, the banner of the queen."

Rob stared into Arianna's eyes, his face turned to stone.

Arianna's hand flew to her heart. A message from the queen! What could she want now? Of course. She had heard that Rob was rescued and wanted to send her congratulations. That was it, she was sure.

In a moment, the messenger was standing before Rob, saying, "My Lord Warwick, my message is for your wife."

Arianna stepped forward. "I am the Countess of Everly. Read me your message. I have no secrets from my husband."

"Yes, my lady. The message reads, 'Dear, sweet Arianna, it gives me great pleasure to know that your husband is safely returned and that you were instrumental in his release, therefore I wish to honor you with a masque at your earliest convenience and shall expect you and Robert at St. James Palace within a fortnight.' "

Arianna turned to Rob, an anxious look upon her face. "I . . . Rob?"

Rob's lip curled in anger and Arianna knew she could expect no help from him. "I . . . wish to thank her majesty for the great honor but will have to decline. Please tell her the Countess of Everly is with child and in delicate health. Her physician has advised her to limit her traveling drastically. Do you have that?"

The messenger raised an eyebrow. "I have it."

"Good, then I'd advise you to be on your way. If I know Elizabeth, she'll not rest until you return."

The messenger shook his head in agreement, then left.

Robert couldn't believe his ears. "Have you gone completely insane? Why would you tell the queen such a thing?"

"Why? To prove to you that my love for you is

stronger than my desire for revenge. Isn't that what you wanted?"

"Arianna, don't you understand? The queen is sure to discover that you're not pregnant. Then what are you going to do?"

"Robert, aren't you pleased that I want to be here with you? Doesn't that make any difference to you?"

"What makes a difference is that you are still being deceitful. Still telling damnable lies."

"But it's not a lie, Robert. It's not a lie."

Robert grasped Arianna's head with his hands and stared into her eyes. "What's not a lie, Arianna?"

"I am with child, Rob. That was no lie. The babe will be born in six months."

"Do you expect me to believe that? Is there no end to your deceit?"

"It's true, Rob. It's really true. I am going to have another child. Believe me."

Rob's eyes opened wide as the truth hit him, and he pushed her away. "My God, Arianna, it is true. You not only risked your life going to Devil's Harp, but you risked the life of your unborn child. My child! Is there nothing you won't stoop to?" Fearful of striking her, so great was his anger, Rob turned on his heels and strode away, leaving behind a devastated wife.

Arianna had thought he'd be happy now, knowing she'd put her love for him above everyone, everything, but instead, he seemed to despise her all the more. Anger rose inside her and she shouted out her feelings as he walked away. "I risked everything for you, but that doesn't seem to matter! I've tried in every way I know how to please you, thinking I was unworthy of your great love. But I was wrong! Wrong, do you hear

MORE PASSION AND ADVENTURE AWAIT... YOUR TRIP TO A BIG ADVENTUROUS WORLD BEGINS WHEN YOU ACCEPT YOUR FIRST 4 NOVELS ABSOLUTELY *FREE*
(AN $18.00 VALUE)

Accept your Free gift and start to experience more of the passion and adventure you like in a historical romance novel. Each Zebra novel is filled with proud men, spirited women and tempestuous love that you'll remember long after you turn the last page.

Zebra Historical Romances are the finest novels of their kind. They are written by authors who really know how to weave tales of romance and adventure in the historical settings you love. You'll feel like you've actually gone back in time with the thrilling stories that each Zebra novel offers.

GET YOUR FREE GIFT WITH THE START OF YOUR HOME SUBSCRIPTION

Our readers tell us that these books sell out very fast in book stores and often they miss the newest titles. So Zebra has made arrangements for you to receive the four newest novels published each month.

You'll be guaranteed that you'll never miss a title, and home delivery is so convenient. And to show you just how easy it is to get Zebra Historical Romances, we'll send you your first 4 books absolutely FREE! Our gift to you just for trying our home subscription service.

BIG SAVINGS AND FREE HOME DELIVERY

Each month, you'll receive the four newest titles as soon as they are published. You'll probably receive them even before the bookstores do. What's more, you may preview these exciting novels free for 10 days. If you like them as much as we think you will, just pay the low preferred subscriber's price of just $3.75 each. *You'll save $3.00 each month off the publisher's price.* AND, your savings are even greater because there are never any shipping, handling or other hidden charges—FREE Home Delivery. Of course you can return any shipment within 10 days for full credit, no questions asked. There is no minimum number of books you must buy.

4 FREE BOOKS

TO GET YOUR 4 FREE BOOKS WORTH $18.00 — MAIL IN THE FREE BOOK CERTIFICATE T O D A Y

Fill in the Free Book Certificate below, and we'll send your FREE BOOKS to you as soon as we receive it.

If the certificate is missing below, write to: Zebra Home Subscription Service, Inc., P.O. Box 5214, 120 Brighton Road, Clifton, New Jersey 07015-5214.

FREE BOOK CERTIFICATE

4 FREE BOOKS

ZEBRA HOME SUBSCRIPTION SERVICE, INC.

YES! Please start my subscription to Zebra Historical Romances and send me my first 4 books absolutely FREE. I understand that each month I may preview four new Zebra Historical Romances free for 10 days. If I'm not satisfied with them, I may return the four books within 10 days and owe nothing. Otherwise, I will pay the low preferred subscriber's price of just $3.75 each; a total of $15.00, *a savings off the publisher's price of $3.00.* I may return any shipment and I may cancel this subscription at any time. There is no obligation to buy any shipment and there are no shipping, handling or other hidden charges. Regardless of what I decide, the four free books are mine to keep.

NAME

ADDRESS _____ APT _____

CITY _____ STATE _____ ZIP _____

( )
TELEPHONE _____

SIGNATURE _____ (if under 18, parent or guardian must sign)

Terms, offer and prices subject to change without notice. Subscription subject to acceptance by Zebra Books. Zebra Books reserves the right to reject any order or cancel any subscription.

ZB0594

GET
FOUR
FREE
BOOKS
(AN $18.00 VALUE)

ZEBRA HOME SUBSCRIPTION
SERVICE, INC.
120 BRIGHTON ROAD
P.O. Box 5214
CLIFTON, NEW JERSEY 07015-5214

that, Robert! I realize now I can never make you happy. No one can make another human happy; they must do that for themselves. What a revelation! What freedom that gives me! For I'll never have to be responsible for your happiness again."

Arianna's words pierced Robert's heart every bit as painfully as a dagger. He thought she'd be repentant, he thought she would beg for his forgiveness, but instead, she ranted and raved about freedom and happiness as if they were her Godgiven right.

'Twas certain she was Mary's daughter. Her royal blood was a curse on him, for because of it, he could never truly conquer her. Never truly make her his. It was too much for any man to bear.

Chapter Nineteen

Lying on the hard pallet in the quarters for his knights on castle duty, sleep was an unwilling bed partner for Robert. It evaded him, until he thought the night would never cease and he would have to endure the agonizing thoughts that rolled through his head, unbidden and unwanted, forever.

Arianna naked.

Arianna pregnant.

Arianna defiant.

It was all he could think of. Rolling over, he punched his goose-down pillow with his fist several times, then buried his head in the depression. No, not true. He could think of one more unbearable thought: *Arianna with Longfellow.*

Would this agony never end? Must he endure the same thoughts night after sleepless night? Taking the pillow from his head, he threw it across the floor and it landed at the foot of John Neal's bed.

John groaned. It was impossible to sleep with this madman in the room. Robert was his best friend, and when he hurt as he did now, it disturbed John. But

God's teeth, he wished the man would get the inevitable over with and bed his wife, so he, too, could get some sleep.

Robert needed physical activity to wear him down, to dissipate the frustration he must be feeling over Countess Arianna, and in the morning, he'd make sure he got it.

Thinking of ways to keep his friend occupied, John finally fell asleep, whilst Robert stayed awake thinking of another kind of physical activity.

Sexual fantasies of Arianna replaced everything else in his mind as he conjured up the image of her in the water and on the mossy bank, naked, seductive, and completely at home in the wildness of the forest. She was a free spirit in every sense of the word, and he was learning new things about her that amazed and confounded him.

She seemed open to everything, and though that wreaked havoc in his life, it was still an enticing thought. For it freed his mind to think of new ways of making love to her. What was he to do? He could not envision living in the same castle without making love to her. That meant he must either forget all about Longfellow or send her away. Either solution seemed an impossible feat. Hence his sleepless nights. Hence the unbearable pain.

And what of her pregnancy? What about his unborn child? He had been denied the pleasure of knowing Robin until his son was ten months old. If he sent her away, he would be denied that basic right of all fathers yet a second time. Why did life have to be so confoundedly complicated? All he'd ever wanted was his wife and family, safe and secure at Everly, living the simple life of country folk. But thanks to Arianna, that was only a dream.

Close to dawn, Rob gave up trying to sleep and arose, dressed, and crept out of the bedchamber and out of the castle. Walking aimlessly about, he heard a loud thumping in the stables and went to see what caused it.

He found Border Lord, trying to break the stall door down again. "What is it, boy? Don't you like your new home? Or do you smell the scent of Pasha, the last stallion to use your stall? Methinks not, since that was over a year ago."

The horse suddenly bolted, trying to jump over the side of the stall, and Rob realized the problem. It wasn't Pasha he smelled, but Sanctimonious. The mare was in season. Damn. It was a good thing he came out when he did. The stallion could have injured himself trying to get to the mare. There was nothing more dangerous to life and limb than a stallion after a mare ready for mating.

Especially a stallion of his magnitude.

When soothing the animal with his voice didn't work, Rob took off his shirt and tied it around the stallion's head, blinding him and blocking the female's scent. Immediately, the horse calmed down, and Rob quickly led him out of the stable. He would have to board him with Fiona's family until it was safe to bring him back. But first what Border Lord needed— what he needed, too—was a long, hard ride.

He quickly saddled the great grey horse and led him through the gate house, still blinded, then called out to the gatekeeper to open the gate.

The gatekeeper thought it was a strange request so

early in the morn, but the Earl of Everly was his master and it was not his place to question his commands.

Mounting Border Lord, Rob rode through the gate and over the drawbridge, the striking of the stallion's hooves on wood a lonely sound in the misty grey dawn. When he thought he was far enough away from the castle, he removed the shirt from Border Lord and headed down the path leading away from Everly village. He had no idea where he was going, but found himself turning toward the wild cliffs several leagues away where Arianna had given birth to Robin.

Once away from the castle the horse settled down and the ride became enjoyable. The sky was turning gloriously pink, and Rob took advantage of the light and raced with the wind, giving the stallion his head. It felt good to ride free and wild, and it boosted his spirit, making him feel invincible. He rode and rode, until Border Lord was lathered with sweat and Rob too exhausted to continue.

By then he had made it to the cliffs and dismounted, walking his horse to cool him down. Sitting at the edge of the cliffs, he stared out at the lonely sea, remembering how he had felt the morning he discovered Arianna's torn and bloody petticoat on the ledge below, thinking she had fallen into the sea. He had wanted to follow her there and only John's firm grip had kept him from it.

It seemed such a long time ago now, and he realized with a pang of loneliness that once again, in the throes of depression and grief, he was back to the same place. Was that why he chose to ride to this lonely spot, to grieve for his lost wife once again? To mourn the life he had once led, the future that had seemed so wondrously bright just a few weeks ago?

But mayhap his journey here was a hopeful one, for he had lost Arianna once before and she had come back to him. Could they possibly, miraculously regain the life they once had and go on as if nothing had happened? Was it possible their love was strong enough to overcome everything?

Back at Everly Castle, Arianna planned a ride of her own. Sanctimonious was acting out of sorts and she thought the mare might be in need of more exercise. She certainly hadn't spent much time riding her of late.

Enlisting Colin and John Neal as her riding partners, she rode east, away from the village. Mayhap Robert would see her with the two handsome men and get jealous.

Sir John yawned for the third time, and Arianna chastised him. "Are you trying to tell me my company is boring, sir knight?"

"What? Oh, you mean the yawns. No, fair lady, they have nothing to do with you, but with your restless husband."

Arianna's spirits picked up immediately. "Oh? Why is that, John?"

"You know better than I, my lady. Your husband cannot sleep . . . or eat for that matter, I fear. He's been that way ever since I bashed his head on Devil's Harp."

"Are you trying to say the injury is causing him to act that way?"

"No, I'm trying to say, as diplomatically as I can,

that Robert is in a bad way, angry at you but at the same time in great need of you. You're the only one who can help him sleep again."

"Oh, John. I would dearly love to be able to do that. But I truly don't know if we can ever be man and wife again. He doesn't trust me, and I can't blame him for that."

"Aye, that is the problem all right. He still loves you, that's obvious, and God knows he still desires you. He can't get you out of his blood, but whether he'll ever be able to trust you again is another matter."

"Then what am I to do? Help me, John, Colin. You're men. You know how they think. How can I make him my husband again?"

"Get him into your bed, and the rest will follow naturally." Colin spoke boldly, expressing what John thought but was too timid to say to his countess.

Arianna had been thinking the same. "But how? He is determined to avoid me, and when he is near, he stays angry at me all the time."

"Sweeting," Colin laughed, "you don't need to be told how to get him back in your bed. You know better than anyone how to do that."

Feeling braver, John piped in, "I daresay it will happen, whether you do anything or not, Countess. Robert's desire for you will drive him to your bed. I've never met a man so obsessed by a woman."

Arianna smiled softly. She hoped that was true, and she felt better having discussed it with John and Colin. She sighed, relaxing in the saddle.

Sanctimonius whinnied loudly, and Arianna looked around her. Was there another horse nearby?

Colin and John became more alert as well. Each placed a hand on the sword at his side.

Sanctimonious whinnied again, raising her head to sniff at the air. That's when Arianna heard the pounding of hooves on the road ahead. Raising her hand to shield her eyes, she gazed into the distance. A huge grey horse and rider were galloping their way. Rob! What was he doing out here?

Colin and John exchanged glances, each wondering the same thing. Each knowing the ride was about to become more interesting.

Robert tried hard to control Border Lord, but the huge animal was hell-bent on galloping down the road. He couldn't imagine what had gotten into him, until he saw the three riders up ahead. He recognized Sanctimonious. Damn. He should have let the stable boy know that Sanctimonious was in season. It was dangerous for Arianna to ride her now. Every stallion from here to London would try to jump the mare if they got wind of her.

Using all his strength, he tried to stop Border Lord, but the animal was too strong. In desperation, he tried the only thing he knew could control the animal now and pulled hard on his left rein, forcing the horse's head to the side. Border Lord began to ride in tight little circles, whilst Arianna and Sanctimonious came closer and closer.

Border Lord finally came to a halt as Arianna rode right up to him. "Arianna, get off that damn horse now!"

Arianna didn't understand why Rob was so angry, but Colin and John quickly realized what was going on and jumped from their mounts. Colin ran over to the stallion to help hold him back, while John reached up and pulled Arianna from Sanctimonious.

"What are you doing? Have you all gone mad?"

The stallion reared, striking at the air with his mighty hooves, almost spilling Robert from his saddle, lifting Colin off the ground, too, with his great strength. Colin held tight to the bridle until the horse came down to earth again.

John ran over to the other side of the stallion, and together the three men fought to keep Border Lord from breaking loose.

Sanctimonious whinnied and the stallion answered, blowing out of his nose, dancing restlessly in place as the mare very prettily pranced up to him and presented herself.

Now Arianna understood. Grabbing hold of the mare's bridle, she declared, "Oh, no, you don't. I'll not have you mating with that big brute." Sanctimonious was having none of that and bit Arianna's hand. "Ouch!" she cried, stepping away from the mare.

Rob lashed out at her. "Damn it all, Arianna, get out of the way before you get stomped on. It's too late to stop this. The horse will kill one of us if we try to stop him from mating with the mare."

"What about Sanctimonious? I won't have that brute hurting her."

"Does it hurt when I mate with you?"

Arianna looked at Rob wild-eyed.

"It's the same with them. If you would help. Unsaddle her so Border Lord doesn't get his hooves caught. Then hold Sanctimonious's head. Soothe her so she doesn't panic."

Everything was happening too fast for Arianna, but

knowing that the stallion could easily break free at any moment and kill one of the men, she did as she was told, unsaddling the mare as swiftly as she could. When she was done, she took Sanctimonious's bridle once again and this time the mare let her, seeming to understand what was to come.

Using her most soothing voice, Arianna crooned to Sanctimonious as the men wrestled the stallion, now also saddle-less, into position behind the mare.

Arianna saw Sanctimonious's tail switch to the side, presenting her backside, and she knew that, at least, the mare wanted the stallion's attention.

Arianna watched, eyes wide with fear, as the great stallion rose on his hind legs and mounted the mare, a fierce sound emanating from his mouth. Sanctimonious answered with a cry of her own. The stallion grunted loudly and nipped at the mare's back, baring his huge teeth. Arianna cried out, but the mare accepted the bites and she realized they were all a part of the mating.

She knew when the stallion found what he was looking for, for the mare jerked, breathing shallowly from her nose. Her eyes closed as the mating began.

The sight of the two magnificent animals before her was wondrous to behold, compelling Arianna to stare at them, enthralled. Colin and John had stepped away from the stallion once the mating began, and Rob had walked around to stand beside her, holding the other side of Sanctimonious's bridle.

Rob felt a wild stirring inside him, and he turned his head to look at his wife. The expression on her face matched his own, and he knew she felt as he did. As if in a trance, he moved behind her, wrapping his arms around her waist and drawing her up to his body, his eyes drawn back to the mating animals. Arianna didn't resist, so caught up was she in the sensuous spell of the moment.

Arianna released her hold on the mare's bridle, unaware she was doing so, aware of nothing but the wild and beautiful mating of two splendid animals, and of the closeness of Rob's body and the pressing of his manhood into her back. She leaned into him, wanting nothing more than to mate with him that very moment, as freely and as wildly as the two beautiful creatures before them.

Rob understood how she felt, for he was feeling the same, and he knew that if Colin and John had not been there, he would have taken her right there and then. For his need for her went beyond the hurt and the deceit, beyond anything but the most basic need of all, the need to mate with the woman he desired more than life itself.

When the mating was done, Border Lord shook his head violently, then moved off the mare, prancing around her again and again. Sanctimonious responded by rippling the muscles of her sleek abdomen, drawing in the stallion's seed to her ready womb in completion of the act.

Colin and John started speaking at the same time, breaking the sensuous spell Arianna was under. Feeling suddenly self-conscious, she moved away from Rob and took the mare's bridle in her hand again, stroking Sanctimonious's nose at the same time. "There's my pretty girl, there's my pretty girl."

Sanctimonious nickered softly, moving Arianna to nuzzle the velvet head with her nose.

Rob's fervent gaze took in his small, delicate wife and the elegant mare, their beautiful heads locked together, and he realized what a spectacular sight they made. He wanted to capture this moment forever, to remember it instead of the image that haunted him, the image of Arianna kneeling naked before Longfellow. Mayhap he could. Mayhap the healing would now begin.

Chapter Twenty

Shaken by the unexpected and powerful event, Arianna rode back to Everly in silence, her mind awhirl. She dared not look at Colin or John, for fear she would see the knowledge in their eyes. The knowledge that she had been filled with lust for Rob as she watched the horses mating. She must truly be a wicked woman to have felt that way.

Glancing over at Border Lord, now cantering down the road with Rob on his back, Arianna was in awe of the swift change in the stallion. In awe of the powerful force of animal lust. A few moments ago the stallion had been a wild, fierce thing, bent on only one goal, and now he was calm, the only visible sign of what had passed the possessive way he stepped in and out of the mare's path, nickering at her, occasionally nipping at her head.

She had learned something of the nature of males this day. Males of every species, she thought, peering over at Rob. He had wanted her back there, and yet, as soon as they were on their way again, he had become cold and formal to her. Knowing her husband as well as she did, Arianna realized he must be angry at himself for pulling her up against him for those few magically erotic moments.

He wanted her still, of that she had no doubt. His hunger had not been abated as the stallion's had been. Rob would still be in great need. And she would be foolish not to take advantage of that. Colin and John had both agreed that if she got Rob back in her bed, he would soon forget all about Devil's Harp. If they were right—and she prayed they were—if she presented herself, as the mare had to the stallion, could he resist?

Would it be so wrong to use what nature had given her to win her husband back to her bed? She had no other weapon. She had only what every other female had, and if she didn't soon win him back, would he not assuage his need with some other all-too-willing female?

Deep in her heart, Arianna knew Rob wasn't like that. She knew he was too noble. That he would ease his need by his own hand if it became too great. But she had to tell herself otherwise to rationalize her actions.

By the time they got back to the castle, Arianna had made up her mind. Robert was the only man she would ever want. She would do whatever it took to get him in her bed, starting now whilst he was still aroused by the wild scene they had witnessed.

When he helped her off the mare, she made sure to lean into his body, sliding down it as slowly as she could manage, pretending not to notice when Rob pushed her away from him, his arms as stiff as iron. She watched in satisfaction as he strode off with a scowl upon his face. More than his arms had been stiff. His need was evident.

Seeking out Cassiopeia, she asked to borrow her most seductive gown. It was a violet-hued satin overlaid with black lace, and shockingly, it exposed every inch of her breasts. The design was the latest Italian rage, and even Elizabeth herself wore one like it, showing her breasts to everyone at court. If the queen could wear such a gown, then why not she? Why not she, indeed? For once donning the gown, she feared she would not have the courage to appear in it.

Cassiopeia gave her the courage she needed, declaring, "Arianna, take my word for it. No man could resist you now, not even your high and mighty Robert. But here, dab some rouge on your nipples. Your attire wouldn't be complete without it."

Arianna rolled her eyes. "Are you sure?"

"I certainly am. That is a part of the fashion. You cannot have one without the other. Why, you'd be naked." Cassiopeia laughed at the irony, and Arianna nervously joined in, repeating over and over to herself that if the queen of England wore such a gown, there could be nothing wrong with it.

"All right. I'll do it." she said, dabbing her finger into the small earthen container of scarlet rouge. She circled each nipple with the sweet-smelling concoction, then stared at her reflection in the looking glass. "Oh, dear. 'Tis very bold."

Her breasts jutted out from the bodice that encircled them, pointing boldly forward, her nipples startling and erotically red. She could feel the touch of Rob's searching hands already, could feel the desire that restlessly stirred her blood.

She had needs that must be assuaged, too.

Gathering her courage, she walked out of her bed-chamber and down the stairs to the great hall, hearing the laughter and murmuring of the people gathered there for the evening meal. Steeling herself, she walked in.

Rob was talking to John Neal, his gaze turning to the door time and again, waiting for his wife to appear. She filled his thoughts so completely that he knew if he didn't have her soon, he'd go crazy with desire.

Looking to the door again, his mouth dropped open at the sight of Arianna standing there. The shock of seeing her breasts exposed careened through his body, lodging in his groin and then back to his brain, where lust fought with rage for dominance in his thoughts.

Rage won out.

Striding over to her, he turned her around and pointed her to the door, propelling her through it with great force. His low, lethal voice spoke in her ear. "How dare you act like a slut in my home! You're not with your pirate friends now. Go to your chamber and take off that . . . that . . . ungodly dress before I beat you to an inch of your life."

Arianna stared at Rob in shocked surprise. "But . . . but it's all the rage on the Continent. In fact, the queen herself wears a dress much like this one."

Rob started up the stairs with her, his hand digging into her arm as he forced her to go with him. "You dare bring up the name of Elizabeth in defense of your actions? I wonder why that surprises me, since you grow more like her every day."

Rob's words hit home. Could it be true? Was she growing callous and uncaring? "You know that isn't true. You're just saying that to defend your archaic self-righteousness."

"Archaic? So be it, if that means I don't want my wife strutting around like a whore."

Tears scalded Arianna's eyes, but she forced them back. She would not cry. On the grave of her mother, she would not become a sniveling little girl. She had done nothing wrong. If Rob couldn't understand that . . .

"Let go of my arm! You're hurting me," she said as he marched her down the hall to her chamber.

Opening the door, Rob pushed her inside.

Arianna turned to face him, her chin jutting out in defiance.

Rob was too enraged to speak. The long walk up to the bedchamber had given him too much time to think about what she had done. He stood fuming, his chest heaving, staring down at his wife. His eyes moved from her shiny turquoise eyes, sparking fire, to the rouged nipples of her breasts, as if he had been mistaken, as if such a thing were not possible.

Arianna stared back, her breathing ragged as she tried to catch her breath. Her breasts rose and fell in rhythm with her erratic heartbeats. Rob couldn't take his eyes from them. He knew if he didn't leave right now, he'd be lost.

He started for the door, just as Arianna let out a shuddering sigh, and out of the corner of his eye, he saw her breasts rise majestically high. It was too much for him to take. Pulling her to him roughly, he held her tight with one arm, while the other moved greedily over her breasts.

"Is this what you want?" he asked in a strange, alien

voice, his fingers digging into her breast. He had to stay angry. His salvation depended on it.

"No," she cried. "Damn you, not like this."

"Yes, exactly like this." Rob's free hand moved down to hike up the skirt of her revealing gown, until he had it bunched at her waist. He grabbed her bare rump with both hands and pulled her up against his throbbing hardness. "You want it, and methinks you'll take it any way you can get it."

"Rob. No. Not like this. Not like . . ."

Rob cut off her words with his mouth grinding into hers. He pushed her lips apart and forced his tongue into her mouth, penetrating as far as he could as he thrust it in and out with great force. But he stopped as suddenly as he had begun and pushed her away, realizing how close he was to taking her by force.

"You started this. You must be the one to finish it. The choice is yours. Take your clothes off or ask me to leave."

Arianna stared at Rob with glazed eyes. She wanted him. But not like this. She wanted him with love, not in the cold, ruthless way he had planned. But she nodded her head yes, knowing that if he walked out of the room, she might lose him forever.

A triumphant smile came to Rob's lips as watched her undress, his lust growing out of bounds. She wanted it this way, he told himself, else she wouldn't have dressed like a harlot. He was only giving her what she wanted.

When she was finished, her clothing in a heap around her ankles, his eyes raked over her body, taking in every luscious detail, but they were quickly drawn back to her scarlet nipples, jutting straight out like two ripe cherries. They were the most erotic thing he'd ever seen. They were designed to bring out the animal lust in a man, and by Satan's blood, that was exactly the effect they had on him.

In a cold, cruel voice, he asked, "Do you want me, Arianna?"

Arianna swallowed hard. "Yes."

"Then come to me."

Arianna took two timid steps toward Rob, then stopped, looking up at his face expectantly.

Rob tried to keep his anger going, but the sweet way she looked at him was quickly undermining him. Moving his gaze from her face, he took in her breasts again, and it gave him the impetus he needed. Sweeping her up in his arms, he carried her to the bed and laid her down, his hands rolling her over on her stomach.

"What are you doing?" she cried, bewildered.

Rob didn't answer. Instead, he quickly undid the buttons of his trunk hose and pushed them down, freeing his manhood. In an instant, he was pulling her hips up to meet him, his hands moving over her round, plump cheeks, then down between her legs as he sought the velvet lips that guarded her most precious female treasure. Spreading them apart, he thrust into her, feeling vindicated.

She was wet and ready for him.

Arianna blinked with surprise. He had never done this before. She felt his hands move up her abdomen, grasping her breasts tight as he thrust again, more powerfully than the first, pulling her bottom up against him as tight as he could.

It had happened so fast, Arianna was still in shock. He was taking her as the stallion had taken the mare.

And until that moment, she had not known that humans could mate that way, too.

He thrust again and she found herself responding to the primitive mating. She anticipated his next thrust, eagerly waiting for it, and when it didn't come, she wriggled her hips, signaling in the only way she knew how that she wanted more. What was he waiting for? Why didn't he continue? Her primal need was every bit as great as his.

Rob rejoiced at her eager willingness and obliged, releasing the last of his inhibitions. With her permission, he gave in to his overwhelming lust with wave after wave of vigorous thrusting, retreating, thrusting, retreating, lost in the erotic world that held but one coupled pair.

Rob belonged to her again, she thought triumphantly. He desired her enough to overcome everything they had been through, and it didn't matter that he uttered no words of endearment or that the act was more of need than of love. For she knew the love was still there, buried deep beneath the hurt. It would surface again, stronger than before, she was certain of that.

Rob suddenly stopped moving and she heard a loud gasp as he plunged in to her one more time, then felt the throbbing as his seed gushed into her. She hadn't yet reached orgasm, but it didn't matter. All that mattered was she had her husband back.

Rob realized he had left his wife unsatisfied, and he moved a finger down between her legs to rub the swollen bud, slippery from their combined juices. It would give her what she needed.

Arianna shuddered and undulated her hips as her

breath came in little gasps. "Oh, Rob," she cried, and gave herself up to the ecstasy, squeezing tight to his manhood still locked inside her as she was carried away. She needed to keep him with her, a prisoner of their love.

When she caught her breath, releasing her hold on him, Arianna slumped forward, sinking into the soft covers on the bed. Regretfully, she felt Rob withdraw from her and climb off the bed, and she shivered, feeling the sudden cold.

Turning her head, she found him buttoning his trunk hose and tucking in his shirt. She willed him to look at her.

He glanced over and saw her gazing at him, and a strange look came over his face. She realized, in shock, that he was ashamed of what he had done, and Arianna suddenly feared it had been a mistake to entice him to her bed.

She took a shuddering breath and waited for him to speak, but instead, he turned away from her and walked out the door, closing it silently behind him.

Silence. It was all around her. Filling her heart with dread. She couldn't help but think of the stallion after he had mated with the mare. How docile he had become, how protective of Sanctimonious. Not like Rob. But it was wrong to compare Rob to Border Lord. He was no rutting animal, but a man with a head full of complex emotions. And he loved her, whether he knew it or not. Else he would have thought only of his own satisfaction.

He could have left her in need, but he hadn't. He cared for her enough to give her the same release he had enjoyed. And with that knowledge she dared to hope, for even in Rob's rage he had thought of her, giving her a gift no mindless, lustful man bent only on his own selfish desires would ever have given, and she felt no shame for what they'd done. It was the act of two people whose love was too powerful to deny.

She prayed he would come to realize that.

Chapter Twenty-one

Rob roamed the hallways of his castle, restless and alone, unable to escape the self-loathing he felt. He despised himself for his weakness in giving in to the lust he had felt for Arianna and the primitive way he had gone about it. That she took it—nay, more than that, eagerly participated—made him feel even worse.

He thought he knew Arianna as well as any man could know a woman, but he wondered now if he knew her at all. Never in his wildest imagination would he have thought she would wear a garment designed to tease and entice a man to such a degree, but she had. Never had he thought she would accept the degrading way he had made love to her, but she had. And all in the name of love. But was it love that had driven her when she was ready to perform an abomination on Longfellow? Was it love that had made her conspire to have him sent away?

From somewhere deep inside came a small, haunting voice that said, *Love motivated everything Arianna did.* Who could doubt she had loved her mother deeply. Deeply enough to seek revenge on the woman who had caused her death. And who could doubt that she loved him. Enough to sacrifice herself to Longfellow in the hopes of getting him back.

He tried to push away those traitorous thoughts, for if he believed them, then how could he condemn her for what she had done?

Was he trying to rationalize her actions so that he could take her back? Running his hands through his hair, Rob tried to clear his aching head. He needed sleep. Needed to get away from her hypnotic presence if he was to see things as they truly were. Every time he looked at her, his desire for her blocked out everything else. His fingers encountered the wound on his head and he winced in pain, cursing John Neal for inflicting such a powerful blow. The wound throbbed painfully, adding to his already-muddled state.

He would ride his borders. That took several days, and it was certainly long overdue. And he'd ride the stallion. It would be a good way for Border Lord to adjust to his new master, and it would keep the stallion away from Sanctimonious. By the time he got back, the mare would no longer be in season. Having settled that, Rob felt much better and went back to the chamber he shared with the castle knights, and for the first time since his return, he slept soundly.

At dawn, Rob was on his way, taking with him but a half-dozen knights. John Neal, in charge while he was gone, watched from the parapet as Rob rode away, feeling a sense of relief. This was exactly what Rob needed. He only prayed that when the earl returned he would have everything sorted out in his mind.

Sighing, he turned to go back inside and saw

Arianna making her way over to him, her son in her arms. "My lady, what brings you up here so early in the morn?"

"I heard the gate open and came out to see what it was all about. I—I saw my husband leave. Where is he going, John?"

"Why, to ride the borders, my lady."

Relief turned Arianna's frown into a lovely smile. "Oh."

John reached out to touch Arianna's arm. "My lady, I think 'twill be good for him to get away for a while. It's understandable that he's not been able to think too clearly. And I daresay, the blow on his head hasn't helped any. Give him time. I'm sure when he's had a chance to think things over in depth, he'll understand that what you did was the right thing."

"I wish I were as confident as you. But you see, it is hard for Robert to understand me, for I am not nearly as good as he." Arianna smiled softly. "It has not been easy living up to his standards. I fear I shall never be able to do so."

John laughed gleefully. "I fear you are not alone in that. 'Twould be hard for anyone to live up to Robert Warwick's standards. You married a superior man, my lady. But, God's teeth, it can't be easy to live with that kind of man."

Arianna was surprised at John's words. But they did make her feel better, and more than that, they reinforced her determination to be true to herself. Mayhap she was finally growing up.

Feeling much better, she went down to the great hall to break the fast with her son. After eating she sought out Ruth, Naomi, and Fiona, to accompany her out to a meadow to pick wildflowers. When the horses were saddled, she gathered up Robin in her arms and, to his merriment, set him on Sanctimonious.

Ruth and Naomi shared a horse, whilst Fiona rode one of her own, and together they traveled the short distance to the meadow, a carefree outing, long overdue. It would be good to fill her home full of flowers, good to smell their sweet fragrance. When Robert returned, he would find a happy, cheerful home and that would make him feel better.

Her troubles were soon forgotten as she romped and played in the sweet-smelling field, enjoying the summer morning. Robin frolicked joyfully, chasing after butterflies and helping her gather flowers, though his little fingers were not adept enough to cut the stems off. Instead, he pulled the blossoms off the stems, then presented them to her when he had too many to carry.

They would not go to waste, Arianna decided. She would spread them on the kitchen floor to sweeten up the sour smell of rotting straw this time of year.

Feeling a sudden chill, Arianna looked up at the sky and saw it turning dark. It would soon rain. But she wouldn't let that spoil her beautiful morning. She heard Sanctimonious nicker softly, and she looked over at the mare grazing on a patch of clover. "What is it, girl? Do you smell the rain?"

It was then she heard the pounding of hooves and, glancing over to the road, saw Sir John galloping her way. She felt a chill once more and started walking toward him. "What is it, John?"

"I'm afraid I have bad news, my lady. One of the knights just returned from Dover. It seems Elijah

Longfellow and Black Bess have been captured and are being held there by Elizabeth."

In shock, Arianna loosened her hold on the large bouquet of flowers and a sudden wind blew them out of her hands, scattering them across the field. Arianna watched, feeling a sudden dread. Her beautiful day had ended.

"What are they being charged with?"

"My lord Robert's abduction. 'Tis a hanging offense, my lady."

"Oh, no! We owe Black Bess so much, John. I cannot let the queen execute her. I just can't."

"I know what you're thinking, my lady. I, too, hate the thought of that beautiful neck stretched on the gallows, but it is out of our hands."

"Was it out of Black Bess's hands when Longfellow held my husband? She rescued him and she rescued you, and I mean to repay that debt."

Arianna called Robin to her and quickly mounted Sanctimonious. Without waiting for her attendants, she started back to the castle. She would ride to Elizabeth immediately. She'd take advantage of the queen's fondness for her and plead for Black Bess's life.

Her thoughts turned to Rob as she wondered what chance she would have of ever winning him back if he came home and found her gone once again. And yet, how could she let an innocent woman hang? Stars in heaven, were there no questions in her life that could be decided easily?

Rob was the most important person in her life. How could she once again risk losing his love? A love that was, at the most, precarious. If that were so, then what did one more grievance against her matter when an innocent woman's life was at stake? Either he loved her and would accept her, warts and all, or he would not. And for some reason she could not fathom, it was becoming increasingly more important to her to know just where she stood with her husband.

Trying to keep her voice calm, so John would not know what she was thinking of doing, she asked, "Is Elizabeth in Dover? The way she flits from one castle to the other, 'tis very hard to know where she is at any given moment."

"Aye, my lady. She is in Dover, but according to the messenger, she'll not be there much longer. She'll be leaving for St. James soon, so that she might be closer to Leicester."

"Leicester? Isn't he with Elizabeth?"

"No, my lady, have you not heard? Elizabeth has put him in charge of the army. He's made camp at Tilbury. Preparing to do battle with the Spanish in case our ships do not stop the fleet in the channel."

Arianna paled. She had been so busy worrying about her own problems, it had never occurred to her that her father's life was in jeopardy. That settled the matter of her risking Rob's wrath. She would go to Elizabeth, for she had two compelling reasons now: Black Bess and her father.

Seeing the determined set to his lady's fine-boned jaw, John suspected what she was up to. "I pray you do not even consider going to Elizabeth. I'll send a rider out for Robert, my lady. Let him handle it. Let him decide what to do."

"Too late for that. Black Bess could die before Robert's found, and what could he do, anyway? I'm the only one who can influence the queen. I'll go to her,

plead with her for Black Bess's life. The queen probably doesn't have any idea that Black Bess was instrumental in freeing Rob. She'll listen to me. I'm sure of
it."

John knew how much Elizabeth admired Arianna,
and he thought she had a good chance, but if he let her
go, Robert would have his head on a block. "I cannot
let you go, my lady. Whilst Rob is away, I am responsible for your safety, and I take that responsibility very
seriously."

Arianna glared at John. "Sometimes, John, I swear
you are every bit as stubborn as my husband." With
that, she dug her heels into the mare's sides and galloped away.

Her mind was at work all the way back to the castle.
There was no way she could just sit back while Elizabeth executed Black Bess. But first she would have to
get rid of one more obstacle. John Neal. By the time
she drew up before the castle door, she knew what she
would do.

Sending her attendants to her chamber with Robin,
Arianna asked John to accompany her to the wine
cellar. She told him she wanted a strong wine to calm
her nerves and he seemed relieved, thinking she had
given up any thoughts of rescuing Black Bess.

John walked down the steps before her carrying a
lighted candle, and they wended their way through the
narrow hallway to the heavy door that guarded the
wine. John waited for Arianna to unlock the door with
the huge iron key, then stepped in and was about to
ask her which rack the wine was on, when he heard the
door slam behind him, followed by the sound of the
key turning in the lock.

Satan's blood. She locked him in!

Arianna's heart pounded as she made her way back up the stairs and looked around. No one was watching. She had gotten away with it. But she must hurry, for sooner or later someone would have need to go down to the cellar and would hear John pounding on the door. She hated to do it, but he was the only one in Everly who had the authority to stop her.

Finding the Terrible Four practicing their swordsmanship up on the parapet, she commanded them to saddle their horses. She would need them to escort her. They accepted her orders without the slightest qualms, and relieved, she set about readying for the trip.

In less than an hour she was ready to go. She had promised her son she would never leave him again, and that was one promise she meant to keep. Content to go for yet another ride on the beautiful white horse, Robin happily settled into the saddle in front of his mother.

Ruth, Naomi, and Fiona mounted their horses and followed behind her, bewildered. Their mistress had not told them where they were going, but they had been instructed to pack two changes of clothing and a night shift, so they knew they would be traveling a great distance.

Arianna rode through the gate, handing the keys to the wine cellar to the gatekeeper. "Give my keys to Margaret at evening meal, and tell her a special treat awaits her in the wine cellar." The gatekeeper accepted Arianna's words and waved to her as she cantered off. *Now, at least, poor John won't have to stay there overnight, and he certainly won't get thirsty before he's set free,* she mused.

No one thought it strange to see their lady ride over the drawbridge and down the road. The Countess Arianna was a very active woman. The people of Everly waved to her as she passed by, and she smiled and waved back. When she was safely away from the castle she galloped down the road, eager to begin her journey. A life was at stake.

Taking the Terrible Four into her confidence, she explained what she was about to do. They reacted enthusiastically. Thomas spoke for them all when he said, "My lady, what you do is a noble thing. Black Bess is a good woman. It would be a terrible shame for her to die. As for Longfellow, though he's cruel and vindictive, I've never known him to kill a man except in self-defense. But he knew when he became a pirate what the consequences would be if he got caught. He'll take his punishment like a man."

As darkness began to descend, the small party realized they would have to bed down at an inn for the night. Robin had been remarkably good but was now starting to get fussy from his long hours in the saddle. Arianna kissed the top of his head and said, "Just a little while longer, little one. Mama will find us a nice soft bed to sleep in, all right?"

As luck would have it, the next town they rode into had a respectable-looking inn, and the small party settled in for the night. At dawn, they were on the road again, after partaking of bread and cheese and tankards of mead that the innkeeper's wife prepared for them. Arianna folded a thick chunk of bread in a cloth to take along for Robin, and seeing that, the innkeeper's wife packed them all a picnic lunch and a grateful Arianna rewarded her with coins.

The sun was directly overhead as they approached Dover, the sight of it taking Arianna's breath away. Terrence told her it was the most formidable castle in all of England, and she believed it. Never had she seen such a sight.

The castle and its walls covered a great deal of land, sitting upon a large mound called Castle Hill. They would be entering it through the Constable's Gate, Terrence told her. Arianna decided it must truly be the most elaborate gateway in all the land. Her heart pounded with fear, feeling so small, so inconsequential next to such a large and rambling structure. Why, the walls led right up to the very edge of the cliffs overlooking the great sea.

Robin, too, was very impressed and was thrilled when they rode right through the gates into the outer ward. Dismounting, Arianna looked around her, in a quandary as to what to do next. A door opened at the great tower, and an elegantly dressed man stepped out. Arianna felt a flood of relief. It was her father, the Earl of Leicester.

Seeing her, he stopped in his tracks. "Arianna, what in God's name are you doing here?"

"My lord, I could ask the same of you. I thought you were at Tilbury."

"And so I shall be again after I confer with Elizabeth. And you? What is your reason for being here?"

"I'm on a mission of mercy. I mean to talk with the queen and have her free Black Bess."

Leicester frowned. "And why would you be wanting to do that?"

"Because, my lord, it was Black Bess who freed Robert and John Neal. She does not deserve to die."

"I'm afraid Elizabeth has more on her mind right now than a lady pirate. We're in the very midst of a crisis, waiting for the Spanish Armada to strike at any moment, whilst my men are starving and have little in the way of arms to protect the coast. I'm here to convince Elizabeth to loosen up her purse strings. I was just on my way to see her. Then I must hurry back to Tilbury." Seeing the concern on Arianna's face, he added softly, "I regret greatly that I have no time to visit with you now, but I shall take you to Elizabeth and pave the way for you. If what you say is true, Black Bess deserves to be freed."

Arianna smiled gratefully, then touched his arm, whispering, "Father, are you in great danger? I know Elizabeth has made you the captain general of the army and—"

"My dear, if the Spanish attack, we're all in danger. Do not fear for me. I'll be fine."

"But you look so pale and tired."

Smiling softly, Leicester answered, " 'Tis nothing. I had a bout with some ailment, but I'm starting to get over it. Don't worry, child. You should be more concerned with Robin and the babe you carry. This is no place to bring a child. Whatever possessed you to bring Robin here?"

"I promised never to leave him again, and I mean to keep that promise. Do not worry about Robin. He is enjoying his adventure immensely."

"Adventure? My God, Arianna, we are on the brink of war here. Where is Rob? I mean to give him a piece of my mind, bringing his family—"

Holding her head high, Arianna interrupted, saying defiantly, "I left Everly without his knowledge."

Leicester rolled his eyes skyward. "I should have known. I can see the best thing to do is to get you into Elizabeth as fast as I can, so you can be on your way back to Everly." Taking Arianna by the arm, he led her into an audience hall. "The queen will be here at any moment. Since you have no appointment with her, you'll have to wait until I've spoken to her."

Smiling reassuringly, Leicester led her to a gilded bench and sat her down, then walked toward the raised dais as a door opened and Elizabeth walked out.

Arianna joggled Robin on her knee while she watched as Leicester bowed to the queen in a courtly manner. Elizabeth acknowledged him with a smile. Leicester drew very close to the queen and spoke to her in a low voice, nodding his head toward Arianna. The queen's face was stern as she sought Arianna's eyes, looking her over intently. Even little Robin was not immune from her gaze, and Arianna realized it had been a mistake to expose him to the queen. What had she been thinking?

In a moment, Leicester joined her again. "I'm sorry, Arianna, but the queen says she is too busy to speak to you. In truth, she's rather angry."

"But why? I don't understand."

"She wonders how it is that you were not well enough to come to her when she beseeched you but found strength enough to come to the aid of a lowly pirate wench."

Arianna blanched. This was the first time in her relationship with the queen that she had been treated so coldly. "I . . . I, oh, Father, what should I do?"

Steering her toward the door, Leicester declared,

"Do nothing. She is punishing you now for not coming when she bid you, but she'll relent. She's too fond of you to stay vexed for long. Come back on the morrow. Mayhap by then she'll want to talk with you. I did tell her about Black Bess's part in rescuing Rob, and so for now I'd say she'll not order any executions. Whatever she is, Elizabeth does try to be fair."

Arianna felt a terrible lump in her throat. Nothing was going as planned. She had been so confident that the queen would listen to her. It was a sobering thing to know that she could lose favor with the queen so quickly. It made her realize just how vulnerable she was. She had been foolish to think she had power and influence over the queen.

"Now, take that sad look from your face, for there's someone here I'm sure you'll be glad to see."

Arianna couldn't imagine who she would know at Dover, but she didn't have to wait long to find out. Her father led her through a maze of halls and then out to a small rose garden. A man sat on a bench, his head in a book, and when he raised it to look in her direction, Arianna saw it was her brother. "The king of Scotland here?"

"Yes, and for a reason you'd never guess, but I'll let him tell you of it himself. Then you'll have to forgive me for leaving. Elizabeth is expecting me back."

Taking her by the hand, Leicester walked her up to James and placed her hand in the king's, saying, "Your Majesty, I leave the fair Arianna in your care." Then bowing, Leicester turned and left.

Arianna was wide-eyed with wonder at seeing her brother, and she stammered, "Your Majesty, I . . . I don't know what to say. I had no idea you were here."

James's blue eyes softened as he spoke to her in a low, intimate voice. "And I never expected to see you here. 'Tis a great rare treat for me."

Arianna smiled shyly and, looking for something to say, replied, "This is my son, Robin."

James let go of Arianna's hand and gazed at the small boy with open admiration, stroking his cheek with bejeweled fingers. "He favors your husband, but those eyes belong to his beautiful mother."

"Thank you, sire, I . . ."

Robin was in awe of the bright and sparkling jewels on the hand so tantalizingly near and reached out to try and remove one of the king's dazzling rings. James and Arianna both laughed at his frustration when the ring would not come off.

The king promptly removed his ring and handed it to the child. "A bairn after my own heart. He knows what he wants and goes after it. Much like his mother, so I've been told."

"What do you mean, sire?"

"Your adventure on Devil's Harp. You wanted your husband back and went after him. You are a very determined lass, it seems."

Arianna was amazed that the king of Scotland should know about her adventure. "But how . . ."

"I know everything that goes on in your life, Arianna. And when word came to me of your husband's capture and your going to Devil's Harp after him, weel, fearing for your safety, I sailed there with galleons enough to take the island by force, if necessary, to free you."

Arianna's mouth flew open.

"I see you hadn't heard yet."

"I had no idea."

"Mmmm. Well, by the time I got there you were gone, and so I did the next best thing and took Longfellow captive, along with a goodly portion of other scurvy pirates. However, I would have let the bonnie Black Bess go had she not insisted on being with Longfellow."

"It was you who captured Longfellow? And because you wanted to help me? But why, your Majesty? I don't understand."

"Don't you? Think on it a moment, and I suspect you will understand."

Arianna gazed into James's eyes, so much like hers, so much like her mother's, and stammered, "But you couldn't know?"

Taking her hand, James lifted it up and kissed the ivory rose ring. "Wearing this, you still dinna understand? It is the ring your mother gave to ye, is it not?"

"You do know!"

"I know that on the day I lost my mother, a letter from her was delivered to me, telling me that I had gained a sister."

Too choked with emotion to speak, Arianna moved toward her brother and was engulfed in his arms, little Robin squeezed in between them. James leaned down to kiss the top of Robin's head, then took Arianna's chin in his hand, tilted her head up, and kissed her on her lips.

Arianna kissed him back, sealing the bond between them. A bond, she vowed, that could never be broken. For the first time in her life, she felt contentment. James was her brother, blood of Mary, the same as she. Now, if she could but win back her beloved husband, she would have everything she ever wanted or needed in this life.

Unbeknownst to either of them, a pair of furtive eyes watched. Eyes that belonged to one of the queen's spies. He had been told to keep his eyes on James, but never expected to be rewarded with such juicy news to report to the queen. Elizabeth would be more than interested to know that the sweet young woman she favored above all others had rendezvoused with the king of Scotland.

Chapter Twenty-two

Whilst Robin played merrily in the rose garden, unaware that he was witness to a momentous occasion, Arianna talked quietly to James, speaking softly enough to assure that no one could eavesdrop on this very private conversation. She told him of her ordeal on Devil's Harp, sparing him—and herself—the most intimate details of that last terrible night.

"Then it seems I am responsible for your being here. If not for my taking the pirates prisoner and delivering them to Elizabeth, you would not be here now." James touched Arianna's soft cheek. "I can't be sorry for that, but I am sorry about Black Bess. From what you say, it would seem she is worth saving."

"Oh, she is, your Majesty."

"No, please, in the privacy of this bower, call me by my given name."

"James . . . brother . . . it is so good to be able to call you that."

"If I have my way, you'll be able to call me brother quite openly, but now is not the time to talk of that. I must speak to your husband first."

Arianna couldn't imagine what he was talking about, but the mention of Rob brought a stab of pain to her heart, which she pushed away, not wanting anything to spoil the happiness of this precious moment.

"Right now, we must see what we can do for Black Bess. The queen has already decided that Longfellow and the other pirates I took captive will be conscripted into the navy instead of hung. Always the practical one, she knows that in this perilous time with the Spanish she can use all the able-bodied sailors she can find."

"Then Longfellow won't die? I'm glad of that. As much as I despise the man, I don't want to be responsible for him and his men losing their lives. What will happen to them after the crisis is over and they are no longer needed? Will they be allowed to return to Devil's Harp and the families that wait for them there?"

"With your influence, Arianna, I'm sure you can convince the queen to do that. She is already in a quandary as to what to do with Black Bess. Since Bess is a female, the queen's sense of propriety will not allow her to conscript Bess into the navy. Methinks you have come at precisely the right time. Did you say Leicester told you to return on the morrow? That the queen might speak with you then?"

"Yes, but what am I to do until then? I have no lodgings or—"

"That's of no consequence. Remember I am a king of Scotland and future king of this land. Anything I ask for is granted. I'll have my secretary arrange to find a proper manor house nearby, where you and your entourage can stay until this matter is resolved. And after I've dined with the queen, I'll try to get away so I might visit you this evening. I'm eager to get to know my sister."

Arianna smiled brightly. "I'd like that, too. There's so very much I'd like to know about you."

"And I you. For instance . . . I'll wager that when you were a child you played with imaginary friends."

"How did you know?"

"Because I had them, too. My Uncle James—pardon me, *our* Uncle James—Mother's half-brother, told me when I was a wee lad that all Stewart children were so verra special that the fairies chose to keep them company. And since our mother was born a Stewart spelled with a *w* and married a Stuart spelled with a *u*, we are double Stewarts, doubly special. Do ye believe in fairies, Arianna?"

"I believe in a great many things that cannot be explained. And right now, I believe in miracles, for it is a miracle that you and I are together."

"We shall be witness to a great many miracles, I think, in the coming years. But now I must arrange for your lodgings and then, alas, meet with the queen."

By nightfall, Arianna and Robin, along with the other seven weary members of her entourage, were settled into a beautiful home overlooking the sea. It amazed Arianna no end that with just a quiet word from the king, a home could be obtained so speedily. It crossed her mind that if her mother had not been imprisoned when she was born, if she didn't have to be secreted out of that gloomy castle in the middle of the night when she was an infant and raised as a peasant to keep her identity safe, she would now have the power of a princess royal.

But thinking of that was of no use, and truth to tell, she was content to be just a countess. In Everly, she had everything she wanted except, it suddenly occurred to her, security and safety from the queen of England. As long as she lived in England, she would be vulnerable to threat from Elizabeth. Is that what James had been talking about? Did he want her and Rob to move to Scotland? The thought of that took her breath away, but she quickly came to her senses. It was too much to ask of Robert; he couldn't possibly love her so much that he would give up everything for her. No, even if by some miracle she won him back, he would never agree to go to Scotland.

And why should he? He had land, power, centuries of history in Everly. Why should he have to give up all that? If he had married anyone else, it would never even be a consideration. Because of her, Robert had to live in the same jeopardy that she did. Always afraid that the queen would take away his land or take away his life. He would be better off if he had never met her. Better off if now, when he was so angry with her, he put her out of his life forever. But that was unthinkable. How could she bear a life without Robert Warwick in the very center of it?

Taking her mind off her terrible dilemma, Arianna nestled her sleeping son in her bed and tiptoed out of the room. Thomas and Thaddeus had already retired, whilst Terrence and Timothy took their turn at watch. It comforted her to have them there, and she knew she'd be sorry to see them go when Cassiopeia had need of them again. She had grown quite fond of the four rugged men.

Sighing, she sought out Ruth and Naomi, finding them sitting at a wide window overlooking the water. The women were intrigued by the sea and in awe of the majestic waves that rolled against the cliff. As for Fiona, she had disappeared for a while, only to reappear wearing a fresh gown, with her hair combed out prettily. Arianna couldn't imagine what had gotten into her, until she saw the way Terrence stared at her.

Why, the little minx was looking her prettiest for Terrence. What an interesting turn of events. But what an odd choice of men for the prissy, straitlaced maid.

There was no accounting for taste, Arianna thought, delighted that her attendant had finally shown interest in the opposite sex. She would have to contrive to get them alone together, because Fiona would need all the help she could get.

"Fiona. Terrence. I am expecting a very important visitor in a little while. The king of Scotland. I would deem it a great favor if the two of you would sit just outside the door whilst he is here and guard it with your life."

Terrence's chest pumped up with pride. "Aye. The king will be safe as long as Terrence Titwiler is in attendance."

Arianna smiled at hearing Terrence's last name. Somehow that mild little name didn't quite convey the image of the four hardy men. "I'm certain of that. But please, don't make it look conspicuous. Mayhap if you two act like . . . like . . . yes, like a couple courting, it will not be so obvious that you are guarding the king and me."

Fiona's face flamed at Arianna's words, but Terrence didn't notice. He was too busy thinking how fortunate he was to be in the Countess Arianna's employ. For otherwise, he would never have met the enchanting creature who accompanied them here. Fiona. The name was as musical as her voice.

As it grew later and later, Arianna began to worry about her brother. Something must have happened to keep him away. But she reassured herself, remembering he'd only said that he would *try* to get away. There were probably a hundred reasons why he couldn't come, not the least of which was the queen herself. She would be sure to keep him close to her, selfish witch that she was.

When it became obvious that James would not be coming, Arianna swallowed her disappointment and told her attendants she wanted to go to bed. Ruth and Naomi helped her make ready, but Fiona could be found nowhere. Arianna smiled to herself. It seemed her little maid would need no assistance in wooing her man.

At that moment, Robert sat by a campfire talking quietly with his knights after a hard day's ride. It had been a stressful day, for reasons he could not fathom; all he knew was he had the urge to ride back to the castle and had to push that thought from his mind several times.

But the feeling persisted, growing stronger all the time, and he kept wondering if Arianna and his son were all right. Of course they were. The stone walls of Everly Castle would keep them safe. John Neal, his most trusted knight, would keep them safe. So, then, what was it? Why did he feel so strongly something was wrong?

A thundering of hooves on the hard-packed road brought him to his feet and he knew for certain then that his instincts had been correct. The sight of John Neal, dust-covered and weary, confirmed it. His knight would never leave Everly unless something dreadful had happened.

"What is it, John?" he cried as soon as the knight was within hearing range.

"Robert . . . my lord, it's Arianna. She took Robin and a small party and rode off for Dover."

The words seemed alien to Robert. "God's blood, John, why would she do that, and why in Hades didn't you stop her?"

Sliding off his horse, John answered sheepishly, "I tried, my lord, but she locked me in the wine cellar."

Rob's blood turned to ice as he realized the seriousness of the situation. "Is the queen in Dover? Is that why she went there?"

"Aye, my lord, the queen is visiting there, but that's not why Arianna went. She went there to try and save Black Bess from execution. She and Longfellow were captured and delivered to the queen."

"Black Bess captured? My God. Elizabeth will hang her for certain."

"Not if Arianna has anything to say about it. She plans on pleading for Black Bess's life with the queen. And, my lord, if anyone can do it, it's Arianna. You know how much the queen dotes on her."

Robert understood everything now, but it didn't make him feel any better. Arianna was in danger anytime she came in contact with Elizabeth. "You say she took Robin with her?"

"Aye, my lord. Margaret says it 'twas because Arianna promised him she would never leave him again."

Robert's rage was complete. *"Now she decides to keep her promises! Now, when it puts my son in danger! I swear to you, that woman is the most exasperating creature the devil ever spawned, and it is my great misfortune to love her beyond reason and beyond hope."*

"I understand, my lord. When do we leave for Dover?"

Eyeing John, Robert gave out a great sigh.

Morning came, and with it a rush to dress the Countess Arianna in her most beguiling gown. But 'twas not a man she meant to beguile, but the queen of England. For the queen must believe that Arianna Warwick was the same sweet innocent she was so fond of.

It was a task that Arianna found harder and harder to accomplish of late, mayhap because her heart grew colder and darker toward the queen as each new day dawned. She settled on a gold brocaded, pale pink gown of a delicate hue, which gave her an unquestionably young and innocent look with just the right amount of sophistication for her station in life.

Armed now to meet the queen, she gave last minute instructions to Fiona on the care and feeding of Robin, then departed for Dover Castle in the waiting carriage James had put at her disposal. It came in handy to be related to a king. Her heart filled with wonder at the very thought of having James in her life, and content, Arianna enjoyed the ride to the imposing castle.

Arriving, a page escorted her into the audience chamber, where she looked around uneasily. Just like the day before, the room was packed with people, all seeking an audience with the queen. That worried her, for if she didn't get a chance to talk to the queen soon, it could very well be too late for Black Bess.

The hall became still as the queen was announced, and the swish of skirts could be heard coming down the hall long before they were actually seen. Elizabeth walked regally into the hall, followed by her maids of honor, and glanced around as if she were looking for someone.

When her gaze locked onto Arianna's, staying just a second longer than was necessary, Arianna knew it was she the queen had been looking for. But why? She had completely ignored her yesterday, why now would she be so eager to make sure Arianna was there? Who could know what was in the mind of Elizabeth? None but the devil himself.

Elizabeth swept her long skirts aside and, with a flourish, sat down on an elaborately carved, gilded throne, her jeweled crown sending dazzling rays streaming in every direction, Begrudgingly, Arianna was impressed. If nothing else, Elizabeth played the part of queen to perfection.

Speaking to the throng of people gathered there, Elizabeth's voice took on an irritated edge as she said, "I cannot believe that on this day, as the English people totter on the brink of battle, so many of you wish to take up my precious time with your petty little complaints. On the morrow, I shall return to St. James to make preparations for a visit to the army at Tilbury. They are in need of encouragement from their queen whilst they wait for the Spanish to set foot on British soil. Knowing that, I ask only those of you who have pressing business with the Crown to speak, so I might return to the demands of my title."

Narrowing her eyes, she looked around the room and asked, in a dramatic voice, "Who shall be the first to speak?" 'Twas obvious what she really meant was who shall be brave enough to speak. She might as well have said it out loud, for visibly shaken, many people took a step backward.

Arianna took advantage of the long silence and stepped forward, saying, "Your Grace, I have a matter to bring before you that is indeed one of grave importance."

The queen smirked, unable to contain her glee, for Arianna did just as Elizabeth expected she'd do. "And what is this matter of such importance that you would take time away from the serious business of war with the Spanish?"

"Your Majesty, it is a matter of life and death. The life of a woman wrongly accused. Her death would be a gross injustice."

"It is not for you to make that determination, Countess Arianna, but for me. But do tell me your story. You have whetted my curiosity."

"I speak of the pirate lady, Black Bess. It was she who freed my husband and his knight, John Neal; she who made it possible for me to leave Devil's Harp with my virtue intact."

"Hmmm, if it is as you say, Countess, then indeed she should be freed. I must have time to think of this and weigh the evidence. For that, I'll need you close by to confer with."

Arianna was relieved by the queen's words. "I would be happy to stay as long as I am needed."

"That is indeed noble of you, but . . . I wouldn't want you to stay if you are feeling . . . ill."

Arianna knew what the queen was leading up to, but she pretended ignorance. "Ill, Your Grace?"

"Not long ago, I desired your presence at court but you declined, saying you were too ill to come. But not too ill, it seems, to come to the aid of a pirate wench. Do you value her more than your queen, or have you had a speedy recovery?"

"Oh, Your Grace, since you have never been with child, you can't possibly know that the first two or three months can make a woman so sick she cannot lift her head from the pillow, but that it can pass quite quickly, leaving her in the best of health. That is the case with me. I am feeling fine now."

Elizabeth was not pleased to be reminded of her barren state, but then, Arianna couldn't know how very much she had always wished she could have a child. The fact that she had been born with some obstruction to her womb made that an impossible dream and gave her one more reason for not marrying. Why bother to wed if she could not have an heir from that union?

Elizabeth couldn't help but envy Arianna her fecundity and her youthful vigor. Envy her radiant beauty. 'Twas no wonder the king of Scotland was attracted to her. Though it had certainly come as a surprise to her when one of her many spies reported that he had found them together in the rose garden, kissing.

She had always thought Arianna above that sort of thing, devoted as she was to her husband. But the fact that Robert Warwick was nowhere to be seen proved that something was going on. And why had Arianna brought her small boy with her to Dover? Seems an odd thing to do, mused Elizabeth; though, come to think of it, it wasn't so odd after all, knowing Arianna. It was only natural for Arianna to want her son to know his queen. After all, because of her royal benevolence, little Robin was heir to Brambly Castle.

If that was her reason, then 'twas a touching thing to do. But how could she be sure? There was much to ponder. Was it possible there was more to Arianna than met the eye? It suddenly occurred to her that she knew very little about the young woman's background. It had not been of importance before, but with the king of Scotland involved, it became paramount. It was in her best interest to know what went on between a king and a seemingly innocent young woman.

"I am having a small, intimate supper with the king of Scotland this evening and desire your presence. Mayhap then we shall have the time to talk about your pirate friend. In any case, rest assured I shall not decide her fate until I know all the facts."

"Thank you, Your Majesty," Arianna said, curtsying gracefully. "I look forward to it with great eagerness."

Arianna couldn't believe her good luck. The queen had gotten over her anger quickly and would surely free Black Bess once the truth was known. And, as an added bonus, Arianna would get a chance to be with her brother. Feeling jubilant, she turned and made her way to the door, but the queen's voice halted her in her tracks.

"And, Arianna, do bring your dear child with you."

Fear knifed through Arianna. "Robin? I . . . I don't understand."

"Don't you? Even knowing how fond I am of the boy? Fond enough to bestow Brambly Castle on him for his first birthday. It is my wish to get to know your son. I assumed it was your wish, too. Isn't that why you brought him on such a perilous journey with you?"

"I . . . uh . . . of course, Your Grace, but . . . but after seeing how busy you are, with the Spanish fleet so very close, I realized how selfish it was of me to take up your time with such frivolity."

Elizabeth's lips formed a pleasant smile, but her cold eyes belied the warmth. "Frivolity? No such thing. It is every bit as important for a queen to know the smallest of her subjects, is it not? Bring the lad. He shall be a pleasant distraction from my heavy duties." With a gesture of her hands, Elizabeth dismissed Arianna.

Chapter Twenty-three

The sun was low in the sky when Arianna rode back to the formidable fortress, uneasiness and dread keeping company inside her as she anticipated the meeting between her small son and Elizabeth. Not even the presence of the Terrible Four riding escort could make her feel secure. Had she made a fatal error in bringing Robin to Dover?

She knew . . . had always known . . . that the farther away she stayed from Elizabeth and her omnipotent power, the safer she and her loved ones would be. And yet . . . yet, she had deliberately chosen to expose her precious son to the queen.

Was she so proud of her influence on Elizabeth, so sure she could manipulate the queen in any way she chose that she had been blinded to the danger?

Dear God in heaven, don't make my son pay for my sin of pride. He is so sweet and innocent, so deserving of a happy, carefree life. . . . If anything happened to him because of my stupidity, I don't know what I'd do.

A shiver worked its way up her spine, but she pushed her troublesome thoughts aside. Surely, oh, surely, she worried needlessly. The queen's request was no more than a whim. So like Elizabeth. And it was true that Elizabeth had given Brambly Castle to Robin. True that she had a special interest in him since his birth. It was only her own guilty knowledge that made her worry. Knowledge that the queen did not possess.

There had never been a hint that the queen knew Arianna was daughter to her hated enemy—daughter to Mary and to Leicester—or that Robin was grandson to that illustrious pair, and it was a secret Arianna was prepared to take to her grave.

She would have an enjoyable evening, and as a bonus, Robin would get to know his uncle a little more. She would think of that and no more.

Happy to be included in the outing, Robin was quite merry, climbing into the carriage seat, then jumping off, repeating his proud accomplishment over and over until Arianna lost patience with him.

"Robin. Sit. I want you to behave like a good little boy for the entire evening, do you understand?"

Robin's eyes grew round and large, unused to hearing his mother speak in such a brusque way. Giant teardrops slid silently down his cheeks.

Arianna's heart broke at hurting her son's tender feelings. It was only her nervous worry about Elizabeth and Robin together for an evening that had caused her to speak in an irritable way. "Mama's sorry, Robin. Come sit in my lap and you'll be able to see out the window better."

Robin's tears melted away as he smiled brightly and climbed into his mother's lap, his little booted foot making a scuff mark on her pale taffeta gown. It both-

ered her not at all. For what was a mark on her gown
that could be washed away compared to the hurt in a
little boy's heart that could last a lifetime? She hugged
him tight, kissing the top of his sweet-smelling head.

They arrived at the castle and were shown upstairs
to the queen's private presence chamber, whilst the
Terrible Four watched helplessly. They were forbid-
den to follow, ordered by the captain of the queen's
guards to wait for their lady in the inner ward.

Arianna clutched Robin's hand tightly as she entered the small tapestry-draped chamber and made her
way over to the square table where the queen sat with
the king of Scotland. It surprised her to see that there
were only four trenchers set at the table, and she realized she and Robin would be the only other guests.
Arianna swallowed hard and curtsied to the queen.

Robin bowed deep from the waist as he had seen his
father do and the queen laughed in surprise. "He acts
the part of the courtier already. How delightful."

Beckoning to him with her finger, she said, "Come
to your queen, little Robin. I have a present for you."

Robin's eyes lit up. He remembered the nice man
sitting across from the queen who had let him play
with his sparkling gems and he hoped for a repeat
performance. Walking boldly up to the lady, he asked,
"Will you wet me pway with your jewels, too?"

The queen laughed all the harder. "A boy after my
own heart. I have a toy galleon for him, but methinks
he will settle for nothing less than the royal jewels.
Which of his doting parents has so foolishly given him
gems to play with? I wager it was you, Arianna, for I
think his father would not be so foolhardy."

Robin was happy at being so admired by the lady

who wore so many pretty baubles, and wanting to please her even more, he pointed at James, declaring proudly, "Him did."

Arianna's heart was in her throat. The last thing she imagined would happen this evening was Robin revealing the fact that he had met the king of Scotland before.

A puzzled look crossed Elizabeth's face, and she turned her head to stare at James. "You must be mistaken, child. Do you have any idea who this man is?"

Robin nodded his head solemnly.

Intrigued, Elizabeth inquired, "Tell me, then."

"King of Scots."

"My, my, but you're a smart little boy. Tell me how you know the king."

"Him wet me pway with his gween ring and his wed one, too."

Elizabeth's eyebrow raised as she turned to James. Here was a chance to have a little fun with the too-serious king. In an exaggerated mocking voice, she said, "I didn't know you had a penchant for little boys, James."

Gripping his goblet tight, James envisioned Elizabeth's scrawny neck in his grasp. "If I thought you were serious, I would take it as a deep insult, but knowing the dry wit of the English, I shall let it pass."

Ever so sweetly, Elizabeth answered. "Of course, I was jesting with you. Methinks your eye doth wander to the mother and not to the child."

James laughed wryly. "So that's what this is all about. Have you arranged this intimate little supper to try and ascertain if Arianna and I are having a tawdry little affair?"

"You belittle yourself, James. An affair with you could never be tawdry. Why, there isn't a woman in all of England or Scotland who would decline an invitation to share the bed of a king. But since you have raised the question, let me just say that it has been reported to me that you and Arianna were seen kissing in the rose arbor."

"Did your spy also report that little Robin was in his mother's arms at the time? Hardly a romantic arrangement."

"Hmmmm. I wasn't told that. Still . . . 'tis quite unusual behavior for a king and a woman he hardly knows, wouldn't you say? Or am I mistaken about that? How long have you known each other?"

"Elizabeth, one has to wonder why you find a harmless little kiss so important when you are faced with an imminent attack by the Spanish."

"Aha!" Elizabeth exclaimed, pointing a bejeweled finger at James. "My thoughts exactly. You knew before you set sail for Devil's Harp that the Spanish Armada prowled the channel, and yet you went there anyway to rescue Arianna. Why else would you risk your life if not for the woman you love?"

"Your Grace," Arianna said softly, shaken by the queen's wicked thoughts, "His Majesty sailed to *Robert's* rescue, not mine. I was never in any danger. Had not Black Bess rescued my husband, I would have paid a ransom for him and left."

"She speaks the truth, Elizabeth. If you know me at all, you know I pay my debts. I was indebted to Robert for saving my life. How could I do otherwise?"

"I suppose it is the romantic woman in me that wished you had gone to Devil's Harp to rescue the fair maiden, but it is the sovereign ruler inside me that applauds the king of Scotland for being such an honorable man." Laughing, Elizabeth clapped her hands together and her servants stepped up to the table to serve the food.

Relieved at her reprieve, Arianna relaxed and enjoyed the sumptuous meal and stimulating conversation, happy that Robin, too, was cooperating. He seemed entirely entranced by the presence of two such illustrious beings, as if he understood that he was in the company of royalty. But no, at his tender age, it most likely was their brilliantly hued clothing that captivated him.

When the meal was finished, Robin climbed up into James's lap and proceeded to admire the golden torque around his neck.

Elizabeth watched, amused at the antics of the charming child. She was glad she had asked Arianna to bring him. It wasn't often she had a chance to interact with small children and her fondness for Arianna made it all the more enjoyable. She envisioned a delightful future visiting with Arianna and Robin and the child soon to be born, thinking that if she couldn't be a mother, then at least she could become a well-loved aunt to Arianna's children.

She watched as James lowered his head to kiss Robin's cheek, touched at the gesture. A smile spread across her face, then vanished as she stared at the two heads side by side in shock.

Two pairs of identical blue eyes stared back at her.

If ever two people had the same eyes, it was the king of Scotland and this little boy. Her first thought was they must be father and son, but she remembered well how much the child resembled Robert Warwick . . . except for his eyes. No, Robert was indeed the child's father. Then what? What was it about the two of them that struck such a note inside her?

For some reason she could not fathom, Elizabeth was suddenly compelled to look at Arianna's eyes, and when she did, from deep within her came a burst of understanding, a cacophony of knowledge so strong it flooded her senses and sent her head reeling.

Arianna's eyes matched those of the king and the child's.

Why had she not seen it before?

These three were related in the only other way they could be.

James was uncle to Robin, brother to Arianna.

There could be no other explanation.

And if that be true, sweet Jesus, that meant *Arianna was Mary's daughter*. Mary's daughter, but so much more than that . . .

Leicester's child.

The child she had wanted so very much but was denied. The child she had searched for so long ago, in need to hold in her arms, to raise as her own. The child she never found until this fateful day.

Taking her goblet in her hand, Elizabeth drained it, then set it down on the table with a heavy hand, whereupon it was immediately refilled by a servant.

The dull thunk of metal on wood drew Arianna's attention from her son and her brother at play, and she lifted her head to look at the queen. A strange sensation washed over her then as she saw something . . . different in the queen's eyes. She shivered, then spoke, suddenly afraid of what the queen might say. "Your Grace . . . are you . . . all right?"

Elizabeth focused her eyes on Arianna, hiding her shock behind a veil of composure. "I'm fine. 'Twas just a twinge in the region of my heart. But 'tis gone now."

An icicle of fear shot through Arianna, though she knew not why. Robin's sudden laughter drew her attention and she gladly dismissed her strange feelings, blaming it on an overactive imagination. Robin had managed to get James's torque from around his neck and had placed it on his head like a crown.

Beaming with pleasure at Robin's antics, Elizabeth said, "It seems the boy has plans to replace you as king, James. You had better watch out for him."

"Queens, too, must take care in keeping their crowns," James retorted, "not to mention . . . their heads."

Arianna stared at James, her face drained of color. Was he speaking of their mother? This evening was taking a deadly turn and she suddenly feared where it might lead.

Elizabeth took another drink of wine, relishing the moment. She had in her presence the son and daughter of her lifelong enemy, and it gave her great pleasure to know that if Mary could see what was taking place this very moment, her bones would rattle with rage.

In life, the Scottish queen had never been with her children for more than a brief time, and that only when they were infants. In death, Elizabeth knew Mary's children better than their own mother ever had. Such irony. Such justice.

It was strange, though, how very fond she was of

Mary's daughter. No! Leicester's daughter, she thought, that was the most important element. She loved Leicester more than any woman ever loved a man, therefore it was only natural that she should love his daughter.

Her gaze traveled over Arianna's diminutive beauty, appraising her critically. She couldn't help wondering if Mary Stuart had been that beautiful, but Elizabeth pushed that painful possibility right out of her mind. Better to think of Arianna and what was to be done about her.

How much did the girl know? Was it possible she wasn't even aware that she was Mary's daughter? For if she did know, how could she be so affectionate to the woman who had signed her mother's death warrant? Unless . . .

Unless, it had all been an act. But she couldn't believe that. Arianna was truly fond of her. It would be diabolical if she had been pretending affection all this time. No. Arianna was not capable of such duplicity. It was her very nature to be natural and honest. Those were the very virtues that had attracted her to the girl in the first place.

Turning her attention to the Scottish king, Elizabeth wondered what part he had to play in all of this. Was he aware of Arianna's true identity? Was the kiss in the garden a brotherly gesture, or simply admiration for a beautiful woman? The latter seemed the most likely, for hadn't she seen with her own eyes the way James had looked upon her. It was the look of a man for a woman, not that of a brother toward a sister.

Truly, she had much to think upon. Much to decide

about Arianna. But one thing was for certain: She had already decided the fate of little Robin. Raising her goblet high, she proclaimed, "Let us have a toast."

Puzzled by the sudden intensity of her manner, James and Arianna looked at each other, then raised their own goblets, waiting for the queen to speak.

Elizabeth stared deep into James's eyes, then Arianna's, then Robin's, holding her gaze on the small boy as she proclaimed, "To the glorious state of motherhood."

Arianna and James exchanged puzzled glances, then followed Elizabeth's lead and drank from their goblets, each wondering what had prompted the queen to give such a strange toast.

Arianna wanted to believe it was nothing more than a spur-of-the-moment gesture with no hidden meaning, but her churning stomach told her otherwise.

James, too, sensed something ominous, but he hid his true thoughts behind light banter in hopes of breaking the sinister spell surrounding them all.

Heady from the effects of wine and power, Elizabeth stood up and gathered Robin in her arms. Hugging him to her, she kissed his cheek, declaring, "You are a very special boy, Robin, very special."

Panic filled Arianna as she watched Elizabeth and the possessive way she held her son.

"So very special that I want to make sure you grow up to be the very best that you can be. I'm sure your mother wishes the same for you." Elizabeth turned her gaze to Arianna, waiting for a response.

Arianna was afraid to speak for fear that whatever she said would lead her into a trap. She held her breath, waiting for the queen to speak again.

"Yes, your mother wants the very best for you, Robin, that's why we shall have a nice little talk now, whilst you go outside with your *Uncle* James."

Arianna rose from the table, clutching her chair for support, while James watched in silence, absorbing the scene as he would a chess game, carefully plotting what move he should make next.

"My dear child, did you think you could keep your secret forever?" Her voice rose in volume and pitch as she continued. "Did you think you could keep Leicester's grandchild from me? Did you? And do not insult my intelligence by denying what my eyes so very clearly can discern."

Knowing it was useless to deny it, Arianna was at a loss just what to do. "Your Grace, I am so glad to be rid of the burden of secrecy. It was only yesterday, here, in the rose arbor, that James and I found each other. I . . . I'm so happy now to be able to share that with you."

Elizabeth had not expected that reply. She had to hand it to her, Arianna was courageous. "I see. James, what do you have to say about all this?"

Rising to his feet, James put his arm around his sister's waist. "I say hallelujah. I have gained a sister and a nephew, and you, dear Elizabeth, have gained another cousin. Shall we now rejoice in the expansion of our family, or—"

"I rejoice, cousin. Indeed, I do. I have always been fond of Arianna, and now that I know why, I shall feel all the more so. But . . . above all else, I feel it is my sacred duty to make sure Leicester's grandson receives every opportunity for advancement, worldly goods, and prestige that only a queen can give him, therefore

. . . I mean to make him my ward starting this very night."

Involuntarily, Arianna's arms reached out for her child. "No!"

Robin felt his mother's fear and started to cry, kicking at Elizabeth to let him go. The queen's grip tightened on the child, and she called out to her attendants to take Robin into her bedchamber.

Not wanting to frighten Robin any more than he already was, Arianna calmed her voice and spoke soothingly to him. "It's all right, Robin. Mama is here. You go with the nice ladies and play, and I'll see you in a little while."

Robin's cries turned to whimpers as he was carried out of the chamber, the sound tearing Arianna's heart in two. "Your Grace, I implore you—"

"Save your tears and your words. They'll do you no good."

"But . . . but, Your Grace, how can you in good conscience take my child from me, from his father? Oh dear God, Rob, I don't know what he'll do when he finds out. I . . . I . . ."

"My dear, you're overwrought now, but when you've had a chance to think about it, you'll see that it is for the best. And, besides, you will have another child soon. In time, you'll get over the heartache."

Arianna shook her head back and forth again and again, not believing what she was hearing, while James tried to comfort her.

"Elizabeth, are you sure you want to do this? What will your subjects think when they hear of this? Let Arianna keep her child. Compromise. I'm sure she would agree to moving to Brambly Castle, where you could see the child anytime you wished. You could have the family you always wanted without rancor, without bitterness."

"So, as usual, James, your role is to be that of peacemaker. Well, it won't work this time. I've waited for this moment for more years than I care to think about. Spent countless hours agonizing over the knowledge that my lover's child was somewhere in the world. Somewhere outside my reach. I wanted Leicester's child. Wanted to carry it in my womb but was denied that pleasure. Do not ask me to give up his grandchild. For, James, even you have not enough power to force me to do that."

James knew she spoke the truth. His power was limited in this country until Elizabeth's death, and he fervently wished for that most heartily at this moment. The only chance he had of getting the boy back was to steal him back, and by God, that's exactly what he would do.

But first he had to keep Arianna from making a mistake that could cost her her life. Taking his sister in his arms, he spoke to her in a gentle voice. "Arianna, can ye not see the uselessness of fighting her? If you ever hope to see your son again, accept this."

Arianna looked around, wild-eyed. Even her own brother was against her. How could she ever accept the loss of her son? Sobbing loudly, she held her fist over her mouth to keep her son from hearing.

"Listen to James, Arianna. He's trying to save your life. Accept this, and you can have your freedom. You can go on living as you did before, in my good graces, a member of my inner circle, with all the benefits that come with that. Or . . . you can fight me on this, embarrass me in public so that I am compelled to lock you . . . *and your husband* . . . away. The choice is yours to make. I advise you to think carefully about it."

It was all Arianna could do to keep from flying at the queen with her teeth and nails, but she composed herself, knowing the futility of that action. She was helpless, had no one to turn to, for who had the power to fight the queen of England? Not even her own brother, a mighty king in his own right, had that kind of power.

The best she could do, for the moment, was to keep her freedom, for without it she would never be able to help her son. Without it she would end up as her mother had, imprisoned by Elizabeth for almost two decades before she was finally executed.

Dear God, she could not let history repeat itself.

"I know that nothing I say will make a difference to you, Your Grace, and so I have no choice but to accept. But I pray you let me see him from time to time. I could not bear it if I could not see him . . . know that he is well and happy in your care. Will you promise me that?"

Triumphant, Elizabeth spoke magnanimously. "I can promise you that and more, but now is not the time to speak of it. I leave for St. James on the morrow. You shall accompany me there. I will provide an apartment in the palace for you to stay in whilst I visit the army at Tilbury. Then, when I return, we shall have a nice long chat. Your son will bring the two of us even closer than before, you'll see."

Elizabeth contemplated a moment, then added, "And, since you are being so cooperative, I shall grant you a boon and release that Black Bess creature to your care. She, too, will travel with us to St. James. I'm sure my court will find her amusing." Then remembering James was there, she said, "As for you, James, dare I ask what your plans are?"

"I was going to leave for home this verra day, but now that my relationship to Arianna is out in the open—among us three, at least—I'm thinking of sailing my ships up the coast, with your permission, visiting with my sister for a time in London, then heading back to Scotland."

Gazing at the young king, Elizabeth carefully weighed the advantages and disadvantages of his proposal in her mind before coming to a decision. "I can think of two very good reasons why I should grant your request. The first being that the presence of your ships near London might help deter the Spanish from attacking, and secondly, because you are Robin's uncle and future king of England, it is wise that you and he become well acquainted."

Raising her hands as if giving benediction, she continued. "And now, I think we've both experienced enough emotion for one evening. Get some sleep, Arianna, for we have a long ride ahead of us on the morrow."

The rage inside Arianna almost got the better of her then. She was being dismissed as if she were a child, with no thought to the fact that she had just been torn from her son. But then, what did Elizabeth know of compassion? What did she know of family? She had executed her own cousin, Arianna's mother, a sovereign queen of Scotland. There was no end to the evil she was capable of.

Straightening her shoulders, Arianna gathered her

strength and walked out of the small chamber without her son, her arms aching to hold him, her heart breaking with each step that took her farther from her baby.

She must go on.

She must endure.

She must keep her head.

As God was her witness, she would find a way to free her son, and, oh, oh, if justice existed anywhere in the world, let it reign for one brief moment here, so that she could exact her long-overdue revenge; so that Elizabeth could feel the prick of her thorns and know that Arianna Warwick was blood of the ivory rose.

Chapter Twenty-four

Robert Warwick's mood was foul as he rode into London shortly after dawn, accompanied by his small band of knights. He had been on the road for two days straight, with little nourishment and even less sleep. His long ride to Dover had been for naught, he discovered soon after arriving, for Arianna had already accomplished her mission and had left for St. James with the queen and her entourage. Bitterly disappointed, he had stayed long enough to eat a quick meal, then rode off again, anxious to find his wife and child.

Something was amiss. Of that much he was sure. In the inn where he and his men had supped, he had been informed that Black Bess had been released to Countess Arianna's care. If that was true, why would Arianna travel on to London? The Arianna he knew would never have been so irresponsible, at least not with Robin with her. But then, what did he know of the Arianna who had returned from Devil's Harp? The Arianna he knew would never have exposed her breasts for public display.

The image of her cherry-red nipples caused his manhood to pulsate and surge with energy, and his mind brought forth other provocative images of his wife. He tried in vain to drive the erotic images of Arianna away, knowing he was condemned to desire her for the rest of his life.

The rest of his life might be very short if he didn't get some sleep soon, he thought bitterly, for he was too groggy to think clearly. At the urging of his knights, he stopped at The Stag's Horn, a well-kept inn on a curve in the Thames River, in search of lodging for the night. Hopefully, after he had slept he would be in a better frame of mind and better equipped to find his family.

As he made his way into the inn, he happened to notice an unusually large crowd of people lining both sides of the river but was too tired to be curious. Finding the innkeeper, he inquired about rooms.

"You're in luck, my lord. The Duke of Norbridge just gave up his rooms this very morning. So's the whole of the second floor is available now."

Will? What was he doing in London? The last time he had heard from him was on Robin's second birthday. He and Felicia had ridden to Everly especially for the occasion. "The Duke of Norbridge is an old friend of mine. Would you happen to know where he went?"

"Can't say that I do, but I'm sure it wouldn't be hard to find out. When a duke comes to town, the news travels swiftly."

Rob made sleeping arrangements for his men, had Border Lord stabled and fed, then went up to his room overlooking the river. He had chosen the inn well. The room was clean and attractive, the only thing unpleasant about it being a slight mustiness that permeated the air.

Throwing open the window to freshen the room, Rob was about to sink onto the bed when he heard the enthusiastic cheers from the throng of people outside. Turning his attention back to the view from the window, he saw the procession of elegant barges gliding down the river. The queen! Satan's blood. Where was she off to now?

Listening to the individual voices that drifted up to him from beneath his window, he heard enough to make out that the queen was on her way to Tilbury to boost the morale of the men camped there with Leicester. Groaning wearily, he wondered if Arianna was on this journey with the queen, too. For if she was, he would have yet another long ride ahead of him.

Scanning the passing barges, Rob searched for his wife's golden head amongst the passengers, but there was none so fair as her aboard any of the barges. Thank the stars. As the last barge glided by, he was about to turn away from the window when out of the corner of his eye, he saw a curious sight. A small boy, sitting on the lap of an attendant. Turning back to get a better look, he found the image had vanished as the barge continued on its way. What had possessed the queen to bring a child along on her journey? Seemed strange, but then, there was no accounting for the bizarre actions of that woman.

He sank down on the bed, too weary to think properly, and fell instantly asleep, the last thought on his mind the lonely image of the small child traveling in the company of the mighty queen and her impressive entourage.

When Rob awoke, something nagged at the back of his mind, but for the life of him, he couldn't remember what it was. He rationalized, thinking his mind was already full of worry over his wife and son. He remembered the small boy on the barge and felt a twinge of pain, then pushed the thought out of his mind as he bathed in the wooden tub provided by the innkeeper, then ate a hearty meal.

He had to put on the same dusty clothes, having left in too great a hurry to remember to bring a change of clothing. Obviously, that wouldn't do. He'd have to purchase new clothes at one of the many shops near St. James Park. 'Twas obvious that in his station of life, he couldn't travel about London like a ragamuffin.

Weary of riding, Rob chose to walk and was glad about his decision. It felt good to loosen up the muscles of his legs and buttocks. Good to be alone with his thoughts. Glancing down the street, he noticed how hurried everyone seemed to be. All in a rush to get somewhere. What a dreary existence, he thought, feeling lonesome for Everly and the wonderfully easy pace of living there. He hated being in the crowded city, but at the moment, he had no choice if he was going to find Arianna and Robin.

Stopping at a shop recommended by the innkeeper, Rob was about to enter when the door opened and a familiar figure walked out. Black Bess, dressed in an obviously new outfit of men's clothing.

"Robert! I can't believe you're really here. My God, man, have you any idea what's been going on?"

Robert's heart sank. Taking her by the arm, he steered her over to the entrance of the park. "No, but you're going to tell me." He plunked her down on a rugged wooden bench and hovered over her. "Where are my wife and son?"

Black Bess almost lost the courage to tell him. She didn't want to have to be the one to break such terrible news to Robert. "Arianna is in seclusion at St. James Palace."

"And?" Rob asked impatiently, wanting to hear it all.

"Before I begin, let me just say that your wife and son are both in good health."

"I thank God for that much, but I fear you have more to say."

"Oh, Rob, it's all because of me. Arianna went to Dover to save my life and she succeeded, but, oh, dear God, she . . . she . . ."

Rob's face turned ashen as he waited to hear the dire news.

"Robert, Elizabeth took Robin from Arianna and declared him her ward."

Head reeling, Robert sat down beside Bess on the bench. The news was much worse than he expected. Robin, with Elizabeth? It was unthinkable. "Why in God's name would the queen ever do such a thing? Why?" But he knew the answer to that. There was but one reason the queen would do that. She had discovered Arianna's identity.

"Arianna! What has the queen done with her?"

"That's the good news, Rob. Arianna wisely accepted the queen's decision and was given her freedom. It seems the queen thinks they can continue on as before. What a fool Elizabeth is to think that. For Arianna is only biding her time, waiting for the moment when she can get her son back. She is a determined woman, Rob, and very courageous."

"No need to tell me that, for I know it too well. It

is that very foolish courage that so often gets her into trouble."

"It took a very wise woman to hold her emotions in check at such a horrendous moment. Give her credit for that much."

Rob gritted his teeth as if in pain. "If she is finally growing up, it's just a little too late. Why didn't she reach this new maturity before she lost us our son?"

Bess caressed Robert's shoulder. "I know the pain you must be feeling, and I wish there were something I could say that would ease it, but I know nothing anyone could say would help."

Tears formed in Rob's eyes, but he blinked them back. Tears would not bring back his son. Action would. And . . . help from the most powerful man in England. "Where was Leicester when all this was happening?"

"Leicester? What would he have to do with it? As far as I know, he was in Tilbury."

"Then he knows nothing of this?"

"He will soon, for the queen left to join him this morning."

"I know. I saw her procession of barges from the window of the inn I'm staying at." Then suddenly, the image of the small boy in the barge flashed in his head and he smashed his fist into the palm of his other hand. "Robin! Elizabeth took him to Tilbury with her, didn't she?"

"Aye, she did. How did you know?"

"I saw him. Dear God, I saw him, but I didn't know it was my son." Laughing maniacally, he went on. "But then, how could I have known? How could I know that my son would have been subjected to? . . .

How could I know that Arianna would act so rashly? How? How?" Rob couldn't go on. He was living a nightmare, nay, much worse; nightmares ended when you woke up. His would not end so easily.

"Robert, pull yourself together. Take a lesson from your wife's actions and stay calm."

"Calm? Do you have any idea how much I want to throttle Elizabeth this very moment? And Arianna's neck is no safer."

"I know, believe me, I do. I share your feelings about the queen, but there is only one effective way to deal with the power she has and that is with deception. There's not a nobleman in London who has not learned that trick to keep his neck safe. Nay, confronting the queen is folly; you must work behind her back."

Robert knew Bess was right, but oh, it was hard knowledge to swallow. He had spent his life living by his honesty and honor, and now, it seemed, the only way he could accomplish his goal was to become deceptive. But what was honor and honesty when the well-being of his wife and son was at stake? He would do whatever it took to save his family, play whatever game was necessary.

Filled with resolve, his mind was already at work. "I am prepared to do just that, Bess, but I'll need your help. I haven't worked out a plan yet, but I know one thing for certain: If I am to get my son back, I'm going to have to distance myself from Arianna. The queen must believe I am divorcing her, and think me that shouldn't be very hard to believe. God knows, I have reason enough for it."

"That would be a wise move, my lord. You will have

much more power to act if you are not associated with Arianna. But the queen will be back in a few days. You don't have much time. How can I help?"

"Are you sure you want to do this? I would think you'd want to stay as far away from that woman as you possibly can."

"Robert, you wound me. I pride myself on my daring; in fact, I believe I verily thrive on it. If you know of a way I can help you get your family back, then I am eager to hear of it."

Rob took in Bess's alluring form, realizing what a powerful weapon it could be. "We pretended to be lovers on Devil's Harp, why not again? With you on my arm, the whole of London will know very quickly that I am done with Arianna. And for my part, the sooner that is accomplished the sooner Elizabeth will believe it is true."

Taking Rob by the hands, Bess pulled him to his feet. "Then what are we waiting for? Let's begin. I trow, I've always wanted to be the plaything of a handsome nobleman."

Rob almost smiled. "Not so fast. We must think out every detail if this deception is to be convincing."

"Right you are, and the first little detail to be considered is a new wardrobe for you. Your attire is much too provincial."

Looking at her incredulously, he said, "I hardly think this is the time to worry about men's fashions."

"Trust me, my lord. The way you dress is an important consideration. Especially in this town. Come with me. We're going back to the shop where we met. I saw the perfect outfit for you there. Every woman in London will swoon at the sight of you."

"God's teeth, Bess, that's the last thing on my mind."

Bess laughed heartily. "Do you want to be believed? Then take my word for it. You'll be able to carry out your plan much easier if the queen believes you are so bitter over your marriage to Arianna that you deliberately sought the life of a sophisticated courtier. If nothing else, it will keep her off guard. What do you have to lose?"

Clothes were of no importance to Rob and hardly the first step he would have taken to get his son back, but he knew Bess was right. He would wear the latest fashions to match the splendid Bess. That would be one detail easy to accomplish, and one that would have the quickest results. For when the gossips of London got a glimpse of the new Earl of Everly, they would be sure to report it to the queen.

Laden down with packages from various shops, a weary Rob returned to The Stag's Horn that afternoon accompanied by Black Bess. He immediately informed the innkeeper that he wanted to rent the whole of the second floor as the Duke of Norbridge had before him. It would give him a base of operations and at the same time keep him in the thick of things. The Stag's Horn was a popular inn and had the reputation of being quite naughty. Many an Englishman brought his mistress there for an enjoyable evening's entertainment.

It was rumored that the queen herself had gone there in disguise one night, bent on seeing for herself the lascivious goings-on, and had been so scandalized that she returned three more times. The old girl was a bit of a bawd, it seemed.

Bess agreed to stay at the inn with Rob, grateful that she had a roof over her head. Her beloved ship, now lost to her, and the wild isle of Devil's Harp, almost deserted now, what with so many of the pirates conscripted into the service of Elizabeth, had been the only places she could call home. She would have to find a new life, and London was a good place to begin.

It had been too close a call for her when she had been imprisoned at Dover, and she never wanted to be put in that position again. As for Longfellow, if he survived and came back from the war with the Spanish unscathed, she would have to decide whether she wanted him in her life again. She would most certainly consider it if he gave up his life as a pirate, but what use in thinking of that now? She would be undertaking a venture that was not without danger. If Rob's plan backfired, her neck would be in jeopardy once again.

By the next afternoon, word had gotten out that the Earl of Everly was in residence at The Stag's Horn, and he received several calling cards from local lords and ladies, all with invitations attached to various dinners and balls.

Sorting through them, he found an engraved card from his old friend Will. It seemed the Duke of Norbridge was having a ball at his new manor house, overlooking St. James Park, that very night. Reading the scribbled message in Will's hand on the invitation, his heart began to pound. Arianna would be there.

It seemed as if it had been a month since he had seen her instead of a few short days, and yet, his first thought was to decline the invitation, to stay as far away from her as he could. But reason won out, and he decided to go. It would be the perfect occasion to show the world that he was estranged from his wife.

With Bess as his escort, there was sure to be a scene with Arianna. That it would be reported to the queen, he was certain. The question was, how was he going to keep his composure when he faced his wife? He loved her beyond reason, but he was also angrier with her than he had ever been in his life. Because of her, his son was in the hands of Elizabeth. Because of her, his life was falling apart.

He had already spent a small fortune today, but had only just begun to gather the props he needed for his deception. Before he was finished, he might have to go through his entire inheritance to get his son back. But what use was there for an inheritance if his son was lost to him? He would spend his last farthing to get Robin back. No, he had no idea what would happen when he was face to face with Arianna . . . but, oh God, he could hardly bear the wait.

Chapter Twenty-five

"Here now, my lady," Fiona pleaded, "you've been dallying long enough. The Duke of Norbridge's carriage is waiting for you."

"Send it away, Fiona," Arianna answered listlessly. "I haven't the strength to go."

"Why did I know you were going to say that? Well, 'twill do you no good to whine. You're going, and that's that."

"Oh, Fiona, I haven't the heart to spend an evening chattering mindlessly to lords and ladies with nothing more on their minds than having a good time, whilst my son is stolen from me."

"I'll tell you how and I'll tell you why you're going. You haven't seen young Will for nigh on a year now. The very sight of him will cheer you considerably. He's always been your champion, my lady. Tell him what's happened and he'll help you think of what to do."

"I can't involve him. I can't put his life in danger that way. And it would be. It wouldn't take much for the queen to remember that the Duke of Norbridge has always been a special friend of mine."

"Nonsense! The queen has no interest in the duke. She has no interest in anyone but you, my lady. Go to the party. Be amongst friends. If nothing else, it will do your heart good."

Arianna smiled wanly. "Do my heart good. Oh, how I have a need for that, for my heart is so full of pain and sorrow I don't know how I can go on."

Fiona covered her ears long enough to say, "I don't want to hear that kind of talk." Approaching Arianna with a silver comb, she pleaded, "Sweeting, let me put the finishing touches on your hair—that is, if those two . . . heathens will get out of the way long enough."

Fiona glared at Ruth and Naomi as they finger-talked at a furious rate. "What's all that flitting about with their hands? What are they saying about me now?"

Arianna almost smiled. "If you would learn their finger-talking as I have, you'd know what they're saying."

"Speak with my fingers? Never. Why, it's . . . it's barbaric." Then realizing that Arianna was guilty of that same barbaric practice, Fiona tried to remedy her slip of tongue. "That is to say, it's primitive. I mean, it's—"

"Enough of your prattling. I'll tell you what they said if you're so very curious. Naomi thinks I look too pale in blue and Ruth agrees."

"Well, I cannot disagree more. What do Ruth and Naomi know of paleness? Everyone is pale next to their skin. The blue is exactly the right color to wear. Shows off your delicateness and the paleness of your skin."

"Did you say *paleness* of my skin?" Arianna asked teasingly to make her point.

"What I meant was the lightness of . . . uh . . . I mean fairness of . . . I mean your delicate fairness. That's it. That's what I meant."

"Oh, Fiona, you're impossible. I'll be glad to leave this place, if only to get away from you. I vow, I don't know what Terrence sees in you. Have a care or you'll drive him away with your sharp tongue and stubborn ways."

Fiona blanched at Arianna's words.

"Oh, Fiona, I didn't mean it, truly I didn't. It's just my nerves are so tight. I don't want to face the world without my husband and son at my side, but since I must . . ." Taking a deep breath, Arianna steeled herself for the ordeal ahead. "Don't wait up for me. I will be in no mood to talk when I return." With that, Arianna walked out the door, out of the palace, and into the waiting carriage.

In a moment, she was being helped inside by a brightly dressed liveryman, her eyes opening in astonishment at the sight of the single occupant of the coach. "Will! I never expected you'd be here to escort me to your own home."

Smiling broadly, Will rose from his seat and helped her inside, hugging her in the process. "I couldn't wait to see you. My God, Arianna, you look magnificent. You're turning into a most enchanting beauty."

"You don't think I'm too . . . pale?" Arianna quipped, feeling suddenly high-spirited at the sight of her old friend.

"Pale? Yes, sweeting, you are very pale, but after the ordeal you've been through, 'tis no more than I expected." Drawing her down on the seat beside him, Will put his arm around Arianna and held her close. "Now begin at the beginning, and tell me everything."

By the time they reached Will's new home, Arianna had related the whole dismal story to him. "And . . . and now I am determined to find a way to get my son back."

"And what about Rob? Do you hope to get him back, too?"

"Oh, Will, I cannot dare to hope that much."

Will looked into her eyes, amazed to see no sign of tears. "I think you would dare anything, my girl. Anything at all."

As the coach pulled to a halt and the liveryman opened the door, Arianna became aware of her surroundings for the first time. "Oh, Will, I haven't begun to ask you anything. How's Felicia? Is she well? And why in God's name are you living here in London?"

Will laughed and took her by the arm, escorting her down the path to the house. "I wondered when you were going to get around to asking me that. First of all, Felicia is fine, as you'll soon see. She is expecting our first child. Which comes to my reason for renting a home in London. I want her to have the best of care from a physician. And that meant coming to London."

"I don't understand. If she is well . . . oh, dear, is Felicia having a difficult pregnancy?"

"No, no, nothing like that, but knowing how Colin's wife died in childbirth, I'm taking no chances with his sister. Just as soon as the babe's born and Felicia's strong enough, we'll be going back to Norbridge where we belong."

"I'm glad for that. London is no fit place to raise a child." Realizing what she had said, a lump came to her throat. *Robin. Oh, Robin.*

Will took her hand and kissed it. "My dearest friend, it grieves me to see you like this."

Before he could say any more, the manor door opened and Felicia's cheerful face peered out. "Oh, there you are, Arianna. I've been waiting ever so impatiently for you to come."

Embracing Arianna, Felicia looked over her shoulder at her husband, asking with her eyes how things were. The slow, solemn shaking of Will's head told her everything she needed to know. Putting on a cheery voice, Felicia guided Arianna into her house. "Come. It's time my friends met the most beautiful countess in all of England."

Smiling softly, Arianna put herself in her friend's hands and was soon being propelled from one group of people to the next, nodding her head and pretending interest in the lighthearted chatter surrounding her. But inside she was numb. It had been a mistake to come. No one in this huge house could possibly know what she was going through. No one here could help her get her child back. She would find a quiet corner and hide away, so as not to hurt Will and Felicia's feelings. Not for all the world did she want to spoil their party.

Remembering a small room to the right of the entranceway, she turned to go there . . . and almost walked into a man dressed elegantly in peach satin and velvet. She tilted her head up to apologize and was jolted by the sight of familiar brown eyes.

"Rob!"

Rob wasn't prepared to see Arianna looking so fragile and white. It was obvious that she was suffering mightily, but he steeled himself, remembering the part he was playing. "I should be flattered you remember my name, since you've obviously forgotten everything else connected with me."

Arianna's heart sank hearing the coldness in Rob's voice. She tried to answer him but was too choked up to speak. What use, anyway? She had nothing to say in her own defense. He had every right to be angry.

She looked away, avoiding his direct stare, and was tortured with the sight of Black Bess looking exquisitely beautiful in a velvet gown of soft grey. A dull pain enveloped her chest. Rob and Bess together. Looking as if they belonged to each other.

It was hard for Rob to continue with his act, seeing how stricken Arianna looked, but for the sake of their future together, he would force himself to be cruel. "Seems you've forgotten several little things, like marriage, home, family, a little boy with bright blue eyes and brown hair."

The room began to swim. "And you, Robert, have you not forgotten something, too? Have you not forgotten the vows you took to forsake all others when you married me?"

Her voice was weak and tremulous, but Rob persisted, knowing that their confrontation was being witnessed by some of Elizabeth's greatest gossips.

"Those sacred words sound foreign to your tongue. Too bad you didn't remember them before you went traipsing off to Dover." His words came out more forceful than he planned and he realized he was no longer play-acting. Held back too long, they now spilled out like a battering rain. "Too bad you didn't think of Robin then. You remember Robin, don't you, Arianna? He *was* your son."

His anguished words hit her like a blow, and she cried out, "No more. Please. No more." In the tense and fragile state she was in, Rob's anger was too much to take. A searing pain tore through Arianna's abdomen, doubling her over, and she clutched at her stomach, cradling it with her arms.

Rob watched in silent horror, his anger forgotten in his concern for his wife. Instinctively, he reached out for her. "What is it?"

Realizing what was happening, Bess shouted, "It's the baby. In the name of God, it's the baby. Do something."

Comprehension flooded Rob's senses and he reacted instantly, scooping Arianna up into his arms and striding up the stairs two at a time, Bess and Felicia following behind.

Directing Rob to a bedchamber, Felicia ran into the room and pulled down the coverlet while Bess turned up an oil lantern so they would have more light to see by.

Arianna gave a little shudder as Rob laid her on the bed, squeezing her eyes shut in pain, then suddenly she went limp, her breathing becoming shallow.

Rob's face was white as he leaned over her, calling her name. "Arianna, Rose Petal." There was no response. Fighting for composure, he turned to Felicia, "Do something."

Pulling herself together, Felicia exclaimed, "Help me undress her. And Bess, go back downstairs and help Will with our guests. There's nothing you can do here."

Bess was happy to oblige. She couldn't help but feel partly to blame for what had happened. She *and Rob.* What had they been thinking to deliberately upset Arianna in her delicate condition?

Rob and Felicia worked on Arianna's clothing, removing her bodice first. The sight and sweet touch of her soft skin flooded Rob's senses with longing for the wife he had lost, and he felt an even greater sense of loss knowing she could die.

"Don't dawdle. Help me. Lift her hips so I can pull her skirts off."

Rob pulled himself together and lifted Arianna's hips, his eyes never leaving her breasts. The soft rising and falling of her chest reassuring him that she was still alive. In a moment they had Arianna out of her clothing and lying under a sheet on the soft feather bed.

Felicia quickly noticed that every time Rob touched Arianna, she responded in some way, and she knew he alone could bring her around. "Rob, put your hands on her belly."

Rob stared at her as if she had gone crazy.

"Do it. Massage her abdomen with gentle strokes."

Rob obeyed, praying Felicia knew what she was doing. Laying his hands on her gently rounded belly, he began to massage her, happy to be able to help in any way. He had been a fool to let his anger get the best of him. He had observed how delicate and pale she looked. Had known she was in no condition to hear his tirade. But he had persisted. It would be no one's fault but his own if she lost their child.

Hearing her moan softly, Rob realized she was responding to the touch of his hands. He saw her head moving back and forth in rhythm with his stroking, and he knew that somewhere deep within, she was aware of what he was doing. Encouraged, he worked harder, speaking to her in a soft voice, relieved to see the pained expression disappear from her face.

He continued his gentle stroking, aware of the small life that caused the small contour of Arianna's stomach. So small a contour that none but the most observant would ever realize she was carrying a child.

The massaging was helping her relax, and it was having the same effect on him. All he had needed was to touch her and everything was right. It had ever been so.

"Arianna? Can you hear me? Wake up, Rose Petal."

Arianna heard her husband's voice from a long distance away. In a dream-like trance, she answered him, unaware she was speaking out loud. "Don't make me wake up. Please, no. I don't want to wake up to a world where my son is gone and my husband despises me. Let me sleep and dream forever. Let me remember what it was like to be Robert Warwick's wife . . . to be Robin's mother."

Rob listened to Arianna, and all the while his heart was breaking in two. Overcome with emotion, he knelt at the side of the bed and buried his head in her belly, sobbing.

Touched by the emotional scene, Felicia gave Rob a few moments alone with Arianna. He was all the medicine she needed.

When she returned, he was still kneeling at her side.

Speaking softly, she placed her hand on his shoulder. "It's all right, Robert. The danger has passed. If she were going to lose the child, it would have happened by now. All she needed was to feel her husband's touch. You eased her pain and suffering, and the terrible anxiety and tension she's had so much of. She'll sleep soundly now."

Rob took a deep, shuddering breath and composed himself before standing up and facing Felicia. "Praise God for that. Felicia . . . will you take care of her for me? I cannot stay."

"I don't understand."

Taking Arianna's hand, he kissed it tenderly, then placed it on her chest. "I can't explain anything to you now, Felicia, but I've got to distance myself from Arianna so that I can retain my freedom. Without it, I won't be able to help her or Robin. Can you understand that? Their future depends on my being able to act, to defend what's mine."

"Oh, Robert, of course I'll take care of her. You needn't worry about that. But, dear God, why did this have to happen?"

"No use in thinking of that. It has happened. Now I must find a way to remedy it." Striding to the door, he said softly, "Stand by her, Felicia. In the coming days, when she hears of my . . . my petition for divorce and other disturbing news, she'll have need of a friend such as you."

Rob took a step toward the door, forcing himself to do what he must do. He walked down the stairs and out the door, oblivious to the elegantly clad lords and ladies who stared at him with curiosity, oblivious to

Black Bess who stood watching with compassion in her eyes.

He was aware of nothing but the effort it took to place one foot in front of the other, knowing each step he took was a betrayal of his heart's desire. Knowing every step took him farther and farther away from the one he loved most.

He was deliberately walking away from Arianna, and it was the hardest thing he had ever done in his life.

Chapter Twenty-six

From a great distance, Arianna heard her son crying. The heartbreaking sound of his voice penetrated her very soul, pulling her from her bed in desperate need to soothe away his tears. But . . . something was wrong. Where was his bed? Where was he? Where? Where? Where? She had to find him. He needed her.

Something scratched at her arm, and suddenly aware of her surroundings, she saw she was in some sort of maze made up of lifeless shrubbery, barren of leaves. Everywhere she turned Arianna was surrounded by the dead bushes, and the dull brown, sterile branches jabbed at her, stabbed at her, as she tried to make her way through the maze in search of her son.

She ran on and on, haunted by his cries, but each time she tried to find her way to him it turned into a dead end. No, oh no, she had to find him, she had to find her way. Robin needed her. He needed . . .

Her body jerked violently, and her eyes flew open. It was only a dream. No, it was much more than a dream. It was a warning that Robin was in need of her.

The thought of him frightened and alone was more than she could bear. Dear God, she had to get her son back before something happened to him.

Stop it! It did no good to think of such heartbreaking things. The only way she could go on was to keep her head and, oh God, her sanity, if she was ever going to get her baby back.

Baby! Her hands flew to her stomach, reassured that the soft little mound was still there. Her new babe was safe. She hadn't lost it. She remembered the gentle massaging of her belly and the release of anxiety that followed, and she knew the touch of Rob's hands had eased her pain and made her contractions stop. Oh, Rob, I need you so.

Sensing suddenly that she was not alone in the room, Arianna sat up. Please let it be Rob.

A soft feminine voice murmured to her from a chair in the corner of the room. " 'Tis me, Arianna."

Swallowing her disappointment, Arianna smiled at Felicia. "Have you been sitting there all night?"

Felicia stood and stretched her arms. "I have, and it is a most comfortable chair. I mean to recommend it to Will when I am going through the long, weary hours of childbirth."

Making her way over to the bed, Felicia sat down on the edge. "How are you feeling this morn?"

"I'm fine. Really. I think it was just the jolt of seeing Rob. . . . Oh, Felicia, it was the hardest thing I've ever done, facing him . . . knowing that I had lost him his son. Where is he? I thought . . . after last night that I'd awake to find him sitting here. Tell me he isn't angry with me anymore. Tell me he has forgiven me."

"Arianna . . . he's gone."

"Gone? Where? When will he be back?"

"He won't be back, Arianna. He has to stay away if he is to find a way to get Robin back. He prays you understand."

"Oh, no, he mustn't try to get Robin back. It's too dangerous. I'm in a much better position to get Robin. Send Will to him, please. Tell him not to do anything rash."

Felicia could see how close to breaking Arianna was. Caressing her shoulder, she said, "My poor, sweet Arianna. You're in no position to do anything now. Why, for heaven's sake, you almost lost your child. You must rest, gather your strength. Don't worry so about Rob. He won't do anything foolish. He'll stay safe."

"I wish I could believe you, but I know too well that everyone who comes near me gets hurt."

"Oh, fah, that's not true and you well know it."

Close to crying, Arianna said, "Please, let's talk no more of this. 'Tis much too painful."

"Then we'll talk about me and my ungainly shape." Felicia patted her swollen stomach. "I look as though I've swallowed a boulder, and methinks the child is every bit as heavy as one. Can you believe it's not due for another month yet? Will swears it will not be another week. Do you suppose men have an instinct for knowing those things about their wives?"

"Husbands as sensitive as yours do."

Felicia smiled warmly. "He is a dear, isn't he? If not for you, I'd never have met him. I owe you for that."

"And I mean to collect. Would it be presumptuous for me to ask if I could stay with you and Will for a little while? I . . . don't want to go back to St. James. The queen will be back soon, and . . . and . . ."

"Oh, Arianna, there was no need to ask. Will and I already discussed it. Of course we want you to stay."

"Good. That solves one problem. I want to stay close to Robin, but I don't want to stay at the palace with her. I'm afraid I couldn't trust myself around her. My urge to kill her is too strong." Seeing Felicia's shocked look, Arianna steeled her jaw. "Don't look so shocked. I'm sure there are a number of people in this country who wish the same of her, but I warrant, none as much as me."

"Arianna, you've always been so gentle, I can't believe you would ever deliberately harm anyone."

"Then you know me not."

"Oh, yes I do. I don't think you really want her dead. Think for a moment of actually doing it. Visualize it in your head, then tell me you could really go through with it."

Arianna had never really thought it out clearly before, and what Felicia said gave her pause. Was it possible that she didn't have what it takes to actually kill the woman, no matter how deep her hatred?

Delving deep inside her mind, Arianna thought about it in great depth before she answered. "You know, on the surface, it's easy for me to say yes, but deep down, when actually faced with Elizabeth standing before me, I really don't know if I could do it or not. Don't misunderstand me. The thought of her being dead gives me great satisfaction, but being the one to plunge a knife through her flesh, to cause her death . . . In truth, I don't know."

Felicia was astonished at Arianna's answer. For

Arianna to even ponder the question showed how very serious she was. It made her all the more grateful for her life with Will. She never wanted to be in Arianna's predicament, for she doubted she had the strength to survive it. Shivering, she said, "You're right. Let's put our dreary thoughts away and think of pleasant things."

A sad little smile played across Arianna's face. Pleasant things? If only it were possible. If only she had her husband and son. If only . . .

By late that afternoon, Arianna was settled in Will and Felicia's new home, along with her three attendants, who made the short trip from St. James Palace riding in the luxury of the duke's carriage. It was a happy reunion that lasted late into the night as Arianna and Felicia talked, catching up on the events of the past year.

Ruth, Naomi, and Fiona listened in fascination. The three attendants were assigned the small sleeping chamber off of Arianna's larger one, and they went to bed that night breathing much easier away from the lofty world of St. James Palace.

By the time the sun was high in the sky the next day, Elizabeth had returned, and by that very evening a page had been sent to the manor informing the Countess of Everly that her presence was desired at St. James Palace at once.

There was no escape from the queen, it seemed. No escape this side of death. That dismal thought jolted Arianna into rebellion and she set her jaw, determined to become victor in whatever deadly game Elizabeth was playing now. Reassuring her friends and attendants that she would be fine, she accompanied the page back to St. James Palace.

Arianna grew angrier and angrier as she climbed the stairs that led her to the queen, and that anger made her stronger. She was tired of being a pawn, a victim to the selfish queen's desires. She was tired of living with the threat of Elizabeth's wrath always hanging over her head. From this moment on, she would live by her wits as she never had before, do whatever she must to be reunited with her son.

Following the page into a room, Arianna braced herself to face the queen and was surprised to find she was in Elizabeth's own bedchamber. Her eyes quickly scanned the room for Robin, but he was nowhere to be seen. With a heavy heart, she curtsied.

Impatiently bidding her to rise with a flourish of her hand, Elizabeth proclaimed haughtily, "I expected to find you waiting here where I left you, Arianna, and was greatly disappointed to find you gone."

Arianna bit down on her tongue to keep from answering as she wanted. Did the queen regard her as she would a piece of furniture? Did Elizabeth think her only reason for living was to cater to the queen's selfish whims? Keeping her voice under control, she answered, "Forgive me, Your Grace, I thought it was only my son you wanted to keep. You did tell me I was free to do as I wished, or did I misinterpret you?"

Elizabeth narrowed her eyes. She had expected a docile, broken little girl but instead found a woman still unbeaten. Damn, if she didn't admire her all the more for that. Was it Leicester's blood or the Scottish queen's that gave her such a strong will?

"You did not misinterpret me, but rather it is I who

have misinterpreted you. I thought you would be eager to stay here so that you could be near your son."

"You made it clear that I will not be able to see him for some time, and believe it or not, I agree with you. 'Twould be too hard on Robin to see me, only to be torn from my arms again. It was for his sake that I left."

"You are an extraordinary woman, Arianna, I'll give you that. But then, I have always admired your compassionate, unselfish nature. And knowing your motive was for the most loving of reasons, I shall concede. It would not be good for you to see Robin right now. He's being . . . ah . . . quite persistent in his desire to leave. It will be some time, I fear, before he will be ready to see you again."

Arianna's heart sank. Her dream had been right. Robin must be truly heartbroken and lonely. *Damn you to hell, Elizabeth. Damn you to hell!*

The rage inside her threatened to break loose and she knew she had to get away from the queen quickly. "Then if we are in agreement, I'll take leave of you—"

"Not so fast. There is yet another matter I wish to speak to you about. Upon my return, I was quite puzzled to find a petition of divorce signed by your husband. To say the least, I was astonished. I thought Robert's love for you unconditional. Was I wrong?"

Arianna blinked back her surprise. *Divorce! Rob!* That was something she had never considered. Shocked beyond belief, Arianna tried to digest the news, but it seemed too incredible. No, Rob would never do that. He might lock her in the tower of Everly Castle, he might take her over his knee and spank her thoroughly, he might stay angry with her a long, long time, but this . . .

Elizabeth saw the shock on Arianna's ashen face. "Dear child, I'm so sorry. I thought you knew. If you do not want to dissolve your marriage, then I will see that you have your way. Whatever you wish in this matter shall be the course I take."

Recovering from her shock, Arianna answered in a too-quiet voice. "Let him have his divorce. I have been a willful wife. He deserves much better."

The answer pleased Elizabeth much. Arianna would be free now to be at her beck and call. In the past, she had always resented the short time Robert allowed Arianna to spend with her. All that would change now.

"So be it. I will set the action in motion. Before long you will be free of him. He's shown his true colors now, methinks, deserting you when you have need of him the most."

"Your Grace, don't think less of him for that. Because of me, he lost a son. For that reason alone, he deserves to be free of me."

Elizabeth did not like to be reminded that she had taken a child from his parents. It ruined her good spirits. "Well, we'll speak of it no more. Put the past in the past, I always say. Today you start a new life, and I will make sure that it will be a happy one for you. In two weeks time I shall be having a grand masque, with pantomimes and entertainment of all sorts, and you shall attend. I promise you it will be quite an inventive evening. Instead of holding it in the palace, it will be under the stars in St. James Park."

"That sounds lovely, Your Grace, but—"

"I will hear no buts. You *will* attend and . . . your husband will be there, too, though it certainly gave me pause inviting him after I learned where he was staying."

"I don't understand."

Elizabeth gave Arianna a sympathetic smile. "Of course you don't, my dear. Robert is staying at The Stag's Horn, an inn that caters to the most, shall I say, sophisticated tastes. 'Tis quite a scandalous place. Oh, dear, I see I'm upsetting you. Don't give it another thought. Just be glad you are rid of him, my dear."

So, Elizabeth was going to dismiss her marriage as easily as old straw swept from a castle's floor. Was the masque supposed to make her forget all about Rob? All about her son? Was she supposed to blithely forget that her family had been destroyed? How would Elizabeth feel if she lost Leicester? Arianna realized what she was thinking and superstitiously tried to take it back. Nothing must happen to Leicester. No. She couldn't bear it if she lost her father, too.

"As I was telling you, the masque will be quite inventive. I will be giving away a purse of gold for the most daring costume. That should prove to be most entertaining. And, Arianna, I shall be most interested in seeing what kind of costume you come up with."

"I shall be most interested in seeing that myself. I imagine the more jaded members of your court will be quite daring. It will be hard to top them, I warrant."

Elizabeth laughed. "Not if you put your delightful creative mind to use. I'm sure you'll come up with something much more daring than Black Bess."

"Black Bess?"

"Oh, didn't I mention that she will be there, too?

She's a very striking woman, is she not? Beautiful enough to attract a man vulnerable in his separation from his wife, don't you think?"

Arianna realized what Elizabeth was up to. She was being tested. The queen obviously wanted to know how she felt about Rob. Wanted to see how she reacted to Black Bess's interest in her husband. Well, she wouldn't disappoint her. "Do you mean to imply that Black Bess is trying to steal my husband?"

"Oh dear, I've upset you."

"Upset me? Oh, yes, enough to make sure that I show up that little witch. Daring costume, you say? I have a costume in mind that will definitely make an impression on Black Bess *and* my husband. Next to me, Black Bess will look like an inconspicuous unkempt little boor, and Robert . . . Robert will see a side of me he's never seen before."

Elizabeth's eyebrow arched high. She had no doubt that Arianna's costume would be exceptional. It was going to be enjoyable having her around. She was sure to keep things very lively at court.

Arianna left the palace feeling much stronger and more alive than she had in a long time. She had been challenged, and it felt good. For there was finally something in her life she could do something about. She would meet Elizabeth's challenge and excel. She would be the most daring of all at the masque, and all of London would know that she was a woman to be reckoned with. That when Arianna Warwick set out to do something, it got done. That she was not a victim, but a woman of bold action.

It would be the first step in her revenge upon the queen. The first step in winning back her son, and yes, she couldn't help but think of one other thing her daring costume would accomplish. For, without a doubt, it would make Robert take particular notice of her. If he thought the gown that bared her rouged breasts had been daring, wait until he saw what she planned on wearing to the masque.

Stepping lively, Arianna ran down the stairs and out the door, breathing deeply of the scented breeze that blew in from the park. Things were definitely looking better.

Upstairs in her bedchamber, Elizabeth preened, sighing like a cat lapping cream as she thought of how well things were going for her. The Spanish rout had never transpired, their ships washed up on many shores, driven there by terrible storms and by her own brave men, Arianna's pirate friends amongst them. And though her brave countrymen must stay ever alert, it seemed England was safe for the moment.

The biggest problem she had to deal with now was Leicester. She frowned, thinking of his reaction to the sight of his grandson accompanying her to Tilbury. He hadn't been pleased at all to hear that she had made the boy her ward.

It was no more than she expected, and she knew it shouldn't matter to her, for if Robin's separation from Arianna was painful to Leicester, it was no more than he deserved, having slept with the sluttish Scottish queen. But still, it did bother her greatly, for she wanted him to be happy that she would raise his grandson. She wanted his loyalty to *her* to override even his love for his daughter.

But that was not to be, and she couldn't help but feel a little jealous that he loved another woman, even if that woman was his daughter. Jealousy was a new and alien feeling to her concerning Leicester. In truth, in all the time he was married, she had never been jealous of Leicester's wife. And why should she? Leicester had always been her creature, his love for her as powerful as hers for him. But she would learn to live with these new feelings, and in time, mayhap little Robin would draw them all closer together.

A sudden shiver snaked its way up her spine, causing a momentary lapse in her reverie, but it soon passed. Nothing was amiss. Of course not. Robin belonged to her. Arianna was hers to command, and Leicester, her dear lover, would always be at her side.

Chapter Twenty-seven

Will and Felicia were amazed at the transformation in Arianna when she returned from St. James Palace. Except for her pale countenance, she looked her old vibrant self. But they soon found to their dismay, that it was rage that gave Arianna strength, the need for revenge that gave her purpose. In sooth, Arianna was almost feverish in her determination, and that made them all the more worried about her.

Hoping to distract her from such destructive thoughts, Will brought her out to the small mews behind the house and introduced her to a peregrine falcon he had just purchased for Felicia. "What do you think of her?"

A tinge of sadness flickered in Arianna's eyes for a moment as she thought back to the wonderful carefree days at Will's castle in Norbridge, when she was disguised as a boy, and he and Robert her comrades. She had taught them the art of falcony, and they had taught her the meaning of friendship. "She's a beauty, Will. Have you flown her yet?"

"No. Before I trust the bird with Felicia, I'd like you

to fly her. You have such a way with birds, 'tis uncanny."

"If you think I have a way with birds, you should meet Black Bess. She teaches birds to talk, and to . . . and to . . ."

"And to what?"

The image of Black Bess and her parrot swam through Arianna's brain. The parrot had flown to Longfellow on command and knocked his hat from his head. It came to her, then, the way to have her revenge upon the queen, and without spilling a drop of her blood. Elizabeth's vanity. Her incredible, mindless vanity was the key to her revenge.

"It's not important, Will. I'll be glad to try the hawk and, if you don't mind, teach it an amusing little trick."

"By the devilish look in your eye, I have a feeling you have more than an innocent little trick in mind, and I think it would be very wise of me not to ask what you are up to."

"You know me better than anyone, except Rob, of course, and sometimes I think perhaps even better than he."

"I have no doubt of that, since it was I who put you up to going after Robert in the first place. Go ahead. Teach the peregrine your little trick. If it will help put roses back in your cheeks, I'm all for it."

That night, Arianna could not sleep. Her mind was too full of what was to come. She had the weapon for her revenge, for it would take no time at all to teach the bird that simple trick, but she would have to have the means to carry it through. Thinking of the queen's challenge to her to wear the most daring costume, it suddenly hit her how to carry out her revenge. The queen loved to be entertained in new and innovative ways. So . . . she would plan an evening's entertainment that Elizabeth would not soon forget.

But to do that, she would have to disarm the queen so she would not be suspicious. That shouldn't be too hard. If she met the queen's challenge and showed up at the masque in the most daring costume of all, it would go a long way toward making Elizabeth believe that Arianna was putty in her hands.

But . . . what she planned was not without danger. Arianna would have to make sure that no one would be endangered by her act, including herself. She was more than confident she could do just that. After all, Black Bess had certainly carried out her little trick with the parrot without anyone ever suspecting it was a deliberate act.

She would have her revenge and at the same time get her son back, for when the queen stood before her people bereft of hair, the pandemonium it caused would give her ample time to reach her son and carry him to safety. All it would take was a little luck, a peregrine falcon, several brightly colored doves, and . . . a lot of courage to pull it off.

Two weeks later, Robert made his way into the inn with Black Bess and heard boisterous voices coming from the tavern room. He knew immediately whom they belonged to. He steered Bess toward the table where the four giants sat, guzzling down tankards of ale. The Terrible Four and one other, he thought, counting five heads instead of four.

"My lord, you've finally come," Thomas proclaimed. "If we had to wait any longer, none of us would be sober enough to navigate."

"So I see," Rob said, folding his arms across his chest. "What brings you to The Stag's Horn? Last I heard you had accompanied my wife to Dover."

"Uh, that's what we wanted to see you about. To apologize for interfering in your affairs. I swear to you, we had no idea that your wife and child were in any danger, else . . . else . . ."

Rob cut him off in a curt tone. "What happened in Dover? Why didn't you stay with her? The very least you could have done was to stay by her side."

Terrence stood, his huge frame blocking the light from the window behind him, and addressed the earl in a solemn voice. "My lord, we tried very hard to do that but were not allowed to accompany the countess inside to see the queen. And then, when she didn't come out that last time . . . well, we immediately made inquiries and were told to be on our way, or we'd be conscripted to fight the Spanish along with Longfellow and his men. I swear to you, we had no choice but to leave."

Robert tried to stay angry at them but could not. He knew what it was like to try to protect Arianna and fail. "I don't blame you men, I blame myself. If you're still willing, I'd like your help." Then remembering there was a stranger amongst them, Rob said pointedly, "You've picked up a new friend along the way, I see."

"So have ye," the stranger answered back, nodding his head toward Black Bess.

Rob recognized the voice, but certainly not the garb

of James Stuart VI, King of Scotland. Dressed in the simple hunter-green of a woodsman, James sat there looking for all the world as if he were one of the common lot.

"Your Ma—"

A finger over James's mouth warned Rob not to identify him as king. Rob complied, all the more curious as to what was going on.

"I've been hearing disturbing things about you, Robert. Not the least of which involves this lovely young lass."

Looking at Bess with interest, he continued. "You're a bonnie thing to behold, lassie. Too bonnie, I'm thinking, for a married man to be seen with. It wouldna be hard for people to mistake an innocent friendship for much more than that."

"That's all for the good," Rob said, bracing himself for an argument with the king of Scotland.

"That's a curious thing to say, man."

Speaking in a low voice, Rob said, "Elizabeth has made my son her ward."

"Aye, I know. I was there when she took him. God strike me, I dinna know how Arianna got through that terrible moment without breaking down. She's taking it much better than I imagined, but she needs you, lad. Needs you bad."

"You're a fool if you really believe she's taking it well. Did you know she almost lost the child she's carrying? In truth, she may have lost it yet, for all I know. I have no way of knowing. I had to leave her with her friends."

"And why did you have to do that, Robbie lad?"

"So that the world—no, bugger the world—so that

Elizabeth will think I want to divorce Arianna. I can't risk having the queen imprison me now. I have to disarm her long enough to find a way to get my son back."

James saw the deep sorrow etched on Robert's face and knew the man was suffering greatly. "I'm working on that goal meself," James said in a low voice. "If we join forces, we can accomplish that task all the faster."

"It can't be fast enough for me." Running his fingers through his hair, Rob's voice grew hoarse. "It's eating me up not knowing how she is."

"My lord," Terrence said cheerfully, "there's nothing to prevent me from going over there and seeing for myself that she's all right. No one will think anything of it since I am courting Fiona."

Rob's face brightened. "Good thinking, Terrence. If you do that, I'll be very grateful. Thank you."

" 'Tis the least I can do to help make up for the harm we've done. And 'twill give me a chance to see my sweet Fiona. Damned if she isn't the most desirable woman I've ever met."

Rob smiled to himself. It never occurred to him to think of Fiona as a desirable woman. Beauty was in the eyes of the beholder, most definitely.

"That's settled, then," James said. "Which leads me to business I need to discuss with Robert . . . in private. Shall we adjourn to your rooms?"

Turning to Black Bess, James bowed low. "Forgive me for taking away your escort, but I think ye'll find these three fine lads will more than compensate for one missing earl."

Addressing the giant men, he continued, "Lads, sorry I canna stay, but it's been lovely. Did you know,

Robert, the Terrible Four is thinking of making me one of their own. What was it we were going to call ourselves? . . . Ah, yes, the Fabulous Five." Laughing uproariously, James slapped each of the men on the shoulder, then left with Robert.

A few moments later, fresh tankards of ale in hand, Rob ushered James into his rooms. "What business do you want to discuss, James?"

"Family business," James answered, downing the ale quickly with a tilt of his head. "Methinks it's time to think seriously of getting your family out of England, and the sooner the better."

"I've been thinking the same myself, but right now, there's not much of my family to move, is there? My son is in Elizabeth's hands and my wife . . . she . . . well, that's it, isn't it? She isn't my wife anymore."

"Is that the way you want it, Robbie?"

"What I want seems to have very little to do with anything. Did I want her to go riding off to Dover? No! Did I want her to expose our son to the queen? No! Did I want her to sail to Devil's Harp or undress for that bastard Longfellow? *No! No! No!*"

"I understand, Robbie lad, and methinks I'm asking the wrong question. Rather I should ask you if you still love her enough to be her champion . . . rescue her from Elizabeth?"

"You know the answer to that."

"Then, to do that, you will have to remove her from England. And, Robert, I wouldna take too long about it. She's liable to do something drastic to get back her son and that could have a disastrous result."

"No need to tell me that; I know her far better than

you do. But the dilemma is . . . until she has her son in her arms, she'll never agree to leave England."

"I expected no different. So . . . between the two of us, smart lads that we are, we should be able to come up with a workable plan."

Rob grinned, suddenly buoyant. "How can I lose with a king on my side!"

"Aye, a king who has five ships at his disposal, enough to carry everyone in Everly Castle who wishes to go with you to Scotland. If it meets with your approval, I'll send three of my ships up the coast on pretense of taking on water and food and goods the Earl of Everly so generously donated. In truth, the purpose will be to load your belongings and the people who want to go to Scotland with you."

Robert's chest felt tight and heavy when he answered. "I know that is the only way my family will ever be free of Elizabeth, but oh, 'tis a hard thing to do."

"Is it too soon for you, lad? Would you rather have more time to think about it?"

"Time is a luxury I cannot afford! No, send your ships. It won't come as too big a shock to my mother. I have often discussed with her the possibility of having to move to Scotland."

James patted Rob's hand. "I feel for you, lad, but truth to say, I canna be sorry that you'll be living in my own sweet country. I'm selfish enough to want my sister nearby, and my wee nephew. And as for you, Robert, you're an extraordinary man. It will be good to count you as my friend and confidant. I'll make certain you never regret making this momentous decision."

Downing his ale, Rob thought of the uncertain future and of the woman who was responsible for his having to leave his beloved homeland. She was the author of all his joy and of all of his anguish. She was his sweet Rose Petal, but she was also the thorn of the rose, pricking his heart, causing him incredible pain. Would there ever come a day when he could have the sweetness without the thorns?

James and Robert worked on the details of moving his family to Scotland, then turned their thoughts to how they would rescue Robin, whilst Rob grew more and more anxious to hear from Terrence. Hearing a knock on the door at last, Robert flung it open, greeting Terrence impatiently. "Well? Tell me. How does she fare?"

"I . . . don't know how to tell you this, my lord, but . . ."

Robert's heart sank. "She lost the child?"

"No. She's fine. Nay, more than that. She is veritably brimming over with energy and busily engaged in . . . in . . ."

"In what?"

"I really can't say, my lord. 'Tis all very strange. The countess was making a strange concoction, a . . . a brownish, powdery sort of mixture that—"

"Terrence, what Arianna was cooking is of no—"

"But, my lord, that's just it. She wasn't cooking it. The mixture isn't meant to be consumed, but . . . but to be rubbed on the skin. I mean to say . . ."

"James, have you any idea what this blithering fool is trying to say?"

" 'Tis puzzling to me, too. Terrence, didna Arianna explain what she was doing?"

"No, she was too feverishly busy for that, and I do mean that sincerely. But—and this is going to sound mighty strange—she did ask me to expose my arm and proceeded to rub the mixture on me." Rolling up the sleeve of his shirt, he said, "You see? It turned me arm every bit as brown as Ruth and Naomi; in fact, she did compare the color to theirs and seemed pleased at the result."

Rob and James examined Terrence's arm carefully, turning it over and over. "She's up to something, James, but I vow I don't know what."

"What was her mood, Terrence? Perhaps that would give us a clue. You say she was brimming with energy, and you said feverish. Is that an exaggeration, man?"

"Not hardly, Your Majesty. I've never seen her so full of life since the day I met her. And restless, my lord, and . . . and strangely elated, too."

Rob looked at Terrence as if he had gone mad. "Elated? My God, she just had her son torn from her arms. How could she be elated?"

"That was my first thought, too. I don't know what to make of it, and I haven't half explained her mood yet. On top of everything else, she was acting . . . uh . . . quite . . . bold."

"Explain what you mean, lad," the king said, trying to understand what possessed Arianna to act so strangely.

"Well, here's how it was. After she finished anointing me flesh with that brown concoction, why, she looked me up and down, squeezed me arms some, and then proceeded to ask me if I was strong enough to lift her over my head. Well, when I told her I could, she wouldn't take me at my word but insisted that I demonstrate on her person, right then and there."

Rob groaned. "She's up to something, and it has something to do with the masque!"

"Then, we'll be sure to stay close to her there. Prevent her from doing anything rash. But it won't be easy. The park is quite large. We'll need your help, Terrence, and that of your brothers, too. I'll find costumes for all four of you to wear so that you won't be conspicuous. We'll all keep our eyes on her."

"Begging your pardon, my lord, but you won't need a costume for myself. The countess has already ordered one for me to wear. I'm to be some kind of god of the hot'n'tot people, whoever they be. And I am to spend tomorrow with her, rehearsing my part. She hasn't told me what I am to do, but said that I will be accompanying her and Ruth and Naomi. 'Tis very odd, but Fiona wasn't invited to come along."

Rob and James exchanged looks, reciting in unison, "She's up to something."

Chapter Twenty-eight

The group gathered in the Earl of Everly's rooms at
The Stag's Horn was a strange sight to behold. Robert, Thomas, Thaddeus, and Timothy were all dressed
as Roman gladiators. Their masculine chests were
bare, except for the leather straps that crisscrossed
from shoulders to waist, their legs naked in the fashion
of ancient Rome. The only female present, Black Bess,
was garbed in a revealing costume of her own. It
looked like one the women of ancient Greece once
wore, one-shouldered, with a single breast exposed for
the world to see. The men found her costume most
provocative, circling around and around her as they
shouted out their guesses as to who she was supposed
to represent.

Bess was insulted that they didn't immediately know
who she was. "If you were at all learned, you'd know
I'm dressed as an Amazon woman."

"An Amazon? No wonder I couldn't guess," Robert
teased. "You forgot a most important detail."

"Oh, and what is that?"

"Amazons didn't *bare* their breast, they lopped it off

so it wouldn't interfere with their aim when they shot their crossbow."

Bess made a face at Robert. "Very amusing, my lord, but I think I'll forget that gruesome little detail if you don't mind."

"Don't listen to him, dearling," Thaddeus said. "It doesn't matter who you're trying to portray. It only matters that you'll win. If it was up to me, you'd win the purse of gold for sure, and I vow every man in this room will agree with me."

A chorus of ayes greeted those words, making Black Bess feel like a winner already. For who but she was lucky enough to count all these splendid men as friends?

When it was time to go, Rob walked out the door, his stomach churning at the thought of seeing Arianna in a few short moments. What was the little witch up to? He knew that whatever it was, it would not be to his liking. He only prayed it would not be something that would put her in jeopardy.

A clap of thunder greeted him as he stepped out into the night air, and a sultry breeze blew across his face. The promise of rain heartened him, for he felt entirely too foolish in his brief costume and hoped a downpour would end the masque before it began.

Leading the small group down the road the short distance to the park, Rob was surprised to see how many revelers shared the way, and he suddenly realized it wouldn't be easy finding Arianna in the crowd.

As they approached the entrance, a cheer went up from the spectators who thronged the edge of the green. Their mood was festive, for it was a rare treat to watch the parade of elegant lords and ladies who

strolled by in their dazzling costumes. Some of the
town's artisans and craftsmen were well off enough to
have costumes of their own made, and they joined the
noblemen in their revelry, adding color and creativity
that easily outdid the lords and ladies in their expen-
sive rented costumes.

Rob gave last minute instructions to Timothy,
Thaddeus, and Thomas, then went his separate way, in
search of Arianna. Black Bess held tight to his arm,
suddenly shy at the attention she was attracting. She
was used to a scurvier lot, not to the fine lords and
ladies who surrounded her now. Never had she seen so
rich an array of fabrics adorning both women and
men, making her all the more aware of the handmade
costume she wore.

Rob felt her body tremble as he took her by the arm,
and he realized she was not the fearless woman he had
imagined her to be. She was obviously not at ease in
her daring costume, but then what decent woman
could be? None but Bess would be so brave as to walk
around half naked for all the world to see.

Circling the perimeter of the park, they searched for
Arianna but could find no sign of her. Then crisscross-
ing through the grounds, they gazed at every woman
they passed, but still Arianna was nowhere to be
found. Had she decided not to come after all? No. He
couldn't be that lucky. She would show up and, he had
no doubt, wreak havoc on his heart once more.

Coming to the center of the park, Rob saw a
brightly decorated platform built as a dais for the
queen. Seeking Arianna's form amongst the lords and
ladies awaiting the queen's arrival, he was disappointed once again.

" 'Tis obvious this gaggle of geese isn't competing for the purse of gold," Bess commented, gazing with contempt at the very conservative garb of the nobles waiting for the queen. "If it weren't for their feather masks, I'd never know they were supposed to be in costume."

Trumpets blared, and Rob braced himself to face Elizabeth. Mayhap Arianna would be with the queen. Turning his attention to the queen, he was amused to find her costumed as an aging Cleopatra. She had on a black wig that made her skin look bloodless behind the garish rouge on her lips and cheeks. His gaze took in her ladies in waiting and the other nobles who accompanied the queen, and he spied the king of Scotland.

Rob smiled to himself, seeing James dressed as Neptune, the God of the Sea, in a toga of sea-green and carrying a gilded trident. He wondered if James had deliberately dressed like a god so that for one night he would outrank the powerful queen.

The King of Scotland seemed to be in a jovial mood, but Rob knew he must be tense, waiting as he was to see what Arianna would do. Damn her. Where was she? Must this agony be prolonged?

Hearing his name being called, he looked up to see the queen beckoning to him. "Damnation. The queen wants to see us."

"Oh, Rob, what am I to do? I've never met royalty before."

"Just take your cue from me and stop worrying. One look at your costume and the queen will be too tongue-tied to speak."

Far from being reassured, Bess hung on to Rob's

arm all the tighter as they walked over to the platform and paid homage to the queen of England.

"Ah, Robert. I see you had no trouble finding an escort to my masque. The infamous Black Bess, is it not?"

Rising from a graceful curtsy, Bess answered, "You flatter me, Your Grace. We met only once, and yet you still remember me."

Elizabeth snickered. "But, my dear, you don't do yourself justice. Everyone knows of you and your exploits. I fear you will find my little masque tame in comparison to the life you are used to."

Elizabeth's words gave Bess back her abundant confidence and she immersed herself into the role she was playing. "Tame? No, I find it quite stimulating. Especially as viewed from the arm of my handsome escort."

Hmph! Elizabeth thought. The wench fairly purred her contentment over Robert's attentions and seemed unashamed of her liaison with a married man. Where was Arianna? It should be most entertaining to see the way she reacts to her husband's very attractive companion.

Giving Bess a close scrutiny, her eyebrow arched at the sight of the wench's bare breast and the bare legs that seemed to go on forever. Quite daring, but then, she would expect nothing less of a coarse female pirate. Arianna was a different matter. The girl had been raised in a convent. Had always acted in a sweet, demure way. It would be quite interesting to see how daring her costume would be.

Arianna was certainly bright enough to know she had been challenged. Bright enough to know she could win favor with her queen if she won the contest. It would be interesting to see how she met the challenge. But, ah . . . well, she was quite prepared not to be too disappointed if Arianna didn't live up to a queen's sophisticated idea of daring. After all, Arianna lived such a sheltered life. She'd most likely come dressed as a mermaid, with her long hair covering her breasts most demurely, or perhaps an Arabian harem dancer; they seemed to be most popular tonight.

A strange rhythmic beat drifted to Elizabeth's ears and she thought at first it was the low rumble of thunder. She cocked her head to hear it better, realizing it was not the looming storm she heard but a hypnotic, man-made sound. What was it? Where was it coming from? As the sound grew louder, she felt a stirring in her blood. The deep, probing vibrations were a kind of erotic music that pulsated through her like a living, breathing thing. Never in all her life had she heard the likes of it.

Looking around, she noticed the music was affecting everyone the same way. How strange. As she turned toward Robert, she noticed him exchanging knowing glances with Bess and realized they were familiar with this music. She was about to ask about it when she saw a sight that rendered her speechless.

Above the heads of the myriad costumed lords and ladies, yeomen and maids alike, floated a near-naked maiden of dark skin and long ebony black hair. The crowd roared their approval and astonishment, enthralled by the exotic sight.

As the shapely form floated closer and closer, Elizabeth was relieved to see her eyes had not been playing tricks; rather than float, the woman was being carried aloft by a giant man, who was dressed in a dazzling outfit that befitted a prince.

The crowd parted, making way for the spectacle, and Elizabeth could finally see the source of the strange music. Two half-naked African women marched before the giant godlike creature, beating on exotic drums tied around their lovely necks.

Elizabeth could not contain her glee, her eyes moving from one figure to the next in wonder, but the mysterious dark-skinned woman carried above the giant's upstretched muscular arms drew her attention the most. The nubile beauty was naked from the waist up, her skin a rich shade of brown that glowed warmly in the light from the torches that lined the park. She was lying on her side as if she were comfortably draped on a bed instead of being balanced between two brawny hands. One of her graceful hands was propped on her hip, whilst the other was somewhere behind her, and the only clothing she wore—if clothing you could call it—was a short skirt made of peacock feathers that barely covered her round little rump.

The image came to Elizabeth of a pagan goddess being carried to some ancient ceremony, and she had no idea what prompted that thought. When the strange quartet came to a halt in front of her platform, Elizabeth found herself holding her breath in anticipation of what would happen next.

Rob, too, held his breath. The dark beauty was a sensuous feast to his eyes and his manhood agreed, hardening to steel. Who was this pagan goddess? 'Twas obvious she came from some primitive country of Africa where nudity was not unusual, for she wore her nakedness like a queen wore her cloth of gold.

Tearing his eyes from the goddess for a moment, he gazed at the dark beauties who played the devil drums and a jolt of recognition coursed through him. Arianna's attendants! Oh, God, no!

Swiveling his gaze to the giant for the first time, he recognized Terrence and his heart stood still. Afraid to look but even more afraid not to, his gaze swept up the giant's body to the floating goddess and took in the bright blue eyes of Arianna.

If he lived to be one hundred, he'd never forget the shock of seeing his wife, bare, brown, and almost naked; never forget the excitement that coursed through his veins as shock turned to awareness of her on a level he never knew existed. She had always been a very sensuous, desirable woman, filled with surprises, but this . . . this went beyond anything he could ever have imagined in his wildest fantasy.

And it fueled his imagination with erotic thoughts that overrode the part of him that was orderly and controlled, the civilized part of him that had always been in the forefront. He should be furious with her for exposing herself like that, but instead, he felt great admiration. He knew Arianna better than anyone alive. It took great courage to do what she did.

As Rob turned his attention back to his wife's attendants, they moved, as if on signal, each making her way to a different side of the giant. In an instant, Arianna was falling to earth, only to be caught by an ankle and wrist just inches above the ground. The crowd roared as the goddess arched her back, posing appealingly, suspended between the giant's strong hands.

Rob caught his breath, realizing it was part of the

act, and watched in awe as Arianna moved lithely to a standing position, her bare feet finally coming in contact with the earth. Immediately, his ears were filled with the thunderous applause as everyone cheered at the spectacular performance. Rob was too stunned to do anything but stare at the woman he loved beyond reason and beyond hope.

Arianna heard the applause from somewhere way off, aware only of the regal woman she was trying to impress and of her husband standing there, too shocked to hide his feelings.

Closing her eyes, she blinked away her husband's image, knowing she must finish what she started or it would all be for naught. With arms outstretched, she fell dramatically to her knees.

Elizabeth laughed delightedly, realizing that the exotic goddess was paying homage in the primitive way of her own far-off land. She was well pleased to see so beauteous a creature on her knees, her breasts bared, and when the girl raised her hands over her head, then lowered them to the ground in front of her to complete the homage, her lovely face touching the earth, the queen applauded as loud as any of her spectators.

"Rise, girl, and come here where I might get a good look at you."

Smiling brightly, Arianna walked toward the dais, moving like the lithe, wild creature she portrayed. She couldn't help but watch Rob out of the corner of her eye as she walked by and was pleased to see that he was staring at her with a look that told her all she needed to know. He wanted her. Still wanted her, despite everything that had happened. And knowing that, she could face anything.

Walking up the steps to the dais, Arianna knew every eye was upon her, and she held her head high. She was surprised to find she felt very little self-consciousness, attributing it to the brown powder that covered her nakedness. To her, it was like wearing a thin layer of clothing, for it hid her white skin behind a veil of brown.

And too, dressed in the black wig and peacock skirt, she felt like the brown goddess she portrayed, and that gave her all the more confidence. Clothed in this knowledge, Arianna stood as tall as her diminutive body would allow and waited for the queen to speak.

"My dear young thing, you must give me your name so that I can introduce you to my countrymen."

"Your Grace, do you not recognize your loyal subject?"

Elizabeth almost fainted at the sound of that familiar voice. Clasping her bejeweled hand over her heart, she cried, "Arianna! Sweet Jesus, is it you?"

"Have I pleased you with my costume, then?"

"Pleased is too mild a word, my dear, dear girl. *Ecstatic* is a word more to my liking. You have surprised me to a degree that I never thought to experience again. And for that I very heartily thank you. Indeed, you are so very creative. It is my fervent wish to see what mischievous delights you can come up with next."

"Then let me plan an entertainment for you, Your Grace. A very special entertainment." Arianna could hardly contain herself. The queen was playing right into her hands. She would have her chance for revenge, and more importantly, she would have a chance to get her son back.

A dart of suspicion flared in Elizabeth's eyes at the thought that Arianna was planning something, but it disappeared quickly. Arianna was not the devious type, which was one of the reasons the queen had been so attracted to her in the first place. "You intrigue me. How can I do other than give you my approval? Speak to my secretary for any special arrangements or moneys that you need. Just when do you think you can stage this entertainment?"

"I will need no more than a day or two for what I have in mind."

"And just what do you have in mind?"

"I'd rather keep it a secret. 'Twould have more impact that way, but I will give you a hint. It involves a form of gambling I have invented. I think you will find it most entertaining."

That answer seemed to relieve the queen, but Arianna realized she would have to tread carefully. Now that Elizabeth knew she was Mary's daughter, it would not be as easy to manipulate her.

Elizabeth remembered that Robert Warwick was there and she turned to him. His presence was fortuitous, for he could be used as a bellwether to see how trustworthy Arianna truly was.

"Robert, you've been very quiet. Do you not have something to say to your . . . wife?"

"Your Grace, what I have to say to her is best said in private."

"Don't you share my enthusiasm over your wife's creative efforts this night?"

"You are a very wise woman. Methinks you already know the answer to that."

Elizabeth laughed craftily. "Methinks I do. Poor

man. Your little virgin has become a very knowing woman, has she not? But methinks you cannot possibly object to that as much as you profess, and I mean to prove it. Come. Stand next to Arianna for a moment."

Robert clenched his jaw and made his way to Arianna's side. He had no idea what the queen was up to but knew it would not be to his liking. He was right. He couldn't believe it when Elizabeth took hold of his wrist and placed his hand on Arianna's bare breast.

Immediately, the crowd was in an uproar, thinking it was part of the entertainment.

Rob felt the heat of Arianna's soft flesh permeate his hand and tried to pull it away, but the queen held tight, insisting without saying a word that he obey.

His face grew crimson as his hatred for Elizabeth threatened to overpower him. She violated every law of decency.

Arianna's breathing grew shallow and quick as she gazed into Rob's eyes, in a quandary what to do. The expression she saw on his face froze her heart. It was a look of sheer hatred.

He blamed her for this.

As Robert's rage grew, he was afraid of losing control, but the sweet softness of Arianna's breast brought him slowly to his senses. His love for her overcame the other powerful emotion fighting for prominence in his heart. The pure love that washed over him freed him from his bondage of hate, from the embarrassment and disgust at the queen's act. The love he felt for his wife was strong enough to triumph over Elizabeth's evil intent. It was so eminently strong that Elizabeth must surely feel it, too, through her contact with his skin as she held tight to his wrist.

Elizabeth held so tight to Robert that she felt his pulse through his wrist and . . . something more . . . something every bit as palpable as the beating of a heart. She knew what she felt was the passion this man had for his wife. Enthralled, she let the feeling possess her for one long, enchanting moment.

It was a wondrous feeling to know that a man and a woman could feel so much, and she wished, oh how fervently she wished, that she could be the recipient of so much emotion.

Her envy of Arianna threatened to overpower her, and in need of denigrating the love between this man and this woman, so that it would not count so very much in her mind, she removed Robert's hand from Arianna's breast and raised it to her face, pretending to study it carefully.

Speaking in barely more than a whisper, she said, "Such a nice hand, Robert. Masculine and strong." Her hands moved over his fingers, then caressed his palm. "You can tell much about a man from his hands. Did you know that? Some say one can even tell the size of a man's cock by the size of his hands."

Rob squirmed inside but kept his face expressionless, dreading what was sure to come next.

"Yours must be very large."

Arianna couldn't believe what the queen was saying. How dare she talk like that! Wasn't it enough that she had to endure the queen's humiliation? Must she humiliate her husband, too? It was obvious Elizabeth was testing her again. How much more was she expected to take?

Gazing out at the throng of people who watched intently, she realized they had no idea what the queen was saying. Would they think any less of her if they did know? She doubted it would have any effect on them at all. They were her subjects and she was their queen, well liked by all. Almost all, she thought bitterly, for her hate counted for something.

"Tell me, Arianna, is my assumption true?"

Damn her. The queen was forcing her to answer. "Why don't you ask Black Bess? She has had more experience with men than I." An inspiration came to her then, and smiling broadly, she said, "Ask her about the pirate Longfellow, Your Grace."

Surprised and intrigued by Arianna's answer, the queen replied, "Well, Black Bess. What do you have to say on the matter?"

Bess had no qualms about answering the queen. If the old girl wanted to be titillated, she would oblige. "If you are really interested, Your Grace, I can only say I believe there is a correlation between the size of a man's hands and his cock. Elijah Longfellow's hands are very large, and as for his cock, I can only say 'tis so enormous, it puts all other men's to shame. Think of what a stallion's root looks like and you'll be close."

Elizabeth was both shocked and pleased at Black Bess's words. If this Longfellow was so impressively immense, she would see to it that he was brought to her for . . . how would she put it? Rehabilitation.

Turning to the king of Scotland, who had not said a word since his sister appeared, Elizabeth said, "James, you have done me a great service in bringing me Black Bess and Longfellow. They will be most invaluable in instructing me on . . . pirate life."

James was seething inside at the queen's reprehensible behavior. He kept it to himself, but it made him all the more determined to get Arianna away from Elizabeth's reach. The more he got to know the queen, the more he realized how dangerous she was.

It came to him that the reason she had never married was so she would not have to share her power with anyone. She was used to getting her own way, and that made her all the more dangerous. For without a husband to temper any rash decisions she might make, her actions could become more and more self-serving, and she was in danger of becoming out of control.

There was yet another reason to get Arianna away from the queen, he thought, gazing at his scantily clothed sister. Arianna was under Elizabeth's influence, whether she believed it or not. He would hate to see just how far she would go to stay in the queen's good graces, if this evening was any example. No, if Arianna didn't leave England soon, she was in danger of becoming, ironically, the kind of woman she hated the most. A woman like Elizabeth.

Having achieved what she wanted, the queen dropped Robert's hand and stepped closer to the crowd. "I think you will all agree that the Countess of Everly has proven to be the most daring of all, not only in the costume she wears, but in her performance, too. Therefore, I proclaim her to be the winner and award her this purse of gold."

As the people applauded and whistled in agreement, Elizabeth took the black velvet purse from an attendant and handed it to Arianna. Arianna thanked her and started to leave, but the queen was not done with her. Taking a wreath of white roses from James, Elizabeth placed it on Arianna's head.

Snapping off one stray rose that dangled too close to Arianna's eye, Elizabeth felt a stab of pain in her finger and realized she had been pricked by a thorn.

Wincing with pain and angry that the stupid wreath maker had overlooked cutting off one thorn, Elizabeth looked down at her finger and saw the blood dripping from the wound.

Arianna saw it, too, and had a hard time containing her joy. It was an omen. An omen that foretold of her victory over Elizabeth.

But Arianna's joy was short-lived. Elizabeth threw the white rose to the platform floor and angrily stomped it with her foot.

Arianna saw her victory turned to defeat. If the rose was truly an omen, then it was now an ominous one. She, the living symbol of the ivory rose, would be ground into dust.

Chapter Twenty-nine

Arianna couldn't take her mind off the crushed rose lying on the floor by her feet. She tried to tell herself there was no significance to Elizabeth destroying the delicate bloom, but it didn't work. She couldn't shrug off the feeling of impending doom, and she knew it was her own fault for conjuring up the omen in the first place.

As long as she could remember, she had been thinking up new things to be superstitious about, and she blamed it on her Celtic blood. She truly believed the Celts were the most superstitious of all the races that peopled this earth.

Superstitious yes, but also creative, and for that inheritance from the ancient Celts she was most appreciative, for without it, she would have had a difficult time surviving in a world where kings and queens had omnipotent powers. If only that inbred creativity would help her get back her husband and son, she would count herself among the blessed.

The sky suddenly lit up as a jagged firebolt stabbed the night, and a torrent of rain fell on the revelers, sending them fleeing in every direction. Elizabeth, too, disappeared from the dais, so quickly Arianna felt as if she had been spirited away. She couldn't be sorry for that. Elizabeth was becoming very unpredictable, and that made her dealings with her precarious.

Aware that only she and Rob remained standing on the dais, Arianna was suddenly very self-conscious of her nudity. The pelting rain washed ribbons of brown dye off her skin, leaving it striped like some exotic zebra, and she knew she must look a strange sight indeed. Suddenly, she wished she was dressed in her most feminine of gowns, her hair brushed until it shone like gold, for then she could face her husband without shame.

Taking off her black wig, she let the rain soak into her hair, wishing it could penetrate to her very soul. Wishing it could cleanse away all the heartache she had caused her family, wishing it could make her feel clean and innocent once more.

She and Rob stood there, two half-naked figures, two living statues, cascading water flowing off their arms and legs, breasts and hair, two living crystal waterfalls with hearts that had always beat as one, gazing at one another as if they were the only creatures left in the world. And oh, how she wished that were true.

A bolt of lightning crackled across the dark sky again, scaring Arianna out of the spell she was under, and she gave out a little cry. Rob stood like stone, unaffected by the thunder and lightning or the stinging rain. He spoke not a word, and that terrible silence was much worse than anything he could ever say to her.

He still had not forgiven her.

She should have known better than to hope for that impossible dream.

Wiping the water from her eyes, she cried out her frustration, needing to break the barrier of silence between them. "Say it. Get it over with. Tell me what a miserable wife I've been, what a terrible mother, losing our son to Elizabeth. Go ahead. Say it. *Say it*. Then leave."

Speaking in the low, ominous voice Rob used when he was ready to explode, he warned, "I'm done with talking, Arianna. It comes too cheap." Taking off the cloak draped over his shoulders, he wrapped it around her nakedness, then took her arm with a firm grip and led her off the dais.

"Where are you taking me?"

Rob didn't answer. Instead, he guided her through the park, oblivious to the rain, his lower lip jutting out grimly.

"Let go of me, Rob, or you'll ruin everything."

"Ruin what, Arianna? What little scheme are you hatching now? Not that it matters. You've done just about all the damage you can do. You've lost your husband, lost your child, lost your pride and dignity, even your sanity, I fear. What's left to lose, Arianna? Tell me."

Arianna dug in her heels, refusing to be led any further. "I'm close to getting Robin back, but that won't happen if you interfere now. You made it obvious that you were distancing yourself from me. That was the right thing to do. Why did you change your mind?"

Robert came close to hitting her then. "You dare

ask me that after parading around half-naked? Damn you to hell." He started tugging on her arm again, but she refused to be budged. "If that's the way you want it . . ." Reaching down, he grasped her around the knees and lifted her over his shoulder like a sack of wheat, then started on his way again.

Arianna kicked her feet and pummeled his back to no avail, soon tiring of that useless act. Rob seemed to be made of stone. No. Stone was cold and dead. Rob was vibrantly alive, and she could feel the warmth of his body beneath her, a stark contrast to the cold rain unmercifully pelting her back. Her heart fluttered wildly as hope sprang deep in her soul once more. For surely he must care for her still, or he would have left her standing in the park.

Suddenly, she felt Rob's body jerk to a stop and, looking over her shoulder, saw that Terrence's huge body was blocking the way.

Rob reacted with an angry shout. "Get out of my way, Terrence!"

"Not until you put the Countess Arianna down, my lord, and I know she's all right."

"Did you think she was all right when you carried her over your head for all the world to see, you stupid oaf? Whatever possessed you to participate in this lunacy? Letting her appear practically naked? Did you think *that* was all right, man? Get the hell out of my way or I'll—"

Terrence could see how angry the earl was and didn't blame him a bit, but he was sworn to protect the Countess Arianna, and that was what he would do. "My lord, begging your pardon, but I must insist on your releasing her . . ."

Before he could finish, Rob was setting Arianna down and balling up his hand into a hard fist. Terrence saw it coming, but was unsure how to handle it. Robert was the last man he wanted to fight.

The fist slammed into his jaw, sending him reeling.

Rob watched Terrence stagger backward and waited for him to right himself before striking again, but Arianna grabbed ahold of his arm, preventing Rob from hitting him again.

"Stop it. I won't have you two fighting over me. Terrence, go away. I don't need protection from my husband."

Terrence stroked his aching jaw with his hand. "Now you tell me. Very well, my lady. If you have need of me, I'll be with Fiona." Shaking his head, he walked away, wondering if he would ever understand females.

Arianna turned to her husband, her hands on her hips. "And as for you, Robert, since when have you resorted to taking out your anger on innocents?"

Grabbing Arianna by the arm once again, he glared down at her. "Since my wife has driven me to it."

Glaring at Rob through rain-clogged eyes, she answered, "Then, by all means, take me with you. I wouldn't want to be the one to drive you over the edge." Trying to free herself from his grip, she pulled on his arm to no avail. "You can let go of my arm. I promise I won't try to run away."

Rob laughed bitterly. "Your promises are not worth the breath it takes to utter them. No, I'm holding tight to you until you're safe in Will's care, though, come to think of it, he wasn't much use in preventing you from your silly performance, was he? What in God's name ever possessed you to do that?"

Arianna didn't answer. What could she say to a man who never made the terrible blunders she was so prone to? She kept quiet on the short walk back to the manor, having all she could do to keep from tripping over the hem of Rob's cloak. She was glad to have it, though, to hide her naked body. Whatever had possessed her to appear in the park in such a wild, primitive costume?

Was she losing her mind? By morning, everyone in London would know of her daring appearance. Would she be censured for it or admired? Did it really matter? Did anything really matter anymore besides the man who held her arm so tight and their little son? She shivered and pulled the cloak tighter. As they approached Will's home, Arianna wondered what would happen next. In truth, she couldn't even begin to guess.

Will answered the pounding on his door and was shocked at Arianna's appearance. She looked as if she had been to hell and back, and he imagined she probably had. And Robert. He looked very close to breaking. What in the world had transpired in the park? Whatever it was, he was sure the queen had something to do with it.

"Arianna, Felicia thought you could use a nice warm bath. She had Fiona fill a tub for you in your chamber."

Mustering up what little dignity she had left, she managed a polite thank you and started up the stairs. She heard Robert's footsteps on the steps behind her, and her heart beat wild with hope.

He was following her up to her bedchamber.

If there was one place where she had a chance to win him back, it would be there.

Entering the room behind Arianna, Rob saw she wasn't alone; Ruth and Naomi sat at a small table staring at him as if he had two heads. "Out!" he commanded, and they obeyed quickly.

Arianna watched as Robert closed the door and locked it. Her heart skipped a beat as he walked over to her and took her arm, but her hope died when she felt the tightness of his grip.

Turning her toward an oval mirror on the wall, he yanked the cloak from her body and said, "Take a good look at yourself. See what you've become."

Arianna looked into the mirror and almost gasped out loud. She looked like a wild, unruly animal, hair matted and wet, streaks of brown running down her face and body. She closed her eyes, trying to erase that awful image.

"Open your eyes, Arianna. Don't shut it out. I want you to remember this. I want you to see what your quest for revenge has wrought."

"Robert. Don't."

"*Look,* Arianna. Open your eyes and look, or so help me I'll pry your eyes open."

Arianna opened her eyes and stared at her image in the mirror, then her gaze moved up to the vision of her husband standing behind her, knowing he saw what she did. "That's not me, Robert. I swear to you that's not me."

"Who else can it be, Arianna? Who? Tell me. It's not the falconer's apprentice, Aaron. Isn't that what you called yourself then? And it's not the troubadour who ran off to try and play for Mary in her prison. And it surely isn't the sweet young virgin who told me she was raised in a convent. Which is the genuine you? You've taken on so many disguises in your life, I don't believe you know yourself who the real Arianna is. But believe me, I do. She is a woman who is so blinded by her need for revenge that she is willing to risk everything to achieve it. Even her family."

"That's not true. I love you more than life, Rob. How can you doubt that when everything I've ever done was to protect you and Robin from Elizabeth? Can't you see that, Rob? It isn't my need for revenge that drives me, but my need to keep you safe from that evil woman."

"And don't you see that it is your need for revenge that has endangered me, endangered Robin. He'd be safe in your arms right this moment if you hadn't gone riding off to Dover with him. Deception is your mother's milk. I think you thrive on it. I think without it in your life you would be bored. Admit it. All your life you've manipulated people in order to get your way. Sweet Jesus, you went so far as to deliberately set out to win me as your husband. And I swear to God, I don't know whether you did it because you loved me or as a way to escape the peasant life of your foster parents."

"Robert Warwick, you know the answer to that as well as I do."

"I thought I did. But how can I trust anything you say anymore? Everything you say is a lie. God help me, I was so desperate to get my family back I thought that I, too, had to be deceitful. You had me convinced that that was the only way I could live my life without fear of what the queen might do. But tonight, standing up there on that dais, when Elizabeth put my hand on your naked breast, I came to my senses."

"I know, it brought me to my senses, too. Truly it did. I realized that because of me, you were forced into that humiliating experience."

"Because of your *deceit,* I was forced into it. Can't you see that all your manipulations and deceit have brought you nothing but grief? I swear if you don't see that now, you're lost. We're lost."

"Oh, Rob, don't even think it. We can be together again. After tomorrow night, everything will be over and we can be happy again."

"What are you talking about? What will be over?"

Arianna's face lit up with a radiance Rob had not seen in a long, long time. "My revenge. She's played right into my hand, and tomorrow night, I will humiliate her. That's all, just humiliate her. I won't shed a drop of her blood, just as I promised you. And then, once we have our baby back, I'll be free of her forever."

"Arianna, haven't you heard a word I've been saying?"

"Of course I have, and you're right. You're always right. My need for revenge has torn us apart, but no longer. I have arranged for a sporting event, a very ingenious sporting event involving a peregrine falcon and some doves, each dyed a different color. The queen was quite thrilled about it. She thinks I have a very creative mind."

"Arianna, I don't want to hear this."

"But you must, Rob. It is such a perfect plan. You see, all the fine lords and ladies at court will bet on which color bird the falcon will attack when the doves are released. It will be great fun for them but even greater enjoyment for me, because, you see, Robert, instead of attacking a dove, I've trained the hawk to pull Elizabeth's wig off her in front of the entire court. Now, that might not be so great a punishment for most people, but for the queen . . . well, that's a different matter entirely."

"Enough, Arianna. I don't want to hear any more."

Arianna could not stop now, not when she was so close to fulfilling her revenge. "Don't you see how simple it will be? Everyone knows how vain she is. It is her Achilles' heel, but none but a few know that she is so very vain that she had a man beheaded for seeing her without her wig. It seems she is quite bald and looks like a pitiful old lady without her bright red wig."

Rob listened to Arianna's fevered speech in shock. She was much more obsessed than he had ever imagined. "Obviously, you're too far gone to hear or understand anything I said. You've made your choice. Now live with it."

"What are you talking about? What choice?"

"The choice between loving me . . . living with me . . . or continuing your miserable dance of death with the queen."

Robert started toward the door.

"Robert! Don't you dare walk out on me now. I listened to you, now you listen to me."

"What's left to say, Arianna? Your hatred for Elizabeth is more powerful than your love for me."

"My hate is a powerful thing, I admit. But it is unfair to compare it to my love for you. Put yourself in my position just for a moment. Think how you would feel if Elizabeth had taken your mother captive, kept her locked away from you for all of your life. Deprived you of your mother's love and then, after nineteen long years, had her beheaded on trumped-up charges. Yes, I have always wanted revenge, but now I actually thirst for it. *She has taken my son from me.* Surely you must feel the same way? Robin is your son, too."

"Don't bring Robin into this, for after tomorrow he'll be with me and you'll no longer be able to use him as an excuse."

Arianna looked at him with her mouth open. "How?"

"Never mind how. In your state of mind, I don't dare trust you with that knowledge. You see, there is no need for your little gaming evening. Robin will be safe hours before your event. So . . . it comes down to this, Arianna. Is your love for me stronger than your need for revenge? Or will you carry out your long-awaited revenge and lose your husband, for I'm telling you what you decide this very moment will determine whether we have a future or not."

"You can't mean that."

In a seductively soft voice, he answered, "If you know me at all, Rose Petal, you know that I do mean it. So . . . what is it to be?"

Tears flooded her eyes as she realized he would not back down. "Damn you, Robert, just one more day, that's all. My revenge is so close I can taste it. How can you ask that of me now? It's inhuman. It's . . ."

Rob hardened his heart to her crying and started for the door. It was too late. Too late. Her heart was too filled with hatred. The only way he could save his son, save himself, was to leave her to whatever destiny awaited her. Rob clenched his teeth and forced himself to walk through the door.

Chapter Thirty

Arianna stood there stunned, the silence of the room a lonely thing. *He left. He actually left. How could he leave me alone when I need him so much? What am I to do? I can't give up my revenge now, not when I'm so close to fulfilling my vow. It's wrong of him to expect me to. He'll be back. He'll . . . He . . . he . . . he . . . won't . . . be back. He means it. Dear God, he really means it.*

Fear struck Arianna like a crushing blow to the chest. She started from the room at a fast walk, then broke into a run to the top of the staircase. Where was he? She flew down the stairs and flung open the door, shouting, "Rob!"

She saw him then, walking toward the road, shoulders hunched against the rain, head bent low. Didn't he hear her? Or was he ignoring her? Was it already too late? In a panic, she shouted again, her voice a high-pitched shriek, "Rob!"

Rob turned to look at her, not daring to hope, not daring to breathe in case it was just his fevered brain that heard her call to him. Just an illusion he saw before him, brought on by his deepest desire.

Running after him, she came to a halt a hairbreadth away, suddenly timid. "Oh, Rob, I've loved you since the first time I ever laid eyes on you in the mews at Norbridge. You were all legs then, coltish and gawky with the face of a young god, and you took my breath away. I loved you then, but not half as much as I love you now."

Expelling his breath in a rush, he spoke in a low, hushed voice. "Enough to give up all thoughts of revenge?"

"Yes!"

"Enough to come with me to our new home in Scotland?"

Arianna's eyes were shining bright. Oh, yes, my dearest, dearest love. The only home I need is in your arms."

Rob's voice grew husky as he drew her into his arms. "Then come home, Rose Petal, come home."

Arianna couldn't remember how they got up to her bedchamber. All she knew or cared about was that Rob still loved her, wanted her, needed her. She gave herself up to him, mindlessly, eagerly, wanting him to guide her toward the rapture she knew awaited.

Before she realized it, she was in the tub and his hands were moving over her, slippery with soap, cleansing her skin of its brown stripes with long, silky strokes, until she thought she'd go out of her mind with desire.

There was nothing this side of heaven that felt as good as Rob's hands moving over her body, claiming with caresses everything that belonged to him.

It had ever been so.

She had always loved the feel of those wonderful

hands, those talented hands that could evoke such incredible feelings inside her, and she had been without them far too long. Been without her man an eternity too long. "Rob?"

"Mmmm?"

"Am I not clean enough yet? You've been rubbing me so long I fear you'll wear my skin off."

"That's not the only part of you in danger of being worn out. Let me demonstrate." With that, he lifted her from the water and carried her to the bed.

"Rob! I'm all wet. Don't put me down on the covers." Too late, she thought, as she sank into the soft feather bed.

"What use in drying you when in a moment I'll have you all wet again."

"Rob!"

"If you insist." He threw a towel at her, undressing whilst Arianna lay on the bed drying her arms and breasts and abdomen. She was about to dry her legs, when Rob grabbed them and separated them, lifting them to his face. Before she could protest, she saw his tongue dart out, and Arianna yielded her body to him, delighted at the masterful and oh, so manly way he held her.

In a second she was crying out her pleasure as his tongue searched between her thighs for her golden treasure, delving between the moist lips.

"Rob. Don't. I'll come too quickly."

Lowering her legs, he said huskily, "Come. I want you to. I want to watch your face as you come. I want to know that I have such power over you."

Lifting her legs again, he buried his head between them once more, continuing his assault. Using his tongue, he circled her opening, then plunged inside her again and again, raising and lowering her legs. It was a strange way to make love, he knew, but it gave him great satisfaction to have such control over this will-o'-the-wisp woman who had always done just as she wished. Now she would belong to him truly, and he needed to demonstrate that to her.

Arianna's eyes were glazed with pleasure as Rob handled her body. She understood his need to dominate her and was surprised to find she enjoyed being a slave to his love. He wanted her to come, and she was eager to comply. It had been too long. As his tongue did its magic, her desire escalated, until she couldn't have held back any longer if she tried. "Oh, Rob, oh, oh, oh." Wave after wave of ecstasy engulfed her, but it was just a tease compared to what she was waiting for.

She had to feel him inside her or die.

But Rob had other things on his mind. Instead of covering her with his body, she was astonished when he straddled her, sitting on her abdomen.

She watched as he pushed his manhood between her breasts, holding them together with his hands, and it crossed her mind that he had been fantasizing this act a long time. She smiled to herself, knowing she had a few erotic fantasies of her own.

Her breasts made a soft cocoon to undulate back and forth in, and soon he was doing just that, an intense look on his face as he moved in and out of the incredible silkiness.

A dreamy look came over his face as the ecstasy came in a rush, his seed flooding the tight space between her breasts. But he was not done with her yet.

Enjoying the sudden slipperiness, he moved back and forth in it, gazing deep into Arianna's eyes as he did. His hips rose and fell in the dance of love, showing his woman with every movement that she belonged to him; that her body was his to love in every way.

Arianna lay there enjoying the feel of him between her breasts and the knowledge that she could give him such great pleasure. When he hardened again, she smiled up at him, glad that their lovemaking would not have to end yet. She throbbed to have him inside her.

And that's just where he wanted to be.

It was time for the serious business of claiming her as his own in the one way males had been doing since the beginning of time. Sliding down her belly, he embedded himself in the petal softness of her womanhood.

He was home.

Lifting his body a little, he stared down at the only place that touched her, his manhood buried inside her. "Look at us," he commanded.

Arianna knew what he meant and turned her gaze to the place they were locked together. The dark of his hair surrounding his manhood mingled with the golden hair of her Venus mound, in a startling contrast of colors. She saw only the root of him, and seeing it was as exciting as feeling it inside her. It was as if the very sight of him like that proved that they were meant to be. And oh, she didn't doubt that for a moment.

"We're joined, Arianna, as closely as it is possible to be joined, not only in this wonderful physical way, but in a deep and abiding spiritual way, too. My soul was lost without yours as companion, my heart lonely without the sound of yours beating next to it. Do you understand what I'm trying to say?"

"I do. I feel the same way. I always have. I always will."

"And no one can take that away from us, Arianna. Not even the almighty queen of England."

Sighing with happiness, Arianna circled his neck with her hands and drew him down to her.

Rob didn't need to be told what she wanted, and he obliged, thrusting into her. Watching the expression on her face change as desire overcame her, he thrust again, enjoying the emotion he aroused in her.

Arianna received each thrust of him as a gift of love, and she let him know with her body and her voice how much she was enjoying it. He belonged to her and she would never let him go. She wound her legs around him, holding tight, and let him ride her into heaven.

Within the tightness of her hold on him, Rob freed the last of his control, giving himself up to his over-powering need. He used his body as he never had before, wanting her to know how much he loved her.

Arianna felt the force of his thrusts and moaned her pleasure, answering him with movements of her own. They came together, in matched rhythm, their bodies slick with sweat, their muscles tuned to the singular chore of gratifying the need of the other. Holding tight, their voices blended in ecstatic harmony as they gave up their bodies to blissful release one last intense time.

Then they lay panting, Rob sprawled on top of her, until they could catch their breath. Then, with one last burst of energy, Rob raised his head and took her face in his hands, kissing her fervently. "I adore you." And oh, he did. She was his sun, his moon, his shining stars, and he thanked God she belonged to him once more. He knew he would rather die than lose her again.

Staring back at her beloved husband, his loving face reflected in her eyes, Arianna responded with a smile. She knew how lucky she was. She had the one man who could make her happy, and they could start a new life. A new life . . . She suddenly remembered what Rob had said before they made love and had to hear it again to truly believe it. "Oh, Rob, are we truly going to Scotland?"

Rob laughed joyously. "Is that all you have to say after I've pleasured you so many ways? At least tell me what a great lover I am! Men need to hear words of love, too."

"Robert Warwick, you are the most fantastic lover the world has ever seen and I am so lucky to have you as my own. Now, you beast, tell me, are we truly going to Scotland?"

"Aye, we are, and it's a great sacrifice, too."

Arianna swallowed hard. "I know it is, Rob, and I would never have asked it of you. Giving up your lands is too great a sacrifice."

"My lands? Nay, I was speaking of having to wear a kilt."

Arianna laughed gaily. "That is the great sacrifice you'll be making, wearing a kilt?"

Grinning wickedly, Rob answered, "Now that I think of it, it might not be so great a sacrifice. I'm thinking of how easy it will be to make love to you. Nothing to untie, or unbutton, or unstrap . . . And if I'm not mistaken, the Scots wear nothing under them

. . . pretty ingenious, I'd say. Always at the ready. Mmmm, I'm beginning to warm to the idea."

"Oh, Rob, you are so very dear to me. When I think of how close I came to losing you—"

"Hush. Let's not speak of the past. 'Tis too painful to us both."

"But I have to. Just for a moment. I truly can't explain what caused me to be so . . . so crazy. When you stood there on that platform with your hand pressed to my breast, I realized how humiliating it must be for you, and I—"

"No. You're wrong. It wasn't humiliation I felt, but something entirely different. I knew then that my love for you was more powerful than anything the queen might do. That I could rise above it all if I stayed true to myself. That the only thing that could defeat me would be the knowledge that you no longer loved me or wanted me in your life."

"Oh, Robert, how could you ever doubt my love for you? It is my strength and my weakness. Whatever foolish and dangerous things I've done, I've done in the name of that tremendous love."

"I know that. Oh, God, how I know that. But knowing doesn't make it easier to take. I thought when I saw you kneeling before Longfellow that I could never forgive you."

"Oh, Rob, I know how hard it was for you to see that; it was even harder to do. But I couldn't bear the thought of losing you. I did it because I love you so much. I only wish you could understand that."

"Unfortunately, anger and hurt cannot be changed by mere understanding. But I do know, too well, for I would have done the same to spare you. Did you know

I begged Longfellow to take me in your place, to humiliate me in front of all those spectators? . . ."

With a sob, Arianna cried, "Oh, Rob, I didn't know, I didn't know. If that had happened . . . Oh, dear God, if Longfellow had done that to you, I wouldn't want to live another day! The pain would be too much to bear." Suddenly realizing what she said, she looked at Rob in horror. "Is that what you felt, seeing me with him?"

Rob gazed at her with sorrow-filled eyes.

Arianna covered her face with her hands, sobbing as if her heart would break. And she wanted it to, willed it to, so she would not have to bear the knowledge of what she had done.

"Arianna, don't, it's over now. It's over. We'll put it all behind us and go on with our lives. What we've been through has taught us a most important lesson. Think of that and be happy. Tomorrow, with your brother's help, I'll rescue our son and we'll be on our way to a life happier than we've ever dared imagine."

"Oh, Rob, I'm frightened. You'll be in such danger. I couldn't bear to lose you again."

"You won't, believe me. James and I have planned it so the danger will be minimal. But the timing is crucial. Elizabeth grows suspicious about James lingering in England so long. He has no choice but to leave very soon. That makes it imperative that our plan succeed tomorrow morning."

"How will you do it?"

"The one sure way we can. Did you know that Elizabeth has arranged for little Robin to ride in St. James Park every morning?"

"No. I didn't know. Oh, Rob, he's much too young for that."

"He only rides a small pony, an attendant by his side. But don't you see—he'll be outside the castle walls, where it will be easier to abduct him. And his escort is but one female attendant, with a liveryman to walk the pony. We won't have to contend with battling her guards. Evidently, it hasn't entered Elizabeth's mind that I might try to rescue my son."

"Of course it hasn't. She knows that only a fool would try to do that. For where in England could you hide from her? Oh, Rob, it could truly work. Elizabeth would never suspect that you would leave England, leave all your holdings, all your belongings, to save our son from her. Because she cannot even begin to imagine the kind of love we share."

Rob pulled her up against him. "So you see, my darling girl, everything will be all right. In the morning, we'll get our son back and sail away on high tide to a new life in Scotland."

Arianna nestled into Rob's arms, feeling secure and safe. Everything would be all right now.

She drifted off to sleep listening to the falling rain.

Chapter Thirty-one

Arianna was content. Waking to the patter of rain on the window and the warmth of her husband snuggled up to her back was a wonderful way to start the day. She would never again take for granted the pleasure of feeling him beside her in bed, and she would never forget how lonely her life had been without him.

Rob stirred, sighed, then pulled her up against his hardness. He was ready and eager to continue where they had left off the night before, but something . . . something . . . bothered him. Suddenly realizing what it was, he jumped out of bed and ran to the window. "Damn. What the hell do we do now?"

Startled, Arianna sat up in bed, crying, "Rob, what is it?"

"It's still raining. That's the one thing we failed to consider in our plan for rescuing Robin. The weather. Don't you see? Elizabeth won't let him have his riding lesson in the rain. He'll be kept in the castle. We won't be able to get him."

Arianna's heart sank. "Oh, Rob! I had such hopes.

I just knew we'd get our son back today and everything would be fine."

Rob made his way to the bed and took Arianna in his arms. "It will be, Rose Petal, it will be. It just means waiting another day."

"But you said James will have to leave soon. What if it rains again tomorrow?"

" 'Tis useless to worry about something that might never happen. We have to take this one day at a time."

"But, Rob, tonight I'm supposed to put on my sporting event. I'll have to go through with it, or Elizabeth will know something is wrong."

"No. We agreed there would be no revenge."

"But there won't be. It's a simple matter of substituting the falcon I trained for another one. Any other hawk or falcon will do what comes naturally and attack one of the doves. Elizabeth will be in no danger of having her wig pulled off. I promise you."

Looking deep in her eyes, Rob searched for the truth.

"I know how hard it must be to trust me now. But, Rob, if we are ever to be truly happy again, you will have to start believing in me. Do it now. I won't betray you. On Robin's life, I promise you that."

Rob let his breath out in relief. Arianna would never take an oath on her son's life lightly. "I believe you, Arianna, but I still don't like it. You're right, though, now is not the time to get Elizabeth upset. We're too close to being free of her. *Free of her.* Just saying the words makes me feel better."

Lifting her in his arms, he twirled her around the room, then kissed her heartily. "All right. You go ahead with your plans, make whatever arrangements you have to for tonight. Meanwhile, I have to report back to the inn immediately. James will be trying to contact me there. He'll be worried if he doesn't hear from me soon."

"Will I be seeing you before I go to the palace tonight?"

"I wish I could say yes. I wish you could accompany me to the inn for all the world to see, but I fear it would be too dangerous. If Elizabeth knows we're back together, she'll be cautious. She might even put extra guards on Robin and make it impossible to get to him."

"Rob, don't even think it. I could never leave England without my son. Could you?"

"To save your life, I could."

Arianna knew he meant what he said, and it sobered her considerably. They must succeed. They must get back their son. Anything else would be unacceptable.

After conferring in private with Fiona, Ruth, and Naomi, Rob left for the inn. He told them about the move to Scotland and asked whether they wanted to come along. Without hesitation, Fiona answered yes, and Ruth and Naomi shook their heads up and down in vigorous agreement. Excited at the prospect, they set about packing the countess's few belongings and their own.

Arianna dressed and went directly to the mews, making sure all was in readiness for that night. Feeding the falcon she had trained, she couldn't help but regret that her revenge would not be taking place. She was human, after all. But a lifetime with Rob was so much more important to her than one brief moment of victory over the queen. If only she had realized that before all this began.

Thinking about her handsome husband and the many ways he pleased her, in bed and out, her heart was light. It wasn't until late afternoon that she started to worry about whether her sporting event would actually be successful or not. She knew birds well enough to know how unpredictable they could be, and the peregrine falcon she would be using was not familiar to her. But she put it out of her mind, remembering Rob's words: *'Tis useless to worry about something that might never happen.*

At The Stag's Horn, Rob sat at a table with the Terrible Four, drinking an ale to help relieve the tension that grew stronger and stronger as the time for going to the palace drew near. Black Bess joined them, sitting down next to Rob.

"There's something different about you today, Robert. What is it? If I didn't know better, I'd think you'd spent a satisfying evening in bed with a female. But knowing how stingy you are with your cock, saving it all for the Countess Arianna, I must be wrong."

Rob smiled. "Nay, you're right on target. Arianna and I are together again."

"No! Is it true? I'm happy for you, Robert. I wish I was as lucky with matters of the heart as you are. I've just come from seeing Longfellow, and you'll never guess what that bastard's up to now?"

"Longfellow? I thought he was conscripted into the navy."

"Oh, he was, until I had to open my mouth to the queen last night. Never in my wildest dreams would I have imagined that Elizabeth would be so intrigued by what I had to say about the size of him. So intrigued, in sooth, that after she found out his galleon was in port, she had him sent to the palace first thing this morning. Can you believe that? She doesn't let any moss grow under her feet."

"Where did you see him? Surely you weren't at the palace this morning?"

"Not likely. Elizabeth and I are not exactly fast friends. No, I bumped into him at the same men's clothier where I met you the other day, Rob."

"Don't tell me. Elizabeth wants him as a lover." Rob laughed joyfully. "I almost feel sorry for Longfellow. I fear he's met his match in Elizabeth."

"Not from the way he tells it. He told me they had a private—and I emphasize the word *private*—conversation, whereupon Elizabeth was inspired enough to set him up in an apartment on the same floor as hers, then sent him off with a purse of gold to buy a new wardrobe. I guess she likes the men in her life to live up to her standards."

Rob whistled. "It seems Longfellow has come a long way since Devil's Harp. But the poor fool's playing with fire, and he's too stupid to realize it."

"Aye, I tried to tell him that, but he accused me of being jealous."

"Are you?" Thomas piped in. "Or have you finally gotten over that worthless piece of scum?"

Making a face, Bess said, "It's not that easy, man. If you have ever been in love, you'd know that. I can't help it. I still love the bastard. Do you know, he had the nerve to tell me that we could still see each other on the sly. That we could still be lovers. That what Elizabeth didn't know wouldn't hurt her."

"Probably not. But it could hurt you." Rob spoke solemnly, wanting to be sure that Bess got the message. "If Elizabeth found out that you were seeing him, she'd have your head off before you had a chance to miss it."

"Don't worry about me, Robert. You have enough to worry about with Arianna. She's just as much the queen's creature as Leicester and Longfellow. When the queen asks her to jump through a hoop, she obliges. As witness last night's very entertaining performance."

It irritated Rob to have Bess think Arianna was such a spineless thing. Against his better judgment, he blurted out, "You're wrong, Bess. She was never the queen's creature. She just pretended to be. She hates Elizabeth. Enough so that until last night, she had every intention of causing her harm, but thank God, she came to her senses in time to prevent a tragedy."

Bess laughed raucously. "Arianna doing damage to Elizabeth? That little puffball? Surely you couldn't have been seriously worried about that?"

"More than you'll ever know."

"What could she possibly do to harm the queen?"

"She could humiliate Elizabeth so terribly the queen would never truly recover from it."

"Not without danger of losing her head."

"She had that all worked out. Actually, her plan was really ingenious. But then, you ought to know, Bess. She got the idea from you."

"Me? You must be jesting."

"No. I'm quite serious. She told me how you trained your parrot to attack Longfellow's hat and pull it off him without him being any the wiser that the bird was being commanded by you."

"I did do that. But . . . you don't mean to tell me she

was going to do that to Elizabeth with a trained hawk?" Bess laughed harder. "Gads, but she has guts. I'll say that for her."

"Yes, she does, but damned little sense. Thank God, I convinced her not to carry it out, or this evening's entertainment for the lords and ladies of the court would have been much more exciting than anyone bargained for."

Black Bess's face lit up at the thought of seeing the queen with her wig flying through the air. Too bad Rob had talked Arianna out of it, she mused.

While Rob and the Terrible Four drank and chatted, Bess sat deep in thought. She couldn't help but admire Arianna Warwick. Though she was small and frail-looking, the woman had a mind of her own and always seemed to know how to get her way. Why couldn't she follow her example and find a way to get Elijah back? If Arianna could learn something from her, there was no reason why she couldn't learn from Arianna.

The rain ended by mid-afternoon, and Arianna became hopeful that it would stay clear through the next day, long enough to rescue her son and sail for Scotland. She tried not to think of what might happen if something went wrong with the rescue, concentrating instead on getting ready to go to the palace.

She was dressed as a falconer's apprentice once again, but this time she was not trying to deceive anyone. It was just an appropriate costume to wear for the evening's entertainment, and she was sure the queen would find it amusing. Topping off the breeches, shirt, and sleeveless leather doublet she wore, Arianna placed a jaunty hat on her head with a fluffy white plume attached. Looking in the mirror, she smiled at her reflection. Yes, that was exactly the right touch.

With the help of Terrence and her three attendants, each carrying a cage containing a brightly colored dove in each hand, she made her way across the park to the palace, the hooded falcon on her shoulder. Spectators gawked at her and her entourage as she passed, and they shouted out encouragements, recognizing her as the daring young lady from the masque.

When they arrived at the palace, they were escorted into a great hall already brimming with people. Arianna recognized several very high officials from Elizabeth's court and sighed, wishing that they would be witness to the queen's humiliation instead of to a game that would be harmful to no one but a poor, sweet little dove. She regretted that a bird would be killed, especially when it was for naught, but it was too late to back out now.

As soon as she entered the hall, she was recognized. It was as if the lords and ladies had been waiting for her to come, and she supposed they had. After all, she was supplying them with yet another evening's entertainment. They began to applaud and Arianna smiled, thinking it wasn't so bad to be a celebrity. She bowed like a man, sweeping the hat off her head in a flamboyant gesture, and the crowd laughed and applauded all the more. Well, at least they were in a festive mood. That should help make the evening a success.

Setting herself to the task, she had her attendants place the cages on eight different tables. Then she enlisted the help of eight volunteers to man the tables, taking bets on that particular colored dove.

Arianna had invented the game for only one purpose, to humiliate the queen, but denied that pleasure now, she found herself caught up in the excitement. Not because of the blood sport, but because of her fascination with the antics of the spectators.

It was very amusing to see how seriously the nobility took their gambling. Some of the nobles actually sized up each bird independently before placing their bet on the one they thought the feeblest and therefore most likely to be caught. Arguments broke out amongst more than one group of spectators over which color bird would attract the falcon, lemon-yellow being the most popular color of choice.

Whilst Arianna was watching the spectators, Elizabeth was watching Arianna. She was glad she had kept her head and not done anything rash once she discovered Arianna's true identity. It would be a pity to lock away this beautiful free-spirited girl.

To think that Arianna might have been her own daughter if she had been able to have children. But since she was denied that pleasure, this was the next best thing. At least, Arianna was Leicester's daughter. That counted for a lot. And thanks to Arianna, she now had a son to raise. Albeit, a very obnoxious little boy, who refused to have anything to do with her so far. It would take much longer than she planned to win him over.

The pony had been a good idea. Robin delighted in riding him each day. Mayhap she would take him out riding herself in the morning. It would help bring them closer together. Yes, that was a splendid idea.

Hearing a murmur amongst her people, the queen looked around to see what was happening. She frowned when her vision took in Black Bess, dressed in her black velvet pirate outfit, a brightly colored parrot on her shoulder. She obviously knew how to make an entrance, too. In fact, she had to admit Black Bess and the Countess Arianna were equally interesting young women.

It was obvious from the response of the crowd that Bess was admired, and Elizabeth had to admit that the woman was very attractive. Too attractive. For she turned the heads of all the males present.

Which reminded her . . . where was Robert Warwick? Why wasn't he escorting the pirate wench tonight? And where was Elijah? She was eager to see him dressed in fine clothing. The man struck quite a handsome figure clothed, and an even more enticing one unclothed. Yes, she was looking forward to seeing Elijah Longfellow, both here and in the privacy of her bedchamber.

Another murmur of voices caught Elizabeth's attention, and she turned her gaze in time to see Longfellow walk into the hall dressed so elegantly that he fairly took her breath away. The presence of the man was something to behold, demanding and bold and oh, so completely masculine. Not since the first time she laid eyes on Leicester had she felt her heart palpitate so wildly. This one was going to be someone special in her life, of that she was certain.

And none too soon. Leicester was getting fusty and feeble of late, and he never wanted to dance anymore. As much as she loved the man, she couldn't help but be perturbed that he didn't court her the way he used to. But that was to be expected, for surely they were like an old married couple who knew each other too well to still become excited.

Longfellow promised to remedy that. The way he had carried on about her this morning gave her plenty of evidence that they would have a pleasing liaison. Following his progress through the hall, she saw him walk over to Arianna. By the looks of it, Arianna wasn't too pleased to see him. She couldn't blame her for that, after the pirate had captured her husband and set into motion everything that had happened to her since.

Something else to be grateful to Longfellow for. If he had not captured Robert Warwick, she would never have discovered Arianna's identity and she would not have little Robin to raise as her own. How very appropriate that the child had been given the name of his grandfather. There would always be a Robin in her life now. How comforting that thought was.

Arianna tried to ignore Longfellow, but he wasn't having any of it. "Don't push your luck, Longfellow. The queen is very fond of me. One word to her, and you'll be out on your ear."

Elijah looked at her as if she were a simpleton. "The queen is even more fond of me, or hadn't you heard? She isn't about to make her new fair-haired boy leave. Anyway, I have no desire to fight with you, Arianna. You intrigue me. I heard about your exploits in the park. You can't imagine how sorry I am to have missed that. It seems we have a lot in common."

Arianna couldn't help but laugh. "You and I? You're truly demented if you think that. What could we possibly have in common?"

"We're both selling ourselves to please the queen, and you know what that makes us."

Arianna lashed out at Longfellow, striking him

across the face. The sound reverberated through the air, catching the attention of everyone around. Her face flamed as she walked away from him and right into her husband, who had just entered the hall.

Rob had come just in time to see Arianna slap Elijah, and he was tensed and ready to do battle with him. Arianna pleaded with him with her eyes not to confront Longfellow, and knowing the queen could very well be watching, he complied, curbing his anger. But oh, it was going to be a hard night to get through.

James made his way to Rob and spoke to him confidentially, "Be patient, lad. In just a wee time, we'll all be on our way to Scotland."

"I can be as patient as I have to, James. Don't worry about me. I won't do anything to jeopardize our plans."

James took Arianna's hand and kissed it, murmuring, "Do not linger too long, lass. The queen will wonder what you and Rob have to say to each other."

"Can't a girl talk to her *brother?* Will Elizabeth find even that strange?"

"No, of course not, especially since this will be my last night in England. I haven't had a chance to tell you yet, but the queen has decided I must leave on the morrow. It seems I've overstayed my visit."

"Then the timing will be perfect, James." Rob said. "If the queen expects you to leave tomorrow, you'll be able to sail away without any suspicion. And she certainly won't suspect my family will be on board your ship."

"But if it rains . . . or if for some reason little Robin is not brought to the park . . . then what?"

"Then it will be up to me. You'll have done all you

can. Don't worry. Your ship is not the only way we can travel to Scotland. If we have to, we'll ride."

" 'Twill be more dangerous by horse."

"So be it. We'll do whatever it takes. But mark me well. We will get to Scotland. You'll not get out of giving us that castle so easily."

Smiling, James took Arianna by the arm and led her away from Rob. "Better to err on the side of caution, I always say."

"Then if I were you, I'd spend the evening close to Elizabeth. After all, this is your last night here. The queen will be expecting you to be attentive."

"My sister is a very wise woman. I suppose I can endure one more evening, knowing that in a short time, I will be able to speak to my sister whenever I wish." With that, he bid her adieu and took his place beside the queen.

Elizabeth was glad when the threesome of Robert, James, and Arianna broke up and each went in a different direction. It made her too uneasy having them together. After all, they were all three related to little Robin. They all had reason to wish he was not in her custody. She was glad she had insisted on James leaving in the morning. That would be one less person to be concerned about.

After James spoke his amenities, Elizabeth asked him, "Have you told Arianna that you'll be leaving tomorrow?"

"Aye, and she understands. I told her I would invite her for a visit next spring, when the Highlands are in color."

The queen narrowed her eyes but said nothing.

"Surely you cannot òbject to my sister visiting me for a short while."

"A short while? Possibly. But I'm sure she wouldn't want to stay away too long. Her son will stay here."

"She understands that too well. Mark me, Elizabeth. I haven't said anything to you about your making Robin your ward. That's between you and my sister. But don't think that I'll stand by if you do anything to harm her physically. That's where I draw the line. Do you understand?"

"I understand, and I can't tell you how much it pleases me to know you care enough about your sister to look after her. You have nothing to worry about from me. I have no intentions of harming her. Indeed, I am quite fond of her. I fear the court would be a dreary place without her."

James smiled to himself, knowing his sister would soon be far away from the court of St. James. And none to soon, either. And he didn't doubt that the court would be a much drearier place. Arianna had a way of making everything that surrounded her brighter.

Arianna unhooded the falcon, preparing him for his part in the evening's event, then waited until the moment was right to start the gaming. Waited until everyone had been properly softened up by the wine and ale that flowed unusually freely. Finally, when she felt confident enough to begin, she made her way to the center of the hall with the falcon perched on her shoulder and signaled to a waiting herald to blow his trumpet. Immediately, the hall became hushed and she knew everyone was eager for the game to begin.

"Your Grace, my lords and ladies of the court, if all

the bets have been placed, let us begin. At the count of three, the birds will be released from their cages simultaneously, and at the count of seven—a very lucky number, by the way—I shall release the falcon." Turning to Longfellow, she said, "Would you count off the numbers for me?"

Longfellow smirked and bowed low. "By your leave." If this was her way of making up for the slap, it was far short of what he wanted. He'd settle for nothing less than a slap of his own . . . across her deliciously rounded bottom.

"One . . . two . . . three . . ."

Suddenly, the air was filled with the sound of flapping wings as the birds took to the air, a graceful blur of rainbow colors.

"Four . . . five . . . six . . . seven."

The falcon was free, ruffling his feathers, dilating his eyes, and then with a great thrust was flying toward the high ceiling of the hall. Aware of their danger, the doves flew in a panic to get away, some of them diving at the spectators as if seeking a safe place to alight. This caused great pandemonium. Men swiped at them with their hands while women shrieked in hysteria when the birds dove too close to them.

Arianna was astonished. Her great game was falling apart before her eyes. It had never occurred to her that the doves would seek refuge amongst the spectators. Suddenly, her eyes opened in horror as the falcon dove straight down, in chase of an apple-green dove who was alighting in the upswept hairdo of an elderly lady. "Oh, no!"

Her voice was drowned out amidst the cheerful shouts of the few lucky lords and ladies who had chosen the green dove to bet on. Before the blink of an eye, the falcon had the dove in its talons and the elderly woman prone on the floor, to the delight of Elijah Longfellow, who couldn't keep from laughing out loud.

The seven lucky doves who escaped the grim fate still flew about like chickens with their heads chopped off, desperate to find a way to escape. More than one lord and lady was anointed with the watery droppings from the doves' nervous digestive systems as they wheeled overhead.

Elizabeth, at first horrified, now laughed hysterically, until her side hurt too much to laugh any longer. Never had she seen such a hilarious sight. And poor Arianna. She seemed dismayed at the way things had turned out. How could she have known that the puddle-headed nobles would panic at the sight of a diving dove? Oh, it was such fun to see.

Coming to her senses, Arianna commanded the falcon to fly to her wrist, carrying its prey with it. She hooded the falcon quickly and removed it from the hall. Immediately, the doves calmed down and order was restored.

It suddenly came to Elizabeth that she had bet on the green dove, and that made her ecstatically happy. She made a big show of collecting her winnings, and a bigger show of handing them over to the poor old woman who had fallen down. In all, Elizabeth thought it had been an enjoyable event.

Black Bess stroked the head of her parrot as she watched the festivities from a quiet corner of the hall. Elizabeth seemed quite pleased with herself. Too bad. *Too, too* bad. Her eyes scanned the hall for Elijah and found him sloshing ale down his throat. The bastard. He's just brimming over with self-assurance now that he's found a home in St. James Palace.

The thought of him becoming the queen's pet was more than she could take. She had thought he was better than that. Oh, how she wanted him to be better than that. Wanted him to love her, but obviously that wasn't to be. A myriad of emotions swept over her, doing battle inside her until she thought she'd go crazy if she didn't do something. Anything to keep Elijah from feeling too smug.

She would best him at what he did the most proficiently, playing games, and she would show him that if she couldn't be his love, she would be his worthy opponent. Striding over to him, she took the tankard from his hand and downed the liquid herself, then wiped her mouth on her sleeve. "How would you like to place a private little bet with me?"

Elijah was taken aback by Bess's sudden boldness, but at the same time he was intrigued. He felt like kissing the arrogant look off her face but didn't dare risk it with the queen present. "A private bet? Hmmmm, sounds . . . seductive. And you know how much I love seductive games. What shall we bet on?"

Damn him. She didn't need to be reminded of the sexual games they had played on Devil's Harp. Not now. Not when he was staring at her like that. Not when she wanted him so. But, he wanted her, too. Oh, yes, he wanted her, there was no doubt about that. It wouldn't be hard to get him to leave with her right this minute, but to what end? Tomorrow he'd be back with the queen. "Well, I can think of any number of things, but the one that strikes me at the moment is this: I'll bet you can't get the queen to wear the blue feather you have on your hat."

Longfellow's eyes lit up. "What a bizarre idea. But tell me, just what is it you want from me if I lose?"

"I want—"

"Yes?"

Bess knew she would have to make the bet a challenging one to goad him into doing it. "I want . . . *The Reluctant Reward.*"

"My ship? You want me to bet my ship?"

"What's the matter, Elijah? Aren't you sure you can do it? Doesn't your charm work on queens?"

"Woman, I don't know what's eating you, but whatever it is, it is getting on my nerves. What is my incentive for doing this? It better be something of equal value."

"Name it. What do you want from me, Elijah?"

"You don't have anything I want."

Blinking back the hurt, Bess wanted nothing more than to slap him, to force him to see how much he truly cared for her, but instead she continued her pretense. "I see. Is that your coy little way of getting out of the bet? I thought you liked to play games."

"Actually, I'm getting a little tired of games. The outcome is always uncertain. But I can think of something alluring enough that's worth the risk."

"And that is?"

"You, Bess."

His words knifed into her chest, twisting around her heart. "What do you mean?"

"If I win, I get exclusive use of your body for a full year's time."

Shaking inside, Bess tried to keep her voice from shaking as well. "You can't be serious."

"I'm deadly serious."

Bess thought about the consequences of that, since she was certainly counting on him winning, and her heart leaped in anticipation. Isn't that what she'd wanted all along? "Very well, you've got a bet, but it has to be tonight, within a reasonable amount of time. All right?"

Longfellow grinned from ear to ear. "More than all right. She'll be wearing my blue feather before you have a chance to warm up to the fact that you'll be spending the night with me this very night."

"You haven't won yet."

Gazing around the hall, Longfellow spotted Elizabeth and started over to her, calling over his shoulder to Bess, "You can start undressing. I won't be long."

Suddenly realizing that he was actually going to do it, Black Bess sat down at the nearest table, feeling weak in her knees. Unconscious of what she was doing, she began to stroke her parrot's head.

Her eyes never left Longfellow as he joined Elizabeth on the dais, watching as the queen invited him to sit beside her. Watching as the queen raised a tankard to his lips, then drank from it herself. He was going to do it. The bastard was going to do it. Elizabeth was in his thrall.

Able to relax for the first time since she had arrived at the palace, Arianna sat at a table where she could keep her eye on Robert. He sat directly across the hall from her and she longed to go to him, to feel his strong arms around her, comforting her after the disastrous events of the evening. But she could not. It would be unwise.

Turning her gaze to the other tables, she saw Black Bess sitting by herself, an intense look upon her face. She seemed to be staring at someone, but whom? It certainly wasn't Rob, for she was looking away from him. Then whom? Following Bess's gaze, she homed in on Elijah sitting with the queen. Of course. Poor thing. It was obvious she still loved him. If only she realized he wasn't worth . . . Suddenly, she saw Elijah's arm move. Saw something blue in his hand, something he was raising to the queen's auburn wig.

A blue feather.

Oh, God, no. A blue feather!

He couldn't be. She couldn't be. No! This wasn't happening. Arianna's hand flew to her heart. A heart that had ceased to beat for a second but now beat out of control. Her gaze went back to the female pirate and the colorful parrot perched on her shoulder.

She was raising her hand to her mouth. She was going to do it! She was going to do what Arianna had been dreaming of doing for so long.

From across the room, Robert saw the strange expression on Arianna's face and became suddenly frightened. Something was going to happen; he could see it on her face. His gaze immediately shifted to the queen. The queen . . . and the blue feather she wore in her wig. What had Arianna told him? That Black Bess had trained her parrot to attack a . . . blue feather!

He stood up, then froze. What could he do? If he stopped it now, the queen would want to know how he knew about that trick and Black Bess would be in serious trouble. Damnation. His gaze swept back to his wife and the look of fascination on her face . . . as Black Bess coughed twice into her hand.

Chapter Thirty-two

A silly little nervous giggle burst from Arianna's mouth as the parrot took flight, and she bit down on her fingers to keep from laughing again. She watched in awe as the bird flew through the air, skimming the tops of everyone's head; watched as the bright-colored conveyer of her revenge lit into the queen's false hair, lifting it off, along with the blue feather woven through the auburn strands.

It was as if the world stood still for just a moment, as Arianna watched the spectacle. And indeed it did, for the whole of the congregation held its breath as it took in the ungodly sight of Elizabeth with her bare head exposed. A bald head, but for a few wisps of greyish yellow hair. A head that gave the queen the appearance of an ancient hag instead of the graceful, ageless queen they had always known.

It happened so quickly that it took Elizabeth a few seconds to comprehend, then feeling the cool air on her scalp, she realized what had occurred, and that knowledge hit her like a cruel blow to the heart.

Nay, more like a woman beheaded, for as she saw

her hair drop from the parrot's mouth and fall to the floor, a few feet away, she remembered what she had been told of Mary's death, how her head had fallen from its wig in the executioner's hands and rolled across the floor. Could that have been any worse than what she was experiencing now?

Her hands flew to her head, trying to cover her baldness, whilst at the same time she scrambled from her chair, knowing she must reach her wig before anyone saw. But it was too late. Stopping in her tracks, she looked around her and saw that every eye was on her, every mouth opened in shock at the sight of her.

She knew then she would not grovel on the floor for her wig. She would not give them the satisfaction of seeing the queen of England in such a demeaning position.

Then what? What could she do to erase the memory of her appearance from everyone's mind? She wanted to scream, to shriek with horror, but instead she held her head high. She was still the queen of England. No one could take that away from her.

Arianna no longer felt like giggling. Watching Elizabeth was painful. Her revenge had been handed to her on the wings of a parrot, at the hands of a female pirate, and she should have felt triumphant, but instead she felt like crying.

Enough. Let this be the end of it.

Standing, she walked over to where the wig lay and picked it up. It looked so insignificant off the queen's head that she wondered how such a small thing could make such a difference in the way Elizabeth was perceived.

Making her way to the queen, Arianna suddenly

realized how awkward it would be to hand Elizabeth her wig. She thought of offering the queen her jaunty hat but realized that would be just as demeaning, so instead she simply asked, "Can I assist you in any way, Your Grace?"

For a full second, the queen stared at Arianna, as if she did not know her and could not understand her spoken words, then a smile of recognition lit up her face. "Arianna, walk out with me. I suddenly feel tired. I fear the excitement has been too much for me."

Arianna smiled reassuringly at Elizabeth and guided her from the hall, chatting lightly with her every step of the way. They walked past the highest officials in the land, the noblest of lords and ladies, without so much as glancing in their direction.

Elizabeth's face displayed her usual queenly expression, but inside she was ready to collapse. Indeed, she would have if Arianna were not there. She would be eternally grateful to the girl for that. For she was the only one brave enough to come to her rescue. The only one with the presence of mind to act as if nothing had happened.

Once they were out and the doors of the hall closed behind them, Elizabeth was able to speak. Taking Arianna's hand in hers, she said, "Thank you, Arianna, I'm in your debt."

Arianna never got a chance to answer, for the next thing she knew a servant was running up to the queen, shouting, "Your Grace, it's Leicester. He's taken a turn for the worse."

Elizabeth gripped Arianna's hand tight, her nails digging into her flesh. "I must go to him at once."

"Let me go, too. He's my . . ." She stopped, knowing they were not alone.

"You may accompany me. But I must see him alone first."

"I understand, but . . . Your Grace, you'll want to put on your wig. There's no reason Leicester has to know what happened tonight."

The queen took the wig from Arianna's hand, then remembering the servant was still there, she sent him away before putting her wig back on. "Is it on straight? I don't want Leicester to see my hair in disarray. He has always been so fond of my auburn . . ." She could go on no further. Too choked to speak, she wiped away the tears that welled her eyes.

Arianna reached up and tugged the wig in place, standing much closer to the queen than she had ever been. She saw wrinkles now that she had never seen before, an aged woman where once she had seen a woman in her prime. From this day forward, she would remember her as she was now, a fragile, broken woman, very close to collapse.

It had never occurred to her that Elizabeth had any feelings, that she was just as human as everyone else, and Arianna suddenly felt pity for her. She wished with all her heart that she did not feel that way, for it would be so much easier to go on hating her for what she had done to her mother. For what she was doing to her son.

They walked up the stairs to Leicester's bedchamber, alone together for the first time in their lives. The two women who loved him most, united in their worry and concern. Each dreading what they might find when they walked into his room.

When they reached the door, Elizabeth took Arianna's hand and, in a shaky voice, said, "I'll send for you as soon as I've had a little time with him."

Arianna nodded her head and waited by the door.

The quiet of the palace seemed ominous after the robust clamor of the festivities below, Elizabeth thought as she made her way into Leicester's bedchamber. Afraid of what she would find, she slowly opened the door and peered in. Her breath expelled in a loud sigh of relief when she saw Leicester propped up in his bed, an attendant hovering over him with a bowl of broth in hand.

"I thought to find you on your deathbed and instead find you enjoying a meal."

"You can't get rid of me that easily," Leicester answered in a weak, tremulous voice.

Bending down to kiss his forehead, she whispered, "And why would I want to get rid of you, Robin? Have I not put up with your foolishness for all these years?"

"And I yours."

"Hmph. If you were feeling better, I'd wallop you good for saying that to me."

"And if I were feeling better, I'd . . ." Leicester's face wrinkled with pain. "Ahhh."

"What is it, Robin? Shall I call my physician?"

"No, he was here a short time ago. There is nothing further he can do. The only thing he had to say was to urge me to take a trip to Kenilworth. To the baths. I fear he is grasping at straws, for he's truly at a loss for what else might help."

"No such thing. 'Tis a brilliant idea. I have every confidence that the baths shall be the perfect cure. Just as soon as you're strong enough to travel, you will go there."

"I'll go tomorrow. Before I am too weak to go at all. Do you understand what I'm trying to say, Elizabeth?"

Taking his hand, Elizabeth pressed it to her lips. "I understand." Her eyes brimmed with tears.

"Good. And now, since I may never have the chance to speak my mind again, I want to be as forthright with you as I know how to be."

"No, Leicester, this is not the time to speak of—"

"If not now, when? I may never get another chance to speak, and I deeply need to tell you that what you are doing to Arianna and her family is shameful and wrong. Give her back her son. You are much too old to be raising a small boy. He needs his mother."

"I will not hear this, Robin."

Her warning tone was not lost on him, but he pressed on, speaking more openly then he had ever dared before. "You will hear it. And you will heed my advice. Don't punish Arianna for something with which she had nothing to do. Have you not already exacted all the revenge you need from the death of her mother, Mary Stuart? She paid with her life. Is that not enough?"

"Stop it, Robin, before this goes too far."

"It has already gone too far, Elizabeth. Way too far. Speak your mind. Tell me what you never have in all these years . . . that you were hurt by my betrayal, that you have never forgiven me for making love to Mary? Tell me, and clear your heart of all the anguish you've been carrying inside."

"Very well, if you insist. I *have* wanted to punish

you, but at the same time, I've wanted your child to raise as my own. *It should have been my child.* You talk of punishment, well think of that. I have been punished most cruelly by not being able to bear your child. Now I have another chance. Don't you see? I can make up for all those empty years by raising your grandchild as my own."

"No, Elizabeth. No. I won't have it. Little Robin belongs with his mother. If you don't return him, I'll make sure that you regret it deeply. I'll make sure that before I die, the whole world will know that I slept with the Scottish queen and that she bore my child."

"Even you wouldn't dare so much."

"What do I have to lose, Elizabeth? I'm near death already. Would you pull me from my deathbed to lop off my head?"

"Robin, please, don't talk like that. I will not hear of you dying."

Leicester tried to laugh, but it came out sounding more like a whimper. "Even your power doesn't descend beyond the grave, my darling. I will die, whether you will have it or not."

"Don't. Don't even speak of it. The world would be a much sadder place without my Robin in it."

With a shaky hand, Leicester reached over to pat Elizabeth's arm. "Do you truly love me as much as that?"

"How can you doubt that after all these years?"

"Then for my sake, for my very soul, so that I might rest in peace, give my grandson back to his mother. If you do not, then *every word of love you have ever said to me will be a lie.*"

Through tear-clogged eyes, Elizabeth gazed at the

man she loved so dearly. "Don't say that. Don't even think it. You are the one true person in my life. I have never doubted your love for me for one solitary moment. And surely you have not doubted mine."

"I repeat, every word of love you have ever said to me will be a lie if—"

A light rapping sounded on the door, and Elizabeth quickly wiped away her tears. "What is it?"

The door opened and the king of Scotland's head appeared. "Forgive me for interrupting, but there is someone here who urgently needs to see Leicester."

"Are you mad? I told my attendants Leicester was not to be disturbed by anyone, and now you—"

"It's Arianna, Elizabeth. 'Tis cruel to make her wait outside for news of her father."

Opening the door wider, James stood aside so Arianna could enter. Looking very pale, her eyes sought out her father, and when she saw him, she ran to his side and knelt beside his bed. "Oh, Father, I was so afraid—"

Elizabeth started to say something, but when she saw the concern on Arianna's face, she could not. Funny, but she hadn't realized that Arianna might actually love the man who had fathered her. She hadn't been in his life for more than two years, and yet the love was there between them.

"Hush, child," Leicester said. "There is nothing to fear. As you can see, I'm far from dead. I'll be leaving for Kenilworth tomorrow. The physician is certain the baths will be the perfect cure, and when I return, I shall be feeling much better, I assure you."

Gazing at her father's wan face, Arianna was shocked to find he had deteriorated so much since last she saw him, and she knew it would not be long before death found him.

"You see," Elizabeth said in a commanding voice, "you upset yourself for nothing. He is just a little tired. There was no reason for you to come running in here like that. I told you I would let you see him. I—"

All of Arianna's old feelings toward Elizabeth returned in a rush of anger, and she could hold it back no longer. She stood and faced the queen. "No reason? I have every reason. He is my father. You may not want to believe that. You may not be able to accept that, but by God, nothing can change the fact that he and I are kin every bit as much as I am kin to James."

"Don't raise your voice to me, girl. I'll warn you but once."

"Is that so? And what will you do to me if I do? You've punished me as much as you possibly can. Do you think I fear dying at your hands? Not anymore. No. Death would be a blessing if I am never to have my child again."

Elizabeth was shocked at Arianna's passionate speech. "Fah. I don't believe that for a moment. You have your husband and a new child on the way. You have everything to live for."

"Do you really believe that?" Placing her hands on her belly, she cried, "I live in fear that you will take this child, too? It may be a little girl. Wouldn't you want to have a sweet little daughter to raise, too? Why not? It will be Leicester's grandchild, too. No. It would be better to die and take the child with me than to have it torn from me like my little Robin was."

James exchanged glances with Leicester, and in silent communion with each other, they decided not to still Arianna's tongue. What she said needed to be said.

Tears flooded Elizabeth's eyes. "Stop. I can't bear to hear any more talk of death this night. Do you think I'm made of stone? Do you not think I bleed when I am pricked? I love this man more than life, and I love his daughter, too, though I never knew who she was. I swear to you, I want no more retribution. I am done with revenge." Turning to Leicester, she cried, "Are you happier knowing that, Robin? Will it soothe your soul to know that?"

"You know what it will take to soothe my soul, Elizabeth."

"Do not ask it of me."

"I will. I must. Bring my grandchild to me."

James realized what was happening and a jolt of excitement coursed through him. "Elizabeth, shall I go to the nursery to get him for you?"

Elizabeth jerked her head in James's direction, fire in her eyes, but it was quickly extinguished, knowing what she must do. Turning to Arianna, she gazed into her eyes as she uttered the fateful words to James. "Bring him to me."

Arianna didn't dare breathe. It couldn't be. She couldn't bring herself to believe that Elizabeth would back down. She stood frozen, waiting for her brother to return. Elizabeth and Leicester, too, were silent, each deep in thoughts of their own, each knowing that something momentous was happening.

James returned in a moment, the sleeping Robin nestled in his arms, and bluntly asked, "Who shall I give him to, Elizabeth?"

Elizabeth practically choked over the words. "To the one who gave him life."

Arianna's knees buckled then, but she righted herself as her son was placed in her arms, and she hugged him to her breast.

"My love is not a lie. Will you believe that now, Robin?"

Tears streamed down Leicester's cheeks as his body shook with happy sobs. "I believe."

Close to breaking down, Elizabeth walked toward the door. Too much had happened to her this day. She needed to be alone, if just for a few moments. Fearful that she could not speak without crying, she left the room, closing the door behind her.

Immediately, the atmosphere in the room brightened, and James hugged Arianna to his chest, child and all. "You see, everything has turned out all right, just as I promised you."

From his bed, Leicester spoke, his voice weak but urgent. "Do not trust her, Arianna. After I am gone, it is very likely she will change her mind and take him back."

"I know that, Father, but there's no need to worry. Tomorrow Rob and I will sail away on James's ship. We'll go to Scotland and live out our lives there, where she cannot harm us ever again."

Leicester reached out his hand for her, "That is a great relief to me, daughter. I can die happy now, knowing you and your children are safe."

Arianna took her father's hand and squeezed it tight. "Don't talk like that. Why, after your trip to the baths, you'll be full of vim and vigor. You can come to visit us in Scotland and we can have a grand time together."

Knowing how much Arianna needed to believe that right now, Leicester forced a smile. She would never leave England now if she believed he was about to die. And he knew without a doubt the importance of her leaving as soon as possible. "I'm looking forward to that. Send word when the new child is born, and I'll ride there and spend some time getting to know my newest grandchild."

"Oh, Father, yes. You'll see, we'll be so happy, so . . ." Arianna couldn't go on. Sobbing loudly, she handed her son to James and sat on the edge of the bed to embrace her father. She was shocked at how frail his once-strong body felt beneath her.

Somewhere deep inside her, she knew this was the last time she would ever see her father alive. She knew it, yet still found the courage to say goodbye to him, to walk away from him as if she would be seeing him again soon. Walking out of the room with her brother by her side, her son nestled in his arms, she took one last lingering look at her father . . . a look that would have to last her a lifetime. Then, giving him her brightest smile, she closed the door behind her.

Out in the hall Arianna walked no more than three or four steps before collapsing in her brother's arms, crying as if her heart would break. She wanted to shout to the heavens how unfair life had treated her. How every time she gained someone dear to her, she lost someone she loved. She had lost her mother to gain her brother, now she must lose her father to gain back her son. It was inhumane, and so very cruel.

Then suddenly, she heard the one voice that could

still her tears, and Arianna saw Rob running down the hall toward her. His look of joy as he saw his wife and son together brought a genuine smile to her face, and her sobbing turned to cries of happiness.

Rob pulled her and Robin into his arms, showering their faces with kisses. "Does it mean what I think it does? Has she truly given us back our son?"

Arianna shook her head yes, so blinded with tears she could not see the ones in Rob's own eyes. "Yes, yes, yes."

Pulling the hat from Arianna's head, Rob set it sailing through the air. "You'll have no more need of that, then."

Arianna laughed, knowing how very much Rob wanted her to be his wife, fully, completely, with no need of masquerade or subterfuge. She wanted that, too. Oh, how she wanted that.

Speaking in an excited voice, James exclaimed, " 'Tis time to go. The bonnie hills of Scotland are calling to us. Do ye hear them, Arianna? Do ye hear them, Robbie?"

Reaching out, Arianna took her husband and brother by the arm, a tiny figure between the two tall men, and led them toward the door, toward the new life that awaited in the country of her mother's birth.

Epilogue

Scotland, Spring, 1590

Sitting on the wide back of Sanctimonious, her baby daughter in the saddle in front of her, Arianna gazed up at the wall of the ancient castle as if it were a holy shrine. Linlithgow. The birthplace of her mother. A carved heraldic panel on the wall displaying the Scottish Royal Arms stared down at her proudly, making it known to all who passed through this gate that a queen had once lived here.

In her childhood, raised as a peasant by Peter and Sybille, she had never dreamed that she was the daughter of that great queen, never dreamed that she would one day reside in Scotland, her mother's land, and she certainly never dreamed she would one day bring her own little baby daughter to visit the great castle where her namesake was born.

It was a proud moment for her, but a very poignant one, too, for she wished with all her heart that her mother could have lived to see her grandchildren. Little Robin and baby Mary would have been greater for having known their grandmother.

Bending her head down, she kissed the top of her daughter's golden-curled head, then clicked her tongue at Sanctimonious and started through the arched entranceway to the castle courtyard. Sanctimonious cantered gently, her head held high, as if she, too, were aware of this was a special occasion.

Sensing this was a heartrending moment for Arianna, Rob kept his silence, delaying his progress into the courtyard to give his wife time alone with her thoughts. Turning toward the riders behind him, he spoke to Colin and Cassiopeia. "Let her have a few moments alone."

Colin nodded his head, knowing well how emotional this journey must be for Arianna. But he also knew how much she wanted to come. From the moment the invitation came from the king, she had been restless, riding back and forth between Evermore, the picturesque castle the king had given her, and Colin's own manor home a few leagues away, in need of Cassiopeia's help in preparing her wardrobe for the journey.

Smiling contentedly, Colin thought of the past few months' events in wonder. He had worried how Rob would react when he found out that he and Cassiopeia were living in Scotland, too, under James's protection.

But it was all for naught. Rob had accepted it quite easily. Mayhap it was the birth of his son and Rob's daughter that had healed the wounds and brought them back to the friendship they had had so long ago, but whatever it was, he was grateful. The four of them had become very close. Close enough to be invited along on this pilgrimage to the Queen of Scots' birthplace.

With his own son seated on his saddle and Cassiopeia riding beside him, Colin cantered into the courtyard and dismounted. When the rest of the entourage had dismounted and readied themselves to meet the king of Scotland, they were led up the stairs to the great hall, renowned throughout the country for its size and grandeur.

Arianna carried her daughter to the hall in silence, her eyes darting everywhere, eager to absorb all that she saw. Her mother had been born here. Had most likely spent many happy days here when she was queen. She could almost hear her laughter echoing through the halls. Hugging little Mary to her breast, she made her way through the double line of nobles, nodding her head and smiling as she went along, feeling suddenly as though her mother were there beside her, guiding her way.

What an odd feeling. But she had learned a long time ago not to question things like that. Rob said it was her Scottish blood that made her so superstitious, so loyal to her blood ties, and she couldn't argue with that answer. She was proud of the Scottish blood that ran through her veins, but never so much as at this moment, amongst her mother's and her brother's people.

When she was, at last, standing in front of the dais where her brother sat, looking every inch a king, Arianna curtsied and waited for him to summon her. It seemed strange that he was being so formal. He usually acted much more exuberant. She looked to Rob for reassurance and saw the grin on his face.

Looking back at James, she saw he wore the same silly grin and realized they were up to something. But what?

A sudden explosion of voices soon gave her the answer. From behind the brocaded curtains at the rear of the king's throne came Will and Felicia, with their new baby, and Peter and Sybille, her dear, dear, foster parents. And oh, no, was that Black Bess with a swollen belly about to burst?

In a moment she was surrounded by her family and friends, and crying in her foster mother's arms. Sybille cried, too, at the sight of little Mary. "She looks exactly as you did at that age, Arianna. Exactly."

Peter stood back and waited, knowing how much Sybille needed to embrace her beloved foster daughter. His turn would come. He had so much to tell her, so much he wanted to hear. He thought of all the times when she was growing up when he would ride her past the many castles where Mary, Queen of Scots, had been held prisoner, just so Mary might get a glimpse of her daughter from behind the barred windows, and he knew that strong bond between mother and daughter could never be broken, not even in death.

Bowing his head, Peter said a silent prayer for Mary, hoping she was at peace at last. In his heart he felt she somehow knew that her daughter and grandchildren were safe here in this wild and beautiful country.

And here in this ancient castle, the circle of life was complete. Now Arianna and James were united, and he and Sybille lived once again in the land of their birth. And with the birth of Robin and little Mary, a new circle was beginning.

Mary started crying at all the noisy strangers surrounding her, and she was handed to her father, who soon had her quieted. Robin, on the other hand, decided to be brave and walked up to his Uncle James and held his hand.

When Arianna had at last caught her breath, she sought her brother. He was standing near the brocade curtains with Robin, and she could swear that a moment ago, from the corner of her eye, she had noticed a woman standing beside him dressed in the most beautiful gown she had ever seen. She would have to remember to ask him who that was, for she would dearly love to have a gown its equal. "James, whatever possessed you to bring my family and friends here?"

"Rob and I thought you'd like to have your friends about you so you wouldn't feel lonely and threaten to return to England."

That struck Arianna as being very funny. "Return to England? Not a chance. Scotland has always been my home, but I didn't know it until I stepped off that galleon onto Scottish soil." She wanted to tell James about the strange way she felt that her mother was there with her, but Arianna knew this wasn't the time. But she couldn't help wondering if he ever felt that way, too.

Glancing around her, she saw all the people she loved and felt a sense of contentment. Saw all the new babies that had been born in the past year. Her own little Mary, snug and safe in her father's arms; Orion, Colin's and Cassiopeia's son; and Felicia's child, William, named after his father. What a happy time they lived in.

She saw Bess approach, so swollen with baby she

could hardly walk, and Arianna almost laughed out loud. It was a sight she never thought she'd see. She could almost forgive Elijah Longfellow for the evil he had done, seeing the happiness in Bess's eyes. Almost. It would take a long time to get over the anguish that man had caused.

"Well, Arianna, what kind of mother do you think I'll be?"

Bess glowed with maternal beauty. "You'll be a wonderful mother, but you could have done a better job at picking the father. Where is that fiercesome pirate lord?"

"Out to sea. It's in his blood, I fear. He promised he'd be back in time for the birth. James has promised him safe refuge as a favor to me."

Arianna looked up at her brother with love in her eyes. "He was right to do so. I've finally come to realize the value of forgiveness."

"What's that? Are you talking about me?" Rob circled Arianna's waist from behind.

"Conceited devil, isn't he? What makes you think we're talking about you? And by the way, I have a bone to pick with you. Why didn't you tell me everyone would be here? I would have chosen my garb more carefully."

"That's very amusing, considering how many trips you made to Cassiopeia's for articles of clothing that you absolutely had to have. Between the two of you women, I'll wager you'll keep the dressmakers of Scotland busy for the next two years."

"Without a doubt. And I mean to corner that woman in the exquisite gold gown, too, and find out who makes her clothing."

Bess looked around, eager to see the gown in question. "Where is she?"

Arianna's gaze skimmed the hall for a glimpse of golden satin and gauze, but saw no sign of the woman. "That's odd. I don't see her anywhere." A shiver crawled up Arianna's spine unbidden, but she shrugged it off. Then her foster father was there beside her and she forgot everything but the joy of having him near.

When the evening grew late, she and Rob climbed the stairs to the chamber, the king himself showing them the way. Their children had long since been bedded there, snug in a gilded bed James had made for them.

"I've put you in your mother's chambers." James said solemnly. " 'Tis the rooms she used whenever she came to Linlithgow, so I've been told."

Arianna paused before the open door, glancing at her husband with panic.

"Rose Petal, if you'd rather not sleep here, I'm sure James can find us another chamber."

"Oh, no, Rob, I do want to. It's just . . . how can I explain how overwhelmed I feel being here tonight? The only place I've seen my mother is in a prison cell, but here I feel her presence, and I see the way she lived when she was queen. I'm glad you invited me here, James. It makes her feel all the more real to me."

James nodded his head in understanding, then left, closing the door softly behind him so as not to wake the sleeping children. He felt a little overwhelmed himself.

Arianna walked over to the window and looked out at the darkened sky. "Rob, she must have looked out this window just as I am now. I wonder what she thought. I wonder what made her laugh. Why did she have to die? You have no idea how much I wish she were with me right now."

Rob blew out the candles, thinking about what she said. "Rose Petal, I do know, and I wish I could bring her to you. I wish . . ." One tiny flickering firefly flew between him and Arianna just then, bringing back memories of their wonderful wedding night when their bedchamber had been filled with them.

He looked at his wife, loving her more this minute, if that were truly possible, than he had that wonderful evening. He fervently wished that he could make her truly happy by granting her wish. "I wish that the firefly was a magical wishing star so that I might wish upon it and bring your mother to you."

Arianna reached for his hand, squeezing it tight. "I love you dearly, Robert Warwick."

Rob drew her into bed and held her in his arms until she fell asleep, drifting off himself as he watched the flickering firefly wend its way around the room.

Something woke Arianna, she knew not what. Opening her eyes, she saw a soft glow and at first thought it was the wandering firefly. But no, the glow illuminated the corner of the room where her children lay asleep. Pulling back the covers, she started to rise, when she saw a woman bending over her children. The same woman who wore the beautiful golden dress.

Suddenly frightened, she climbed out of bed, but something kept her from calling Rob. The woman . . . looked so very familiar. So . . . very . . .

Sensing her presence, the woman stood up straight and slowly turned her head to look in Arianna's direction.

Tears welled in Arianna's bright eyes as she reached out for her, whispering in reverent awe, "Mother!"

Mary, Queen of Scots, smiled softly at Arianna, stretching out her own hand toward her daughter as she glided slowly toward her.

"Oh, Mother, you're here. You're really here."

Mary gazed at her daughter with such love that it broke Arianna's heart to see it. Their hands touched, and for just a moment Arianna felt the firmness of her grip. Bliss enveloped her. "I love you, Mother."

Mary nodded her head just a little, and Arianna realized it was beyond her capacity to speak. She knew then that her mother could not stay, and she swallowed hard. "I'll love you always."

Mary's image began to flicker and fade.

"Arianna." Rob was there beside her, pulling her into his arms.

Tears spilled from her eyes as she cried out, "She was here, Rob. My mother was here. You brought her to me with your firefly wish. Oh, my darling husband, you gave me my dearest wish."

Rob's face was lit with wonder. "I think, for just a moment, I saw her, too."

"I'm so glad you did. Oh, Rob, she was looking at the children when I saw her. Her grandchildren. How can such a thing be possible?"

"Don't question it. Just accept. When it comes to the Stuart women, anything is possible. Anything at all." Bending down to kiss his daughter's forehead, he whispered, "I have a feeling it is an inherited trait."